Also by Wendy Isaac Bergin:

The Piper's Story: A Tale of War, Music and the Supernatural

The
THRESHOLD
of
EDEN

The

THRESHOLD

of

EDEN

Wendy Isaac Bergin

The Threshold of Eden
© Wendy Isaac Bergin

Published by Clay Bridges
www.claybridgespress.com

ISBN 10: 1939815193
ISBN 13: 978-1-939815-19-4
eISBN 10: 1939815207
eISBN 13: 978-1-939815-20-0

Cover image: A Golden Dream, 1893 (oil on canvas), Gotch, Thomas Cooper (1854-1931) / Harris Museum and Art Gallery, Preston, Lancashire, UK / Bridgeman Images

Special Sales: Most Clay Bridges titles are available in special quantity discounts. Custom imprinting or excerpting can also be done to fit special needs. Contact Clay Bridges.

In memory of my paternal grandparents,
Josephine and Feyood Isaac,
in memory of Annie Mowad Vestal,
for the Syrian Christian community of Louisiana,
for all the people of the Gulf Coast,
and, naturally, for all the Saints

For the LORD shall comfort Zion: He will comfort all her waste places; and He will make her wilderness like Eden, and her desert like the garden of the LORD; joy and gladness shall be found therein, thanksgiving, and the voice of melody.

~Isaiah 51:3

Nor shall fail from memory's treasure
Works by love and mercy wrought,
Works of love surpassing measure,
Works of mercy passing thought.

~Richard Mant, 1824

Contents

Prologue: May

I t was the morning of an ordinary day. The garden, warmed by the light and heat of an ancient, incandescent star, blossomed into summer. Dew diamonds bejeweled the thick, green grass; they sparkled on the red geraniums, the velvety roses, the scarlet hibiscus, and the purple trumpeted morning glories. Birdsong bespangled the air: trills, roulades, chirps, whistles, calling and answering. The fruit trees, bending and swaying in the morning breeze, waited to bear their pomegranates, pears, persimmons, figs, mayhaws, mulberries, and pecans in due season.

A bumblebee, wholly unconcerned about its aerodynamic impossibility, traversed a winding, erratic aerial path, rising, falling precipitously, rising, buzzing left and suddenly right amongst the potted geraniums. Drifting over to the roses, its wayward path zigzagged over the bent head of a young girl sitting cross-legged on the grass, half-hidden in the shade of the tall, green elephant ears. Though she rode on a planet spinning at one thousand miles per hour and hurtling through space at untold velocity in a universe expanding to infinity, she read and turned the pages of her book, absorbed and unperturbed, as though her garden were the calm, still center of the universe, which, of course, contrary to all observable natural laws, it was.

Twenty feet away, high in the mulberry tree, a fledgling blue jay, bright-eyed and curious, craned his spindly neck upward to peer out of the nest. Inquisitive and drawn perhaps by his kinship to the cloudless azure sky that matched his own dark blue, he left his siblings and hopped up onto the uneven twigs of the nest's perimeter. Unafraid and unaware of gravity or its laws, he hopped forward to see the verdant world, teetered precariously, lost his balance and plummeted, immature wings flapping vainly, to the uncut grass twelve feet below. His squawks of alarm startled the girl, who looked up, saw the struggling bird, and rose, drawn by its frantic cries.

Neither the girl nor the bird, though it was not a sparrow, nor even the bumblebee, went unobserved. They and their stories, written long ago, were known, as they traveled, borne at high velocity on a spinning planet, warmed and bathed in the light of an ancient star, on the morning of an ordinary day.

CHAPTER 1

June: The Mulberry Tree

J oshua Brightman sat alone on a park-style bench in a half circle of shadow, the only shade in the backyard. It was late on a Friday afternoon, and he had only ninety minutes of freedom until the return of the Beast. He dragged deeply on a cigarette to calm his nerves and watched the smoke rise in a straight column until it disappeared into the thick, glossy-leaved arms of the tree above him. The day was hot and windless, and the wide-spreading tree branches leaning over the wooden privacy fence at his back gave him respite from the sun.

The backyard was a large rectangle of thick green, perfectly clipped and perfectly boring grass with a hidden sprinkler system. The monster brick house, with its French doors and concrete patio looked as uncomfortable on its tiny lot as an NFL offensive lineman squashed into an airline seat. Looming and ugly, it not only suited the Beast, it resembled him, with rooms too big and windows too small.

Joshua's heart sank as he observed the house and yard. Removed from his native Brooklyn, like an apple tree uprooted and set into a tropical garden, he had a bad case of transplant shock. The place was too quiet; the climate was too humid, too hot, and there was too much sky, all lorded over by the brilliant, pitiless sun. Except for the morning exodus to work in the city, there was no street traffic and not a sign of a human being. In the three weeks since he and his parents had moved to the nether regions of the universe, otherwise known as south Louisiana, he had been under virtual house arrest. Here he sat in boring Chalice, surely the most insipid New Orleans suburb there ever was.

Joshua noticed a line of ants marching from the base of the park bench to an ant hill just outside the area of shade.

Strip him. Tie him down hands and legs to four stakes in the ground. Cover him with honey and let him lie for days in the sun 'til the ants eat him alive.

His hand trembled slightly as he took a deep drag on the cigarette. He was dying for a beer, but since the near disaster in San Francisco, there was no alcohol in the house. Well, correction: there was alcohol, but not for him. The Beast had taken care of that. He quickly counted the ants. Twenty-four. He was twenty-four.

$24 = 2 \times 12, 3 \times 8, 4 \times 6$
$14 + 10, 12 + 12$ and $12 \times 12 =$

A sudden rustle in the leaves above startled him. There was no wind, so maybe there was a bird up there. As Joshua looked up, he heard a distinct click followed by a soft whirring sound. He watched wide-eyed as a small white rectangle descended out of the tree and halted in midair, six inches from his nose. In place of a hook, a paper clip at the end of a weighted nylon fishing line held a 2 x 3 notecard with a mechanical pencil clipped to it.

Well, it certainly wasn't a bird. Joshua followed the line upward with his eyes, but it disappeared into the canopy of the tree. Craning his head left and then right, he could just see the straight edge of a wooden platform high in the tree, but no sign of the person who had to be perched on it. He returned his gaze to the dangling card. Something was written on it. He reached out and steadied it with one hand.

> Would you please not
> smoke under my tree?

Joshua took the pencil, cradled the card in his left hand, and wrote: *Who the hell are you?*

As soon as he reattached the pencil, the card was reeled upwards and disappeared into the foliage. Just to show who was in control, Joshua lit another cigarette. In less than a minute, a new card descended.

My name is Sam. What is your name? Are you the piano player?

By the way, please do not use cuss words like hell, damn, shit, fuck, or son of a bitch. That is not polite.

P.S. You did not answer my question. Are you going to stop smoking under my tree?

Joshua turned the card over and wrote: *My name is Joshua, and I am not polite, but I will consider your request. Yes, I am the piano player. Do you have asthma?*

Away went the card. He dragged deeply on his cigarette, stretched out his legs, crossed them, and leaned back on the bench. Just to show off, he tilted his head back and blew three smoke rings skyward while he awaited the reply.

Asthma? I <u>will</u> have it if you don't stop smoking under my tree.

If you don't have asthma, then why does the smoke bother you?

It gets in my eyes while I'm reading.
Smoking is not good for you, but don't
worry, I have the solution. Just wait.
Don't go away.

Wondering why anyone would read in a tree, Joshua wrote: *What is the solution?*

The card retreated upward. After a moment, Joshua heard a high-pitched giggle, bright as birdsong, and then he was pelted hard on the head and shoulders by a shiny hailstorm of round, red and white cellophane-wrapped peppermints.

"Ouch!"

He heard a sliding sound, followed by a thump, then running footsteps. Joshua jumped up on the bench and looked over the fence in time to glimpse a young, dark-haired boy just before the backdoor slammed shut behind him.

"You little turd."

Joshua lingered a moment, spellbound as the Englishman in *Lost Horizon* who discovers the hidden kingdom of Shangri-La. Compared to the sterility of his backyard, this was a slice of paradise. The yard had a dense, tropical air, as if nature, barely restrained, might run riot and subsume the entire property. The perimeter was shaded by banana plants with thick, fleshy stalks ending in tall green fronds, wide-leaved fig trees, pear, and several other types of trees he didn't recognize. The sun-dominated center was a large, rectangular vegetable garden with neat, well-tended rows of staked tomato plants, yellow squash, and green beans growing from the rich, black earth. The sea of uncut, ankle-deep grass ringing the garden stretched from a dilapidated, tin-roofed tool shed at the back to the tall white frame house with dark green shutters and gabled roof at the front. The house itself seemed to have materialized from another time; it recalled the character, atmosphere, and charm of the nineteenth century. A narrow concrete stoop led from the house to the flagstone patio, which was inhabited by three Adirondack chairs and a riot of potted roses, hibiscus, and geraniums, framed by a forest of large green elephant ears.

"Sam, you lucky dude." It was so very inviting and peaceful that he wanted to climb over and explore, but he dared not.

Reluctantly, he hopped down and gathered up ten peppermints from the ground and the seat of the bench. Then he sat down again, smiling, feeling somehow comforted. After a moment, he sighed, dropped his cigarette butt on the ground and stamped it out with his foot. He unwrapped a peppermint and popped it in his mouth. The cool, minty taste was almost as calming as nicotine. It wasn't really a solution, but maybe it would make it just a little easier to face the Beast.

CHAPTER 2

Weapons

The tension he felt when he entered the house reminded him of returning to New York after a vacation and deplaning at LaGuardia: his pulse quickened, his blood pressure rose, his senses heightened in wariness, and his muscles tensed for combat. As he opened the French doors to the living room, that same on-guard persona took over, but all that assaulted him at the moment was the warm, homey smell of pot roast and onions.

"Joshua, come and set the table," his mother called from the kitchen. "I still have to make the salad and put the dinner rolls in the oven."

Whatever else she might be, his mother was a good cook.

"In a minute, Mom," he called. He glanced to his left at the eat-in kitchen, seeing only the rectangular dining table and chairs. His mother was out of sight, probably working at the counter. The late afternoon light behind him cast his shadow across the living room to the wall of weapons. Naturally, the Beast had mounted his weapon collection in the room where they spent the most time.

The Beast's fascination with guns began when his college roommate at Ithaca took him deer hunting in the Adirondacks. Hunting became a perfect outlet for the Beast's aggression. Later, when he had a full-time job and could afford it, he bought his own rifles, beginning with a Browning, a Remington, and a Ruger. He found he had a taste not only for guns, but for all the instruments of war, and he satisfied his appetite by collecting them. Two Civil War swords, crossed with points aimed downward, were the centerpiece of the display. They were surrounded with WWI and WWII German Lugers, Mauser pistols, a British Webley 6-shot revolver, an Italian Carcano Carbine rifle with a folding bayonet under the barrel, a WWI German Imperial Trench Axe and a Lion Head sword, as well as daggers from Japan, Italy, and a British V-42 stiletto.

> *Kill the bastard. Disembowel him with the stiletto. Finish him off with the Luger—one shot through the temple.*

Joshua drew in a quick breath.

> *Avoid the weapon wall. Turn right. Seven steps past the sofa, turn left, seven steps past the fireplace to the hall. Turn right. Three steps to the bathroom. Safe!*

He locked the door behind him, wiped the clammy sweat from his brow, and regarded himself in the mirror. Normally pale, his face, framed by curly auburn hair, looked unnaturally white. His eyes were two wide hazel pools above the olive green of his polo shirt and his khaki shorts. Thin as ever, he stepped on the scale to be sure, sandals and all. Still 130 pounds. He washed his hands three times. After peeing, he washed three more times.

As he popped another peppermint in his mouth, the ringing started in his ears. Hungry as he was, he didn't think he'd be able to eat.

The slam of the front door made his stomach lurch. Only a matter of seconds now.

Four staccato raps on the bathroom door. "Hey, what are you doing in there? Hurry up, time for dinner. Don't be late!"

Joshua lowered the toilet seat, sat down, and counted to one hundred. Slowly.

When he entered the kitchen, his parents were already seated for dinner. His father, Billy "The Beast" Brightman, loomed at the head of the table, knife in hand, like an executioner clad in a Brooks Brothers suit. Swarthy, with a shaved head and black goatee, he had the muscular but aging body of an ex-athlete. Joshua's mother Amy sat to his right, small, plump and bottle blond, like an overripe apricot. Their two sets of eyes, his menacing and dark, and hers a vague, watery blue, accused him before he even sat down.

Holding his fork and knife with clenched fists, as if he were going to dissect Joshua instead of his food, the Beast glared at his son. "Your mother asked you to set the table, but since you were hiding in the bathroom, I had to do it."

Consumed by his anxieties, Joshua had actually forgotten his mother's request. If he had to forget something, why couldn't it be his parents? How he was descended from these two, he could not fathom. Maybe his real mother had left him with the Brightmans, like a cuckoo laying her egg in a serpent's nest. He shook his head and sighed. Surely, a warm-blooded bird should not grow up among reptiles. Maybe his real mother was daft as a cuckoo, which would explain his craziness.

Interrupting Joshua's thoughts, the Beast laid down his fork and knife, made a fist with his left hand, wrapped his right hand around it, pressed hard, and cracked his knuckles loudly.

Joshua winced at the sound. Whatever his true origin might be, he knew his parents certainly did not give rise to his musical talent, which must have come from a distant ancestor, since his father was tone-deaf and his mother enjoyed elevator music.

"Yeah, sorry, if she'd have waited a minute, I would have done it."

Joshua sat down across from his mother and drank a long sip of water. He couldn't focus and his vision began to blur. His hands and feet and face, especially around the mouth, felt numb. Wouldn't be long now. Trying to conceal the tremor in his hand, he served himself some pot roast and potatoes.

"Dinner," proclaimed the Beast, "begins at six. It is now 6:10. You are late. You are always late, mister, which is exactly what got you into trouble in San Francisco. Your problem is you have it too easy. All you have to do is practice the piano every day, play a few concerts here and there, and you're done. You don't know what it is to work hard for a living."

Right. He had just practiced three hours a day since he was ten, and then five to six hours daily from college to the present. Joshua clamped his jaws around a chunk of pot roast and ground it between his teeth. Why did people, including his parents, think musicians never really worked at all; they just enjoyed themselves, "playing" mindlessly for hours on end?

"Really, Dad? Well, I don't think working as an attorney at Leviathan Oil is exactly hard labor."

"How would you know, since you've never had a full-time job in your life? Believe me, we're working nonstop. Since the criminal trial, which already cost the company billions, Merrick has ratcheted up the pressure. In August, we face prosecution by the federal government in the civil trial, where we stand to lose billions more, as well as the looming litigation by every Gulf coast state and thousands of private citizens. It's unbelievable; it's like Gulliver besieged by the Lilliputians, those tiny-brained, pompous, self-important hypocrites. A slew of the private claims are motivated by pure greed; people falsify and exaggerate their losses. They want to use the oil spill to their advantage, to cash in and milk us for money."

He rubbed his eyes, "Except for today, we've been working ten, twelve hours at a time. God, I'm so fried I can hardly see straight."

The Beast buttered a dinner roll, and shook his head. "Truth is, when I chose this field, I had no idea how hard attorneys work. In terms of preparation and research, it's like frantically cramming for a final exam—every single day. But back then I didn't know; I was just glad to get a job where I didn't have to inhale drywall dust, paint fumes, and insulation fibers, or break my back outside in dangerous conditions in all kinds of weather. And then after all the job stress to get ridiculed for going. . . Ah, hell, fuhgeddaboudit."

Bald. Joshua mentally filled in the blank. As he had to acknowledge, the Beast's history truly was a tale of very hard work. When Billy was fourteen, his father, an iron worker, died in a fall. For the next four years, until his mother remarried, he helped support her and his three younger sisters by working construction jobs evenings, weekends, and summers. Large for his age, he worked for his uncle, a building contractor, bringing in twenty an hour. The income kept the family afloat, but the mental and physical stress of school, work, and sports manifested itself in early hair loss; he had bald patches at fifteen, which grew progressively worse. At school they called him Baldilocks.

The ridicule and embarrassment, devastating to an adolescent, fed Billy's anger, and he took it out with grim determination. He spent hours throwing sizzling fast balls over and over to his cousin Lenny either in his backyard or at baseball practice where Lenny was the first string catcher. Billy somehow managed to work, play on the high school baseball team, and make acceptable grades. College would have been impossible without his baseball scholarship.

Joshua ate some pot roast, tender and flavored just right with garlic, onions, salt and pepper. "It's good, Mom."

"Thanks."

"Have some wine, dear." The Beast made a display of filling her glass and his own with red wine. He gazed at his son, "None for you, mister."

Amy made a rare plea on her son's behalf, "Billy, the incident in San Francisco happened over a month ago."

Encouraged, Joshua spoke up, "Dad, you know it was a one-time thing."

The Beast refused to budge. "Was it? Maybe you ought to do some soul searching. The real question is *why* you got drunk. That's what led to the whole sorry mess that followed." He shook his head, "The fact that the press got hold of it jeopardized your career."

"Well, I got good reviews and my management didn't drop me."

"Doesn't it matter to you that Shapiro labeled you 'The Bad Boy of Classical Music'? It's a smear on your professional name."

Shapiro? Completely nonplussed, Joshua blinked rapidly, astounded that his father had actually *read* the review and knew the critic's name. That must be a first; the Beast's disdain for his son's music career was as constant and glacial as the cold in Antarctica.

"It's time for you to grow up, son, and stop behaving like a spoiled brat." The Beast clinked his glass against Amy's. "Here's to those who are punctual, sober, and really work for a living." His mother smiled weakly and took a sip.

Although he was tempted to throw it at the wall, Joshua simply picked up his water glass and gulped. So what if the Beast denied him alcohol? In the end it was hopeless; a bathtub of scotch, a vat of merlot, an ocean of gin could not erase scenes like this from his memory or still the angry voices in his head.

The Beast added in a jovial voice, "Cheer up, son, it's for your own good. Count your blessings; think how lucky you are to live here rent-free while you pay off your debt." He punctuated his sentence by cracking his knuckles.

Rent-free, but never pain-free. Joshua gulped down a bite of pot roast that seemed to inflate itself like an airbag and block his throat. The only way to end this nightly punishment was to move out and live on his own, something he had never done. The astronomical rents in New York had made it impossible. His performance fees were not that high yet, and his manager's commission was twenty per cent of the monthly gross. Moving out might be economically possible here in the South, but did he have the guts to do it? He really didn't know.

"By the way, Joshua, tomorrow, I'm going to teach you how to drive. Since we're not in New York anymore—"

"No kidding."

"Don't interrupt me." The Beast glared at him. "And don't make flippant remarks. You think I'm rough on you? *My* father would have knocked me across the room if I talked to him like that." He stabbed a potato with his fork and then continued. "Since Chalice has a transit system that is practically worthless by New York standards, you're going to have to learn how to drive. We start tomorrow at eight a.m."

"Don't they have driving schools in this town? I can go to a school and save you the trouble." Shit—if he'd only learned to drive sooner, but his priorities had been practicing and performing. In New York he got around fine by subway and bus. But now, here he was, stuck in this humid, suburban, car-dominated hellhole. The pounding in his head made him squint in pain.

"It's cheaper if your dad teaches you," said his mother.

"How much can it cost? I'll pay for it!" He said it so vehemently that a chunk of beef and gravy flew out of his mouth onto the white tablecloth.

"Clean that up!" the Beast roared. "Now!"

Joshua pushed his chair away from the table with a scraping sound, and dabbed at the fleck with his napkin. He succeeded in smearing it and making the spot twice as large.

"Get a dish towel and dip it in cold water," said his mother.

He did and returned to the table to scrub out the spot. "I can't eat anymore," he said, with his head down, as he worked to make the brown stain disappear. "I've got a migraine coming on and I have to go lie down."

"Figures," said the Beast. "Every Friday night, just like clockwork."

Joshua tossed the towel back onto the counter and turned to leave the kitchen.

"What a pussy."

"Billy, hush!"

Through the blinding pain, Joshua saw his mother's complicit smile as she glanced at the Beast, lifted her glass and sipped the wine which swirled in the cup, red as blood.

CHAPTER 3

Annie

Tourists did not drive out of their way to see the New Orleans suburb of Chalice, which began life as a small town on the West Bank of the Mississippi, or as the locals say, "ova da rivuh." Of course, directions in New Orleans are not what they are in the rest of the world, since everything is relative to the river, as in Uptown and Downtown. But even then it gets confusing. For example, the West Bank, home to Chalice, is due south of the city.

Built around a U-shaped bend in the river and narrowing to a long tail, Chalice's name was derived from its wineglass shape and from one of the strongest influences in south Louisiana, the Catholic Church. In the late seventeenth century, René-Robert Cavelier, Sieur de La Salle, claimed the Mississippi River and the vast lands drained by it and its tributaries for France, naming it Louisiana after Louis XIV. From then until a century later when the French ceded Louisiana to the Spanish, the European colonists brought their culture and their religion to bear on the New World. Their Roman Catholic influence remains; it is present in names, in institutions, in the heritage of the people. Instead of counties, boot-shaped Louisiana has sixty-four parishes. Eleven parishes, intoned in order, could serve as a litany: Assumption, Ascension, St. Bernard, St. Charles, St. Helena, St. James, St. John the Baptist, St. Landry, St. Martin, St. Mary, and St. Tammany. They are situated in the southeastern part of the state in and around New Orleans.

There were two convents and three Our Lady churches, as Sam called them, in Chalice. The natives never used their complete names, such as Our Lady of Prompt Succor, they just called them Prompt Succor, La Salette, and Queen of Angels. Even in the secular world, the Catholic influence was evident. All schools had a week off for Mardi Gras; spring break coincided with Easter, and in the not too distant past, children in public schools ate fish on Fridays.

Sam's neighborhood in Chalice was old, a little run-down, not a clipped-lawn neighborhood landscaped by professionals and photographed for the covers of home and gardening magazines. At least not yet. No, it was a bit shabby and unkempt with a smattering of uncut lawns and broken, uneven sidewalks, cracked and pushed skyward at odd angles by the roots of ancient live oak trees. Overall, the neighborhood had a certain disheveled, haphazard Southern charm. The houses, on large lots of lush, green St. Augustine grass, sat well back from the street. Old oaks and sycamores shaded the yards, and in spring and summer, the reds, pinks and whites of flowering crape myrtle, azaleas, and magnolias provided color. The wood frame houses on high piers had been built at the turn of the twentieth century. Modest in size, with steeply pitched gables and generous porches, many needed paint or new roofs.

It was the type of neighborhood that sharp-eyed, salivating realtors surveyed, gauging it ripe for progress. Progress, of course, meant tearing down the old houses and replacing them with oversized brick monstrosities on concrete slabs. The newer houses, like the one on the west side of the Faris family home, dotted the neighborhood and pushed up against their frailer neighbors like school bullies, self-satisfied, hulking and contemptuous.

The Faris family's three-bedroom house was built to last in 1920 by Sam's great grandfather Khalil. It had stood its ground for almost a century, through summer heat, fall hurricanes, hail storms, and tornados. Painted white with dark green shutters, it had twelve-foot ceilings with crown molding, well-maintained wood floors, and one bathroom with the original claw-foot tub. The house faced north with its living room, dining room, and large kitchen on the west side. The master bedroom, the bath and two smaller bedrooms opened off a hall on the east side.

When Khalil died, his son Albert inherited the house where he and his wife Annie raised their sons George and Joseph. After Albert's death in 1995, Annie's younger son Joseph bought the house from his mother, and he and his wife Diana moved in with her. When Sam was born, Joseph rewired the house, modernized the kitchen, and installed central air.

"Sitti, Sitti!" Sam shouted as the door slammed behind her. She ran into the kitchen, almost breathless. "There's a boy next door who plays the piano—the one we hear all the time now—his name is Joshua! His hair is dark orange, like the rolled apricot candy Uncle George brings us from Levant House." She skipped around the spacious kitchen in a circle, humming and clasping her book in one hand.

Her grandmother Annie laughed in surprise and relief; she hadn't seen Sam so animated in months. "*Albi*, you are so excited, you hop like a lamb in springtime. Since you mention Uncle George, he and Aunt Cat are coming tonight after the store closes to take us to Vespers at St. Basil's."

"I know. I hope he brings some baklava."

Annie Faris stood at the gas stove, spatula in hand, watching over two deep cast-iron frying pans. Her smooth, olive skin was flawless, and her white hair was pulled back into a French twist. Her profile with its strong high cheekbones and slightly hooked nose was the living image of Mediterranean queens minted in high relief on ancient coins.

"Yum," cried Sam, breathing in the rich smell of the ground sirloin patties with onion, mint, and cracked wheat frying in olive oil. "Kibbeh and French fries for supper!"

"With fresh sliced tomatoes," added Annie. "And that's your job. Leave the book and go out and pick two nice, ripe ones. You can slice them up for me." Annie's heart rejoiced that after months of quiet grieving, the old Sam had emerged, cheerful, outgoing, enthusiastic. Whoever this Joshua might be, he was a blessing.

"Sitti, wasn't Joshua in the Bible?"

"Yes, he was the leader of the Israelites after Moses. He led them across the Jordan into the Promised Land."

"Joshua, Joshua!" Sam skipped around the room, and came back to hug Annie, dark eyes flashing and cheeks flushed. "Let's read that part tonight after Vespers."

"All right, but first we have to eat, and we can't do that until you go and pick the tomatoes."

"Okay!" Sam dropped the book on the kitchen counter and raced out the back door to the garden.

She was back in two minute with two tomatoes. "Look, Sitti, how round and fat."

"Just like me." The old woman smiled and held out her arms and the young girl ran into them. Although she was almost thirteen, and soon to enter high school, Sam looked about ten. Her head only reached her grandmother's chest, and when Annie wrapped her in a tight hug and kissed the top of her head, Sam was completely enveloped.

Since the death of Sam's father Joseph in January and the onset of her mother's illness, Annie had been Sam's rock of stability. Though she was seventy-nine years old, Annie Faris had remarkable energy. She was always cooking something: lentil soup, *mahshi* (stuffed grape leaves), *laban* (yoghurt), fig preserves, mayhaw jelly, or Syrian bread: round, relatively flat loaves that formed pockets when baked. She even made *shankleesh*, a very smelly white cheese. She planted and tended the garden. She did the wash and kept the house clean, and on weekends, she took Sam out for ice cream and the occasional shopping trip.

"All right," said Annie, releasing her. "You slice the tomatoes and put them on a plate, then go call your mamma to supper. The kibbeh and French fries are done."

Sam quickly sliced the tomatoes, and then ran through the hall door to her mother's room and tapped lightly on the door, "Mamma?"

"Come in, Sam, I'm awake."

Sam opened the door and bounded across the dimly lit room to the bed where her mother lay.

Wincing with the effort, Diana sat up. She held out stick-like arms and hugged her daughter. "I haven't seen you this cheerful in ages. You must have had a good day."

Sam could feel each rib of her mother's skeletal body. "I did," Sam murmured, as she breathed in the familiar scent of her mother's skin and hair, still sweet and pleasant despite her illness. With her face still pressed against Diana's neck, she asked, "Are you feeling okay tonight, Mamma? 'Cause Sitti has dinner ready. It's kibbeh and French fries."

With a last squeeze, her mother released her. "Isn't it a little early to eat dinner?"

"Well, Uncle George and Aunt Cat are coming to take Sitti and me to Vespers at St. Basil's."

Diana raised one eyebrow, "Really? No one asked me about that."

"We didn't think you'd mind. Besides, you were resting and we didn't want to bother you. May I go?"

Diana sighed, "Yes, but you'll have to change into a dress and brush your hair, which as the hymn says, is 'prone to wander'."

"I will. Thanks, Mamma. We won't be gone long. So will you come and eat with us?"

"Yes, I think I can eat today." There were dark circles under Diana's blue eyes, and her fair skin was pale and tinged with yellow.

"Can I let Eliot out?"

"After dinner, Sam. Although it may have some nutritional benefits, I don't relish bird poop on my French fries."

"No, it's much better on cornflakes."

"You little smart aleck!" Diana aimed a playful swat at her daughter, as Sam laughed and scooted out of range, glad to get a rise out of her mother.

Wearing a white dressing gown, Diana sat with her mother-in-law and Sam at the dining table beside a bank of four windows overlooking the backyard. Ceiling fans in the center of the living room and above the dining table rotated slowly, circulating the air. It was almost as green and lush inside the house as outside. The dining area and living room, separated by a graceful, curved archway had the feel of an outdoor courtyard. The profusion of potted palms, a tall and elegant Norfolk Island pine, spider plants, hanging ferns, and fichus trees, had allowed Sam's former pet, Franklin the flying squirrel, to circuit the rooms from branch to frond without ever touching the floor.

"Mamma, I met the boy Joshua who lives next door. He's the one who plays the piano."

"How did you meet him?"

"Well, he sits on the other side of the fence and smokes under the mulberry tree where I read sometimes, and the smoke bothers me. So I got one of Daddy's old fishing poles and put a lead weight and a paper clip on the end of the line. Then I attached a note card and a pencil to the paper clip and lowered it in front of him. I asked him what his name was—I wrote it on the card—and then I asked him to please stop smoking under my tree."

"Clever like Joseph," remarked Annie.

The corners of Diana's mouth turned down, but Sam smiled at the mention of her father.

"We didn't talk, we wrote." And then between bites of kibbeh, French fries, and salad, Sam told the rest of the story, strategically omitting the part about the cuss words. "And so I gave him peppermints to help him stop smoking."

"Well, that was nice of you."

Sam grinned.

Just then the doorbell rang. "Oh," said Sitti, "that's George and Catherine."

Sam ran through the living room and opened the front door.

"Sam! Just the person I wanted to see," said George. He reached down, gave her a hug and then handed her a cloth shopping bag. "Take a look!"

Uncle George always smelled like cigars, and he moved and gestured with a strong, male energy that Sam missed in the house since her father died. The white swatch in his combed-back black hair and the high bridge and sharp downward curve of his nose reminded Sam of an eagle. Aunt Cat, on the other hand, was a swan, quiet, long-necked and graceful.

With George and Cat following her, Sam brought the bag to the dining table, set it down and peered inside. "Pistachios, baklava, and apricot rolls! Thanks, Uncle George, you know just what I like."

"Yes, 'cause I remember all the things your daddy used to bring you."

George held up two more bags to show Annie. "Mamma, I have a gallon of olive oil, five pounds of cracked wheat, some cardamom tea, and a pound of French feta for you. And, hello, beautiful Diana, glad to see you up and about."

He bent down and kissed his gaunt sister-in-law on the cheek.

"Hope you don't mind if we shanghai your sassy daughter and take her to Vespers."

Diana smiled in spite of herself, "She likes to go, and I don't mind really, George, but I wish someone would have let me know first."

Annie leaned forward, "I'm sorry, *albi*, I should have told you and I meant to, but I didn't want to disturb your rest. And when you got up, I was busy serving dinner and I completely forgot."

Diana felt the sting of resentment return. They always kept her in the dark, just like they did with Joseph. She speared a piece of kibbeh so forcefully that the fork clinked loudly against the plate. "Sam, go and change clothes, and brush your hair."

Swallowing a mouthful of French fries, and fleeing her mother's harsh tone, Sam dashed off to the bedroom. Catherine seized the moment to put a hand on her sister-in-law's shoulder. A thin, willowy brunette, almost as tall as her husband George, a six-footer, she spoke in a low, quiet voice. "Diana, thank you for letting us take her to St. Basil's. Would you like to come, too?"

Diana's shoulders slumped, "Cat, I'm just too tired. I don't have the stamina."

"Well, I'm so glad to see you up and eating. I remember how little I wanted to eat when I had the tumor three years ago."

And now you're well and taking my daughter with you, and I'm sick and no amount of treatments or medicine or prayers has helped.

Catherine patted Diana's shoulder gently. "You need to keep up your strength."

Diana glanced down at her half-eaten kibbeh and untouched fries, trying to restrain the swirling wave of jealous anger that threatened to undo her in front of them all. Distrusting her voice, she nodded mutely.

After they left, Diana poured herself a mug of tea and heated it in the microwave. She took the hot drink to the sofa, and sat down heavily, thinking about another occasion, three years earlier, when George brought Cat here to the house. He had delivered groceries that time as well, and as soon as he put them down in the kitchen, he spoke to Annie. "Mamma, I want you to pray for Cat. As I told you, they found a tumor up here," he touched his left temple, "on Monday. She's been havin' bad headaches for quite a while now, and well. . ." His voice trailed off.

"All right. Let me get the anointing oil."

When she returned with the small round chrism of sanctified oil, Annie beckoned them to come and lay hands on Cat's shoulders, something as foreign to Diana as it was familiar to Sam, who had participated in many of Annie's healings in the Syrian-Lebanese community.

Catherine sat on a dining room chair with George at her left and Sam and Diana to her right. It was the first time Diana had participated in a healing. After they laid their hands on Cat's shoulders, Annie rubbed her finger in the oil-soaked cotton and made the sign of the cross on her daughter-in-law's forehead. "In the name of the Father, the Son, and the Holy Ghost." She placed her hands on Cat's temples, closed her eyes, bowed her head, and began to pray aloud quietly, but with great intensity, "Lord Jesus, You have promised that where two or three are gathered together in Your Name, You are also present. Grant healing, Lord, for Catherine in her body, mind, and soul. To You all things are possible, and You are able to heal any illness no matter how great. . . "

As the prayer continued, Diana held her breath, struck both by Annie's words and the way she uttered them. The energy and intensity of the prayer was palpable. With bowed head and eyes squeezed shut, the old woman prayed with all her heart. Like a generator creating electricity, she emanated a force field, and the power of it jolted Diana. She had experienced nothing like it in her Midwestern Protestant background. She believed in God, but as a distant entity addressed by the pastor and the congregation in formal prayers on Sundays. Annie prayed as if God, her friend and helper, stood present in the room.

"Remove the tumor and every cell of cancer from her body, all pain and all fatigue. Restore her to perfect health. Cast out all fear or anxiety from her and strengthen her faith. Grant her new and unending life in You, to the honor and glory of Your Name. In Jesus' Name we pray. Amen."

Annie released her hands and after a moment, Cat stood up, dwarfing the older woman in height. "Thank you, Annie," she said in an unsteady voice. As she hugged Annie and kissed her cheek, Diana noticed the glitter of tears in her sister-in-law's eyes.

As George reported one week later, "Catherine's headaches stopped entirely; she hasn't had any since Mamma prayed for her and, well. . . " his voice trailed off and he shook his head in wonder, "the MRI she had on Friday showed no trace of a tumor."

A miracle, just like that. Diana sipped the hot tea. *And for six months Annie has prayed for me to no avail whatsoever.*

As soon as Sam and Annie returned from Vespers, Sam tried again, "Mamma, now may I let Eliot out?"

"Yes."

When Sam left the room, Annie sat on the sofa beside Diana and apologized again, "*Albi*, I didn't mean to upset you. I would have told you about taking Sam to Vespers, but I didn't want to trouble you, that's all. You have enough to deal with now."

"Well, it surprised me. I guess I'm still hypersensitive because when Joseph gamb—" Diana halted in mid-sentence, hearing Sam's footsteps in the hall. She dropped her voice, "And you knew and—"

Aware that Sam was about to return, Annie sighed and hurriedly whispered. "I know. I should have said something then, and you know how sorry—"

Annie shrieked and Diana ducked involuntarily as Eliot, flying low and fast as a missile, zoomed between their heads, only inches away. After one dazzling, swift circuit of the living room, Eliot the blue jay landed in a Boston fern hanging near the back door, jarring the basket into motion.

Following swiftly behind the bird, Sam re-entered the room. "Mamma, were you talking about Daddy? What did he do?"

"Come sit with us." Diana patted the sofa, while Annie caught her breath.

When Sam sat down, Diana held her by the chin, "Your father gave you his big brown eyes, his sense of humor, and your curiosity about everything in life. That's what he did." She released Sam's chin and sat back, "But of course you got all your brains from me." She leaned forward and kissed her daughter on the head, inhaling the scent of her hair.

"You smell like incense. Did you enjoy Vespers?"

"Yes, I love to look at the icons, especially the angel ones. But now let's read about Joshua."

Sociable, and naturally interested in all things biblical, Eliot flew over and perched on Sam's shoulder, ready to hear the story. Sitting between Diana and Annie, Sam read aloud from the first chapter of Joshua when God appointed him leader of the Israelites. Her favorite part was God's promise of protection to Joshua and His reminder about the Law:

> *"There shall not any man be able to stand before thee all the days of thy life: as I was with Moses, so I will be with thee: I will not fail thee, nor forsake thee. Be strong and of a good courage: for unto this people shalt thou divide for an inheritance the land, which I sware unto their fathers to give them. Only be thou strong and very courageous, that thou mayest observe to do according to all the law, which Moses my servant commanded thee: turn not from it to the right hand or to the left, that thou mayest prosper whithersoever thou goest.*

"After that, Joshua fought many battles, didn't he, Sitti?"

"Yes, he did, and with God's help he won them."

"Well, sleep is winning the battle with me," said Diana, kissing her daughter goodnight, "and it's bedtime for you, too."

Too tired to protest, Sam returned Eliot to his cage in the room she shared with her grandmother. Shaken by her father's death in January, she had deserted her own room for Annie's. Once she was dressed for bed, Sam knelt and said her nighttime prayers.

After cleaning up the kitchen, Annie was also ready for bed. She returned to the room just as Sam finished praying. Annie changed into what she called her blue chemise and took the pins out of her hair. Sam sat cross-legged on her bed in her yellow nightshirt, and looked across at Sitti, who brushed her long white hair as she sat up in bed. Their twin beds were separated by a nightstand bearing a lamp and a clock radio.

"Sitti, remember how God healed Aunt Catherine?"

"Yes."

"Well, if He healed Aunt Cat and the other people you pray for, why won't He heal Mamma, after all our hard praying?"

Annie laid the brush in her lap. Separated by the space between the beds and the life experience of almost seven decades, the wise old woman and the inexperienced young girl regarded each other with the same dark, liquid eyes. "*Albi*, just because He hasn't healed your mamma yet, doesn't mean He won't. We have to be patient. God does everything at the right moment, in His own good time."

"Are you sure, Sitti?" Sam glanced anxiously at her grandmother.

"*Albi*, I am absolutely sure. Don't worry; God hears our prayers and knows all the desires of our hearts. He can heal your mamma at any time."

Reassured, Sam replied, "I know, but I sure wish He would hurry up."

With that, she hopped off the bed, gave her grandmother a goodnight kiss, dove back into her own bed, and two minutes later was sound asleep.

CHAPTER 4

In the Garden

Early the next morning, Sam and Sitti ate a breakfast of scrambled eggs, bacon, and buttered homemade biscuits smeared with mayhaw jelly. Afterward, they took mugs of hot, milky tea outside to the shady patio to enjoy the short-lived cool of morning. Sam, flanked by her tea mug on one broad arm of the Adirondack chair and her current book on the other, had also brought Eliot. He perched on her index finger, secured to her wrist with a lightweight bird harness.

"If Eliot had been a soldier in 1861, Sitti, in his blue and gray uniform, he would have fought for the Confederate army. I'm reading a book about the Civil War," she announced. Sam stroked the bright blue feathers on his lower back while Eliot flicked his long, barred tail. "It's funny how his chest is gray and his upper back is a bright blue."

"That's God's design for blue jays," said Annie.

Sam continued to stroke the bird gently. "But, Eliot, I hate to tell you your Rebel hat is all wrong. You have a crest where you're supposed to have a flat top." Although he loved affection, Eliot was a sucker for bright, shiny objects. He suddenly hopped from his perch on Sam's finger to Sitti's shoulder and pecked at the back of her gold hoop earring. Sitti hunched her shoulders, laughed, and jerked her head to one side like a boxer avoiding a punch.

"Eliot!" They shouted at the same time.

He fluttered up into the air in a short arc and landed on Sam's head, protesting with a succession of liquid notes, followed by whirrs and gurgling sounds.

"Eliot, you're not a pigeon. Get off my head!"

Clearly contrite, he fluttered down to Sam's shoulder.

"Look, Sitti," Sam pointed at the crystal drops on the potted flowers beside her, "the dew is still on the roses! Just like the song Mamma sings sometimes." Unselfconscious as the blue jay, she sang in a clear, true voice:

> *I come to the garden alone,*
> *While the dew is still on the roses,*
> *And the voice I hear falling on my ear,*
> *The Word of God discloses.*
>
> *And He walks with me and He talks with me,*
> *And He tells me I am His own,*
> *And the joy we share as we tarry there,*
> *None other has ever known.*

Sam felt a hand on her shoulder. "Mamma!" Both Sam and Annie turned their heads in surprise. Diana had come up quietly behind them.

"Sam, except for the hymns you have to practice for youth choir, I haven't heard you sing on your own like that for six months," Diana said. She caressed her daughter's head, "That was lovely."

"Mamma, are you okay?"

Diana's dark blue eyes, underscored by purple half-circles of exhaustion, stood out starkly against the yellowish cast of her skin.

"No, honey, I'm not feeling well. Been turning my stomach inside out all night. Now it's the dry heaves."

"*Albi, albi*, take the medicine for nausea."

"Can't." She drew a pill container out of her pocket and shook it. "Empty. Annie, could you please go to the pharmacy and refill the prescription for me?"

Annie rose from the chair, "Of course."

"Can I go too, Sitti?"

"You stay with your mamma."

"Let her go," said Diana. "There's nothing she can do for me right now. Eliot will keep me company. I'll be all right. But, Sam, brush your hair before you go."

"I already did!"

"Really?" The corners of Diana's lips curled upwards slightly in a ghost-like smile.

"Yes, really," Sam laughed, glad her mother still had the spirit to tease her about her cloud of unruly hair. Once inside the house, Sam handed Eliot to Diana and gave her mother a quick, wordless hug before she and Annie left for the pharmacy.

Annie drove her ancient green Ford sedan with one foot on the accelerator and one foot on the brake. The moment the car gained a little speed, she applied the brake, so the car advanced like a rowboat in a succession of head-bobbing lurches.

They arrived safely at the pharmacy, thanks more to God than the internal combustion engine. While they waited for the prescription, Sam spied the candy.

"Sitti, can I have some peppermints? I gave Joshua all the ones I keep in the mulberry tree."

"All right, *albi*." Although Annie lived on a fixed income, she always had enough money to buy treats for her Sam.

On the return trip, as they advanced down their block in a series of jerks, a shiny, silver BMW pulled into the driveway of the enormous brick house next to theirs, and two men stepped out of the car. The driver was a slim young man with reddish, curly hair, but the passenger was a massive, scowling older man, bald as an egg.

"Sitti, Sitti," yelled Sam, "see the red-haired boy? That's Joshua!"

Startled by Sam's outburst, Annie missed the turn into the driveway by a foot and hit the curb. Airborne for a moment, they landed with an ominous metallic clank as the ancient shock absorbers took the blow. As they bounced toward the house, Annie jammed on the brake, gripped the steering wheel with one hand and clapped the other over her chest, "You scared me!"

Oblivious, Sam remarked, "Aw, heck, they already went into the house."

Annie handed Sam the bag containing Diana's prescription. "Here, *albi*, you're quicker than I am. Run in and give this to Diana."

At the same time Annie entered the front door, she heard the backdoor slam. She hurried to Diana's room to check on her. Like the academic she was, Diana had made the spacious room more library than bedroom. Her large computer desk and work table stood against the eastern windows, opposite the door. Across from the bed and its side table, floor-to-ceiling bookshelves filled the southern wall. With four large windows, the room could have been cheerful and bright, but since Joseph's death and her illness, Diana kept the curtains drawn, and the room remained dim even in the middle of the day.

"Sam delivered the goods and scampered outside," said Diana. "Thank you, Annie, I just took a pill." She was sitting up in bed with one hand resting protectively over her stomach.

"Let me make some peppermint tea," Annie offered. "That's good for nausea."

"Thank you, I'll try anything." Diana smiled wanly. "But first, Annie, sit down for a minute." She patted the bed. "We need to talk while Sam is out."

Annie sat down on the edge of the bed.

"I have a doctor's appointment at the Medical Center on Monday. They're going to evaluate how I'm doing." Diana bit her lower lip. "My gut feeling is that I'm going downhill. If the radiation has failed, then really all that's left is pain control. If that's the case, then we'll have to discuss what arrangements we can make for Sam after my death."

"*Albi*, it's too early to give up."

"I'm not giving up; I'm just telling you how I feel." Diana's tone was sharp-edged. "I hope I'm wrong, but in any case, I'll get the report on Monday. It's just that I have, well, not a premonition exactly, but just a kind of knowing that—"

They heard the slam of the back door and the sound of running footsteps. Sam appeared in the doorway, "Mamma, would it be all right for Joshua to come over?"

"Is he coming now?"

"Umm, I haven't asked him yet, but I want to." She looked expectantly at Diana.

The hope in Sam's eyes decided her. Although company at the moment was the last thing she wanted, Diana simply couldn't disappoint her daughter after all the grief Sam had endured. "Yes, you can invite him."

Sam's whole face lit up.

"He can eat lunch with us, if he wants," added Annie. We're having—"

"Oh, Annie, please don't mention food!" exclaimed Diana with a grimace.

"Oh, sorry."

"Thank you, Mamma!" Sam turned on her heel and rushed back out to the backyard.

"It's wonderful to see Sam so excited and enthusiastic again," said Diana. "The doctors are wrong; all I really need is an energy transfusion from her. With that I could survive anything."

Eliot flew into the room with his own burst of energy and landed on the headboard of Diana's bed with a chirp. He cocked his head and eyed the two women with a questioning look.

"Hello, you beauty," said Annie. With her eye on the bird, she said, "Sam saved your life, didn't she?" And transferring her gaze to Diana, Annie added, "And this Joshua might just save Sam, I think. She's beginning to be her old self again."

"It appears so," replied Diana.

Annie rose. "Before I make the tea, Diana," she said, "I would like to pray for you again."

"You are so persistent, Annie, but I think it's hopeless."

"It's never hopeless. Let me pray for you."

Diana sighed, and her shoulders slumped, "All right."

While Eliot watched the proceedings with great interest, Annie made the sign of the cross upon Diana's forehead. She gently laid one hand on Diana's back and one hand on her abdomen. Surprising Diana, although Eliot took it in stride, Annie changed tactics, praying fervently in Arabic, "*Ay'yuhar-Rab'bu(d)-(d)aabi(t)ul-kul Ilaahu aabaa'ina, na(t)lubu ilayka fastajib war(h) am. Ir(h)amna yaa Al'laah ka`a(th)eemi ra(h)matika, na(t)lubu ilayka fastajib war(h)am. . .*"

For several minutes, the liquid syllables and occasional soft gutturals flowed musically and hypnotically, rising and falling, capturing the ear like birdsong. But though they listened intently, neither Eliot nor Diana had the least idea what she said.

CHAPTER 5

Bookings

To Joshua's relief, his mobile phone rang as soon as he entered the house. For a few minutes at least, the Beast would have to hold his fire about the driving lesson.

"Joshua, it's Nathan, callin' with good news this mornin'."

Nathan Weiss' nasal voice with its heavy New York accent and staccato delivery cheered Joshua immensely. He had the cheekiest manager in the world, of that he was certain.

"Get a pen and dust off your calendar, we've got two new bookings for the fall."

Joshua walked quickly to the music room, where his glossy black seven-foot B-model Steinway resided in solitude across from a large window overlooking the front lawn. He opened his planner, which lay on the piano, and took a pencil from the music rack. "Okay, shoot."

"Block out these dates: October fifth through seventh, Seattle Symphony, Brahms first. Then November twenty-third through twenty-fifth, Thanksgiving weekend, Detroit Symphony, Mozart twenty-one. I'll call later with rehearsal details." Nathan paused for a moment. "Got it?"

"Yeah. Business has really picked up."

"You can thank San Francisco for that. Shapiro's review in the *Chronicle*, 'Brightman, the Bad Boy of Classical Music,' got attention and the calls have started comin' in to BG Artist Management. You're suddenly a risin' star with the thirty-five and under demographic, just the crowd all these orchestras are tryin' to pull in. As they say in showbiz, notoriety is not a bad wave; you better ride it while you can."

"I can guarantee that notoriety was not my intention."

"I'm glad to hear it, 'cause the flip side of this is not so pretty. We've been friends ever since high school, so I'm tellin' you this for your own good, Joshua, and I'm only gonna say it once. In the world of classical music, talent is paramount, but reputation and reliability are the keys to longevity. You put us both in danger when you showed up late for that rehearsal. Ninety union musicians sat idle while the orchestra management paid them for every tick of the clock. When they couldn't locate you, they called me."

"Nathan, I know—I apologized already."

"Yeah, but what you don't know is that when the Seattle Symphony and Detroit called, they were interested, but very leery. They were so nervous about hiring you, I had to talk 'em into it."

Other than one engagement with the Boston Pops, playing the Tchaikovsky first piano concerto in May with the San Francisco Symphony had been the highest profile gig he'd ever had. Alone in the hotel room the night before, he had tried to drown the demons of obsessive-compulsive disorder, the irrational fears and intrusive thoughts, the perpetual counting, which always grew worse under stress. After downing half a bottle of scotch, he spilled the rest on the bed and the carpet. Drunk, and furious with himself, he hurled the bottle at his reflection, shattering the mirror. He promptly fell asleep in his clothes, overslept, and showed up late for the morning rehearsal.

By the time he arrived, only thirty-five minutes of the allotted rehearsal time remained, not enough for the entire concerto. Halfway through the last movement of the Tchaikovsky, management stopped the rehearsal; they refused to pay the orchestra overtime. Then the hotel slapped him with a large fee for damages. Thank God he had played well that night, and the critics liked it, even though someone tipped off Shapiro about his misbehavior at the hotel and the rehearsal snafu.

Bringing himself back to his ever-present anxiety about money, Joshua asked, "Nathan, did you finalize the fees?"

"Yeah, after I hooked 'em. Ten grand each."

"Really?"

"Yeah," said Nathan, and Joshua was relieved to hear the smile in his voice. "The price goes up for the Bad Boy of Classical Music."

Nathan cleared his throat. "But seriously, Joshua, from now on, keep to the straight and narrow. This was a close call. Mister CEO Bruce Grifaldo came within an inch of cannin' your ass. Only my inspired and eloquent defense saved you."

"And what was that?"

"I pleaded your youth, your great talent, your heartthrob good looks."

"Thanks, Nathan."

"No problem. Just remember you owe me dinner next time you're in New York."

Joshua smiled, "Sure thing."

As he pocketed the phone, he felt a small stirring of hope in his chest. Maybe, just maybe, if his bookings picked up and his fees increased, there might be a way out.

He heard the heavy footsteps of the Beast and his stomach muscles tightened. He thought his father was either going to jeer at him for hitting the curb four times on the turns, or make him pay to fix the alignment. But this time his father surprised him.

"Who was that?" The Beast loomed in the doorway, practically filling it. His father's eyes were small, but they probed, penetrated, and burned like lasers. No place to hide.

"Nathan, my manager."

"Why do you look so depressed?" Suddenly changing his expression to one of mock surprise, he pointed his index finger skyward. "Ah, let me guess: BG Artists dropped you from their roster."

With the tip of his finger, Joshua tapped the sharp point of the pencil he still held.

Slam his head against the wall, then gouge out his eyes.

His fingers suddenly seemed boneless. The pencil fell from his hand and clattered on the wood floor.

"So what was the call about, Fumble Fingers?"

Joshua wanted to counter with his own question: *Why, Baldilocks, when you know what ridicule feels like, do you always have to ridicule me?* But he held his tongue and stuffed his sweating hands into the pockets of his shorts. "Two new bookings for the fall—Seattle in October and Detroit in November."

The Beast sniffed. "Well, at least you still have a career."

"And the fee went up. I'll make ten thousand for each."

"Hmmph," The Beast shook his head. "Just a drop in the bucket against your student loans and the cost of the Steinway." He smiled and cracked his knuckles, satisfied with himself, "Your mother and I are going out to play eighteen holes with Charles Merrick and his wife, and then we're eating lunch at the country club." As he turned to go, he added, "As for you, I guess you'd better tie yourself to the bench and practice."

As the Beast turned to go, Joshua's anxious thoughts swirled.

Brahms 1 + Mozart 21 = 22

22 = 2 × 11 = 2 × 7 + 2 × 4

Three steps to the door, turn right, four steps to the hall, turn left. Three steps to the bathroom. Safe!

Joshua lathered and rinsed his hands three times, and then washed his face with cold water. He still felt weak from the effects of last night's migraine. Glancing at the red stubble on his chin, he decided to shave. He slowly smoothed shaving cream on his cheeks, wishing the Beast and his consort would leave.

By the time he rinsed and dried his clean-shaven face, he heard the sound of the BMW pulling away. He put his right hand in his pocket and discovered a round red-and-white peppermint. He had fallen asleep in his clothes last night and though he had changed his shirt, he still wore the khaki shorts from yesterday.

He unwrapped the peppermint and put it in his mouth. Why a piece of peppermint candy should give him such a sense of well-being, he didn't know, but it did. For a moment he couldn't remember the kid's name. After last night, their encounter seemed like a week ago. *Sam*, that was it. Sam and his notecards.

Joshua retrieved his cigarettes from his bedroom while his empty stomach growled loudly. He had vomited up the pot roast and potatoes during the night. In the kitchen he poked around in the refrigerator, but nothing he saw seemed appealing. Well, the peppermint would suffice for breakfast.

He stood at the patio doors with his lighter and pack of cigarettes in one hand. He wondered what kind of tree it was that leaned over the fence, shading the bench. In his backyard, devoid of any living plant but grass, the tree drew the eye. He knew it was an old tree by the great thickness of the trunk. The morning breeze ruffled its leaves and the topmost branches swayed slightly.

He wasn't going to practice now. He'd save that for when the Beast was home. No, he was going to enjoy some peace before his parents returned. He thought about the yard he'd glimpsed next door. It was a garden, really, a little Eden teeming with various plants and flowers. To his great surprise, he was suddenly overcome by a ridiculous sense of longing. He wondered if the kid was up in the tree.

Only one way to find out. Joshua opened the patio door.

CHAPTER 6

Playing Catch

He paced off eighteen steps (an excellent number) to the tree. Before sitting on the bench, Joshua peered up into the canopy from different angles, trying to see if Sam the kid was up there, but as before, he only saw the edge of the wooden platform high up in the tree. He waited quietly for a minute or two, but nothing. No sound, no movement, no kid.

Ridiculously disappointed, Joshua sat down and laid his cigarettes and lighter on the bench beside him. He crunched the last bit of peppermint, leaned back, stretched out his legs, and enjoyed the cool early morning breeze. He looked up at the Louisiana sky, which seemed almost as vast as his debt. One hundred thirty-five thousand dollars to pay off his student loan and the Steinway, down from one-fifty. The Beast and his consort allowed him to live for free while he paid off the debt in big chunks every month. Moving from home into an apartment had been impossible in New York; only broom closets rented for under a thousand there. But if the rents in New Orleans were cheaper, and Nathan could get him more bookings and higher concert fees, he might be able to escape.

He took a deep breath, released it, and looked up at the endless blue sky. The Adagio of Beethoven's fifth piano concerto came to his mind unbidden, the melody so serene and heartbreaking. That was where he wanted to live. The only place Joshua really had peace was there, in the music. For as long as the music lasted, whether he played it or listened to it, his world was a pure and perfect construction, untouched by fear or shame or ridicule or anger. There he dwelt in perfect peace, like Adam in the Garden before the Fall.

"What the—?" Joshua ducked involuntarily, startled by a large brown object which sailed over the fence and hit the grass in front of him with a dull thud.

It was a worn leather baseball glove, a fielder's glove, evidence of a kid not seen. Well, at least it wasn't a catcher's mitt. He remembered the endless Saturdays when the Beast pitched fastball after fastball at him while he crouched behind a catcher's mitt in a grim, unspoken battle to see what gave out first, the Beast's arm or Joshua's hand. Many times Joshua's left hand swelled and he couldn't play piano for two days after.

He picked up the faded, musty-smelling glove to throw it back over the fence, and then he couldn't resist. He stuffed his left hand in it, only to find something stiff and crackling inside. He pulled out a folded piece of lined school paper which he opened.

Dear Joshua,

If you want to play catch with me, hop over the fence. My mom says it's okay. You can eat lunch with us too.

Your neighbor,
Sam

Joshua smiled; he liked this kid. Surely Sam couldn't throw as hard as the Beast. Besides, what else did he have to do—he wasn't going to practice until later. Joshua put the note in the pocket of his shorts, stepped onto the bench, and looked over the fence.

No one was there.

Unsure of what to do, he surveyed the yard. He delighted again to see such a riot of resplendent life. The trees across the way were heavy with fat brown figs, and beside them stood a small tree loaded with reddish-orange flowers. But where was Sam? He searched with his eyes from the vegetable garden to the swaying elephant ears near the house. Plenty of plant life, but no sign of a human being. The kid must have gone back into the house.

Joshua hesitated. Should he toss the glove back into Sam's yard and retreat, or should he hop the fence, and return it—step into the unknown? The garden was so inviting, and after all, he *had* been invited. Curiosity and hope propelled him. With the glove in his hand, he stepped onto the top of the bench, climbed over the fence, and hopped down, landing in a patch of thick grass beside the massive trunk of the tree.

He saw the series of short horizontal boards nailed to the tree like the rungs of a ladder, making it easy to climb up the thick, rough trunk. From this side of the fence, the small platform high up in the branches was more visible, but as far as he could tell, the kid was not up there. He climbed up three rungs, craning his neck upwards to see. "Sam?" he called.

No answer.

Joshua hopped down again and walked toward the old wooden tool shed at the back of the property. Just inside the open door stood a red gas-powered push mower. The ankle deep grass certainly needed cutting. Guessing that Sam was hiding in the tool shed, Joshua peeked in. It was inhabited by an assortment of yard tools, but no young boy.

Joshua put the glove on his left hand and smacked his right fist into it a couple of times. It felt good, but for whatever reason, it didn't seem like he was going to play catch. He turned and walked toward the house to return the glove. He could just lay it on one of the Adirondack chairs on the patio and then he'd hop back over the f—

"Heads up!"

Motion caught his eye. A white softball lofted up from somewhere on the patio. Surprised, but keeping his eyes on the ball, Joshua followed its arc, jogging forward and to his right to catch it. As soon as it smacked his glove, Joshua looked toward the house.

A small, sturdy boy looking about ten years old, emerged from among the potted flowers and elephant ears on the patio. He sure needed a haircut; his cloud of wild, dark hair fell in waves to his chin. Dressed in a yellow T-shirt, blue jean shorts, and sneakers, he raised the fielder's glove, which looked enormous on his left hand, and beckoned Joshua to throw the ball.

Joshua lobbed the ball in a slow, high arc and watched Sam calculate the trajectory perfectly. The boy caught it, and immediately wound up and threw it back with all his force, straight at Joshua's chest. It didn't have much speed on it, but it was accurately thrown.

"Come away from the house," Joshua called. "I don't want to hit a window or any of the flowers."

Joshua jogged backwards and Sam skipped forward about ten feet. They began to throw the ball back and forth until they found a kind of easy rhythm. Joshua had a practiced ease in throwing, while Sam had to use more effort with the heavy softball, which looked too big for his hand. Surprisingly strong for his size, he put everything he had into each throw. As they played, they talked in a conversation punctuated by the smacking of the ball on leather and Sam's soft grunts of exertion.

"That's my dad's glove. He used to play catch with me a lot."

"Doesn't he have time anymore?"

"He got killed in a car wreck in January."

"Oh." Joshua winced—only six months ago. *Wish it had been my dad instead of yours.* Without thinking, he threw the ball with fierce speed.

It hit Sam's glove with a resounding smack. "Ouch, Joshua, that was a hard one!" He took his hand out of the glove and shook it.

"Sorry," Joshua called, and he truly was. *Shit, why can't I do anything right?* The last thing he wanted to do was to hurt the little guy.

"Well," said Joshua, "my dad used to play catch with me, but we used a hardball. How about you? Did you ever play hardball?"

Sam put the glove back on and threw the ball to Joshua. "Nope."

"Why not?"

"'Cause girls play softball."

Girls? Sam was a girl?

"Oh." Well, now the hair made sense. Joshua felt a little ridiculous. Why hadn't he caught on sooner? He wound up and threw the ball back and watched him. . . *her* leap to catch it.

He scratched his head and tried to adjust. He was playing catch with a little girl. The Beast would mock him to the end of time if he ever found out. Well, at least she hadn't invited him over to play with dolls.

"I played on a softball team last summer, but then my mom got sick and this year I couldn't."

If her father was dead and her mother was ill, then who took care of her? "Do you have any brothers or sisters?"

"No, do you?"

"No." He was out of his league; he had no experience with young girls. In fact, apart from Nathan, he had never even had many friends. He was a loner, a social disaster.

She grinned, "Looks like we're a pair of spoiled-brat only children, then."

The remark was so unexpected, Joshua laughed. But at the same time, the Beast's comment surfaced in his mind. *It's time for you to grow up, son, and stop behaving like a spoiled brat.* He wiped his brow. The sun blazed directly overhead and the heat threatened to melt him. "A spoiled brat—I've been accused of that before."

"So what?" She threw the ball to him and suddenly darted across the yard to a fig tree. She plucked two figs, popped one in her mouth, turned and hurled the other one at him.

"What the hell?" He caught it in his free hand.

"Take a bite, Joshua, and never give a fig about what other people think!" She bolted for the house, "C'mon, let's get some ice water."

"Good idea on both counts." Joshua smiled and ate the fig. He tucked the glove and ball under one arm and wiped his brow again. Feeling a little sheepish and unsure of what to expect next, he followed her. She had surprised him all along, with her notecards, the peppermints, and finally the invitation enclosed in a baseball mitt. As he walked toward the house, he tossed out all preconceptions: forget about sugar, spice, and everything nice; this girl was a firecracker.

CHAPTER 7

Here's My Heart

"Sitti, Sitti, Joshua's here!"

As Joshua followed Sam into the bright, airy kitchen, a stout, white-haired woman standing at the gas stove turned to greet him with a broad smile. She wore a white cotton apron over a blue dress, and she looked as soft and round as a teddy bear. "So you are Joshua. I am Annie Faris, Sam's grandma."

Surprised by her foreign accent, he immediately tried to place it. At the same time, seeing Sam and Annie together, he was struck by their strong resemblance. Despite the age difference they had the same high cheekbones, the same smooth, fair skin with olive tones, and most welcoming to him, the same kind and gentle light in their deep brown eyes.

Joshua guessed it must be Annie who took care of Sam. He shook her outstretched hand, "A pleasure to meet you."

Inhaling deeply, he gestured at the great covered pot on the stove. "Whatever you're cooking smells wonderful."

"Please stay and have lunch with us," said Annie. "I'm making *mahshi*—stuffed grape leaves, and we'll have yoghurt salad."

Noticing his flushed face, she tapped Sam on the shoulder, "*Albi*, give Joshua something to drink."

Sam hurriedly filled two glasses with water and ice and gave one to Joshua, who drained half his glass immediately.

"Thank you for inviting me." Joshua wiped his brow. "I love stuffed grape leaves, but what's in a yoghurt salad?"

"Cucumber, salt, garlic, and a little mint from the garden."

Unable to contain his curiosity longer, he asked, "Your accent, is it Greek?"

Annie smiled, "And I think I sound so American. My family is from Beirut. For many years we spoke only Arabic at home."

"Oh. When did your family emigrate?"

"They came here in 1915. They were hoping for a better life, more opportunity. Many, many Syrian Christians like us came to America, beginning in the late 1800's. And then they all went into business," she laughed. "Sam, please set the table and then go and get your mamma. She's resting."

Joshua helped Sam carry the plates, glasses and silverware to the dining table. He glanced out the bank of windows at the backyard where he could see the roses, geraniums, and hibiscus on the patio and the neat rows of the vegetable garden in the brilliant sunshine. He wished his own backyard had been as beautiful and full of life.

It pleased Joshua greatly that the interior of the house was as inviting as the yard. The high ceilings created a sense of space and peace, while the shining oak floors and the bright oriental rugs added color and cheer. A graceful archway separated the living and dining rooms. In the living room, comfortable sofas and armchairs were grouped around a coffee table, and he was glad to see a large old upright piano with a round wooden bench against the left hand wall. The slowly oscillating ceiling fans and the profusion of potted plants on both sides of the archway gave the house a very exotic atmosphere. He reveled in the warm, welcoming space, so unlike his own home.

Once the table was set, Sam ran off to get her mother, and Joshua returned to the kitchen to help Annie bring the food to the table. "Why does Sam call you *SIT-tee?*" he asked.

"It means *grandmother* in Syrian."

"Is Sam's real name Samantha?"

"Yes."

"But you call her *EL-bee.*"

"It means *my heart.*"

Joshua nodded. "She could easily steal one's heart, couldn't she?"

Annie just smiled.

Joshua set a platter of steaming stuffed grape leaves on the table, and Annie brought a basket with several loaves of homemade Syrian bread. Lastly, she set out a bowl of cool yoghurt salad. The smell and look of the food set off a monsoon in Joshua's mouth. Surprised that he almost forgot, he blurted, "Oh, may I use the bathroom?"

As soon as he was safely in the bathroom, he washed his hands three times. When he returned, he strolled over to the upright piano and played a few soft arpeggios to check the sound of the instrument and its tuning, which was fine. A battered hymnal stood open on the music rack with a box of tissues beside it. There was a small icon propped on an easel on top of the piano, Christ the Good Shepherd, robed in red and carrying a sheep across his shoulders. But Joshua's attention was drawn to a large framed photograph of a young sailor hung on the wall above. The sailor's white cap contrasted with his black, curly hair, olive skin and dark eyes. He wore V-necked dress blues with three white stripes on the edge of the broad collar. The white eagle insignia on the left arm of the shirt was underscored by something that looked like wings with lightning bolts in the middle, and under that two red chevrons.

Annie came and stood beside Joshua. "That's my husband Albert. He was a Radioman in the Naval Air Force during World War II."

"Where did he serve?"

"He was stationed at Clark Airfield in the Philippines on Luzon."

At that moment, Sam returned. Standing under the archway, she announced, "Mamma's feeling much better. She's getting dressed!"

Hearing a strange thrumming sound, Joshua turned and then dodged sideways as a bird, appearing out of nowhere, darted directly at his head. It happened so fast, he didn't even recognize what kind of bird it was. It circled the living room, shot past Sam through the archway, skirted the ceiling fan in the dining room, and landed on the edge of a hanging spider plant.

"A blue jay?" he blurted, staring open-mouthed as it flew from the plant and landed on Sam's shoulder.

"This is Eliot," Sam announced. "He fell out of the nest this spring, and I raised him."

Joshua had no idea that a wild bird could be tamed. "Well, hello, Eliot!"

At the sound of his name, Eliot cocked his crested head and regarded Joshua with a stern, beady look. He could have presided over the Supreme Court; there was judgment in that eye.

Joshua hoped he passed muster.

When Sam took a few pistachios from her pocket, the bird fluttered down and ate them from her hand. Joshua was fascinated. He stepped cautiously forward; he had never been so close to a wild bird. The blue jay was such a vivid and beautiful presence. The violet blue and white-flecked wings contrasted with his blue and black-barred tail feathers.

"Sam found him under the mulberry tree when he was just a fledgling."

All Joshua's attention had been focused on the bird until Sam's mother spoke. He lifted his eyes from the blue jay to the woman who walked slowly toward him. He estimated that she was about forty, maybe fifteen years his senior. But the fullness and richness that should have been high summer in her had been robbed by her illness. Cancer, he guessed. There was an aura of resignation about her. Looking jaundiced, frail, and brittle in her loose blue blouse and white slacks, she moved carefully and slowly like one old and infirm, holding a hand protectively over her stomach. Only her masses of thick, wavy light brown hair and her wide-set eyes, the rich, dusky blue of a northern sky, seemed youthful.

"Joshua, so glad to meet you." Her smile brought the fleeting return of summer to her face. She held out her hand, "I'm Diana Faris, Samantha's mother."

Her Midwestern accent surprised him almost as much as the coldness of her hand. "I'm Joshua Brightman."

"Joshua Brightman," repeated Sam. "Your name is like the hymn I memorized for youth choir last week, *Ye Holy Angels Bright*. I have to sing one more tomorrow, the fifth one, and I'll get my own hymnal with my name printed on it in gold."

"Do you attend an Orthodox church?" asked Joshua, glancing at the icon.

"No," answered Diana. "Sam's father Joseph was Orthodox, but I was a lowly Methodist, so when we married, we split the difference with the Episcopal Church. What about you?"

Good question. At age twenty-four, Joshua didn't know who he was anymore. Brooklyn-born, a city boy transplanted to alien southern suburbia, he had lost his identity; he felt faceless as a mannequin.

"My family is Jewish, but we were never observant."

Hell, even his family had no real identity—secular Jews so divorced from their tradition that apart from his Bar Mitzvah eleven years ago, there was nothing that made them particularly Jewish. They had no tradition. They never went to synagogue; on Friday evenings they never had Shabbat dinner. And how many New York Jews loved hunting and collected weapons like the Beast?

"My parents aren't religious at all." Feeling uncomfortable, Joshua changed the subject, "So Sam, what is the song you're singing tomorrow?"

"*Come Thou Fount of Every Blessing.* May I sing it, Mamma?"

"Of course."

With Eliot perched on her finger, Sam stood framed in the archway and sang:

> *Come thou fount of ev'ry blessing,*
> *Tune my heart to sing thy grace;*
> *Streams of mercy, never ceasing,*
> *Call for songs of loudest praise.*
> *Teach me some melodious sonnet,*
> *Sung by flaming tongues above;*
> *Praise the mount—I'm fixed upon it—*
> *Mount of thy redeeming love!*

Joshua sat down on the piano stool and clasped his hands together. His fingers itched to accompany Sam, but he decided against it; he didn't want to draw attention away from her.

He recognized the tune she sang, an old American melody in triple meter with an easy, rocking rhythm. Familiar though it was, it had a strange effect on him. Somehow, and he never knew if it was the singer or the song, like gamma rays penetrating stone, it cut through all his defenses to reach the innermost chamber of his heart.

As she came to the end of the verse, Joshua lowered his head. Sam sang as purely, sweet and true, as an English choirboy, but instead of a stiff white ruff and flowing choir vestments, she was clothed in innocence and the complete trust and faith that she was loved by those around her. She smiled as she sang and her eyes kindled with light.

Though he was always sensitive to and keenly affected by music, he didn't know why a simple song, an unadorned melody, should touch him the way it did. He was ambushed, utterly disarmed by her singing. His heart, hardened from childhood by continual emotional assaults, had turned to ice. Now the ice cracked; his heart melted. His vision blurred, and he fought to retain control of himself.

By the time he got his bearings, she was singing the final verse.

> *Oh! to grace how great a debtor*
> *Daily I'm constrained to be!*
> *Let thy goodness, like a fetter,*
> *Bind my wand'ring heart to thee!*
> *Prone to wander—Lord, I feel it—*
> *Prone to leave the God I love;*
> *Here's my heart—O take and seal it—*
> *Seal it for thy courts above.*

As the song ended, Eliot flew off and found a comfortable perch in the potted Norfolk Island pine. Looking like an unseasonable Christmas ornament, he sang his own wordless solo, warbling and bright, while Annie and Diana applauded Sam.

Joshua grabbed a tissue from the box on the piano and wiped his whole face, especially his eyes. "Whew, still sweating from the heat," he said. "Well, Sam, I'll bet that tomorrow, not only will you win the hymnal, but you will be the very best singer of all."

Sam's smile could have encompassed the whole Crescent City. "I hope so," she said, eyes alight with innocent pleasure, unaware of how much she had affected them all.

"I know so," Joshua affirmed. In fact, he had a very strong hunch that Samantha Faris was gifted in many ways, and he surmised that whatsoever she did, she would do it very well.

For her part, Diana felt a surge of new energy, her heart lifted in a way she had not felt for months. Because of Joshua, the old Sam had returned, and Diana, positively buoyant with thankfulness, could have kissed his hand.

Annie's delight took a practical turn, down to earth and basic, a tenet of Middle Eastern hospitality. "*Yalla, yalla,*" she urged them, smiling and extending her arms to hurry them toward the table. "Eat, eat! Time to eat while the *mahshi* is still warm!"

CHAPTER 8

A Prediction

A t the dining table, Joshua sat across from Sam with his back to the windows. Diana sat on his left and Annie on his right, nearest the kitchen. "We always say a blessing," said Annie. She and Diana reached for his hands and Sam's, and once the circle was complete, they bowed their heads. Joshua could not remember the last time he had held anyone's hand or the last time he had been included in a prayer.

Annie prayed aloud, "O Lord Jesus, we thank You for this day, for the life You have given us, and for our time together."

Joshua shifted uneasily in his chair. He would have felt uncomfortable in the presence of a rabbi who prayed aloud, much less a devout Christian like Annie. To his embarrassment, his hands began to sweat.

"We ask Your blessing upon this house and upon Joshua and all his family. Grant healing for Diana and all those who suffer in body, mind, or soul."

Suddenly, without the least idea why, Joshua swiveled his head toward Annie. She looked up and met his eyes with an incredibly piercing gaze. It stopped his breath. *What does she know?*

After the slightest pause, she closed her eyes and continued, "Bless this food to our bodies' use and us to Your service, in Jesus' Name. Amen." She, Diana, and Sam crossed themselves.

Thankfully, the prayer was short. Joshua surreptitiously dried his moist palms with a napkin.

As they began to serve themselves, Diana asked Sam to get some butter. "We forgot the mayhaw jelly, too," said Sam, darting into the kitchen. She came back bearing the butter dish and wearing a frown. "Sitti, there's no more mayhaw jelly."

"*Albi*, we've got several more jars. Look on the bottom shelf in the pantry."

Joshua bit into one of the stuffed grape leaves and crossed over into gourmet paradise. The consistency, the delicate intermingling of flavors: meat, rice, tomatoes, a touch of lemon, salt, and the tangy flavor of the grape leaves themselves—forget about New York—they were the best he had ever eaten. In spite of his extreme hunger, Joshua ate slowly, relishing every bite. After he had consumed one, he was able to speak again. "The stuffed grape leaves are delicious, the best I ever tasted. And what is mayhaw jelly? I never heard of it."

Diana explained that the mayhaw was a southern tree with small, red, very tart fruits resembling crabapples. She pointed toward the backyard, "See the slender tree beside the mulberry tree?"

He turned and looked out the window where she pointed. "Which is the mulberry?"

"The big one I read in," said Sam.

"Okay, I see it." It was a small, nondescript, rather scraggly tree with a narrow trunk.

"That's a mayhaw tree, a type of hawthorn. It's covered in beautiful white flowers every spring, and the fruit ripens in May, hence the name."

"Mamma, I can't open this." Sam handed the Mason jar filled with jelly to Diana. She gripped the jar and tried to twist the lid, but she hadn't the strength.

"Let me," offered Joshua, something he never did at home.

Sam watched him carefully. With a little effort he opened it and handed it back to her. As she spooned a blob of the light pink jelly into the pocket of her bread, she asked Joshua, "Why are your hands so red?"

"Oh, they got sunburned." As soon as the lie left his lips, for some reason he couldn't fathom, he looked at Annie, and again she met his glance with a penetrating look. It was eerie, as if she peered right into his heart and discerned the lie. He dropped his gaze, feeling exposed and ashamed.

"Try some jelly," said Sam, sliding the jar back across the table to him.

He did. "Mmmmh! That is delicious, very delicate and light. Did you make this, Diana?"

"No, Annie is our chef. She made everything we're eating except the butter."

Joshua regarded Annie, who, except for the prayer, had sat silent through the entire luncheon. "The bread and the yoghurt, too? Annie, you're a wonder. You should open a restaurant!"

"Thank you, Joshua." She patted her ample belly and smiled, "I love to cook because I love to eat."

After Joshua and Annie finished eating the yoghurt salad (neither Sam nor Diana ate any), Sam and Annie cleared the table and they moved to the living room. Sam set a platter with four mugs, containers of cream and sugar, and a plate of baklava on the coffee table. Annie brought out a yellow teapot steaming from the spout and placed it on a large coaster.

"So, Joshua," said Diana, while Annie poured the tea, "are you a student?"

He leaned forward and poured some cream in his mug. "No, I graduated last year with an Artist Diploma in piano performance."

Sam claimed the biggest piece of baklava and said, "We hear you playing sometimes, and it sounds great!"

"Do you also teach?" asked Diana.

"Not regularly, but I sometimes give masterclasses at universities. For now I'm a concert pianist trying to establish a performing career." He sipped the hot, strong tea.

"What's a concert pianist do?" asked Sam. She took an enormous bite of the pastry.

"Well, I travel to different cities and give solo recitals or play concerts with orchestras."

"Garu ronnapray eerinawlins?"

"Sam, don't talk with your mouth full!"

She chewed fast and swallowed, "Are you gonna play here in New Orleans?"

"I'd love to, but at present I don't have any engagements here." He picked up a piece of the baklava and its scent filled his nose. "My manager in New York books the concerts for me, and if someone in New Orleans calls him and asks for me to play here, I will."

"Good, 'cause I want to come."

Joshua took a bite of baklava. Like all the rest of the food, it was splendid.

"Sounds like an exciting career," said Diana.

"It is—I love traveling and playing music." He hesitated, "It's just that I need more bookings to be able to move into a place of my own. I'm twenty-four and I still live at home."

"If you're interested in teaching, there may be some openings at one of the universities in New Orleans, or at some of the local community colleges."

"Are you a musician?"

"No, I teach English at Tulane, but I'm not working this summer. I'm on medical leave."

"I see." She didn't specify the illness, but if it was cancer as he guessed, Diana did not appear to be winning the battle. He decided to change the subject. "So, Sam, what grade are you in?"

"I'll be in ninth grade this year."

High school? Joshua was taken aback; he thought she was much younger.

"Joshua, do you have a girlfriend?" Sam asked.

"No."

"Good."

He laughed, "Why is that good?"

"Because I'm going to marry you."

"Albi!" Annie's eyes grew wide and she clapped her hand over her mouth.

Diana laughed and shook her head, "Sam, you are twelve years old."

"Almost thirteen." Sam knitted her brows together, "Well, it's the truth. I'm going to marry him when I get old enough."

Struck by Sam's expression of utter certainty, her sincerity and seriousness, Joshua did not laugh. He ate some baklava while he regarded the young girl, bemused. Her wavy dark hair was a perfect illustration of anarchy or Handel's chorus *All we like sheep have gone astray.* Her face was apple-shaped with high, well-defined cheekbones a model would envy. Although her eyes were small, the deep brown irises were shaded by lashes thick and long as awnings. But her real beauty lay in the mobility and animation of her features and in the strength, directness, and intelligence of her gaze. She was strong and independent, and whatever her talents or abilities, it was clear she would be a woman of spirit.

He hoped the light would never go from her eyes and that her brightness of spirit would never flag.

"Well, in that case," he replied, "I think I'll be the lucky one."

Diana, disconcerted by Sam's announcement, realized at once what prompted it. She poured herself more tea and groaned inwardly. Dreaded puberty, that necessary evil, had arrived. Diana pursed her lips. Why couldn't Sam's first crush be some pimple-faced adolescent? Joshua was twenty-four years old! He seemed nice enough, but nowadays, who knew? Joseph would have arranged a man-to-man talk with Joshua, just to feel him out. She'd have to speak to George about doing that. She sipped her tea, gazed at the young man, and tried to make light of it, "Well then, as my future son-in-law, Joshua, could I ask a favor of you?"

He smiled, "Yes."

"The grass is in dire need of cutting, but we can't get the mower started. Could you do that?"

"I can try. In Brooklyn, we lived in a brownstone with no lawn to mow, so I'm not too familiar with those machines." He set his mug on the coffee table and stood. "But of course, I have my raw strength to rely on."

"Good," said Diana, "but sit down. In the South, in the summer, we do heavy labor in the morning or evening; it's too hot in the middle of the day. Could you come back around six or seven?"

"Sure."

"Joshua," said Sam, "once you get the mower started, I'll do the mowing."

"Really?"

She nodded firmly.

"Well," he said to his own amazement, seeing he had avoided physical labor all his life, just to spite the Beast, "I'll be glad to stay and mow some, too."

After thanking Annie for lunch, Joshua climbed the fence, picked up his lighter and pack of cigarettes from the bench where he had left them and walked to the house. He was very conscious of the coiled energy in his muscles—not tension, but anticipation. Although he forgot to count his steps, he did wash his hands three times. That done, he entered his world with a light heart and total concentration. He sat at the Steinway to practice the Brahms concerto. As he played the opening phrases, he reveled in the smoothness of the keys under his fingers, the perfectly coordinated muscular response of his arms, hands, and fingers which conjured up the rich and melancholy sound signature of Brahms. Music filled the room like wine in a chalice, and drinking deeply, Joshua was home.

CHAPTER 9

Diagnosis

"George, I may die of terminal seasickness instead of cancer if Annie drives me into the city for my appointment on Monday. You know how she is at the wheel, and Dramamine interferes with my other medications."

He laughed. "Diana, are you askin' me to drive you?"

"Begging. I have to be at the Medical Center by seven-thirty. Can you help me out?"

"Of course."

"And there's one other matter." She got up and closed the door to her room. Even though Sam had already gone to bed, Diana lowered her voice. "Sam has a new friend, our next door neighbor Joshua Brightman. She has quite a crush on him. I'm glad because it's helped bring her out of her grief over Joseph."

"Well, that's good news."

"She invited Joshua to lunch, and he seems like a nice young man. The problem is he's twenty-four years old."

"Ah."

"It might be good for him to meet Sam's Uncle George just so he knows there's a man in the picture. What do you think?"

"Well, I'd like to meet him just because he's Sam's first crush. I s'pose I can take him out fishin', spend some time with him and lay down the law, if necessary."

"Thanks, George, that would help set my mind at ease."

"Sure thing, Diana. Rest easy and I'll see you Monday."

He picked her up at six-thirty in the morning, and they arrived in plenty of time for the series of blood tests and x-rays, followed by a conference with her oncologist Dr. Wun.

George enjoyed Diana's company, even though she tended to be high-strung and nervous, unlike his quiet Catherine. At the Medical Center, he parked the car, and almost as soon as they located the correct floor and room and signed in, Diana was called in for her first battery of tests.

He sat with an open magazine on his lap and did not read a word. His mind drifted to memories of Joseph and Diana eighteen years ago, long before death and disease intervened. Having observed them over the years, George often wondered what it might be like to marry for love. He had not had the chance, since like so many first generation Lebanese, his parents had chosen his spouse for him. His brother Joseph, ten years younger, had somehow escaped that fate.

Joseph loved to tell the story of how he met Diana. It began when he decided to create a cookbook with his mother's Middle Eastern recipes. To gather design ideas, he went to his favorite Garden District bookshop on Prytania Street to browse through their selection of cookbooks. When Diana walked in, he glanced up and suddenly forgot why he held the book in his hand and why he had entered the bookshop in the first place. Single-minded as a general besieging a city, his entire focus became the capture and capitulation of the striking woman with tousled blond hair and deep blue eyes who sauntered up to Novels—New Releases. Never taking his eyes off her, Joseph reshelved the cookbook and sidled his way through Self Help to Science Fiction and then over to Mysteries. He observed her elegant profile, her slim but shapely figure, her mass of blond, wavy hair, framing the fair, rosy skin of her face.

She chose a novel, paid the cashier, and left the store. Joseph followed her down Prytania past the walled Lafayette Cemetery No. 1 to Washington where she made a left, and walked one block to St. Charles Avenue to wait for a streetcar.

Like many of his sudden, intense interests, Joseph's Middle Eastern cookbook fell by the wayside, but his interest in Diana never waned. With eyes closed, George imagined Joseph hovering near Diana under the majestic old live oaks that make a living green, sun-dappled tunnel of St. Charles Avenue. When she boarded the streetcar, Joseph followed and managed to sit beside her. He struck up a conversation and discovered that she was a Master's student in English at Tulane. Her eyes were a rich, dark blue, and he noticed a single brown freckle in her left iris.

At the time, Joseph was thirty-one, with an MBA from LSU, the bookkeeper at Levant House. At forty-one, George was the introverted manager, a settled family man. Joseph was talkative, quick-witted, charming, and handsome, used to success with women. When Diana rebuffed his advances at first, Joseph became more determined to have her. It took him a year, but in the end, she married him.

"Testing done." Diana, thin to transparency, looking weary and older than her forty-one years, interrupted his reverie. "Time to meet with the doctor."

In the small examining room, round-faced Dr. Wun peered at them through thick glasses and delivered his heavily accented verdict, "Mrs. Faris, despite our best efforts, the cancer has metastasized to the stomach and colon." He showed them the computer scans. "There's nothing more we can do except for pain management." He dropped his eyes, "I'm so sorry."

"How long do I have?" Diana asked quietly.

"Very hard to say, but probably a matter of weeks."

Ironically, Dr. Wun's report of doom did not seem to faze her, perhaps because she had anticipated it for so long. George fidgeted and cleared his throat nervously, while Diana, usually the jittery one, sat immovable, resigned to her fate like a coastal city in the direct path of a hurricane. Here we go, thought George. The onslaught of damaging winds, driving rain, and tornados was inevitable; it simply had to be endured.

On the way to the car, to comfort himself, George lit a cigar without thinking. He drove round and picked up Diana at the entrance. As he turned onto Jefferson Highway, he realized he still had the lit cigar in his mouth. She never let him smoke in her presence. When she remained mute and failed to admonish him, he prompted her, "Aren't you gonna tell me to put out the damn cigar?"

She ignored his question. "I'm thinking about Sam."

Sam, who had lost her father and was soon to lose her mother.

Biting down hard on the cigar, George cracked open the window to siphon off the smoke, while rage at the fate of his sister-in-law built up in him like steam in a locomotive. The pressure rose until it propelled him to action. He blew out a puff of smoke, and his anger exploded, "Dammit all to hell, Diana! Doctors don't know everything; they're often wrong."

Diana flinched at his loud, strident tone.

"Where's your defiance, woman? God is in control, not any effin' doctor in that half-assed medical center. You just might beat this cancer yet."

Pressing her lips together into a white line, she stared ahead at the highway and didn't respond.

George softened his tone, "Listen, I'll make you a deal."

Diana gave him a sidelong glance. "What deal?"

"I'll quit smokin' in the car if you agree to stop off for some *café au lait* and French Market doughnuts at Café Massenet. It's just off I-10 on the way home."

Her mouth relaxed and the left corner pulled up in a half smile. "All right, George," she replied softly, "we can get it to go with extra doughnuts for Annie and Sam."

"Good."

"Now put out that damn cigar!" she shouted.

He grinned, "Thatta girl."

Although the posted menu included gumbo, red beans and rice, and other local dishes, Café Massenet, open twenty-four hours a day, specialized in chicory-laced coffee cut with an equal amount of hot milk and the square, hole-less beignets served piping hot and topped with powdered sugar. Like the vast Atchafalaya Basin to the west, Café Massenet was a gathering place for exotic species, no binoculars needed. George and Diana sat on round wooden stools at the mirrored, marble-topped bar, which was lighted like a backstage dressing room with brilliant rows of globe lights framing the mirrors. It overlooked the larger dining area with battered wooden tables and chairs, perfect for people-watching.

They surveyed the colorful clientele: a table of businessmen in three-piece suits, tattooed bikers, a black family with children in assorted sizes, eager-eyed Japanese tourists wrapped in cameras, a black-clad, dog-collared priest presiding at a table of parishioners, and two drag queens, beautiful, statuesque pseudo-women with muscular arms and deep voices.

While they waited for their order, Diana said, "Remember Cat's illness?"

Having just heard Diana's death sentence, George winced. "Cat?" He grabbed a round metal container of powdered sugar and rolled it nervously between his palms, "Uh, well, she's been fine ever since the night Mamma prayed for her."

"Yes, she has, and I'm very glad about it, George. I just wonder why Annie's prayers haven't done anything for me."

George cleared his throat loudly and blew out a breath. "Diana, maybe it's a test of faith."

Diana smiled wanly. "Looks like I'm failing the test."

"What I mean is that we have to believe that God can cure you, instantly, at any time, no matter how late the hour."

She gazed at him intently, "Do you really think that is going to happen, George?"

He opened his mouth to speak, but nothing issued from it. She dropped her eyes to the counter and nodded. They sat in silence until their order came.

After they left Café Massenet, George turned on the car radio, and they heard a report of the first tropical depression forming in the Caribbean. It was that time of year, June to November, hurricane season. George sighed; they were in it for more ways than one.

Diana reached over and clicked off the radio. "George, before we get home, we need to talk about what happens after. . . well, after I'm gone. I've named you as executor of my will. In order to settle all the debts Joseph created, I think you're going to have to sell the house. As for Sam and Annie—"

"Diana, darlin', don't you worry at all about Sam and Mamma. You know Cat and I will take care of them. Sam is like my own child." George exhaled loudly, "If we have to sell the house, she and Mamma will come live with us." He glanced at her. "I know it's good to be prepared, but please, let's take it one day at a time. We're not there yet."

That night, Diana waited to speak to Annie until after Sam had gone to bed. They sat in the living room drinking peppermint tea. "Annie, Dr. Wun says the cancer has spread from the spleen and liver to my stomach and colon, despite the radiation, and he says there is nothing more they can do."

Annie fingered the olive wood cross she wore around her neck. Her grandfather had carved it in Lebanon long ago. "You know, *albi*, God can heal any illness at any time. He doesn't always agree with the doctor's diagnosis."

Diana placed her mug on the coffee table. "Annie, I know that sudden cures happen sometimes to some people, but I'm certain that I'm not one of them."

"Diana, God can—"

"Enough!" she blurted, suddenly leaning forward aggressively. "I don't want to know what God can do." Her eyes blazed blue fire that was quickly doused with tears. "While God is doing nothing at all, I have to figure out what will happen to my twelve-year-old daughter after I die."

Diana's voice rose in frustration, "If you and George had just informed me about Joseph, I might have been able to stop his gambling. But you didn't. We lost all our savings, he cashed in our life insurance policy, and he put us in terrible straits." She rubbed away the tears with the heels of her hands.

Annie opened her mouth to speak, but Diana cut her off.

"I know you didn't tell me because he had promised to stop; he was going to put it to rights. Well, as we both know, he didn't get the chance. He took out a second mortgage on the house and now we've got that to pay. If—" she stopped herself and drew in a deep breath, "*when* I die—you and Sam won't have the means to stay in this house. Sam will get survivor's benefits from my social security and my teacher's retirement, but the mortgage payments will eat up that and your social security check as well."

Diana dropped her head into her hands. "I told George he'll probably have to sell the house, and I feel terrible about it."

Annie got up and sat beside her on the sofa. Putting an arm around Diana's thin shoulders, she said, "*Albi*, you know that George and Cat will take us in. They have a large house with plenty of room. Their children are grown and gone, and they love Sam like a daughter. Sam will be loved and taken care of in every way."

Diana's tears spattered like raindrops onto the carpet, wetting and deepening the blues and oranges of the rug. "You know, the greatest pain is not the cancer; it's the thought of leaving Sam when she is so young." Diana smiled, "She sang beautifully on Sunday, and she was so proud of winning that hymnal. There are going to be so many moments like that. . ."

"Let me say a prayer for you, Diana."

"No, Annie. I'm done with prayers. They don't do any good."

Seeing Annie's shoulders slump and the downward bend of her head, Diana added, "I know you believe prayers help, and I know you have healed many people, but for me all your praying has been useless." She covered Annie's hand with her own, "Save your energy for Sam and for others."

The old woman nodded with downcast eyes.

Diana patted Annie's hand. "I'm worn out and I'm going to bed now. Goodnight, Annie."

"Goodnight."

Annie watched Diana leave the room. She knew what she had to do. She rose and carried the two tea mugs back to the kitchen where she washed and dried them and put them back in the cabinet. It was eleven o'clock when she turned out the light. She walked slowly to her bedroom and entered quietly. In the pool of golden light cast by the lamp, Sam lay sleeping on her left side, her tousled hair dark against the white pillowcase.

Unhurriedly, Annie changed into her nightgown and wrapped herself in a light cotton bathrobe. She removed the pins from her hair and took down the French braid. She brushed her hair thoughtfully for a long time, pondering the situation. Diana, unlike herself, was young and highly educated. Annie's education had ended at age sixteen, when her parents took her out of school so she could work at Levant House, the import store her future father-in-law Khalil had founded. Her parents had even chosen her husband for her. At eighteen, she married Albert Faris, Khalil's son, nine years her senior.

Had she loved him? She hadn't thought of it that way. She had carried out the duties of a wife; she had cooked, cleaned, borne their two sons. Albert had earned a living, managing Levant House; he had planted the garden and all the fruit trees in the yard. They had never traveled much; they had never known great wealth, and yet Annie did not envy those who were educated and wealthy or those who had married for love and traveled the world. Her world had been her family, Albert and her two sons, and now her grandchildren, Sam, and George's children, Michael and Lucy. She was a simple woman, a mother and housekeeper, not a career woman. She had no education, but in the matter of prayer, she knew Diana was wrong. Prayer opened the door to unlimited power, power greater than that of men and angels, greater than all sickness, evil, and death itself.

Sam murmured something, then shifted and turned in her sleep. After a moment her breathing resumed a slow, regular rhythm. Annie watched her sleeping granddaughter with love and deep affection. The child's mouth was open slightly and her long lashes created feathered shadows on her cheeks. She was Joseph and Diana's only child, beautiful, lively, and pure-hearted. "*Albi*," Annie murmured, "my heart. If only the Lord would heal your mother."

Where prayer was concerned, Annie knew her own position in the world, her humble origins, her small circle of influence did not matter. Prayer and its spiritual power were not bound by time or place or worldly position. To kneel and pray in her bedroom in Chalice, Louisiana for her cousin Zara in Beirut was to be in the instant with Zara in Beirut. And what is more, Zara, in some part of her being, would know that Annie was with her.

The opening phrases of the Nicene Creed came into her mind: *I believe in one God, the Father Almighty, Maker of heaven and earth, and of all things visible and invisible. . .*

The visible and the invisible. The older she grew and the more time she spent in prayer, the more conscious Annie became of the invisible, the unseen world. Like the sun veiled by clouds, the invisible realm was a constant; though hidden, it was always there, and the older she grew, the more she glimpsed it. She had seen the radiant presences, like pillars of light, standing near when she prayed over Catherine, and not for the first time.

But the invisible realm was not only light. The light was opposed by darkness, and Annie felt that as well. *For we wrestle not against flesh and blood, but against principalities, against powers, against the rulers of the darkness of this world, against spiritual wickedness in high places.*

She sensed the darkness hidden in the young man Joshua, how he struggled with it, and she had felt firsthand the unforgiveness and the festering anger in Diana. But these were not insurmountable obstacles. In her long experience, she had actually seen the darkness depart from persons like a black vapor, followed by instantaneous healing. Prayer was the weapon to defeat the principalities that oppressed human beings. But prayer did not always bring healing; it could be blocked by lack of faith or unforgiveness.

Although she did not have all the answers, she did know one thing: the invisible world was coming closer; she could feel it. She could feel the thinning of the veil, the curtain between life and death, between this world and the next. When the veil dissolved like mist before her eyes, she hoped she might see the true Sun in all its glory.

Annie laid her hairbrush on the night table, and then she stood beside the bed and placed her pillow on the floor. With effort and the creaking of her joints, she knelt on the pillow and crossed herself. She placed her elbows on the bed, clasped her hands together, bowed her head, and began to pray softly and intensely in Arabic. She had a plan. Sam needed her mother, and her mother needed Sam. That was natural and proper, and furthermore, Annie decided, the Lord willing, that was how it was going to be.

CHAPTER 10

Lessons

J oshua sat cross-legged on his bed, fighting the impulse to smoke. He had decided to quit the nasty, expensive habit. To distract himself, he rose, selected a travel book on Scandinavia from his bookshelf and took two of Sam's peppermints from the dwindling pile on his desk. He sat down again and popped one in his mouth, but he left the book unopened as his thoughts returned to the time he spent with Sam on Saturday.

It took them fifteen minutes to get the lawn mower started that evening. He pulled the start cord repeatedly to no avail, until he was red-faced and soaked in sweat. Sam tinkered with the spark plug and the choke, and then he pulled again, raring back with all his force. Suddenly the mower sputtered and then roared into life. Sam pushed back on the throttle and mowed the first few rounds of the backyard, and then he took over.

It was the first time in his life he had ever mowed a lawn. Except for the motor noise, he liked it. Pushing the mower, he enjoyed the strain on his arms, legs and back, as he clipped the bearded, uneven grass to a clean-shaven edge. He inhaled the unmatchable scent, sharp and fresh, of the mown grass while he felt the rising heat and clean sweat of physical labor. The whole lawn took only forty minutes, side yards and front yard included.

Afterwards, he and Sam sat on the patio as the sun set, drinking tall glasses of orange juice, filled to the top, southern style, with ice, and devouring an entire bowl of pistachios. Each nut was housed like a clam, delicate tasting and salty, in its bone-white shell. The air was humid, but the evening breeze cooled them, lifting Sam's dark hair and ruffling the sleeves of Joshua's damp T-shirt. Bees hummed and buzzed, seeking nectar in the roses and geraniums. The wind, coming in unpredictable gusts, swayed the flowers and fruit trees, while the sighing and whispering of the leaves rose and fell like the sound of the sea, pleasing to the ear and soothing to the heart.

Joshua surveyed the garden-like yard. "Sam, what is that small tree by the fence with the reddish-orange flowers?"

"A pomegranate tree."

"Does it bear fruit?"

"Oh, yeah. We get more than we can eat usually around September. It's hard to pick them 'cause you can't tear them off; you have to cut the stems and they're thick. If you help me, I'll give you some."

"It's a deal."

Sam ducked as a bumblebee, flying erratically, buzzed past her head. "Joshua, did you know that a bumblebee is aerodynamically impossible?"

"Really?" Joshua sipped his orange juice.

"Its wings are much too small for the size of its body, and yet it flies."

"I see that," he remarked, ducking his head as the bumblebee passed by again. "So how can they fly?"

"God wants 'em to."

Joshua swirled the ice in his drink before he spoke. "You know, Sam, some people, my father for one, think that God didn't make the world. They think it's just random."

"It can't be."

"Why not?"

"'Cause everything is designed, down to the last dust mote."

"Can you back up that statement, *mademoiselle?*"

"*Oui, monsieur.* The bee is a good example. Its design is made up of the number three."

At the mention of number, whether she knew it or not, Sam had Joshua's full attention.

"The egg of a queen bee takes three days to hatch. The queen is fed for nine days, which is three times three. She matures in fifteen days, five times three. The worker bees mature in twenty-one days; the drones mature in twenty-four, all multiples of three."

She broke off to take a sip of her orange juice.

"And," she continued, "their bodies have three sections, a head and two stomachs. Their eyes are compound, made of about three thousand small, six-sided eyes. And in case you didn't realize it," Sam smiled, "six equals two times three. They have six legs. The foot is made of three triangular sections, and triangles, as you may recall, are three-sided. Each antenna has nine sections, and the stinger has nine barbs on each side."

"Sam, how do you know all that?"

"School report," she grinned, "and you know it was the best in the class."

"I imagine it was. Any other examples?" he asked.

She wrinkled up her nose and glanced at the setting sun. After a moment of thought, she answered, "Well, we're sittin' here in the middle of a cosmic clock. The movements of the sun, the moon, the stars, and the revolving of our planet mark the day, the night, and the seasons in perfect time and without interruption or error."

"True."

"And speaking of the sun, the seven colors in sunlight are related to the seven tones in the musical scale. At least the ancient Greeks and some insignificant guy named Isaac Newton thought so." She scratched her head, "I'm not sure about the wavelengths of light, but the notes in the scale are all multiples of eleven. I forget what the actual numbers are, but that's your field."

A-440. Eleven times forty. She was right; he would have to look up the others.

"Sam," Joshua smiled, "if you debated my father, I think I'd put my money on you." How many twelve-year-olds thought like she did?

Just to tease her, Joshua picked up a nut. "What about the pistachio?"

"Well, the story of the pistachio is a little different. The pistachio comes from the tachio tree."

"The tachio tree."

"Good listening, Joshua. Yes, you see, the tachio tree was native to Syria. For ages it produced nuts as white as the shell— pale, without much flavor. But one year there was a terrible drought, so to conserve water, they decided to irrigate the tachio trees fifty-fifty."

"Fifty-fifty?"

Sam nodded. "Fifty per cent water and fifty per cent horse piss. They had a lot of horses in those days."

Joshua smiled. "And that's what gives it its flavor."

"Of course, and its name—PIStachio."

"Sam, you little wiseacre."

She threw back her head and laughed, and the sound was high and musical and sweet.

In some ways she reminded him of himself at that age, precocious, an avid reader with a curiosity about everything.

Fortunately for Sam, she was flowering in a nurturing environment, whereas Joshua had grown prickly as a cactus, struggling for survival in a dry and desolate landscape.

They were quiet for a time after that, enjoying the evening as the garden revived after the heat of the day. Birds sang their liquid, unexpected melodies in short bursts, their voices large and projecting, in inverse proportion to the size of their tiny throats. Then faintly, intertwined with the birdsong, Joshua heard other music, a woman singing. On hearing any music, he automatically tried to identify it, but the faintness of the music, swelling and fading, competing with the sound of the birds, made it impossible.

"Where is the music coming from?"

"From Dr. Leo's house next door." She gestured to the left where over the fence they could see the roof of the frame house with a garage apartment behind it. "He speaks Italian and he loves opera. He has a ton of CDs in his house and DVDs, almost all opera. He lives with Rosie. "

"His wife?"

"His dog. She looks like a polar bear."

He barely heard what she said because he was trying so hard, and unsuccessfully, to identify the opera. Then another powerful sound arose from high up in the trees.

"What the hell makes that buzzing sound?" Joshua asked.

"Katydids or cicadas, or both." Sam smiled, "You hear them, but usually you don't see them, which is probably a good thing. Katydids are okay—they look like walking green leaves— but cicadas are creepy with a capital C. They could win an ugly contest against space aliens and gargoyles."

"Seen any gargoyles lately?"

"Well, actually I have. I'm reading a book about the Gothic cathedrals of Europe. It's got lots of pictures. But as far as I know, gargoyles don't buzz in a chorus. Cicadas do. Just listen, there's a second one answering the first, and soon there will be others, until we have the cicada version of the Mormon Tabernacle Choir."

She described it perfectly. In five minutes or so, the sound was practically deafening, ebbing and flowing in stereo, call and response, from one side of the yard to the other.

As the sun set, the sky's blue deepened to violet, then indigo, making a beautiful backdrop for the entrance of the first silver stars and the cool ivory of the crescent moon. Over all there was the rich smell of the damp earth, mingled with the odor of the newly cut grass and the fragrance of roses. Laying his head against the fanlike back of the wooden chair, Joshua felt a calm, a quiet peace fill him. The frenetic inner voice was hushed, something rare and precious. He rested, serene and silent, watching Night and her starry mantle descend on him and this remarkable girl, his equal, disguised in a child's body.

No, he wasn't in Brooklyn anymore, and for the moment he didn't miss it at all.

Saturday evening with Sam had been the good part of the weekend. Joshua popped another peppermint in his mouth and opened the Scandinavian travel book. Maybe Nathan could book him a recital tour there. He wanted to see Stockholm, Copenhagen, Oslo, and Helsinki. Winter or summer would do, just so long as he was playing music, earning money, and keeping a safe distance between himself and his father.

On Sunday, he had endured another "driving lesson" with the Beast. Like all instruction from his father, it was a chance for the Beast to prove his superiority and to point out Joshua's shortcomings. Nothing Joshua did was good enough for the Beast; the Beast could always do it better. That was the point of every lesson.

The Beast had dreamed of a son who would be an imitation of himself, first a star athlete, then a lawyer. Billy "the Beast" Brightman's size, strength, and accuracy with scorching fastballs, curveballs, sliders, and sinkers had won him strikeout records and low ERA's throughout his high school and college careers. His son's precocious talent for the piano greatly disappointed the

Beast, who had either avoided or sulked through each of Joshua's childhood recitals. Clearly, for the Beast, a piano prodigy compared in value and excitement to a star pitcher like pig slop to a gourmet dinner.

Joshua had spoiled the Beast's blueprint for his son's life. After high school, Joshua was supposed to major in political science or criminal justice and then attend law school, with his father's blessing and funding. True men did not major in music. When Joshua auditioned and was accepted at four of the best music conservatories in the United States and one in England, the Beast vowed that if his son wasted his life by majoring in music, Billy Brightman would not contribute a penny towards his education.

The Beast kept his promise.

Well, so be it. Joshua laid the travel book on his night table and thought about his driving lesson, a necessary evil. No matter what the Beast's comments about his driving, Joshua, ever a quick study, knew he had done well enough in both parallel parking and freeway driving. With a little more practice he could pass the driving test, and the written test would be no problem. He was on the road to independence. By the end of June, in three weeks, he felt sure he would have his license.

Pin him between the car and the house. Crush his legs, shatter his pelvis, break his back.

3 weeks—3 × 7 = 21

In mid-July, his parents were renting a house in the South of France, in Nice. They would be gone for a month. Five weeks away.

3 × 7 = 21
5 × 7 = 35
21 + 35 = 56; 5 + 6 = 11, a good number

Eleven! A-440. Sam had mentioned the frequencies of the musical scale being multiples of eleven. He fired up his laptop and quickly found the frequencies of vibration.

C	D	E	F	G	A	B	C
264 (33)	297 (33)	330 (22)	352 (44)	396 (44)	440 (55)	495 (33)	528
24 x 11	27 x 11	30 x 11	32 x 11	36 x 11	40 x 11	45 x 11	48 x 11

She was exactly right! All the frequencies and even the differences between them were multiples of eleven.

Joshua leaned back against the headboard. Was creation random or not? And how could human beings, with their limited perception know? There were frequencies of sound above and below the range of human hearing and wavelengths of light invisible to the human eye. Could human beings with narrow, finite senses rule out the existence of God? Maybe Sam's theory about the order and design in the world was correct. Maybe it was time to explore that more thoroughly, and maybe, seeing the way the Faris family lived their tradition, just maybe, he should get himself in touch with his own. He sat bolt upright and searched for a book online, found it, and ordered it.

Joshua started when his mobile phone rang.

"Joshua, it's Nathan. You're not gonna believe this—the Louisiana Philharmonic called. Right there in your own backyard. Tian-Tian Chang cancelled for one of their summer concerts on July eleventh. She's goin' back to Beijing for the summer 'cause her mother is ill. Can you sub?"

Eleven is a good number. "Which concerto?"

"Beethoven five."

Five. Five weeks. "Absolutely."

"Cool. The other good news is that you'll be gettin' her fee, which is fifty per cent higher than yours."

"Great. Thanks, Nathan, for helping me move up in the world."

"So how's it goin' down there in Cajun country? Meet any babes yet?"

"Well, as it happens, I live next door to one."

"No kiddin'."

"Yeah, she's quite a babe—a slim brunette with deep, dark eyes. Smart, sassy, and sporty."

"Sporty?"

"Yeah, one of those fit, athletic types. Plays softball, mows the lawn."

"What's her name?"

"Samantha Faris, but everyone calls her Sam."

"So, any sparks there? Is she attracted to you?"

"She invited me to lunch on Saturday, and you're not gonna believe it, Nathan, but right then and there she declared she's gonna marry me."

"No shit, man, just like that!"

"Uh-huh."

"So can she cook?"

Pop. Pop-Pop. Pop.

Joshua tried to identify the muffled popping sounds he heard. "Hold on a minute, Nathan."

He opened his bedroom door and then he knew. "Listen, Nathan, gotta go. We'll talk later."

He walked into the family room. His mother sat sideways on the sofa with her legs up, thumbing through a magazine, her reading glasses perched on the end of her nose. The Beast sat on a kitchen chair about four feet back from the French doors, one of which was open. Holding a .22 rifle to his shoulder, he aimed through the opening and squeezed the trigger.

Pop-pop.

For a moment Joshua stood speechless, uncomprehending.

Finding his voice, he asked, "Dad, what the hell are you doing?"

The Beast lowered the gun and looked at him. "Just firing into the ground to test the gun." He glanced at Amy with an odd, complicit look in his eyes.

"Joshua," said Amy, lowering her magazine, "your father has been working hard for weeks preparing for the trial. He's just relaxing. You know how he loves guns."

The Beast gazed at Joshua and a slow smile spread across his face, "Want a shot yourself?"

"Uh, no thanks—"

"Of course not, don't want to get your lily-white hands dirty, do you?"

As the Beast picked up the gun to fire again, Joshua heard his mother's quiet chuckle.

Batter his head with the stock, fire into his ugly mouth.

Pop-pop. Pop-pop-pop.

Flushing and breaking into a sweat, Joshua turned on his heel, heart pounding.

"That's right, run away, little girl."

Seven steps past the sofa, turn left, seven steps past the fireplace to the hall. Turn right. Three steps to the bathroom. Safe!

He washed his face and then his hands three times, trying to fend off the nausea rising in his throat.

At two a.m., after lying wide awake for hours with a pounding migraine, Joshua couldn't stand it anymore. He got up, put on some shorts and, despite his best intentions, grabbed his lighter and a pack of cigarettes. He unwrapped a peppermint, popped it in his mouth and put the last two in his pocket just in case.

He opened the bedroom door quietly and listened. Except for the hum of the central air unit, the house was silent. Avoiding the weapon wall in the den, he padded barefoot to the patio doors and quietly let himself out. The heavy night air, very humid and mild, was alive with the sound of cicadas. The thought of Sam crossed his mind, but the peaceful time with her seemed very distant. He stood for a minute on the warm concrete patio, breathing too fast, fighting the temptation to smoke. Thick clouds, pushed by a southerly wind, obscured the stars and the moon. Darkness enveloped him.

He inhaled sharply and blew out the breath through his mouth; he wanted to get away from the house. Counting his steps, he walked on the damp grass toward the bench, *One, two, three, four, five, six—*

"Shit!" Pain shot through his foot—he had stepped on something hard-edged and sharp—was it broken glass? As he limped forward, grimacing, his bare foot grazed a soft, wet, lumpy object. He jerked his foot away reflexively, lost his balance, and fell onto the damp grass, landing on his side.

He righted himself and sat up, immediately bending his leg and turning up the sole of his foot. He couldn't see anything in the dark, so he flicked on the cigarette lighter. Two brown, irregularly shaped objects were stuck in his foot, one darker than the other. He held the lighter closer—broken walnut and pecan shells? Sharp-edged little bastards. He brushed them off, rubbed his foot, and then got up.

Keeping the lighter lit, he backtracked gingerly and discovered a pile of nuts still in the grass, some whole and some broken and emptied of their meat. Who put them there and why? He was the only one who ever set foot on the lawn.

Holding the lighter before him, he turned back in the direction of the bench, carefully watching his step, to search for the other thing he had bumped into. Three paces away, he saw a grayish, rounded lumpy thing lying curled in the grass like an old stuffed sock. Maybe it was a stuffed animal Sam had thrown over the fence.

He bent down, holding the flickering lighter closer and then recoiled.

"Uff!" It was a dead squirrel with a bloodied hole where its eye should have been, its body crawling with ants.

Standing upright, he relaxed his grip and extinguished the lighter. Suddenly he knew.

Joshua pocketed the lighter and cigarettes and let his arms hang limply at his sides. He stood frozen, deceptively so, like an Arctic volcano, white and immobile, but seething underneath with internal fire, hidden and ferocious.

Nuts attract squirrels. He knew who put them on the ground. He knew why.

Just firing into the ground to test the gun.

The lying, cruel bastard.

Standing alone in darkness, Joshua jammed his hands into his pockets and gripped the lighter.

Tie him down. Douse him with gasoline, set him on fire. Watch him burn.

CHAPTER 11

Early One Morning

Maybe the culprit was Café Massenet's powerful *café au lait*. Or maybe not—she had drunk it hours ago. But, for whatever reason, as Monday night dissolved into the wee hours of Tuesday, Diana could not sleep. More surprising than that, she did not even feel tired. She stretched out her right arm to the empty side of the bed, vacant for six months. In spite of her anger toward Joseph, she missed him terribly, his vital, electric physical presence, his sense of humor, his way with Sam.

His carefree air, typical of the south Louisiana motto, *Laissez les bon temps rouler,* had attracted her, but it had also led to his downfall. *Let the good times roll.* Although he was an accountant, and good at his job, Joseph was a risk taker. For him, money had been as attractive and dangerous as a full-stocked bar to an alcoholic. During football season, he met his bookie once a week, to collect his winnings or pay his debts on the outcomes of the Saints, Tulane, and LSU games. He bet on the horses, and occasionally he went to the casinos in the city. Most of the time he won, or so she had thought, and she had enjoyed his good luck. With his winnings, he had bought her a diamond pendant with matching earrings, rented them a cabin one summer for a week on Pensacola Beach, bought a nineteen-foot fishing boat with an expensive Evinrude motor. His gambling had seemed harmless at first.

Then, like the diagnosis of her cancer, when she discovered the extent of Joseph's disease, it was too late. He had already wiped out their savings as well as Sam's college fund and embezzled money from Levant House, the family business. And to her everlasting ire, George and Annie had withheld it all from her. The family had closed ranks, like the clannish tribe they were, and kept her in the dark while they tried to get Joseph back on track. George even knew about Sam's college account. It was infuriating and unforgivable. When the initial shock of Joseph's death in the head-on collision subsided, Diana's emotions had seesawed back and forth from grief to anger at the funeral and ever since.

Stirred up by her thoughts and wide awake, she decided to distract herself. She turned on the bedside radio to listen to the WWL news. After the reports of a bank robbery in Uptown, the progress on the RTA improvements to the St. Charles streetcar line, and speculations about the Saints' chances in the upcoming season, the only news of interest to Diana was the weather report, which stated that the tropical depression in the Caribbean was strengthening. Curious about the storm, but too lazy to get up and take a look at it on the computer, she put it off until the morning.

She turned off the radio, laced her fingers behind her head and looked at the dark ceiling, reflecting on the storm she herself had to weather, her doctor's pronouncement of doom earlier that day. The odd thing was, that after hearing Dr. Wun's admission that there was no more he could do for her aside from pain management, a great calm descended. The pronouncement she feared had somehow made her fear vanish. Now that the worst was known, it made it easier to face.

And yet, and yet...none of that accounted for the fact that she felt a new energy. She was actually hungry. She had a sudden craving for breakfast. The red numerals on her bedside clock proclaimed the hour to be 12:45 a.m., and she wanted breakfast? She lifted her eyebrows and shrugged. Well, what the hell.

She got up, put on her white bathrobe and walked barefoot into the kitchen. She decided to eat something rich, something scrumptious. She snapped her fingers and smiled: a three-egg spinach and tomato omelet topped with extra sharp cheddar cheese. She took eggs, milk, cheese, spinach, and tomatoes out of the refrigerator. She also craved strong tea and toasted Syrian bread—with butter and mayhaw jelly.

She heated water for tea, broke the eggs into a bowl and stirred in the milk. Diana had not cooked for ages; just the sight of food had made her nauseated. But now, as she added salt and pepper to the omelet, to her great amazement, her mouth watered. She relished the sight of the yellow egg mixture heating in the frying pan and the rising smell of toast. When the kettle whistled, she poured hot water into the yellow teapot. She grated the cheese to sprinkle on top of the omelet. For a preview, she pinched some cheese between finger and thumb and with only a slight hesitation, popped it into her mouth and waited. No queasiness at all. Smiling, she savored the strong, sharp taste. She had always loved to eat until the cancer—

"No!" Shaking her head, she slammed the door on the thought of illness; she refused to think about it. She would think about health, about this meal, about life. Suddenly George's comment popped into her mind. *God is in control, not any effin' doctor in that half-assed medical center. You just might beat this cancer yet.* She had thought it ludicrous at the time, but now when she felt so much better, it didn't seem quite so far-fetched.

Diana placed the toast on the plate beside the omelet, added a hefty slug of half and half to her tea, and took it to the dining room table. She ate; she enjoyed. *Thanks be to God. Thanks be to God.* The thought traveled through her mind like a jaunty banner drawn by an airplane, flying high and snapping in the wind. Just to have respite from the nausea was exhilarating. Taking a sip of the steaming tea, she knew the moment, brief though it might be, was a gift; this might be the only meal she would enjoy before she died.

Her appetite was quickly sated. After months of eating very little, just a third of the omelet, several sips of tea, and a few bites of the toast seemed like a three-course meal. As she laid down her fork, a deep fatigue descended on her. Rising with effort, she placed the plate with its partially eaten omelet, utensils, and tea mug in the sink. Too exhausted to wash them, she turned out the light and walked weak-kneed to bed.

Diana lay on her back in the bed, bone-tired. The fatigue was crushing; it felt as if she lay already entombed underground, pressed down by a great weight of earth so that she could not move. And yet, as weak and weary as she was, she had the merest intimation that something had altered. In her innermost being, she sensed a change. For the first time in months, in the darkest night, contrary to all logic and reason, she heard the sweet singing of a bird called Hope.

A sputtering, rhythmic sound woke Sam at first light. Disoriented, she rubbed her eyes and tried to get her bearings. When she realized where she was, and that it was morning, the familiar sinking feeling returned; her dad was never coming home. No more breakfasts together, no more jokes, no more hugs and kisses.

But what was that sound? Was something wrong with Eliot? She lifted the cage cover and peeked under it to check on him, but he was fine. She glanced at the other bed, surprised to see Sitti, always the first one up in the morning, still asleep. Then Sam realized the rhythm of the sputtering sound matched the rise and fall of Sitti's breathing—she was snoring!

Smiling, Sam removed the cover from Eliot's cage, and opened the small wire door. Touching her index finger to her lips, she whispered, "Good morning, Mr. Eliot. Be quiet, 'cause Sitti's still sleeping."

The bird, silent and obedient on his perch, blinked, cocked his head and peered at her with a single shiny dark eye. She reached into the cage to stroke the cool, smooth feathers of his back, delighted as always to touch the beautiful wild creature. He was a great comfort in her father's absence. In May, when she found him as a fledgling beneath the mulberry tree, she had taken him in and hand fed him. She had been so frightened he wouldn't survive. "If you had died, Eliot," she whispered, "I would've died, too.

"Stay well, little Eliot. Stay with me forever." She extended her forefinger, and Eliot accepted the invitation. Sam sailed out of the room with the blue jay perched on her finger, preceding her like the masthead of a ship.

In the bathroom, Eliot fluttered up and perched on the shower rod while she peed and then washed her face. Gathering up her courage, Sam attempted the inevitably vain act of brushing her hair. The brush snagged itself in her thick, tangled tresses like a kite in a bramble bush. She tugged on the brush, wincing and grimacing, as it broke through the knots in her hair. When she finished she surveyed the results, wondering why she even bothered. Her hair had the body, bounce, and attitude of a wild kangaroo; it did exactly as it pleased—nothing could keep it down. Frowning at herself in the mirror, Sam pronounced the verdict, "Hopeless."

Laying the brush down with a sigh, she said, "Well, Eliot, on to better things. Let's go get breakfast." Eliot launched himself off the shower rod and flew before her into the living room. Sam fed him a handful of pistachios, and then she ate a bowl of cereal, alone at the table. She rinsed her bowl and spoon, surprised to find dirty dishes in the sink. Sitti usually left the kitchen clean at night. Discovering that the teapot was full, Sam poured some tea into a mug, and added two teaspoons of sugar and some half and half. While she warmed it in the microwave, she retrieved her latest book from the armchair where she had left it.

While Eliot perched in a Boston fern by the window, she set the steaming tea on the coffee table and curled up in one corner of the sofa to read an English translation of poems by Rainer Maria Rilke, whose name she thought rhymed with Gainer Maria Milk. French was the dominant language of her native Louisiana; she could pronounce names like Chargois, Arceneaux, Choupique, and Guillot without a thought. Of German she knew next to nothing; it lurked in her future, not her present.

Gazing at the cover of the book, she asked aloud, "Why did his mother name him Maria?" Instantly, in her head, she heard her dad's voice: *She was just makin' sure he'd be a damn good fighter.*

Sam laughed out loud, and then the memories played out like a movie on the screen of her mind. In the summers he used to take her out fishing in the big boat. They spent many afternoons on vast Lake Pontchartrain, fishing for speckled trout, redfish, and flounder. He taught her how to cast, and if the wind wasn't blowing too hard, he let her steer the boat. Other times he took her crabbing. In the fall they watched the Saints games together, eating popcorn, commenting, cheering, and making beer to soda toasts when the Saints scored. He taught her the rules, he explained the penalties, and he predicted the plays.

The night the Saints played the Super Bowl, Diana decided not to watch. "I don't like football," she said.

"Honey," Joseph declared, "this is not football, this is history!"

The hard-luck, hapless, faltering Saints had made history just to qualify for the Super Bowl, and then against all odds, they won, to the absolute delight of Joseph, Sam, the hurricane-battered City of New Orleans, and the state of Louisiana. It was unbelievable, the fulfillment of Saints' fans wildest fantasies. She and Joseph set off fireworks in the backyard afterwards.

Sam felt a familiar prickle behind her eyes. Everything had changed in January. Now Daddy was gone, Mamma was really sick, and Uncle George had the boat.

Sam watched Eliot fly a circuit of the room before he landed expectantly on her shoulder. "No handouts right now," she told him. Nonetheless, he elected to stay. She sipped some of the hot, sweet tea and then fingered her book, her dad's book. Joseph had loved poetry and often recited his favorite passages from memory. Sam, too, loved poetry, but she didn't stop there. She read everything.

Sam mused aloud, "Maybe I got my love of reading from Mamma, the English professor. What do you think, Eliot?" He shifted position, pondering the question. "I guess I was born into the right family, Mr. Eliot, 'cause we all love books." Sam loved to handle them, to feel their weight and size, to breathe in their smell, but most of all to experience the worlds they opened. To turn from the title page to Chapter 1 made her feel as excited as Marco Polo standing at the threshold of Xanadu, the fabled summer palace of Kublai Khan. The power of ideas, the power of language, the striking images of poetry, and the flow of well-written prose delighted her.

Unlike her classmates, who were addicted to mobile phones, computers, and who spent hours watching television, Sam was a throwback to the nineteenth century. She could type an essay on a keyboard as quickly and well as anyone else, but when she wrote at home, she always began with a legal pad on a clipboard, scrawling her thoughts in longhand. Even the implements of writing, sharpened yellow pencils, ink pens, clean sheets of lined paper, excited her. Why, she didn't know. She simply knew her destiny was set; she was going to be a writer—and—she was going to marry Joshua.

That is, if Joshua would wait for her. She would be thirteen in September, in just two months. She hadn't got her period yet, unlike most of the girls at school, but her body had begun to change; her breasts were beginning to develop. Though physically immature, she knew that her mental maturity surpassed most of her peers; she possessed a formidable intellect.

And now, poised at the cusp of adulthood, Sam's awareness had changed. She had somehow awakened. It seemed to her that she had emerged from the unconscious, self-absorbed world of a child as from a dream. Perhaps her emotional maturity had been hastened by her father's death, but it would have come about one way or another. She simply knew that she was more aware, more present in the world; her mature life was about to begin. Unfazed that her mother and Sitti laughed when she declared she would marry Joshua, Sam knew the power of her own feelings. She had loved Joshua from the first time she saw him. She would always love him, and that was that.

With a rustle of wings, Eliot fluttered over her head and landed on her other shoulder. He cocked his head and peered at the book. He always made her smile. And now there was Joshua who made her heart lift. "Shall I read you some poetry, Mr. Eliot?" Sam opened the book of poems, let her eye fall randomly, and read aloud:

"Extinguish my eyes, I still can see you,
Close my ears, I can hear your footsteps fall,
And without feet I still can follow you,
And without voice I still can to you call.
Break off my arms, and I can embrace you,
Enfold you with my heart as with a hand.
Hold my heart, my brain will take fire of you
As flax ignites from a lit fire-brand—
And flame will sweep in a swift rushing flood
Through all the singing currents of my blood."

at was the way it was, with anyone you held in your heart.
d her eyes, thinking of her father, thinking of Joshua,
her mother might soon die.

xtinguish my eyes, I still can see you,
lose my ears, I can hear your footsteps fall

fluttered down to her wrist. She laid down the book
lifted him to her cheek, closing her eyes and feeling
ol feathers. Eliot was a wild bird, not meant to live
captive. The time was coming, she knew with quiet
when she would have to release him.

And without feet I still can follow you,
And without voice I still can to you call.
Break off my arms, and I can embrace you,
Enfold you with my heart as with a hand.

Sam stroked the bird, thinking how truth and love pierce
the heart like arrows. And yet, even so pierced, the heart loves on.

Annie awoke with a start. It was fully light; she knew it had to be late. She glanced at the bedside clock and was startled to see that it was 8:40, two hours past the time she usually rose.

"*Tatheedi!*"

Then she remembered the dream. Albert had come to meet her. He was the Albert of their youth, slender, strong, and straight-backed, his long, beautiful fingers not yet twisted and misshapen by arthritis. They met in the most beautiful garden she had ever seen. The flowers glowed in brilliant colors, the trees were full of fruit. It seemed to be morning. Somehow, without speaking, he spoke, "It is going to be all right, Annie." She heard it clearly in her mind.

Just the one sentence. She couldn't remember if he spoke Arabic or English. It didn't matter; it was the meaning that was important. *It is going to be all right, Annie.*

She inhaled sharply and sat up. She knew suddenly what he meant. *Thanks be to God, thanks be to God.*

Her prayers had been answered. So be it.

July

The Earth, to those who watch it from above, is a deep blue, watery planet dominated by its oceans, with its smaller land masses appearing in greens and browns. As the planet spins on its axis, half in darkness, half in light, clouds swirl around it, white as the fair linen of altar cloths or puffs of incense.

It is not only the oceans that make the Earth a blue planet. There are also the lakes, the rivers and streams that run to the sea. From on high, the great river that divides the North American continent appears as a broad blue ribbon that twists and curls back on itself, winding thousands of miles from a northern lake to the great curved gulf. As it approaches the coastline, there are other rivers parallel to it, narrow blue ribbons that flow in harmony with their tributaries, creeks and bayous, to form the great estuaries, the watersheds where the fresh water purifies itself, trickling down through marshes and swamps, forming lakes which are not really lakes, whose outlets in turn overflow into the sounds and bays, finally reaching the sea.

The estuaries are places of transition, for not only does the fresh water flow toward the sea, but the denser saltwater of the ocean, governed by the *aestus*, the tide, makes its way north, flowing inland along the bottom of the estuaries. The southward flowing water, filtering through vegetation for miles, does not come empty-handed. With wind, tides, and the action of waves, it brings sediment and nutrients that are trapped by the plants and the grasses.

When the great summer and autumn storms come, the estuaries are a defense against the sea, a refuge for the plants and animals. The watersheds are themselves protected by reefs, barrier islands, and headlands. But sometimes the sea takes its toll and devours the fragile land.

From the rolling woodlands of the north down to the marshes of the coastal plain, the water flows in trickles, rills, creeks, bayous, rivers. It passes over sandy bottoms, mud flats, through the dappled shade of majestic cypress swamps and through miles of marsh grasses, published and open to the sky. The water teems with shrimp, fish of all kinds, turtles, crabs, alligators, otters; it provides life and habitat for birds of a hundred species, raccoons, rabbits, deer, armadillo, opossums, squirrels, black bears, the elusive, solitary panther, and not too long since, the native peoples.

Thus it had been for millennia; thus it was until the coming of the Europeans. It took only a short while, by the reckoning of the ancient watchers, for the greed of men to defile the waters. For situated on this estuary are large cities, teeming with human beings blinded in the pursuit of self-gratification. Dissatisfied, longing, striving after their desires in an imperfect world, they wonder, where is Eden; how have we lost it? Those who watch might say: look about you; it is here.

CHAPTER 12

Excursions

J uly first was going to be more exciting than July fourth, Sam was sure of it. Best of all, Mamma was feeling so much better that Sitti had invited her and Sam to go shopping. The three of them hadn't shopped together for ages. And secondly, Uncle George was taking the boat out to Chef Pass, and he had invited her and Joshua to go fishing with him late in the afternoon.

The reason they were going shopping, according to Sitti, was that the Lord told her to do it.

"The Lord told you to take me shopping?"

Sitti nodded emphatically. "You and Diana. I'm going to buy something for each of you."

"Did the Lord tell you what to buy?"

Sitti threw back her head and laughed. "No, *albi*, we are going to buy something you would like. It's a present—your choice."

"Oh." Drawing down her brows in a frown of concentration, Sam immediately tried to picture something she wanted. Then she snapped her fingers, "I know! I would like to get a new dress for Joshua's concert. He's playing with the Louisiana Philharmonic on July eleventh and he invited us to go. And then Mamma invited him over for July fourth. Oh, and I need some make-up."

"What make-up?"

"Well, lipstick, eyeliner, you know, stuff like that."

Diana was just as surprised as Sam when Annie asked her to go shopping. "Well, thank you, Annie." She quickly added, "Let me drive."

After storming the women's department of two outlet stores in Metairie, Sam had a new white dress, dotted with small blue and violet flowers, a pair of plain blue pumps, and a make-up bag containing lipstick (rose-red), black eyeliner, mascara, and a tawny foundation. Diana didn't think Sam needed any make-up, but she knew she had to let her daughter grow up. She herself needed clothes. After having lost twenty-five pounds since January, her blouses hung loose and her slacks threatened to fall down around her ankles. She chose a new blouse with three-quarter length sleeves, a pair of navy slacks, and a knee-length, A-line khaki skirt. While they tried on clothes, Annie disappeared for a few minutes and returned with something for herself, a hardback journal with blank pages. She waited patiently while they finished shopping.

After Annie paid for all the purchases, Diana said, "All right, let's adjourn to Café Massenet to revive ourselves. My treat this time."

"Yum, *café au lait* and French Market doughnuts!" Sam skipped ahead to the car.

Annie, who had a sweet tooth the size of a rhino tusk, blossomed like the desert after a rain. She quickened her step and smiled.

They sat at a table near the wall in the old-fashioned, high-ceilinged New Orleans landmark. When their order came, coffee for all and three beignets apiece, Diana added a dusting of powdered sugar to hers, while Sam and Annie enthusiastically shook out a white blizzard onto the square doughnuts. They took enormous bites chased by rapid sips of the steaming, chicory-laced brew.

Revived by the hot drink and sugary treat, Annie said to Diana, "You feel much stronger, don't you?"

"It's amazing—I really do," she laughed. "I seem to improve every day."

"I am so glad, *albi.*" Annie patted Diana's hand and said, "Remember when Hurricane Lili approached the Louisiana coast? Sam was two or three years old. It was a big, dangerous storm out in Vermilion Bay. I think it was Category four. They predicted twenty-foot storm surges, and everyone was scared."

While Diana sipped her *café au lait,* wondering if Annie's sudden change of subject, a colossal *non sequitur,* stemmed from fatigue, disorientation, or senility, Sam went along with the flow.

"Mamma, what's a Category four storm?"

"Let's see." Diana looked it up on her phone. "It's got winds from about 130 to 155 miles per hour. The winds create the storm surge on the coast, and they do tremendous damage inland as well. Big hurricanes like that also bring torrential rain which causes flooding, and they always spawn tornados."

"While Lili sat strengthening in the bay, everyone from New Orleans to Lake Charles followed the hourly weather reports, ready to evacuate," Annie continued. "No one knew where it would come ashore. Joseph taped the windows and bought plywood to board them up if the storm came our way."

"I remember that," said Diana.

"What happened, Sitti?"

"Well, everyone along the coast prayed hard—"

"Or in Joseph's words," said Diana, "everybody prayed like hell."

Annie laughed and nodded. "He did say that. And the reason we all prayed like hell was because as a hurricane approaches land over very warm water, it gains strength. They were expecting Lili to strengthen to Category five, the most powerful storm possible."

Diana checked her phone again. "Category five storms have 180 mile an hour winds with gusts up to 200 miles per hour."

Sam was wide-eyed. "So what happened?"

"Before it made landfall it weakened to a Category two storm, the exact opposite of what everyone expected."

"We were all amazed," said Diana. "What an anticlimax. No one evacuated, and it amounted to a couple days of hard rain and gusty winds, not much worse than the normal Louisiana thunderstorm."

"And then it was gone," said Annie.

"What caused it to weaken?" asked Sam.

Annie and Diana spoke simultaneously.

"We don't know," said Diana.

"Prayer," answered Sitti.

Diana turned down the corners of her mouth and looked away, annoyed. Annie regarded Diana patiently.

"So what's the point of this whole story?" asked Diana with an edge in her voice.

Annie bent her head and murmured something under her breath in Arabic, avoiding Diana's question.

"I know," Sam interjected into the uneasy silence between the two women. "It's about why you feel so much better, Mamma. The story means that if prayer can turn the course of weather in nature, it can also turn the course of illness. God is healing you, Mamma, because of prayer." She looked inquiringly at her grandmother. "That's what you meant, isn't it, Sitti?"

Annie nodded.

Sam smiled, "See, God can do the impossible if people believe."

Unconvinced, Diana drank the last of her coffee. She set the mug on the table with a clatter. "Well," she asked, with a clear challenge in her blue eyes, "what happens if they don't believe?"

"Then," answered Sam, unaware of how close she was to the truth, "God goes to Plan B."

On the day he was to go fishing with Sam and her Uncle George, the first social event Joshua had to endure was the lunch his parents hosted for the Beast's boss, the head of Leviathan's legal team, Charles Merrick, his wife Lucinda, and daughter Taylor. The lunch was a big deal to the Beast, and he required Joshua to be present.

Days beforehand, Joshua had even overheard his parents bickering about the menu. He sat on his bed, laptop balanced on one knee and his *siddur*, the Jewish prayer book, on the other. He either muttered transliterated Hebrew phrases from the *siddur*, which had just arrived in the mail, or peered at online maps of New Orleans' waterways in anticipation of his fishing excursion with Sam and George. Suddenly he had a third focus for his concentration; the strident sound of his parents' raised voices erupted from the living room.

When Amy told the Beast she intended to cater the lunch with spring rolls and a light seafood platter from Kim-Ly Nguyen's Vietnamese restaurant, he hissed, "Hell, no! They get their seafood from the Gulf. We're not eating that and we're certainly not feeding it to Charles Merrick and family."

"But Billy, the oil spill happened over a year ago."

When the Beast was angry, his Brooklynese surfaced. "Fuhgeddaboudit, Amy, we're not eatin' that shit. Why don't you cook something yourself? Go with salmon or cod. Figure it out."

Amy served an array of small sandwiches: smoked salmon with cream cheese and capers, chicken salad, cucumber and mayonnaise, alongside a tray of strawberries, blueberries, melon balls, and cheeses, including Brie, Swiss, aged cheddar, and Jarlsberg. They had a choice of white wine, beer, mineral water, or soda.

The Merricks were a trio of tall blonds, each one predatory in Joshua's estimation, but in different ways. He watched them warily. Charles, drawn immediately to the weapon wall, listened with interest as the Beast explained the origin of each gun and sword. His thick, sun-bleached hair flopped over his ruddy forehead like a lion's mane, almost covering his small, shrewd eyes. He obviously fed well; his belly bulged and drooped over his belt like a water balloon dangerously close to bursting. A tuft of graying chest hair peeked out from the green polo shirt he wore over khaki slacks and golf shoes.

Sharp-eyed Lucinda followed Amy into the kitchen, taking in every detail of the house on the way. Dressed in a red short-sleeved silk blouse with tight-fitting capris and leather sandals, she was as sleek, supple, and quietly dangerous as a lioness in her prime. As with many women who tried to appear younger than they were, her platinum hair and heavy make-up only served to accentuate the crow's feet and lines of her thin, angular face and the loose, sagging skin of her neck. As she passed by, enveloping Joshua in a cloud of perfume, her smile seemed to be a function of her facial muscles only; it never thawed the ice in her eyes.

Tawny-haired Taylor was as long and lanky as an adolescent lioness. Flat-chested and slender, she wore a sleeveless blue, low-cut sheath over white shorts that barely covered her round derrière, revealing thin, impossibly long legs. Upon meeting Joshua and realizing he was a head shorter than she, Taylor's interest evaporated immediately. Boredom clouded her face like fog on the Serengeti. She prowled around the room restlessly and then settled on the sofa with one of Amy's magazines.

Ignored by all, Joshua stood alone and flat-footed in the living room. As usual, he felt completely out of place in his own home. Thankfully, Amy put him to work; she asked him to set out *hors d'oeuvres*, napkins and drinks.

Since the Beast required Joshua's presence to keep Taylor company, they were seated across from each other at the table. While the older couples talked investments, golf, and the pros and cons of European vacations, Joshua and Taylor sat frozen in the awkward and excruciating silence which arises when young people who have nothing in common are forced upon each other socially. Finally gathering up his courage, Joshua broke the ice. "Are you a student?"

"Mm-huh." She slid her eyes away and bit into a chicken salad sandwich.

"Here in New Orleans?"

"No." She took a sip of white wine and then concentrated her gaze on her lap.

Joshua waited for the rest of the sentence, which never came. Regrouping, and hoping to stave off defeat, he drank some mineral water, as the Beast still denied him alcohol, and ate a smoked salmon sandwich, trying to figure out his next move. Watching the part in her bent head, he tried again like Custer, expecting the attempt would be vain and very likely fatal.

"So where do you go to school?"

"Vanderbilt."

Whoa, a three-syllable answer! What a pleasure to converse with a pretty girl as animated and articulate as a pothole. Where the shit was Vanderbilt? Rolling his eyes to the ceiling, he drank some effing mineral water. "Well, what's your major?"

"Uh, psychology." Never lifting her head, she brushed him off with as much interest as a cat flicking its ear, momentarily bothered by a fly.

Joshua suddenly realized that Taylor, concealing her mobile phone in her lap, had been texting the entire time.

"You know you'll need a master's degree with that major," he said, raising his voice. "An articulate girl like you could probably write a stunning, eloquent thesis on the psychology of fucking rudeness as practiced by the narcissistic rich, derived, of course, from your own deep well of personal experience."

Taylor actually looked up and regarded him malignantly, eye to eye, "You asshole."

"Goodness, two whole words," Joshua smiled. "That probably exhausted ninety per cent of your vocabulary." He rose and made a half-bow, "Text on to your heart's content." Meeting the hostile glare of all parties, he said, "Excuse me, one and all. Mother, thank you for a wonderful lunch, and as I am not needed here, I will retire to the music room and entertain you all with a Beethoven sonata. Please enjoy your lunch as I play."

He carefully counted his steps to the music room, but more than that, he counted every minute that separated him from his four o'clock fishing trip with Sam and her Uncle George.

It was a first. Joshua had never ridden in a pickup truck. And what a vehicle it was: ancient, dented, stricken with the automotive version of vitiligo, the white paint peeling to expose splotches of gray undercoat. The narrow cab came equipped with splitting seats, a dusty dashboard, and a seven-branched crack in the windshield that resembled a menorah. It rode with the grace of a tank; its deceased shock absorbers, seized by rigor mortis, intensified even the smallest bumps into spine-jarring jerks and jolts.

"This is my second car," George remarked, smiling at Joshua. "Ah."

At least the AC worked, as they rattled and banged down the road, elbow to elbow in the slowly—very slowly—waning heat of late afternoon. Dressed in a one-piece green work overall, George drove, cigar clamped in mouth, exhaling fragrant fumes. Holding a wide-brimmed straw hat in her lap, Sam, dressed in shorts and a Saints T-shirt, sat in the middle, swinging her legs, as her sneakers dangled three inches above the floorboards. Joshua wore a loose Statue of Liberty T-shirt, faded jeans, and sneakers. He jumped and twitched at the occasional explosive backfire, nervously adjusting his Yankee baseball cap to cover his embarrassment.

After a particularly ear-shattering report, George glanced at Joshua, patted the dash, leaving a set of fingerprints in the dust, and remarked in a reassuring voice, "Fear not, she's an old girl, a little temperamental, but she'll get us there and back." In the understatement of the year, he added, "Prob'ly needs a tune-up."

Like a bent, aged, arthritic trainer leading a magnificent racehorse, the pickup truck hauled a sleek, gleaming white boat and motor on a trailer, Joseph's boat. It clip-clopped behind them, docile, obedient, and trusting over New Orlean's heat-cracked, pot-holed roads, adding its own clatter and noise.

Joshua could not have been more pleased; it was paradise compared to lunch with the Merricks.

"Gotta make one stop," George said as he parked in front of a tobacco shop. "Be right back," he said. "Gettin' low on supplies." He left the truck running with the AC on to keep them cool.

"Uncle George has cigars stashed everywhere," Sam remarked to Joshua as they waited. "He keeps boxes of 'em in all his cars, at work, and he has a cabinet for 'em at home."

"What kind does he smoke?"

"All kinds," Sam laughed. "Big, small, fat and skinny, and I get the boxes."

Joshua decided to tease her, "Oh, so it's all right if *he* smokes."

Sam pursed her lips, "Yes, 'cause he doesn't do it under my tree."

"Well, I learned my lesson about that."

George returned with two boxes under his arm. "Now that I'm stocked, we can continue," he smiled, "*after* I light up." He glanced at Joshua, "Would you like one, too?"

Joshua shook his head regretfully, "No thanks, I'm trying to quit, but you go ahead."

"Okay," said George, "Sam, do the honors." She opened the glove compartment and took out a box of large kitchen matches. Sitting behind the steering wheel, George opened one of the wooden cigar boxes, took out a hefty torpedo, and extracted a cigar cutter from his breast pocket. He carefully made a straight cut across the closed end of the cigar. Before he slid the cutter back into his pocket, he showed Joshua the small, flat metal device with loops at both ends. "Double blade guillotine, trusted and true," George remarked. "Can't be too careful; a bad cut can ruin a good cigar, and *sacré bleu*, that would never do!"

Sam lit a match and waited a moment until the flame caught. Then she turned slightly toward her uncle, holding the burning match so the flame rose vertical and still. George placed the tip of the cigar perpendicular to the flame and just above it, slowly and patiently rotating it until the end began to glow. Then he blew on it gently and took the first puff. Satisfied that the cigar was lit and drawing, George opened his window slightly to funnel out the smoke, and drove out of the parking lot.

In the silence that followed the cigar-lighting ritual, Joshua decided to satisfy his curiosity. Always sensitive to sound, he had been trying to analyze George's accent from the moment he met him. The older man's speech was familiar and yet strange, like slow-motion Brooklynese. It intrigued Joshua almost as much as his ride in the exotic truck. "George, you're one hundred per cent Lebanese, right?"

"At least," George smiled. "Maybe a hundred-ten."

"Well, I notice you don't have the same accent as Annie."

George took the cigar out of his mouth and swiveled his head abruptly to stare at Joshua, "Accent?" he repeated, raising his eyebrows, "you think I got an accent?" He pointed his cigar at Joshua. "I'd say *you* got the accent. You're from New York, aren't ya?"

Joshua nodded, "Brooklyn."

"Bingo."

Shaking his head, George glanced down at Sam with an incredulous look, "Hmmph, he thinks I got an accent?" He suddenly erupted into the battle cry of the state of Louisiana, "Who dat, who dat say dey gonna beat dem Saints?"

"Yeah, you right," answered Sam. "And afta da game, we eat ersters, but first we wrench 'em in da zink."

"Ya see," said George, "I grajiated from Cat'lic school," pouring it on for Joshua. "I don't have Mamma's accent 'cause she and Daddy didn't want us soundin' like furriners, so they didn't teach us Arabic. We got da accent from da city, prob'ly originally from da Irish and Italian immigrants, same as you got in Brooklyn. Irish and Italian nuns taught school, and dat's how dey talked: *dis, dat, dese, dem, and dose.*" He laughed, "And dere ya go, da New Orleans accent was born."

"Yeah, and what's really weird," Sam added, "is that people born here have about five ways of sayin' the name of the city." She then proceeded to pronounce them, "New OR-luns, New AW-luns, New OR-lee-ens, New AH-lee-ens, Nyoo AH-lee-uns."

"What about New Or-LEENS?" asked Joshua, humming a famous song about being homesick for the city.

George laughed, "The locals *nevah evah* say dat. Dat's da give-away for a furriner." Satisfied with his discourse on language, he lapsed into silence and puffed on his cigar.

"So how do people talk in Brooklyn?" Sam asked Joshua.

"Very similar to the way you and George talk." Then Joshua launched into Brooklynese, "So I'm wooawkin' da dooahg down Toidy-Toid on a poifect day. So I see my cousin Bevuhly, 'n I says to huh, 'Wanna get some cwafee?'"

Sam laughed and clapped her hands, "Poifect! Dey say toidy-toid heah, too."

"How long ya been in New AW-luns, Joshua?" asked George.

"About a month."

"Well, since we're related by dialect, you should feel right at home."

And the funny thing was, thought Joshua, glancing at bright-eyed Sam and George, encircled by a fragrant halo of smoke, in their company, he really did.

CHAPTER 13

Fishing

Ten minutes later, they arrived at the boat launch near the Highway 90 Bridge. George pulled into the shell parking lot directly in front of Big Skinny's Grocery & Bait Shop. He parked in the shade of a large old live oak with gnarled, spreading limbs. On the far side of the lot, a concrete boat ramp descended into the water, which glittered in the brilliant sunlight. A single brown pelican perched on the railing of the deserted fishing pier.

"Joshua," said George, "we have to get you a fishing license here." Big Skinny's sold an assortment of fishing tackle, live bait, lures, and nets, as well as groceries, and New Orleans specialties such as pralines and freshly made shrimp and crawfish po-boys.

As Joshua discovered, the proprietor was big, but far from skinny. White-haired, bearded, and rotund, dressed in sandals, a gaudy Hawaiian shirt and shorts, Big Skinny resembled Santa Claus on summer vacation. He sat behind the counter with his great girth threatening to overwhelm a battered office chair on wheels. As he extracted himself from the chair to greet his customers, it squeaked and squealed in profound relief.

"Hey, Skinny, how's business?"

"Bait business is boomin', but the actin' is on hiatus for the summer. Only non-equity jobs right now."

"Big Skinny's a stage and film actor, the best and funniest Falstaff I ever saw," George told Joshua. "He lives a block to the west of us in Chalice."

Sam piped up, "This is Joshua our new neighbor."

"Greetings, my man," said Skinny, with a half-bow, "and how can I help y'all today?"

While George purchased the fishing license, as well as beer, water, ice, and bait shrimp, Sam and Joshua roamed about the store, choosing snacks and soda for the fishing excursion. Joshua helped George carry their purchases outside, where they loaded the ice, the drinks, and the round carton of bait shrimp into a large red and white ice chest in the back of the boat.

"Why'd he say the bait business is boomin', when we were his only customers?" asked Sam.

"This place is swamped Thursday through Sunday," George answered, "but it's slow at the beginning of the week, as you can see." There was only one other truck and trailer there. "Best time to come. Good thing the boss let me off today."

"Uncle George, you are the boss at Levant House."

George grinned at Sam, "Exactly." He backed the boat and trailer partway down the incline of the concrete boat ramp and stopped. "Joshua, you and Sam hop out and tell me when the trailer wheels are completely under water."

When Joshua shouted, "Okay," George put the truck in park and got out. He released the winch and let the boat slide into the water. Holding the painter in one hand, he unhooked the bow with the other. The boat bobbed lightly on the water, as George pulled the rope to guide it to the adjacent pier. "Sam, hop in. Joshua, park the truck next to Big Skinny's over there under the live oak."

Sam ran up onto the pier and climbed into the boat, but Joshua did not move.

George looked at him expectantly. "Joshua," he prompted, pointing with his free hand, "the truck. Move it."

Joshua grabbed the bill of his cap and adjusted it on his head. "Uh, well, uh, are you sure you want me to drive it? I just got my license the end of June."

"Son, this is Louisiana. It's summertime; it's damn hot, and until we get goin' in the boat we're not gonna cool off." George wiped his brow with his forearm. "Do you really think you can hurt that sorry vehicle? I don't give a rat's you-know-what if you got a license or not. Move the damn truck!"

Joshua laughed. He moved the truck.

As soon as he jogged back and hopped over the gunwale, George pushed off and started the motor. They donned life jackets and sat as they had in the truck, only with Sam and Joshua now to George's left. Gripping the steering wheel with cigar in mouth, George guided the boat down a short channel to the Grand Canal and then into Chef Pass. As the boat picked up speed, George had to shout over the sound of the motor. "I thought this was the best place to go today because of the wind. There's so much open water on Lake Pontchartrain, we'd prob'ly be navigatin' whitecaps."

"Where are we going?" Sam yelled, holding on to the brim of her straw hat which threatened to sail off her head.

"I'm takin' us a little ways toward Pontchartrain, just to show Joshua, and then we're gonna turn around and pass under the Highway 90 Bridge and continue on to the CSX Railroad Bridge. There's not any traffic noise at the railroad bridge unless a train comes by, and the bridge supports act like a reef to attract the fish."

As they sped through the Pass, Sam excitedly pointed out great blue herons, brown pelicans, kingfishers, red-winged blackbirds, laughing gulls, and egrets. Enjoying her sense of wonder, and sharing it, Joshua smiled and felt the weight of tension drop away from him like a heavy cloak. The deep green grasses and plants of the flat, marshy landscape contrasted with the blue-gray water, sparkling in the sun. Overarching it all was the dark blue sky with its towering snow-white cumulus clouds. It seemed to go on forever.

After a few minutes, George turned the boat around.

"There's the bridge again!" shouted Sam. "The superstructure looks like the backs of three elephants walking in file, head to tail."

"How do the big boats go under this?" Joshua asked as they passed under the eleven foot clearance.

"They don't. They can't do it the way we just did, but this is a swing bridge. See that big central section shaped like a T?" George pointed back over his shoulder. "It's motorized and it pivots around that middle support, until it's perpendicular to the rest of the bridge, opening up two wide pathways for the big boats to go through. The CSX Bridge where we're headed is the same type."

"Is Chef Pass a river?" Joshua asked.

"No, it's not. What we call passes are actually straits. There is another pass, just north of here, the Rigolets."

"Da RIG-o-leez," echoed Sam. "Love the sound of that word!"

"Both passes are natural channels, connectin' Lake Pontchartrain with Lake Borgne, which connects to the Gulf. We call this channel Chef Pass, but its official name is Chef Menteur Pass, and it's only about six miles long. The Gulf tides come in first through Lake Borgne and then through the passes. High tide today was at eleven-thirty this mornin', and low tide will be 'bout eleven tonight."

"When is a lake not a lake?" Sam asked.

George shrugged, and Joshua said, "When it's dry?"

Sam shook her head, "When it's not completely enclosed. Lake Maurepas, which is farther inland, Lake Pontchartrain, and Lake Borgne are not true lakes because they are actually interconnected through the passes. They are part of the Lake Pontchartrain Basin, which is an estuary or watershed. The watershed covers ten thousand square miles with Pontchartrain as the centerpiece."

"How do you know all that, Sam?" Joshua asked.

"School report." She grinned, "You know it was the best in the class."

"I bet it was," he said. She was such a blessed contrast to Taylor Merrick. "Just do me a favor, Sam. When you graduate, please don't go to Vanderbilt."

"Don't worry," she replied with a sparkle in her brown eyes, "I've already decided on Harvard."

As they approached the railroad bridge, George let up on the throttle and then cut the motor. Their momentum carried them close to the bridge supports. As they glided in the sudden quiet, they could hear the cries of the gulls, the lapping of the water against the boat and the bridge, the buzz of insects and crickets in the marshes, and the calls and songs of birds. As the boat slowed, George dropped the anchor. "Hard to believe we're only fifteen miles from the Central Business District and the French Quarter."

"Paradise in the midst of civilization," Joshua replied, gazing up at the deep blue sky and brilliant white clouds. The vivid colors, so clean and suffused with light, seemed to emanate from a higher world, emblems of virtue and purity. Could they be there, he wondered, Virtue and Purity: unstained, unspotted patient entities, watching over mankind?

"Louisiana is called Sportsman's Paradise," Sam announced.

"Well, it would be paradise if you took human beings out of the equation," George remarked. "I'll tell you what, people sure know how to mess up everything, the damn oil companies in particular."

Leviathan Oil, his father's company. He noticed an old tire, resting on the bank, half in and half out of the water and a beer can floating next to it, both ugly, jarring reminders of the presence of man. *It would be paradise, if you took human beings out of the equation.* Returning his gaze to the sky, he wondered, could there be a restoration of the paradise that had been? The sky that seemed so huge to Joshua, almost endless, gave no answer.

Pulling on a black baseball cap emblazoned with the Saints gold *fleur de lis*, George instructed, "Take a fishing pole and bait it." He opened the lid of the large cooler behind the seats and took out the round white container of shrimp.

With her wayward locks hidden under the broad-brimmed straw hat, Sam baited her hook. Joshua, completely out of his element, watched her surreptitiously and copied every move. He made a great effort to appear nonchalant in front of Sam, even as he cringed inwardly in disgust at the feel of the slimy bait shrimp and the tearing sound it made as he impaled it on the hook.

"Cast as close as you can to the bridge supports," George told them. He and Sam let fly, but Joshua just sat there, pole in hand, tugging on the bill of his cap.

By this time, George recognized the signs of inexperience and fear; he had dealt with it in his own children, Michael and Lucy. Well, once a father, always a father. Demonstrating as he explained, George said, "Joshua, hold the release button with your thumb, bend your arm at the elbow like this, and bring the tip of the rod slightly behind your head. Now watch, I'm gonna use my wrist to flick it forward, and when the rod reaches about ten o'clock, I'm gonna let go of the button. That releases the line." George made his cast.

"Okay, your turn. And if you don't get it right, just keep tryin'. We got the rest of the afternoon." George opened a long-neck beer and smiled, raising it like a toast.

Joshua's first two attempts failed, but with George's quiet encouragement, he made an excellent cast on the third try.

"There you go, Joshua!" yelled Sam.

"Hush, girl, you're scarin' away all the fish," admonished George. "Help yourself to a soda, Sam, and hand that red-haired New Yorker a beer."

George caught two flounder and Sam hooked a medium size redfish, but Joshua, to his amazement, landed three big speckled trout. Pleased as he was, he had no idea the day was about to yield much more than fish.

After putting their catch on ice, George started the motor and headed for home. The huge disc of the setting sun turned the sky to deep gold. It shimmered like the background of a Russian icon, and the water mirrored it. As the boat traveled down the center of the gilded channel, creating a V-like wake behind them, a small flock of cormorants flew ahead of them, crisscrossing back and forth over the strait, going before them like a mystical escort of angels. The aerial ballet, so graceful and flowing, took Joshua's breath away. Suddenly, in the strange beauty of the flat, watery landscape, it struck him that all was movement: the fluid motion of the boat, the birds weaving the air above them, the fish surfacing to feed, the blowing wind, the ebbing tide, their breathing, the beating of their hearts and the coursing of their blood, the turning of the earth itself.

Propelled to his feet, he rose, doffed his cap, and grasped the top of the windscreen. Sam stood beside him, and they leaned into the wind. All was movement, like a great and intricate music, and he was part of it, as though he were one moving melody with a myriad other melodies sounding above and below him. He had just entered into the song; he knew it had gone on before him and would continue after him. Suddenly, without a doubt, he knew that someone had called this music into being; it was not random. Surely there was a Creator; there had to be.

Sam nudged him, "You're glad you came, aren't you?"

She had no idea. Joshua glanced down at her and smiled, "I am."

She suddenly raised one arm and let out a long, loud whoop. They looked at each other and burst into laughter.

"All right, sit down, you two," said George. He let up on the throttle and headed into the short channel toward the boat ramp.

The sun hung very low on the horizon by the time they winched the boat back onto the trailer. George told Joshua to get in the driver's seat. "Experience, son, you just need experience."

"Where do you want me to drive?"

"Home."

"What about insurance?"

"What about it?"

"Is your truck insured for other drivers?"

"Are you a musician or a lawyer?" George laughed. "Hell, a third of the cars in New Orleans are uninsured. And yeah, I got insurance, which covers you, but we're not gonna need it, 'cause we're not gonna get in a wreck. Someone responsible like you is gonna be a damn good, careful driver." George climbed into the passenger side after Sam. "So let's go, Joshua. Get behind the wheel and drive."

They didn't go far; they stopped at the first gas station so Sam could use the restroom. George and Joshua waited in the cab with the windows down. "Thanks for making me drive. I'm beginning to feel more confident."

George nodded, struck a match, and lit his third cigar.

"I'm not good at much. According to my dad, I don't do anything right."

"Well, speakin' from my own experience, you're a good driver, a quick study at castin', and an excellent fisherman—you caught the most. In addition, Sam tells me you're a fabulous pianist."

"Oh, that. Well, yeah." Joshua shrugged, "But I suck at everything else. Just ask my dad."

"And what does your dad do?"

"He's an attorney for Leviathan Oil."

"Hmmph. Not a popular company right now in these parts."

"No." Joshua adjusted his cap, "The thing is, my dad was a star athlete, and he wanted me to excel at sports and go to law school like he did. I'm just never good enough for him."

"A star athlete, eh?" George flicked his cigar ashes out the window. "What's his name?"

"Billy Brightman. He was a pitcher. They called him Billy the Beast."

"Never heard of him. Who'd he pitch for?"

"The Ithaca College Bombers."

"Oh. Did he get spotted by the pro scouts? Get any offers?"

Joshua frowned. "Hmm, I don't know. He never mentioned it if he did."

"So he was a star on a college team."

"Mm-huh."

"So then after college he went to law school?"

Joshua nodded.

"So what about you—where do you play piano, besides the upcomin' concert here in town that Sam cannot quit talkin' about?"

Joshua smiled, "Well, I played with the San Francisco Symphony, once with the Boston Pops, the Tulsa Philharmonic, and I have engagements this fall with the Detroit and Seattle Symphonies."

"San Francisco Symphony and the Boston Pops. Sounds like the big time to me."

Joshua smiled, "Well, I'm getting there."

"And does your dad enjoy comin' to hear you play?"

"Nah, he thinks it's boring. If he comes, he usually can't wait to leave."

"Got an agent?"

"I do, in New York."

George puffed on his cigar a moment. "And your dad is a big time attorney at Leviathan?"

"Well, he's one of many lawyers on their legal team. He's definitely not the head of it."

George exhaled a puff of fragrant smoke. "Hmm, let's see what we got here. On the one hand, we got the college star who never made it to the pros and the middle-aged lawyer who's a small fish in a big corporation. On the other hand, we got the son in his twenties who's already playin' with some of the top orchestras in this country, at the beginnin' of a big time career."

Squinting at Joshua through the cloud of smoke, George added softly, "Maybe we got a green-eyed problem here."

Like lightning, George's words struck with devastating impact. Shocked, Joshua stared straight ahead, unseeing, with a buzzing in his ears, all circuits overloaded. Time ceased to exist for him. *Jealous? The Beast jealous of him?* A kaleidoscope of scenes whirled in his mind: his father's uneasiness at the concerts, his lack of praise, his continual fault-finding. It all appeared suddenly in a new and ghastly light. Joshua couldn't breathe.

"Ready?" asked Sam.

Joshua looked at her in disbelief. "When did you come back?"

"Been sittin' here for two minutes. Sorry it took so long, but there was a line for the ladies room."

Somehow he drove home, though he didn't remember seeing the road.

CHAPTER 14

The Prince of Lies

He broke the news as they drove home from the country club. "Amy, we can't go to France next week. We have to cancel our vacation."

Her eyes widened and her jaw dropped in disbelief. He might as well have punched her. "Billy, why?"

"It's the trial. Merrick told me the company is sweating this out, and no one on the legal team gets a vacation until it's over. Prosecutors are looking for a huge settlement, the biggest in history. Leviathan might have to pay billions."

"But we rented the house in Nice. We bought the plane tickets months ago."

"I know, sweetheart, I know. But Merrick says he'll make it up to us." He patted her hand and glanced at her anxiously. "Sweetheart, don't cry."

Despite her long practice at masking her emotions, spontaneous tears of disappointment and frustration flooded her eyes and streamed down her face. Amy fished a tissue out of her purse and wiped her eyes. She had so looked forward to their vacation. France, especially the south of France, was so lovely. She was a New Yorker, unused to the awful southern climate. France would have been a blessed respite from Louisiana's oppressively hot and humid summer, from the ridiculously named Chalice, the godawful wasteland of a suburb where Billy had landed them. Disappointment drained her like a vampire, sucking her blood and robbing her of all energy. She suddenly felt so fatigued that she wondered if she could hold up her head.

"Well wasn't it a great day?" Billy asked, trying to distract her. "Your lovely lunch, golf, swimming, and then drinks at the clubhouse. Charles and I had a great time. Did you enjoy meeting Lucinda?"

"Of course." Amy lied automatically, knowing what he wanted to hear. Yes, she enjoyed Lucinda just the way a heifer revels in the company of a mountain lion. Beside the sleek, athletic Lucinda, Amy had felt like a klutz, plodding along, shooting a 90 while Lucinda, scarcely veiling her contemptuous glee, shot a 78. Afterwards, while Lucinda circled the pool like a shark in its element, pudgy Amy struggled, feeling as attractive and streamlined as a cow in the Bering Sea.

Billy steered the car onto the exit ramp for Chalice. "Everything went well today, except for Joshua's rude behavior."

"Now, Billy, Taylor was the rude one, texting at the table like that. He tried to talk to her, and then she called him an asshole—I heard her."

"Why didn't he come with us? What was that bullshit about having a prior engagement?"

"Well, it didn't matter anyway, because Taylor left after lunch to join her friends."

Billy snorted, "He just didn't want to make a fool of himself on the golf course."

"Maybe so, but I think he did meet friends somewhere."

"What friends? He's hardly been out of the house since we moved here."

"I don't know. He was vague about it, but you know he doesn't lie."

"Hell, Amy, everybody lies. That's how the world works." His mind returned to his all-consuming job. "I see it every day at Leviathan. After the oil spill, the company set up huge funds to compensate people and businesses for their losses. Look what happened—the commercial fishermen and business owners on the coast lied about the amount of damages they incurred. Some of them inflated invoices billed to Leviathan by hundreds of thousands of dollars. Hell, people made completely bogus claims, seeking lost wages from restaurants or seafood processing plants where they were never even employed, trying to cash in."

"Really?" Wallowing in disappointment over the aborted vacation, she was only half-listening. She had grown so inured to Billy's continuous rants about the oil spill that she regularly tuned him out. Feigning interest, she asked, "Weren't there some legitimate claims?"

"Of course, but there again you've got people taking advantage. In those cases, the plaintiffs' lawyers are making a killing. They inflate the amount of the claims and if they're successful, they pocket fees up to twenty-five per cent of the total award."

Billy leaned back in the driver's seat and cracked his knuckles. "I'm damn worried about the civil trial in August. We're charged with violating the federal Clean Water Act."

"Why are you so worried about it?"

"Well, at some point, the company may start laying off people like me to recoup its losses."

With sudden real interest, she glanced anxiously at Billy, "Oh, I hope not! How much will Leviathan have to pay?"

"Probably billions more. Depends on how many barrels of oil spilled into the Gulf and whether the company is found by a jury to have been grossly negligent or to have committed willful misconduct. There are also the issues related to containment of the spill and the use of dispersants. We'll have to pay either a minimum of eleven hundred or a maximum of forty-three hundred dollars per barrel."

"What's the difference?"

"If the company is found grossly negligent, the higher penalty applies."

"But you've told me all along they weren't negligent."

"Of course not. Look, it was just a tragic accident. I'm an attorney, not an engineer, and I don't know all the technical details, but I know Leviathan always complies with industry standards and we meet all government requirements."

She frowned and glanced at him, "Billy, in that case, why did Leviathan plead guilty on several criminal counts in the first trial? What does Leviathan have to say about all those men who died?"

"Sweetheart, people died because the individuals on the scene made some bad decisions. They didn't follow company policy."

"The newspaper articles said the company lied about the amount of oil spilling into the Gulf, the rate of flow."

"That was the spin the prosecution put on it, charging that the individuals involved were trying to minimize the amount of money the company would have to pay." Billy shrugged. "Maybe those involved were overzealous. Sometimes in business, sweetheart, profit comes before people and the environment. But that's definitely not Leviathan's policy."

Turning onto their street, he continued, "The company has spent billions already in the cleanup and restoration of the shoreline, including large payments to the Wetlands Conservation organization and Louisiana Wildlife and Fisheries. Hell, we do our part for this state and the whole Gulf coast, providing thousands of jobs and supporting the economic and environmental recovery. We've cleaned and restored ninety per cent of the entire coastline and brought the seafood industry back to its pre-spill conditions."

If that was the case, Amy wondered, then why did Billy refuse to let her serve Gulf seafood when the Merricks came to lunch?

He shrugged and blew out a noisy breath as he turned into the driveway and parked the BMW. Glancing at his wife, he added, "What more can anyone expect? We've really done our part."

Depressed about the cancellation of their trip to France and tired of the conversation, Amy steered the subject back to her son. "Well, I still don't think Joshua lied about meeting his friends today. But I really don't know the details, so when he comes home, you can ask him where he went."

"Oh, I intend to," replied Billy.

When he got home, Joshua entered the house with mixed emotions. It had been a day of revelations, good and bad; he was still trying to digest it all. After he put his bag of fish in the freezer, he headed for the bathroom. He stripped off his clothes and then adjusted the heat of the water. Easing into the shower, he sighed with pleasure as the hot water sluiced over him, rinsing away the sweat. He washed his hair first and then lathered up his body, thinking about his conversation with George concerning the Beast.

Bam-bam-bam-bam-bam! "We gotta talk," shouted the Beast through the closed bathroom door.

Think of the devil.... Well, the devil could wait. Joshua took his time, letting the hot water soothe him and relax his muscles before he went into battle. When he had shaved and dressed, Joshua emerged from the bathroom in a cloud of steam. The Beast was waiting for him on the sofa, sitting beside Amy.

"Joshua, would you like some ice cream? I'll get some for all of us."

"Sure, thanks, Mom." His mother, known for avoiding confrontation, hurried into the kitchen.

Taking his cue, the Beast began the inevitable interrogation. "Where did you go today, Joshua?"

"Fishing."

"With whom?"

"Friends. How was your day, Dad?"

"Great!" He popped his knuckles and flexed his shoulders. "Your mother and I played golf and swam at the country club. You could have spent the afternoon with us, but you chose not to."

Joshua sat silently in the armchair across from the Beast.

"So who are these so-called friends of yours?"

"Sam and George."

"Ah. And how did you meet Sam and George?"

"One of those chance encounters. I met Sam, and George is Sam's uncle."

The Beast's tone hardened, "Joshua, quit the bullshit. You're making up a story just because you didn't want to embarrass yourself playing golf."

At that moment, Amy appeared in the doorway, holding up a very large plastic freezer bag containing three fish, gutted and cleaned. "Look what I found in the freezer. What are these and where did they come from?"

"Speckled trout, caught by yours truly," Joshua smiled, gazing at his father, "on my mythical fishing trip with my mythical friends."

"Could you just bring the damn ice cream, Amy?" hissed the Beast, highly annoyed.

They ate the ice cream in silence until the Beast announced to Joshua that Charles Merrick had invited them all for a paddle wheel cruise on the Mississippi on July fourth. "No excuses, this time," he added.

"Is Taylor going to be there?"

"As far as I know."

"Well, sorry, Dad, but I've already accepted an invitation to a party on the Fourth at Sam's house."

"Decline it."

"Absolutely not. Sam and George are kind, intelligent people I like. Taylor Merrick is utterly rude with a vacuum where her mind should be. She won't miss me; she's already deleted me like spam from her pathetic memory."

"I said you're coming with us."

"Billy," Amy intervened, "Joshua is twenty-four years old. Let him be with the people he likes. He's in a new place and he needs new friends."

"What is Taylor, chopped liver?"

"Can't be," Joshua remarked, leaning back in the chair, "chopped liver has substance."

"As I told you earlier, Billy, she was rude and she called Joshua an asshole," Amy said, secretly glad to take a dig at sleek Lucinda's daughter. "And frankly, we don't really know if she'll be there or not. She went off with her own friends this afternoon, even though Charles originally told us she would be going along to the country club."

"All right, the hell with it."

"Joshua, tell us about your new friends," his mother prompted. "What do they do?"

"Sam is a student, and George runs Levant House, an import store in the city."

"What do they import?" asked the Beast.

"I haven't been there, but I think it's mostly Middle Eastern food and products."

"Are they Jews?"

"No, Dad," he answered with an edge, "they're Lebanese."

The Beast drew his brows down and stared at Joshua with open-mouthed incredulity. "That's my idiot son, consorting with terrorists on the Fourth of July."

Joshua felt heat rising in his throat and face. He straightened his back and leaned forward, "For your information, they are devout Christians, and Sam's grandfather served in the United States Naval Air Force in World War II. What war did you serve in, Dad?"

"Well, I—"

"The war against squirrels?"

"What the hell—"

Joshua's voice rose with the pressure in his head, "I know what you did. I buried the squirrel you shot. You set out the nuts as bait and then sat inside the house where they couldn't see you. You shot the squirrel when he came to eat." Suddenly dropping his voice, feeling nauseated and blinded by the pain of a migraine, he whispered, "What bravery, what courage, what a superior man!"

Three things happened at once. The Beast sprang up from the sofa, Joshua rose to meet him, and, stunning them both, Amy leapt between them, faster than a wildcat. She braced both hands against her husband's chest, "Billy, do not hit him!"

"I ought to rip his head off," the Beast growled, glaring at his son over Amy's head. He pointed a thick forefinger at Joshua. "You've had your say, you ungrateful piece of shit, and now I'll have mine." The veins stood out on his shaved head as he stabbed himself in the chest with his finger, punctuating each phrase. "This is my house; it's my gun, and my yard, and I'll do anything I please here. You've got one week," he spat, pointing his index finger skyward, "to get your sorry ass out of this house. And take your fuckin' piano with you."

Joshua turned on his heel and strode away. "Gladly," he threw back over his shoulder.

To his amazement, he suddenly felt light, practically buoyant. His headache lifted and the nausea vanished. He was going to move out. He didn't know how, he didn't know where, and he didn't know if he'd survive the stress of moving combined with the pressure of his upcoming concert, but he was moving out. Smiling to himself, he walked by the weapon wall, steadfastly refusing to count his steps.

CHAPTER 15

The State of Louisiana

It was late on a sunny Thursday afternoon, when Dr. Leo DeLuca drove toward his third appointment for the day. The agency which employed him part time, Citizens for a Better Louisiana, had sent him south of New Orleans to Plaquemines Parish, to interview three families impacted by the oil spill. He had already completed two interviews in Venice, the Fishing Capital of the World. His last appointment was with the Clostio family, who lived somewhere near Buras. The long drive on Highway 23 had awakened memories of his youth and focused his mind on his unique and beautiful native state.

Although not as long or elegant as Italy, the state of Louisiana is also shaped like a boot, but a thick, snub-toed working man's boot. The shaft, or northern half of the state, settled by Scottish-

Irish Protestants, is mostly rural, insular, teetotaler territory, defined by its rolling hills and piney woods. Most of the large cities are located in the south, the vamp and toe of the boot, a coastal plain, peopled in large part by hard-drinking, fun-loving Cajuns and Creoles, descendants of the French and Spanish Catholics who colonized the territory.

Like a mythical planet, South Louisiana is its own watery world, bounded on the west by the Sabine River and on the east by the Pearl River and the Mississippi with its far-flung delta. In between lies a lacy, labyrinthine coast line marked by vast marshes, myriad islands, lakes, bays, sounds, and once-pristine beaches. Outside the cities of Lake Charles, Lafayette, Baton Rouge, and New Orleans, the land is sparsely peopled; it is dotted by small towns and even smaller settlements. The melodious names of the bays and sounds, of Native American, French and Spanish origin, ran through Leo's mind like a song: Vermilion, Atchafalaya, Terrebonne, Timbalier, Barataria, Breton, and Chandeleur.

Thinking about music led him naturally to opera, a subject dear to his heart. He had just bought a new recording of *Manon Lescaut*, Puccini's first great success, which also contained one of Puccini's major blunders. The mistake would be obvious to anyone traveling Highway 23, the only possible highway through Plaquemines Parish, a long, narrow peninsula that juts like a crooked finger into the sea. The road was bounded by the Mississippi River levee on one side and the marsh levee on the other; it was surrounded by water.

"Water, Giacomo, H-two-oh!" Leo exclaimed. "Signor Puccini, you were a great opera composer, but a poor student of geography." The fourth act of *Manon Lescaut* famously takes place in the "desert" near the outskirts of New Orleans, where Manon, an innocent girl turned courtesan, has been exiled from Paris. Giacomo Puccini would have been mortified had he known that New Orleans itself had been built on a swamp, and his so-called desert actually encompassed some of the greatest coastal wetlands in North America.

Rather than wandering in thirst through Puccini's desert, Manon would have more likely drowned in the vast, watery marshes or been devoured by a marsh monster. If the 'gators didn't get her, the black bears, panthers, and red wolves might have. One way or another, her choices led her down the long, unhappy road to death.

The controversial story of Manon Lescaut and her lover, the Chevalier Des Grieux, written by the eighteenth-century French novelist Abbé Prévost, got the best kind of publicity possible in France: it was banned. Nothing could have made it more popular. The story was set to music twice, first by Jules Massenet in his opera *Manon*, and later by Puccini. Leo also owned the Massenet version, a recording made from a live performance at the New Orleans Opera in 1967. When the story begins, Manon is an innocent young girl, on her way to join a convent. She falls in love with young Des Grieux and impulsively runs away to live with him in Paris. Although she loves Des Grieux, Manon's downfall is that she loves wealth and luxury more.

Now if South Louisiana was an opera, Leo mused, in story and persona she could be Manon: beautiful and innocent in the beginning, but untamed, sensual, immoral, and doomed by her love of money. Louisiana's story, steered by the passions and greed of human beings, had truly been a tale of pristine natural beauty and abundance sold to the highest bidder and corrupted to the point of environmental catastrophe and death.

For years, Louisiana politicians had bent over backwards for Big Oil, selling the state for its resources, turning a blind eye to the oil industry's toxic emissions and flagrant violations of clean air and water regulations. Putting people in jeopardy, especially minorities and those below the poverty level, was quite all right as long as the state pocketed the cash. Consequently, in addition to having some of the worst pollution problems and highest cancer rates in the country, Louisiana was also the fastest disappearing state in the union. According to some researchers, each day approximately thirty football fields of Louisiana coastal land dissolved into the sea.

Every time Leo visited lower Plaquemines Parish, he saw more open water—saltwater—and less marsh and dry land. There were two prime causes. First, for decades, the natural flow of the Mississippi River had been diverted by engineers who built levees to control and prevent flooding. Blocked from its natural path, the great river could no longer overflow its banks and deposit its sediment to build up and replenish the land as it had for millennia. Meanwhile, the oil companies dredged thousands of miles of canals for pipelines and access to drilling sites, crisscrossing the brackish marsh and opening it to an influx of saltwater, which killed the grasses and plants, destroying the root systems which held the fragile land together. The areas infiltrated by salt water just melted into the sea. In addition, the pumping out of the oil and gas caused the land to sink.

Thirty years ago, as a teenager, Leo had fished in the Plaquemines marshes with his friends. The marsh went on and on, for as far as he could see. He recalled how the flat-bottomed metal boat glided through the winding channels in the early morning chill and how they welcomed the rising sun which warmed them. They found a promising fishing spot, anchored the boat, baited their hooks, and threw in their lines.

In the quiet, Leo heard what he thought of ever after as marsh music: the sighing of the wind, the lapping of the water against the boat, the rustling of the grasses, frogs croaking, the calls of red-winged blackbirds, and other small songbirds he couldn't identify, against the intermittent bellowing of the 'gators and the harsh cries of seagulls. He was transfixed by the loneliness of the vast space, its wildness and danger, and its deceptiveness. It was very hard to tell from a distance whether what looked like solid land was actually *terra firma* or just reeds growing up out of the water. There were so few landmarks, it was easy to lose one's sense of direction, to become lost in the endless channels amongst the tall cord grass, surrounded by gigantic prehistoric reptiles. He had harbored a slight anxiety they would never find their way back to the boat launch and dry land.

Middle-aged Leo pushed his glasses up to the bridge of his nose, remembering the words of Gerard Manley Hopkins, his favorite poet:

> *What would the world be, once bereft*
> *Of wet and of wildness? Let them be left,*
> *O let them be left, wildness and wet;*
> *Long live the weeds and the wilderness yet.*

Long live the magical, mysterious marshes of Louisiana, he thought, O let them be left, and the fishermen who make their living therein, let them be left. Let the marsh restore itself; let the people regain their life and health.

But would the marshes and the people survive? Leo had his doubts; he feared the battle might be lost.

Glancing at his handwritten directions, he turned left off the highway onto a narrow road paved with oyster shells, little more than a bumpy track through the flat, marshy land. He crawled along at fifteen miles per hour. Above the noise of the air conditioner fan, which he had set on high in the ninety-degree heat, he could clearly hear the crunch and crackle of the shells under the Chevy Blazer's tires.

Treeless pastures flanked the road, dotted by grazing cattle. Narrow canals, lined by tall reeds, paralleled the road on either side. Here and there he spotted egrets and great blue herons stalking the edges of the canals. In the water, dark, knobby logs that were not logs glided half submerged, lazily self-propelled by long tails. There were more alligators in Louisiana than anywhere else in North America.

Leo passed a few houses on stilts, all standing stork-like above the flat landscape. Built on thick pilings the size of telephone poles, they stood eight to twelve feet above ground. The road dead-ended at the substantial Clostio house, green with white trim. A flight of wooden stairs led up to the wraparound deck. Heat waves shimmered above the metal roof in the late afternoon sun.

Leo parked at the bare dirt edge of the yard next to a white Chevy pickup and a blue Ford sedan. Two girls' bicycles and a flat-bottomed boat were stored in the space under the house, but no one was visible. Dressed informally in a light blue polo shirt and khaki slacks with cowboy boots, he stepped out of the Blazer, carrying his briefcase into a world of silence and oppressive heat.

He climbed the stairs to the deck, expecting that someone would hear him and greet him shortly, but no one appeared. At the top of the stairs, he wiped his brow, crossed the deck, and raised his hand to knock on the front door just as a woman opened it.

"Hey, are you Dr. DeLuca?" Her shoulder-length brown hair framed a narrow face with weathered skin and dark eyes that were hooded, puffy, and red, as though she had been crying. Barefoot and tanned, she wore a navy blue T-shirt and white cotton knee-length shorts.

"Yes, CBL sent me to interview your family. Are you Mrs. Clostio?"

"Uh-huh, I'm Emma." She shook his hand. "C'mon in."

Leo stepped into the cool of a large air-conditioned room and blinked as his eyes adjusted to the interior after the brilliant sunshine outside.

"Be right back," said Emma. "I'll go get Foreman."

The spacious room doubled as an eat-in kitchen and living room. In the tiled kitchen to his right, he saw a round table holding the remains of dinner, four plates with half-eaten hamburgers and ketchup-covered French fries. There was a thick beige carpet covering the floor of the living area opposite the kitchen. Two brown leather recliners, a sofa and an armchair, faced a large flat-screen television affixed to the wall. A glass-topped coffee table strewn with magazines stood in front of the sofa.

The many large windows gave an excellent view of the marsh, miles of wetlands interspersed with winding channels. To the west he could see the open blue water of the Gulf and the brilliant sun, low on the horizon. A large blue and white fishing boat was moored to a short wood pier that jutted out into the canal behind the house.

It was a beautiful but lonely view. Leo could see high white clouds approaching from the west. The house, perched precariously above the marsh and subject to the wind and storms from the Gulf, like the whole coastline, was so vulnerable. Now, in addition to the power of nature, these people and the dwindling coastal lands had to face the consequences of terrible pollution caused by human error and human greed. Leo sighed and shook his head. Could this ever be righted? Could the purity of the air and water ever be restored? He didn't know if it was possible.

"Dr. DeLuca, this is my husband Foreman Clostio."

He heard Emma's voice before he saw her. She entered the room pushing an older, haggard man in a wheelchair. Unshaven, with dull, sunken eyes, his jeans and khaki shirt could not conceal his thinness.

Foreman held out a hand and arm that were more bone than flesh. "Nice to meet you, Doc. I'd get up, but then I'd prob'ly fall right back down again, like a jack-in-the-box." He gestured toward the sofa, "Have a seat."

After he shook Foreman's hand, he laid his briefcase on the coffee table and sat down. Emma maneuvered Foreman's chair so he sat facing the doctor. "May I bring you a glass of ice water?" she asked Leo.

"Yes, please."

"Sure you don't want somethin' stronger, Doc, a beer, maybe?"

"No thanks, Foreman, I've got to drive back to New Orleans after this."

"All right, Doc, next time."

While Leo took out his clipboard and pen, Foreman pulled out a stained cotton handkerchief and coughed violently into it.

Emma returned bearing three tall glasses of ice water, which she set on the coffee table. She remained standing beside her husband.

"Thank you," said Leo, and took a long pull on his. "As you know," he said, "Citizens for a Better Louisiana sent me to document your story. So, Foreman, why don't you just tell me about yourself, how you were employed before the oil spill and afterwards. Tell me when your health issues arose and what symptoms you have, and so on."

In the heavy silence that followed, Foreman sighed and dropped his head. He still grasped the stained handkerchief, but his hands lay limply in his lap.

Leo adjusted his glasses, then fingered his pen and waited.

"Mamma!" a child called from the back of the house.

"'Scuse me for a minute," said Emma, hurrying toward the hall doorway, "that's my daughter Collette."

Seized by another coughing fit, Foreman bent his head and covered his mouth until the wracking coughs subsided. He spat into the handkerchief, folded it over and then wiped his mouth. White-faced, he lifted his head and said, "Well, Doc, I was a commercial fisherman. Fishin' 'n shrimpin' was my life. I grew up here and it's the only work I ever did." He coughed again and spat into the handkerchief. "Funny thing about it is my dad thought workin' close to home would keep me outta trouble. But it looks like trouble came home to find me.

"Well, me 'n my brother-in-law Ivy were partners. That was before the spill when we could still fish. Made a purty good livin'. Built this house, bought my truck." With a rattling sound, he cleared his throat. "Then, of course, after the spill, being a handsome dude like I am, you know, sorta like a male model, Leviathan scheduled me to star in one of their TV ads about how they've helped the people of south Louisiana and restored the Gulf and the marshes and all that. But somehow, bleedin' from the lungs and havin' short term memory loss disqualified me." He frowned and shook his head, "Doc, I just cain't understand it."

Despite the sadness he felt, Leo laughed softly. "It's a mystery, Foreman."

"Well after the spill, nobody could fish or shrimp. The water was fouled from here to kingdom come. With no money comin' in, we did the only thing we could; we signed on to use our boat for the cleanup, and that's when. . . uh, that's when. . ." A puzzled expression came over Foreman's face and his voice trailed off.

Emma returned. "Sorry. Got two little girls sick in the back bedroom. Collette and Alicia, nine and six. They got some kind of flu-like symptoms which we keep treatin' with this drug and that drug. They get better after two, three weeks, and the next thing you know, they're sick again with the same thing. And on top of that, they both got skin rashes. They scratch themselves 'til they bleed."

"Honey," said Foreman, blinking rapidly, with an anxious look in his eyes, "I cain't remember what I was tellin' the doc. Can you help me out?" He looked at Leo. "Sorry, Doc, I cain't remember shit anymore."

"It's okay." Leo glanced at Emma, "He was going to tell me about the cleanup."

She rolled her eyes. "Well, that's when the party began. We've been havin' a great time ever since, right, Foreman? Just ask the PR people from Leviathan."

She shook her head and paused. "It took a while for the oil to reach us, and we thought it might not be too bad. You know, we been out here all our lives; we weathered some purty bad hurricanes, so we thought we could weather this. But then the oil hit the marsh, stinkin' like diesel fumes. It was so thick and strong, you could taste it on your tongue. Then birds, fish, all the wildlife started dyin'. Foreman and my brother Ivy did the only thing they could do—they hired on with Leviathan. They did what the oil company told 'em, workin' on their own boat, tryin' to burn off the oil on top of the water and layin' boom to contain it. Foreman came home covered in it, thick brown, sticky crude oil. It was all over his clothes, his shoes, his hands and his face. There was no way in hell I could get his clothes clean."

"What did you do with them?"

She flashed a grin, "Torched 'em. Whoosh!" She threw her arms up toward the ceiling. "They flared up in flames bigger 'n hellfire."

A barefoot little girl dressed in pink pajamas ran into the room and tugged on Emma's hand. "Mamma, my throat hurts."

Emma reached into her pocket and gave the child a cough drop. "Here, Alicia, suck on this. Sit on Daddy's lap while I talk with the doctor."

"Hello, Alicia," said Leo.

"Hello." Her brown eyes had the glaze of fever and her cheeks were flushed a bright pink. She gave Leo a solemn look and then climbed up into Foreman's lap. Her father embraced her, and she threw her arms around his neck and laid her tousled head on his shoulder. Leo noted the ugly red rash on her forearms and elbows, crusted with blood and oozing in places where she had scratched it.

Emma continued her story, "Then they started with the dispersant. They had ships sprayin' it in the Gulf, and planes sprayin' the beaches and the marshes, night and day. Sometimes it hit the workers right in the face. There was a constant fog—the air was hazy with a strong chemical smell, and we all breathed it in."

Leaning down, she laid her arm across her husband's shoulders. "He's in the wheelchair 'cause he suffers from severe fatigue and dizziness and his right leg is numb."

"Otherwise, I'd be dancin' the Cajun two-step, Doc."

Emma smiled and punched her husband gently on the shoulder. "He's fallen down so many times, I convinced him to sit in the chair so he don't break his neck. And as you can see, he's coughin' up blood. Sometimes he has these searin' headaches. I get 'em, too." She slowly shook her head. "Between him and the kids, if it ain't one thing, it's another."

Tears welled up in her eyes. "Foreman here is thirty-four years old, two years older 'n me, and he's like an old man. He was strong and healthy and muscular and full of life, and now.... well, you see how it is."

Foreman leaned forward and whispered, "Doc, I think she's tryin' to tell you I'd be good-lookin' if it weren't for my face."

Leo smiled; he admired Foreman for his unfailing humor in the circumstances.

And for Foreman and others like him, the circumstances had forever changed. The Clostio family and the people of the Gulf coast had entered a new era in which time was reckoned by the oil spill: before and after. The residents' stories marked an ominous shift in destiny. Their voices echoed in Leo's ear, resonating and reinforcing each other, solemn and portentous as the tolling of bells. Marshall Ross and his wife Regina, the couple in their early fifties Leo had interviewed earlier that day, owned a seafood restaurant in Venice. Marshall had not even been part of the cleanup, and he experienced nausea, vomiting, and headaches for months. Regina suffered from headaches and dizziness. Their two dogs had had seizures and died.

Another Venice resident, René Guilbeau, a hunting and fishing guide, had run a lucrative business with his wife Cecile and their sons T-René, Gaston, and Marcel, all in their twenties. Using three boats, the Guilbeaus, too, participated in the cleanup, with devastating consequences. René and T-René developed kidney and liver problems; they bled from the nose and eyes, and fought nausea, vomiting, and diarrhea for months.

Gaston and Marcel had rectal bleeding and skin rashes, with dizziness and short term memory loss like Foreman.

Leo knew their symptoms were consistent with exposure to the chemicals found in the dispersant and in crude oil. Crude oil alone contained high levels of volatile organic compounds, some of which were known carcinogens, as well as other chemicals that affected the central nervous system. Add to that the toxins contained in the dispersant, and it was no wonder that the illnesses of those exposed to it for long periods bloomed like algae in a red tide.

The Guilbeaus told Leo how they had to replace the hard rubber impellers in their boat engines constantly because the chemical solvents in the dispersant disintegrated them. Those same solvents, ingested through the air and absorbed through the skin, disintegrated the human body from the inside out, bursting red blood cells and destroying tissue. Human beings dropped dead; they could not be replaced. And what monetary settlement could ever compensate these people for the destruction of their health and their whole way of life?

And what of the life of the Gulf itself, the source of forty per cent of the nation's seafood? He thought about the fish kills, the dead dolphins, sea turtles, the oil-covered pelicans and seagulls. Everything from microscopic plankton up the food chain to human beings, had been contaminated and stained, and now death reigned where there should be abundant life.

"Doc," said Foreman, interrupting Leo's reverie, "there's one other thing maybe you could help us with. We're thinkin' of suin' Leviathan for reparations, but out here, there ain't no lawyers, and we don't know anybody in New Orleans. Got any recommendations?"

"I sure do." Leo took an ivory-colored business card out of his briefcase and handed it to Foreman. "Michael Faris is a young lawyer in New Orleans who is handling several cases just like yours. I'm friends with his family, and I know him personally.

I can assure you he is an honest, hardworking attorney who is passionate about helping people who have been affected by the oil disaster. He's had some success already."

"Thanks, Doc," said Foreman, gazing at the card. He looked up at Leo, "You know, considerin' the state of my health," he coughed and spit into the stained, sodden handkerchief, "perfect though it is, well, if things change and I'm not, well if I'm no longer around, Emma and the kids got to have help."

The two men locked eyes for a long moment.

Leo broke his gaze. "You're right," he agreed.

Foreman nodded, "Well then, Doc, we'll definitely give him a call."

After completing his interview with the Clostios, Leo descended the stairs and walked behind the house to stand on the short pier for a closer view of the marsh. Signs of the catastrophe were everywhere. An iridescent oil slick on the water glimmered in rainbow hues, beautiful and deadly as a serpent. Across the channel, he could clearly see more evidence of the oil; a horizontal red-brown line stained the green reeds at the high water mark. Fifteen dead catfish and red snapper, some spotted with open sores, floated belly up in the channel, exuding the stench of death. Tar balls, dark brown, jelly-like rounded clumps the size of his fist, bobbed on the surface of the water as the strengthening evening breeze stirred the marsh.

His questions remained. Could this magical wilderness ever be cleaned and restored; could these people survive? Would a whole way of life be shattered for millions of Gulf coast residents forever? And where was the public outrage at the damage? Why were the Clostios, the Rosses, the Guilbeaus and their children forgotten and ignored by the media? Why were their stories not broadcast to the whole world? Leo drew down the corners of his mouth and shook his head. Although he believed with all his heart that evil could not ultimately triumph, for the time being, it had triumphed here.

In calculated and chilling self-interest, for the love of money, Leviathan had committed a great wrong against man and nature and then covered it up with lies and media manipulation. The use of dispersants was imperative to disguise the magnitude of the spill, thus reducing the fines Leviathan had to pay. As far as the company was concerned, the lives of the Gulf residents and the entire ecosystem were expendable if they stood in the way of profits.

Corporate greed and illegal pollution were not new or unique to Leviathan; Leo had observed the same scenario when he interviewed people impacted by industrial pollution in Cancer Alley, the same pollution that had filtered down to New Orleans and affected his own life. Although he couldn't prove it, he suspected his daughter's leukemia stemmed from the toxins in New Orleans' water. Leo sighed and shook his head silently. Similar scenarios had played out all over the country in different communities. What was new here was the magnitude of the disaster. This time the scope of the damage was catastrophic, potentially harming the entire Gulf coast and the millions who lived there. Unless the Lord Himself intervened, Leo did not see how this wrong could ever be righted.

He felt helpless and frustrated in the face of it. When he tried to take in the scope of the destruction, it felt like the end of the world. As a physician, he did what he could, documenting their cases, but it was so little. Leo tightened his fists as a sudden rage, fierce and towering, erupted in his heart. He burned with anger against those who had committed this crime, who had harmed this great and glorious creation, and for what? *For the love of money—fucking money.*

In the west, the sinking sun loomed huge and red, and the water of the marsh took on the color of blood. Yes, there was blood on the water, the blood of men who had died because of the oil spill, the blood of animals, and the blood of those, like Foreman Clostio, who were soon to die.

"Damn it!" Galvanized by rage, Leo turned abruptly and strode towards his car. His boot heels struck the ground, pounding like war drums. He got in the car, slammed the door, and started the motor. As his heart cried out for vengeance—blood for blood, he remembered the words of Ezekiel:

> *Because you have had a perpetual hatred, and have shed the blood of the children of Israel by the force of the sword in the time of their calamity, in the time that their iniquity came to an end: Therefore, as I live, says the Lord GOD, I will prepare you unto blood, and blood shall pursue you: since you have not hated blood, even blood shall pursue you.*

Then, as if no time had passed at all, he suddenly found himself at the end of the oyster shell road where it intersected the highway; he didn't even remember driving out of the yard. He clenched his teeth and gripped the wheel white-knuckled. He was a good Catholic, a believer; he knew that evil would not ultimately triumph. Even so, what terrible suffering had to be borne in the meantime by its victims. Judgment would come; it had to come, and as far as Leo was concerned, it could not come soon enough.

He drove north on Highway 23, heading for New Orleans. Instead of the road, he saw the oil-stained marsh and a blood-stained handkerchief. With burning eyes, he looked to the darkening heavens, as a single cry rang in his mind like a trumpet call: *Rise up, Lord. Come quickly to destroy them which do destroy the earth.*

CHAPTER 16

Independence Day

S am woke before it was light. Her first thought was about her new dress and her dark blue pumps waiting in the closet for Joshua's concert next week. Since Monday, she had already experimented several times with the lipstick, eyeliner and mascara. She intended to look quite grown up for Joshua's concert. Lying on her back, she rubbed the sleep out of her eyes and remembered it was July fourth, the day of the Faris family party. Six people were coming: Joshua, Uncle George, Aunt Cat, her cousins Michael and Lucy, and Sitti had invited Dr. Leo. They hadn't had a party in ages, not even for Mardi Gras, which was too soon after Daddy's death. But now Mamma seemed like her old self; she didn't seem sick anymore. They had a lot to celebrate.

Sam glanced over at the other bed where Sitti slept on her right side, facing away. Her grandmother used to be the first one up in the mornings, but ever since she bought the journal, Sitti sat up late each night, writing for hours. When Sam asked what she was writing, she replied, "Oh, nothing much, just this and that." Last night when Sam got up to pee at one-thirty, Sitti was still writing. No wonder she slept in this morning.

Sam dressed quietly and quickly, thinking about the party. Uncle George and Aunt Cat were coming earlier than everyone else because they were going to cook. The menu consisted of fried catfish, corn on the cob, Aunt Cat's fat French fries, salad, fruit, and Uncle George's specialty dessert, chocolate mousse topped with whipped cream.

At ten-thirty, Uncle George arrived with a lit cigar clamped between his teeth and a large watermelon in his arms. Aunt Cat, close behind, carried two big bags of groceries. "Hello, hello!" George greeted Sam and Diana.

"George, take that smelly cigar out of your mouth!"

"What a way to greet your brother-in-law, Diana!" He put the watermelon down on the kitchen counter and set the offending stogie in a saucer to die out. "Where's Mamma?"

"Here I am, *albi*, I slept late like a lazy person." Dressed in her flowered robe with pink crease marks imprinted on her face from the pillow, Annie hurried in.

"Well, you can continue to be lazy," said Cat, "and let us do all the cooking. Have some toast and a cup of tea and put your feet up." As soon as they unloaded the groceries, they and Diana set to work in the kitchen, and Cat put Sam in charge of the salad. "Here's the lettuce and carrots," she said, "now go out to the garden and choose the rest."

When everyone had arrived and gathered in the living room, George handed out longneck beers. He introduced Joshua to his children who were both in their early thirties. Michael, a tall, thin, bespectacled attorney in private practice, had a grave demeanor, but a warm, kindly smile, just like his mother. When Joshua asked him what kind of work he did, Lucy didn't give him a chance to open his mouth. With a hand on Michael's shoulder, she said, "My brother is a boring lawyer, but I, being the creative one, majored in art history at Sophie Newcomb. After college I did some modeling, but I gave up that vapid career to teach art to high school students, which I love."

Joshua couldn't take his eyes off her. Lucy could have been a Mesopotamian queen. She was tall, hazel-eyed, and voluptuous, with masses of black, wavy hair framing an exotic face. Her charm and exuberance played a perfect foil for her quiet older brother. Joshua was smitten, even if she was eight years his senior and six feet tall.

George handed Joshua a beer and drew him over to meet Leo. "I have to make the introductions quickly," he said, "since Catherine will kill me if I don't get back to the kitchen. You two have a lot in common." They stood in the living room beside the upright piano. "Leo, Joshua is a concert pianist. He could probably sit on that piano bench and play for hours."

Turning to Joshua, George said, "And Leo is on the same wavelength. He's got a collection of recordings you wouldn't believe; he's a passionate opera lover."

"Is there any other kind?" asked Leo, laughing. His eyes crinkled and a web of lines shot out from them. He was a fit man of only medium stature, but an imposing presence nonetheless. Blue-eyed and ruddy-cheeked, he had thick light brown hair flecked with gray and a white mustache. His round-lensed wire-rimmed glasses gave him an intellectual air.

As George hurried back to the kitchen, Leo said, "So, you're a concert pianist. You do look familiar. I wonder if I've read about you somewhere."

"Not many articles about me," said Joshua, feeling uncomfortable. To change the subject, he asked, "Is New Orleans a good city for opera?"

"Yes, indeed, now and for the past two hundred years. New Orleans is America's first city of opera."

"Really?" Joshua sipped the ice-cold Abita beer, which tasted wonderful.

"Oh, my boy," exclaimed Leo, clapping him on the shoulder, "the history of opera in New Orleans is quite a story. To give you an idea, the first performance at the Met in New York was in 1883. The first documented performance of opera in New Orleans was almost a century before that, in May of 1796, and there have been operatic performances here on a regular basis ever since."

"How did you get introduced to opera?"

Leo took a sip of beer and adjusted his wire-rims, "My grandfather was an Italian immigrant who worked as a stage manager at the opera house. He sneaked me in when I was a kid, and I got to watch the performances from backstage. On slow nights I sat in the house. We spoke Italian at home, so opera was familiar and easy to understand. I loved it and still do."

"Are you in private practice?" Joshua asked. He sipped his beer and kept an eye on the beautiful Lucy who held an animated conversation with Sam across the room.

"I work part-time at Oschner Medical Center, but my passion, besides opera, is the work I do for a nonprofit agency researching community health, especially those communities impacted by the oil and gas industry."

That subject brought the Beast to mind, but Joshua flicked the mental image aside. "Then I guess you're a busy man here in Louisiana."

Leo smiled, but his eyes were sad. "Indeed I am. This state gives huge tax concessions and structures environmental policies to benefit industry. For example, Louisiana classifies oil-field waste as being non-hazardous, even though it contains carcinogens, radioactive materials, and heavy metals. So the oil companies can dump the waste practically wherever they please. That dumping plus the heavy emissions from the chemical plants results in terrible health and environmental problems."

"Is there a specific location you study?"

"Until recently, most of my research was in Cancer Alley."

Joshua lifted his eyebrows, focusing all his attention on Leo. "What's that?"

"It's a hundred-mile stretch of the Mississippi between Baton Rouge and New Orleans. It's very thickly populated, and, unfortunately, it is also crowded with more than 150 industrial facilities. The industries release millions of pounds of toxins into the air each year, and the consequences are severe. In some communities there are clusters of people with rare cancers, and high incidences of respiratory illnesses, miscarriages, and staph infections.

"Some of the poor black communites waged big battles against the industries for compensation for their illnesses. In fact, my house cleaner Jerrica was one of the leaders. Her group eventually won compensation. After that she moved to New Orleans."

"Where are you working now?" Joshua asked.

"Since the Gulf oil spill, I've been working down on the coast." Leo shook his head. "The destruction there is on a scale I've never seen. The oil and the dispersants have devastated the seafood industry and the environment, and the local fishermen have lost their livelihoods. I'll spare you the details, but many of them are seriously ill." He pushed his glasses up higher on his nose and sighed. "For whatever it's worth, some of my research may be used by the prosecution in the civil trial against Leviathan Oil, which is coming up in August."

While Leo sipped his beer, Joshua tightened his lips and shifted position. "Unfortunately, my father is also involved in that trial. He's an attorney for Leviathan."

"Ah."

"I don't agree with their policies, but the oil companies provide work for thousands of people like my dad."

"Yes, they do. The revenue generated by the industry is in the billions of dollars."

Joshua rubbed his finger against the cold droplets of condensation on his bottled beer. "I guess the issue is balance."

"It should be," agreed Leo, "but it seems that balance usually comes out wanting when it's weighed against the love of profit. It's the question that all prostitutes ponder: morality or money? Louisiana politicians made that choice a long time ago."

"Attention!" Sam clapped her hands. She stood in the center of the living room and surveyed the company. "I have an announcement," she declared loudly.

"Lunch is ready!" guessed Lucy, stealing Sam's thunder.

"That, too," Sam countered, "but more importantly, our favorite pianist, Joshua, is going to be the soloist with the symphony one week from tonight, and you are all invited. Do not miss his performance of Beethoven's Emperor Concerto."

"And I can get you all comp tickets," Joshua added.

"Of course we'll come," Lucy said. "All famous musicians should have groupies."

Sam lifted her nose in the air, and spoke with a British accent, "An *entourage*, I believe it's called, dear Lucy."

"Add me to the entourage list," said Dr. Leo.

"Count me and Cat in," said George.

"Well, Joshua," Diana summed it up, "including Annie and me, your entourage is up to eight people. Not too shabby for the new kid on the block."

"Nine," chimed Lucy, "counting my boyfriend Richard." The announcement, illuminated by her charming smile, broke Joshua's heart.

Lunch really was ready. George and Michael sat at either end of the table. To George's right were Annie, Cat, Joshua, and Sam, who sat on the corner, squeezed in next to Michael. Diana, Leo, and Lucy sat to George's left.

"Let us pray," said George.

There was a soft rustling as they joined hands.

George prayed with bowed head and eyes closed, "Lord, we thank you for this day, for our family and our friends, Leo and Joshua. We remember my brother Joseph, may he rest in peace. We thank you especially for your great power, goodness, and grace in healing Diana, for which we are so grateful. We thank you for your great and holy and splendid creation. . ."

Your great and holy and splendid creation. The phrase, so rich and deep, reverberated like an organ pedal tone, and it created an answering vibration in Joshua. While George continued to pray, Joshua's mind, resonating with memory, transported him back to the boat ride with Sam and George in Chef Pass. He relived the moment of his epiphany—the movement of the boat, the wind, the cormorants' aerial ballet. . .

Michael brought him out of his reverie. "Joshua, would you like some fish?"

The hold of the vision was so strong on him that it took Joshua a moment before he could answer. He blinked rapidly and realized that the prayer had ended and Michael was holding a platter of fried catfish before him.

"Uh, yes. I guess I was daydreaming." Feeling slightly embarrassed, he helped himself to a large serving.

"I can tell by your accent that you're not a southerner," said Michael. "Where are you from?"

"I'm a native New Yorker, from Brooklyn."

"When did you move here?"

"Only a month ago, and now I've got to move again." It just slipped out. He hadn't intended to disclose his personal problems.

Sam looked alarmed, "No! Why? Where are you moving to, Joshua?"

"Well, my dad and I had a disagreement, and for both our sakes, it's better that I leave home. As to where I'm moving, I have no idea, but it has to happen before my concert next week."

"Are you thinking of moving into a house or an apartment?" Lucy asked.

"An apartment, I guess—I can't afford a house. I'm still paying off my student loans and the loan for my piano. But it will have to be a big apartment with tolerant neighbors, because wherever I go, my Steinway goes, too."

"Moving now would be so difficult for you," said Diana. "Can't you delay the move until after your concert?"

"'Fraid not, according to my dad's decree."

Cat regarded her children, "Any suggestions, Michael or Lucy?"

"Thinking on it, Mamma," said Lucy.

"To change the subject momentarily," said Leo, "do you have a dog, Joshua?"

"No." Joshua was puzzled.

"Do you like dogs?"

"Yes. My manager and friend in New York, Nathan Weiss, has a Labradoodle named Buster. Nathan and I used to meet sometimes in Prospect Park in Brooklyn and walk Buster for miles in all kinds of weather."

"What's a Labradoodle?" asked Sam.

"It's a cross between a Labrador Retriever and a Standard Poodle."

"Another question," continued Leo, "do you have a lot of furniture?"

"No, just the piano and my desk. Everything else at home, even my bed, belongs to my parents."

"Then I may have the solution to your problem. You see, I have a garage apartment behind my house, fully furnished by the previous owner. It's been unused for the past five years, ever since I bought the property."

"How does that relate to the dog question, Leo?" asked George.

"Well, I have a dog—"

"Rosie!" exclaimed Sam.

"Yes. She's a Great Pyrenees, and since I travel a lot for my work—sometimes I'm gone for weeks at a time—I have to board her, which I hate to do, or pay for a dog sitter. What I propose,

Joshua, is that you move into the garage apartment for a low rent, say three-fifty a month, and help me out when I'm away by taking care of Rosie."

"Whoa, that is dirt cheap!" exclaimed Michael.

"Is the apartment big enough for a seven-foot Steinway?"

"Should be. It's the same width and depth as the double garage. There's a large living area with a kitchen at one end, one small bedroom and a bath, and there's a room with a washer and dryer downstairs in the back of the garage."

Joshua's smile was beatific. He could hardly believe it—he had not only found a place to move, but it was a place where he could practice in peace without disturbing anyone, and it was next door to this family who had been far kinder to him than his own. He reached across the table to shake Leo's hand. "We definitely have a deal. Thank you so much."

"All right. I'll have my house cleaner Jerrica straighten up the apartment tomorrow, and then you can move in anytime this weekend."

"I'll bring you a check for the first month's rent and call the piano movers tomorrow."

"Hurray," shouted Sam, "you're still gonna be my neighbor!"

"God works in mysterious and wonderful ways," said Annie, smiling broadly.

Diana sniffed, but George agreed. "Yes, he does, Mamma, he sure does."

"Now that's settled," said Lucy, "what's for dessert?"

"Chocolate mousse with whipped cream!" Sam was ecstatic.

"Take it from an experienced attorney," said Michael, "barring alcohol, there is truly no better way to close a business deal than with chocolate mousse." He rubbed his hands together, "What are we waiting for? C'mon, Sam, follow me to the 'fridge, and let's serve these hungry Americans."

CHAPTER 17

Recognition

fter dessert, they moved from the dining table to the living room. Standing near the upright piano, with beers in hand, Michael, Leo, and George discussed the slow start to the hurricane season, "Only two named storms in June, and both of them veered out into the Atlantic," said Michael.

"Let's pray it stays that way," said George, "I don't wish storms on anyone else, but this area has had it rough. Maybe we'll get off easy this year."

"Too soon to tell," said Leo, "there's a tropical depression swirling now a bit east of Cuba."

Annie sat next to Joshua on the loveseat, while Sam sat with Lucy, Catherine, and Diana on the sofa across from them.

Annie addressed Joshua, "It's lighter, isn't it?"

"What's lighter?" asked Joshua.

"The burden you've been carrying."

He gazed intently at the old woman. How could she possibly know he had a burden, much less that it had lightened? He had always concealed his fears and mental distress. Even the people close to him didn't have a clue. Nathan didn't know; his parents only knew about the hand washing, but nothing else. Joshua drew in a deep breath, then puffed his cheeks and exhaled through his mouth. Since Annie knew, he might as well be truthful, "The burden is lighter. How did you know?"

"The Lord told me." She sipped some hot tea. "I sensed the heaviness and the darkness the first day I met you, and from then on, I have prayed for you every day, Joshua."

The Lord told me. He suddenly recalled the intense looks Annie had given him at lunch on the day he met her. In the midst of blessing the food, she had abruptly glanced at him with a penetrating gaze, and she had caught his eye when he lied to Sam, telling her that his hands were sunburned when the skin was raw from compulsive washing. He blinked, speechless.

Nor could he comprehend that she prayed for him every day. To his knowledge, no one in his life had ever prayed for him. He had grown up in a secular household; as far as he knew, his father was an atheist. For his part, he had his new prayer book, which he now read nightly, but as a believer, he was only a beginner, a greenhorn. Annie was like a trick rider, in complete command of her mount, while he was still learning which end of the horse to feed. What did he know, moored in the twenty-first century as he was, taking his first squint-eyed glimpse towards the distant origin of his people, back over the vast gulf of time to Abraham, Isaac, and Jacob?

Could Annie's prayers have had an influence on the chain of events that had led to his moving out? Everything began when he told George how worthless he felt in his father's eyes. For ages Joshua had believed a lie, he had accepted the falsehood that he couldn't do anything right, and he had dismissed his own abilities as unimportant. Of course it wasn't true, but it took someone else to point that out. George's comments had put his relationship with the Beast in an entirely new perspective, shattering Joshua's false self-image like a distorted mirror. And it was his growing sense of self worth that gave him the strength to confront the Beast, a confrontation that forced him to leave. A move, if he was honest with himself, he should have made a long time ago.

Had Annie's prayers started that whole cycle in motion? It was possible. The supporting evidence sat across from him on the sofa, Diana.

"You also prayed for Diana, and you healed her."

Annie corrected him, "I prayed for her, but I am only a channel. It was the Holy Spirit who healed her. And three years ago, Catherine had a brain tumor, and through prayer the Holy Spirit healed her also."

Annie had prayed for Diana and Catherine, and there they were, laughing and talking in perfect health and good spirits. Diana had turned around completely. Pink-cheeked and animated, her eyes sparkled, and she gestured and spoke with energy and vitality. Even though she was still a bit underweight, she was sallow and infirm no more.

What would it be like, he wondered, to be completely free of his own illness?

"All the good food made me sleepy," said Annie, yawning. "I can hardly keep my eyes open, so I think I'll go take a nap."

"Annie," Joshua placed his hand on her arm before she could rise, "will you pray for me? Not right now," he hurriedly added, "but soon?" Slightly embarrassed, he felt heat rise in his face, "You know, the laying on of hands."

"Tell me when you are ready," she answered, "but, as you said, it must be soon."

Sitting across from Joshua and Annie, Lucy draped an arm around Catherine's shoulders. "Mom," she said, "I promised to meet Richard for dinner and then a party at his friend's house in Kenner."

Michael came over at that moment. "I'm leaving, too, Mom. I'm meeting friends at Creole Louie's and then we're going to a concert in the park."

They hugged Catherine in turn, and Lucy added, "We'll see you next week at Joshua's concert."

"Aunt Diana," Lucy said, "you're looking great! We are all so glad for your amazing recovery. You really beat the odds."

Michael leaned down and kissed his aunt on the cheek. "We want you around for decades to come. God bless."

Diana was touched. "Thank you both. Go and enjoy the evening—go lightly on the drinking though."

"Where's Sitti?" Lucy asked. "We want to tell her goodbye."

"She said she wanted to take a nap. The good food made her sleepy," said Joshua.

"She ate very little," said George, sitting down on the sofa beside Catherine.

"I noticed that," agreed Catherine. "She usually has a much stronger appetite."

"Well, tell her goodbye from us," said Michael.

As soon as they left, Sam said, "Mamma, may I go get Eliot?"

"Yes."

"Who's Eliot?" asked Leo, sitting directly across from Diana on the arm of the loveseat.

"He's a blue jay she found in the backyard this spring. He fell out of the nest and Sam raised him. She's crazy about him."

Like a blue-gray rocket, the bird shot into the room, with Sam skipping behind. After two rapid transits around the living room and one around the dining area, he landed briefly in the Norfolk Island pine, jarring the whole tree, and then flew to roost on Sam's shoulder. From his safe perch, he eyed the assembled company with a grave, but curious eye. "Isn't he beautiful?" asked Sam.

"Too-lili, too-lili, too—click-click," remarked Eliot.

"What did he say?" asked George.

"He said, 'Absolutely right'," Leo assured them, "according to my interpretation of the southern blue jay dialect."

Joshua bounced up and covered the distance from the loveseat to the piano in a flash. He picked out the approximate pitches the bird had sung. "Actually, Eliot's singing a song for Sam. Here it is." Playing Eliot's melody with a slow waltz tempo accompaniment, he sang:

Too-lili, too-lili, too,
My heart is telling me true,
Too-lili, too-lili, too
No one's as lovely as you.

Too-lili, too-lili, too,
Meek as a little lamb,
Too-lili, too-lili, too
No one's as kind as Sam.

Too-lili, too-lili, too,
I am your blue-gray boy,
Too-lili, too-lili, too
I wish you only joy!

Sam laughed and the entire company applauded. Eliot, startled by the noise, flew back to the Norfolk pine, deploying a bomb from the rear, which landed on the rug with a splat.

"Lovely," said Diana.

"The turd, the bird, or the song?" asked Leo, making her laugh.

"I don't know about the turd," Sam replied, "but the bird is beautiful, and the song is better than Beethoven."

Joshua grimaced in mock alarm.

"Well, almost," said Sam.

"Honey, you know you'll have to let Eliot go soon. He's a wild bird."

"Mamma, I know that!" Sam's voice rose in irritation, "But not today." Frowning, she bent down to clean the bird poop with a paper napkin.

"No, not today."

Leo broke in, "I have a suggest—"

"Aren't we going to the levee to watch the fireworks over the river?"

"Yes, Sam, we are. Please don't interrupt Dr. Leo." Diana's voice was stern.

"My suggestion," said Leo, "is that, if you like, I will drive y'all to Joshua's concert next week."

"Oh, that would be helpful to me," said George. "If you can take Diana, Sam, and Mamma, Cat could meet me at the store and we'll go from there instead of driving back out to Chalice to pick them up."

"Secondly," said Leo, speaking to Diana, "I'd like to invite you and Sam to come as my guests to a performance of *Die Fledermaus* this Saturday at the City Center."

"You know, I've never been to an opera," Diana admitted.

"Me either," announced Sam.

"Well, this is a wonderful comedy, perfect for first-timers."

"You should go, Diana," urged George. "You're feelin' better and it will do you good to get out of the house."

"I am feeling stronger every day, but just to be sure, I made an appointment tomorrow with Dr. Wun, to check out my condition."

"And?" said Leo.

"And unless he hospitalizes me, which is not going to happen, I don't see why I couldn't go." She paused and shook her head. "An opera and a concert within one week. That's more than I've done all year."

"Me, too," said Sam. "I can't wait. But Dr. Leo, you forgot about Joshua on the night of his concert. Can he ride with us, too?"

"You'll be driving yourself, won't you, Joshua?" Leo asked.

"Uh, well, I don't have a car."

"Not a problem." George grinned, "I have just the vehicle for you, vintage transportation. You can borrow it until you get your own, or you can snap up this classic machine for the bargain basement price of only twelve hundred dollars."

"You mean the truck."

"Uh-huh. A concert pianist should always travel in style. Gotta maintain your image, you know."

Joshua laughed, "That truck has style, all right."

"Ah-ha!" exclaimed Leo, "Now I know why you look so familiar, Joshua. I just remembered the article I read about you."

"Oh, no!" Joshua winced.

"Joshua Brightman, the Bad Boy of Classical Music."

"Okay, Joshua," laughed George, "as Ricky Ricardo said to Lucy, 'You got some 'splainin' to do.'"

"Later," said Joshua, "much later."

CHAPTER 18

Stirrings

On Friday morning, Leo called Jerrica Hobbs to tell her about the garage apartment.

"Oh, my Gaaaawd!" she exploded, with a theatrical tremor in her voice. "It ain't been cleaned in all the years I been workin' for you, Dr. Leo. I'll prolly need a backhoe to clear out the dust balls. You gone throw this on a pore ol' black woman, on top of cleanin' your house and sweepin' up piles of hair from that monstah you call a dawg and what I call a sheddin' machine?"

"I sure am, Jerrica."

"Well, can it wait 'til Monday?"

"No, I've got someone moving in on the weekend."

"A purty woman, I hope. What's a good-lookin' man like you doin' stayin' single all these years?"

He laughed, "Don't worry about my social life, Jerrica, I don't have time for a woman. I'm renting it out to a young man, a musician, who's also gonna take care of Rosie when I'm away."

"Mm-huh. The pore boy prolly ain't seen that animal yet. Whas his name?"

"Joshua Brightman."

"Well, why can't Mr. Joshua Brightman do his own cleanin'?"

"Later on he will. But he's a pianist and he's got an important performance coming up next week. He has to move now, at the same time he's preparing for the concert, so I'm helping him out this once."

"You mean *I'm* helpin' him out. How old is he?"

"You sure are nosy."

"Nevah mind what I am. I asked you how old he is."

"Early twenties. His dad kicked him out."

"Same age as my grandson." She sniffed, "Look at you, layin' all this hard labor on an ole grammaw."

"Don't worry, I'm going pay you for an extra day's work."

"Damn tootin' you are. I just don't know how I put up with you, Dr. Leo."

"Ah, Jerrica, you know you love me."

He was rewarded with a low musical laugh, followed by a theatrical sigh, "Oh, Gawd help me, the sad truth is I do!"

He hung up the telephone knowing that the apartment would be in outstanding shape by the end of the day.

The subject of women reminded Leo of the conversation he had had with George at the party. "Diana has improved dramatically," he told George. "It's unbelievable. The last time I saw her was in late May, and she looked sixty years old, jaundiced and gaunt as walking death. Today, she moves with energy and strength, and her color is good. She's too thin still, but what a beautiful woman."

George glanced at him, "Grab a beer and c'mon outside, Leo. That beautiful wrong-headed woman won't let me smoke cigars in her house."

Once they were ensconced in the Adirondack chairs, and after he lit up his stogie, George continued, "Diana always had movie star looks, but to her credit, much like my daughter Lucy, it never went to her head. Her interests never were superficial. She loves teachin' at Tulane, and she's passionate about good literature. And Lord, don't get her started on politics." George exhaled a puff of smoke, "But sadly, neither Joseph nor I could get that woman interested in the most profound subject of all."

"Religion?"

"Football."

Leo laughed, "Well, even if she is a disappointment in that department, she's making a phenomenal recovery. Her doctor should be very proud."

"Her doctor had nothing to do with it."

Leo's eyebrows rose in surprise. "What do you mean?"

"In June, Dr. Wun told her there was nothing more he could do for her. I was there; he essentially sent her home to die. Told her the only thing left was pain management."

"So this is a spontaneous recovery?"

"In a manner of speakin'. I think it's due to prayer. You know Mamma's reputation as a healer, don't you?"

Leo nodded.

"But this time it worked different." George tapped the ashes off his cigar. "Usually Mamma prays once, and that's it—the person recovers. She's been prayin' ever since Diana got the diagnosis in January, after Joseph died." George shrugged, "It seemed like her prayers didn't have any effect, until just recently."

"Strange," said Leo. "So you really think prayer was the key."

"Absolutely, even though it defies all logic. But I'm glad Diana's takin' the precaution of having Dr. Wun examine her tomorrow."

Leo nodded, "She should. Cancer is a tricky disease."

Cancer he knew about, from firsthand experience. He had not only studied it in the field, but he had endured the roller coaster ups and downs as his own daughter Lisa had struggled with leukemia and lost. Despite chemotherapy, blood transfusions, temporary remissions, and a bone marrow transplant, she died seven years ago, one week after her eighteenth birthday.

It took two more years for his marriage to fall apart. Joyce became increasingly angry as he immersed himself in research for the nonprofit agency and distanced himself emotionally. He was away for weeks in the field, living near and studying the poor, predominately black communities of the river parishes. Documenting the death rates and clusters of rare cancers, asthma, and other illnesses of those who lived in the fence-line communities had been his way of submerging the grief that threatened to overwhelm him at the loss of his only child.

Eventually Joyce's anger hardened her heart, and they parted ways. In the divorce settlement, she kept the house in the Garden District, and he moved out to Chalice. He had lived like a monk ever since, except that monks live in community, while his had been a solitary existence. His only companion was his Great Pyrenees, Rosie. There was also Jerrica, whom he had met down in Lyons when she helped organize the black communities in a decade-long battle against the injustices of an oil refinery in Cancer Alley. She had been his feisty friend ever since. He had given her work cleaning his home in the Garden District, and recommended her to his friends. As her reputation for thoroughness and reliability grew, her work expanded into a thriving business with clientele all over the city.

Jerrica continued to work for him after his move to Chalice. There, in suburban exile from his friends in the Garden District, Leo felt isolated until Joseph Faris made it a point to meet his new neighbor. He had invited Leo for Thanksgiving dinners, Christmas dinners, for crawfish boils, and a New Year's Eve party. Joseph had been a gregarious, fun-loving man, the complete antithesis of the stereotypical gray-faced, pinch-mouthed accountant. Joseph's sudden death saddened him, and gave him concerns about the safety and welfare of the family of women he left behind.

And one of those women seemed to have magnetic qualities. Fair-skinned, blue-eyed Diana was as exotic in the context of the olive-skinned, black-haired Faris family as a snowy owl in a Middle Eastern market. Leo had always enjoyed speaking with Diana, but he knew little about her. An English professor at Tulane, she was a native of some Corn Belt state, Illinois, Indiana, or Iowa, he couldn't remember. He had always thought of her as Joseph's wife and Sam's mother, but at the party, for the first time, he had seen her as a woman, a powerfully attractive woman.

But it was Annie who had invited him to the party. With Joseph gone, maybe thoughtful Annie just stepped into the breach, feeling sorry for a divorced man alone on a major holiday. At the party, although he hadn't mentioned it to George, he had noticed how age had begun to take its toll on Annie. Even though she was eighty or so, she had always seemed vibrant and full of energy, but yesterday there was a fragile air about her; she had lost a lot of weight and she moved slowly and with more effort than the last time he had seen her.

Images from the party kept returning to his mind. He pictured bright-eyed Sam with Eliot the blue jay perched on her shoulder. He knew it would wrench her heart to release the bird. He thought of drawling, humorous George, wreathed in cigar smoke, and how red-haired Joshua improvised a song based on the warbling of a bird. Joshua's embarrassment when Leo called him the Bad Boy of Classical Music was a good sign. There were so many young people nowadays who flaunted their peccadilloes with pride. Thankfully, Joshua wasn't of that ilk, especially since he would be living in the garage apartment. Leo suspected whatever Joshua had done in San Francisco, something to do with drinking and vandalism of a hotel room, was probably a one-time thing. God knew, he himself had done things as a young man that still embarrassed him.

That afternoon, after he bought three *Die Fledermaus* tickets online for Saturday night, he fidgeted with impatience for Friday to end and Saturday, too, so the evening would come when he would take Diana and Sam out for dinner and the opera. *Die Fledermaus* was a tuneful, charming comedy, a perfect introduction to opera, and since the performance would be in English, not the original German, they would understand all the jokes. Finding himself pacing rapidly around the living room in circles, he realized he had to get out of the house before he made a rut in the floor. He got Rosie's leash and took her for a long walk.

After dinner, he listened to his new *Traviata* recording with the superb young soprano Jane Barry, recorded live in her debut performance at Glyndebourne. The voice, focused, plangent, rich and so expressive, the poignant music, and the tragic story, powerful as they were, could not dispel the image fixed in his mind of the healed Diana, pink-cheeked, blue-eyed, and laughing.

Wrapped snugly in her white dressing gown, Diana ate breakfast with Sam and Eliot. Sam, wearing green shorts and a purple T-shirt, sat beside her mother at the dining table, while Eliot, clad in his usual blue and gray, perched just behind Sam on the top rung of the ladderback chair. He bobbed his head and flicked his striped tail, hoping for a handout. Diana had toast and tea, while Sam devoured a heaping bowl of cereal. Diana couldn't vouch for Eliot, but after the late night of fireworks, she and Sam had slept in until nine o'clock. Annie was still sleeping.

"Annie seems so tired lately."

"That's 'cause she sits up late every night writing in her journal," said Sam.

"Does she?" Diana buttered her toast. "She's written letters to her sister in Colorado and her cousin Zara in Beirut, but that's all the writing I've ever seen her do."

Sam held a spoonful of cereal suspended between the bowl and her mouth. "Mamma, do you think Sitti's gonna die?"

Diana cast a sharp glance at Sam. "What gives you that idea?" As she spooned some jelly onto her toast, she tried to formulate a reply that would allay her daughter's fears. "Well, eventually she'll die, Sam, but there's nothing wrong with her now. She may be slowing down as she ages, but I think Sitti will be with us for a long time to come."

"But she didn't come with us to see the fireworks last night."

"Honey, she would have had to stand for a long time in the heat and humidity. We're a lot younger than she is, and we were worn out by the time it finished."

"Well, Daddy died all of a sudden."

The past six months had left their mark. Sam had had to deal with her father's death and the possibility that her mother might die. Diana knew that children had phases in which they suffered from an intense fear of death, even before they experienced the death of a family member. The problem in Sam's case was exacerbated, since her fear had actually come to pass; her father *had* died.

Again, she tried to reassure her daughter. "Yes, Sam, but you know that was an accident. But concerning Sitti, please don't worry, honey. She's all right. People in her family live a long time; her mother lived to be a hundred and eight!"

"Well, what about you, Mamma? Are you going to be all right?"

"Yes, she is, *albi*. Your Mamma is going to be completely well. The cancer is gone."

So intent were they in their conversation, that neither Diana nor Sam heard Annie approach.

"Good morning," they said in unison, looking up in surprise.

"Good morning." Annie sat down at the dining table and took Sam's hand in hers. Her white hair hung down around her shoulders; she had not put it in the French braid yet.

"But, Sitti, how do you know Mamma's going to be completely well?"

"I just know." She squeezed Sam's hand gently, "Why don't you go with your mamma to the hospital today for her appointment? The doctor can show you and Diana the X-rays and you'll see that they are clear. Then you will know for sure."

"That's a good idea, Annie," said Diana. She felt certain the news would be good. "Will you come, Sam?"

"Okay."

"Can I get you some tea and toast, Annie?" asked Diana, starting to rise.

"No, sit, *albi*. I'll get it. I'm going to take a little tea back to my room, and then I'll get dressed. I'm not hungry this morning."

As Sitti walked slowly to the kitchen, Sam fished out a single milk-soaked cornflake and fed it to Eliot. "Mamma, I've decided to let Eliot go tomorrow."

Diana held her piece of toast motionless in midair. "I'm proud of you, Sam. You're doing the best thing for him."

As Eliot pecked at the wilted cornflake in Sam's hand, Diana reached out and stroked the bird's back. "I bet he'll find a mate and stay close. Maybe they'll build a nest in the mulberry tree."

Sam bent her head, and Diana could see she was fighting back tears. Hoping to divert her, Diana pointed to the two books beside Sam's bowl, "What are you reading now, my darling bookworm?"

"The small book is poetry by Rilk."

"Who?"

"Rilk."

Surprised that she had never heard of the poet, Diana said, "Let me see that book."

As soon as Sam handed it to her, Diana recognized it as one of Joseph's books. She smiled, "Honey, the poet's name is pronounced *Ril-keh*."

"Oh. *Ril-keh*. And the big book is a biography of Elizabeth the first of England." Taking the book from her mother and scooting back her chair, Sam rose and said, "C'mon, Eliot, let's go read Mr. Ril-keh."

Diana took her plate and Sam's bowl to the sink to rinse them out. Sam was more vulnerable and sensitive to loss than ever, and Diana knew that releasing Eliot would be very difficult for her. Pleased that her daughter had the courage to do the right thing, Diana knew that Sam would eventually get over the sadness. Going to the opera with Leo would distract her later tomorrow night, and next week there was Joshua's concert.

Thankfully, Joshua had come into the picture, giving Sam another focus for her emotions. Diana smiled as she dried the dishes; her daughter was completely taken with the attractive, red-haired New Yorker. Maybe Joshua would give them a tour of his apartment on Saturday. Diana suddenly wished she could call Joshua and set that up. She made a mental note to get his telephone number from Leo.

And what a kind and extremely generous offer Leo had made to Joshua. No one paid three-fifty a month in rent anymore. The going rate was at least twice that for an unfurnished apartment, much less a furnished one with all appliances. But then, money and status didn't seem to be Leo's priorities. He worked for a nonprofit agency, which could not be very lucrative for a doctor, and he had left his Garden District home to his ex-wife and moved out to Chalice, definitely a downward plunge in the world. No doubt about it—Leo was an unusual man.

On the other hand, George's offer to Joshua was not quite as charitable. Twelve hundred for that rolling eyesore he called a truck! Diana laughed. You could hear it coming—rattling, clanking, shooting flames out the rear when it backfired. *Vintage transportation, a classic vehicle.*

God, what businessmen they were, the Lebanese. Very likely descended from the ancient sea-trading Phoenicians, they flourished, as Joseph used to say, in entrepreneurial endeavors. During the waves of emigration at the turn of the twentieth century, the Orthodox Christians from the Syrian Arab Republic poured off the ships and hit the streets of America with enterprising zeal. Some were peddlers, pushing their carts through the city streets; some opened grocery stores, import houses, restaurants; some sold shoes, clothes, dry goods of all types. As soon as they were established they wrote to the relatives in the Old Country and offered them a place to live.

The struggle to survive in a new country took all their energy, and few were able to go to college. They valued the education which they themselves were so often denied, and so they urged their children to get college degrees. The first generation Lebanese Americans became doctors, lawyers, physicists, journalists, musicians, engineers. No doubt about it; they were an enterprising people, hospitable, quick-witted, and charming.

But as Diana's mother, a war bride from Berlin, had pointed out, "Dey are foreigners. I tell you dey are *stammesbewusst. Wie sagt man das?*"

"Clannish."

"Ja, dey keep to demselves."

"But Mamma, we're foreigners, too. Everybody but the Native Americans are foreign to this country."

"*Liebling*, you know vhat I mean."

Diana had thought her mother's remarks comical at the time, but the Faris family had certainly closed ranks when Joseph gambled away all the money. But now Joseph was gone, and at forty-one, she was a widow, still living with her husband's people. She had fled the cold Indiana winters as a young woman to attend Tulane in the exotic city of New Orleans. She had met Joseph, married, and stayed.

Should she leave now? If she returned to her roots, she would uproot Sam. But she had no real desire to return to Indiana, even though she missed her own family. Her parents and her sister Steffi rarely came to visit. They didn't like the heat and humidity. She and Joseph and Sam had made the trip north every other year. Sam loved the rolling southern Indiana farmland, and the native wildlife: chipmunks, woodchucks, bluebirds, and deer. For his part, Joseph always made himself at home and got along well with her family. But Indiana just wasn't home anymore.

It was all so strange. Just when she thought her life had ended, her health mysteriously returned. Had it been Annie's prayers? She really didn't know for sure. She had seen the results of Annie's healing abilities before; she knew the power of Annie's prayers was real. But why had Annie's prayers for her been useless for so long? Diana had grown so frustrated by her worsening condition that the last time Annie had wanted to pray for her, she had rebuffed the old woman.

Returning to her room, Diana dressed for what she hoped would be her final cancer checkup. Confident that Dr. Wun would be dumbfounded with her amazing recovery and release her, she had elected to drive herself in for the eleven o'clock appointment.

Her interview with the doctor unfolded exactly as Annie predicted; the X-rays showed no sign of cancer. Dr. Wun was shocked into stammering, "Mrs. F-f-faris, the cancer is g-gone. No trace of it." He shook his head in disbelief and showed them the backlit X-rays. "Look at this. C-c-completely clean, all organs healthy. At first, I thought there was a mistake; I thought I had someone else's X-rays, so I double-checked."

Sam reached for Diana's hand and squeezed it.

"Are they mine?" asked Diana.

"Yes, they are."

She felt Sam's hand relax.

"In addition, Mrs. Faris, your blood test shows all levels within a normal range. Your recovery is just incredible." Shaking his head and cleaning his glasses on his white coat, he said, "I know spontaneous healings occur, but yours is the only one I have witnessed firsthand." Gazing at Sam, he added, "You are a very lucky girl. I am releasing your mother; she is well." Diana left the hospital elated, but mystified as to why she had recovered and how Annie knew it with such certainty.

They stopped by Levant House on the way home to tell George the good news, and amid laughter and high spirits, they dined on plates of stuffed grape leaves and kibbeh, followed by Turkish Delight.

On the drive home, Diana felt light, as if a great weight had fallen off her shoulders. Her mind swirled with the new possibilities this sudden change had opened up. She didn't know why she was recovering, but recovering she was. She enjoyed eating again; she had gained weight, and her renewed energy was marvelous. She had reached a new milestone, a marker for the next stage of her destiny. She had known Joseph's weaknesses, but she had loved him fully. Now he was gone and she had to look ahead. Whether she liked it or not, she was poised at the beginning of a new life as a single woman. How strange, how fearful, and yet, how exciting.

CHAPTER 19

Flight

Diana drove the SUV to the feed store, with Sam riding shotgun. It was eight o'clock on Saturday morning. They had risen early; they had quite a day ahead of them. Sam was going to release Eliot later in the morning, and that evening, they were going to their first opera with Leo.

"We have to get the kind that's squirrel-proof," said Sam.

"They make them, I know," said Diana, "but squirrels are such clever little devils, they'll probably find a way to get to the food anyway."

At the feed store, Diana helped Sam choose a hanging bird feeder with a central clear plastic cylinder protected by a round metal cage. There were six feeding ports at different levels in the cylinder. The bronze-colored top was slightly domed with a short chain in the center, designed to suspend it from a tree. It seemed very sturdy, and the label assured them it was squirrel-proof. In addition, Diana bought a twenty-five pound bag of wild bird seed and a lightweight birdbath, a three-legged metal stand topped by a shallow basin.

As soon as they returned home, Sam sat at the dining table and peeled pistachios and raw peanuts, enough to fill a cereal bowl. She had not taken Eliot out of his cage yet. She had decided to get everything ready first. Then, in a large bowl, she created her own custom mix of the bird seed, which consisted of black-oil and striped sunflower seeds, millet, cracked corn, and safflower seeds, with the pistachios and peanuts. When she was satisfied with the mix, she unscrewed the top of the feeder and poured in her own concoction, made especially for Eliot. She refastened the lid securely.

In the backyard shed, she found a hammer and nails in Joseph's toolbox. She took them out to the patio and placed them in the seat of one of the Adirondack chairs, which she dragged through the dew-laden grass to the mulberry tree. After positioning the chair under the lowest limb, she climbed up on the chair so she could reach the branch. She held one long nail against the thick limb with her left hand and pounded it in with the hammer so it angled slightly up, skyward.

Diana brought the filled bird feeder out to the tree. She held the feeder up as high as she could, and Sam took the chain on top, stretched it out, and slipped the ring over the nail. Diana gently lowered the feeder and released it. Sam hopped down from the chair and they observed their handiwork.

"Nice," Diana said. Shaded by the leaves and the thick branch, the feeder hung about four feet out from the massive trunk. Diana set up the birdbath nearby in the shade of the tree, and Sam pulled the garden hose over and filled the basin.

"Perfect," said Diana. "He has food and water, a nice, shady yard full of trees, flowers, and Louisiana's unparalleled assortment of fat, tasty bugs."

She was gratified to see Sam smile. Draping her arm around her daughter's shoulders, she said, "Eliot's going to have a good life, Sam."

"I know."

Diana leaned down and kissed Sam's cheek. "All right, after all this work, let's go eat a big breakfast. How about scrambled eggs, pancakes, and bacon?"

"We haven't had pancakes in ages."

"And we'll drown 'em in maple syrup."

While Sam dragged the chair back to the patio, replaced the hose, and returned the hammer to the toolbox in the shed, Diana cracked eggs, mixed batter, and got breakfast underway in the kitchen. When Sam came in, the stove resembled a three-ring circus, with scrambled eggs cooking in one pan, pancakes bubbling in another, and bacon sizzling in the frying pan. Sam rinsed out the teapot, filled the infuser with English breakfast tea, and then added water to the kettle and set it to boil on the fourth burner.

"Mamma, I'm gonna go get Eliot and wake up Sitti for breakfast."

"Okay," said Diana, spatula in hand like a ringmaster's whip, "I've got everything under control here."

By the time Sitti was up and dressed, Diana had set the table and breakfast was served. Sam volunteered to say the blessing. "Thank you, Lord, for Mamma and Daddy, for Sitti, Uncle George, Aunt Cat, Michael, Lucy, and Joshua. I especially thank you for my blue jay Eliot. Protect him in the wild and give him a long and happy life. Bless this food to our bodies' use and us to your service. In Jesus' Name. Amen."

Sam, evidently famished after her morning's work, finished the mound of scrambled eggs on her plate in three gulps, and then attacked the two syrup-soaked pancakes like a destroying army. Between bites she managed to say, "I'm gonna release Eliot this morning, Sitti." The aforesaid bird, all unaware, sat grooming himself in the Norfolk Island pine.

Sitti sipped black tea. "*Albi*, that is a good thing."

"And tonight we're going to the opera with Leo," said Diana, pouring maple syrup on her pancakes. She ate with gusto equal to Sam's, surprised first by her raging hunger, and secondly by the fact that the pancakes had turned out so fluffy and light, and the bacon was crisp and perfectly done. As a very out-of-practice cook, she was proud of herself. She was a little miffed, however, that Annie put so little on her plate and didn't even eat all of that.

As if she read Diana's mind, Annie said, "Your breakfast is wonderful, Diana. It's very delicious, but my stomach is a little upset this morning."

After breakfast, Sam fed Eliot his favorite snacks, pistachios and peanuts. She was determined to feed him well before she released him. She knew he was not used to fending for himself, and in his new life he would have to forage for food all on his own.

By ten o'clock, Diana had cleaned up the kitchen and loaded the dishwasher. All that was left was to launch Eliot out into the world. "Ready?" she asked.

Sam nodded.

"Annie and I will come with you." Annie, dressed in a green dress, brought a cup of tea, and she and Diana, in a purple sundress, sat side by side in the Adirondack chairs on the patio. Sam walked out last, cupping Eliot between her hands. She stood between the chairs so they could tell Eliot goodbye. They each stroked him gently on the head. "Have a good life, Eliot," said Diana.

"Goodbye, you beauty," said Annie.

Eliot bobbed and craned his crested head, but he did not struggle.

"I'm gonna show him the bird feeder and the water and release him near the mulberry tree, 'cause that's where I found him."

Diana watched Sam walk slowly to the tree, speaking quietly to the blue jay. She smiled; Sam had always talked to him as if he were a person, not a bird. After showing him the feeder and the birdbath, Sam held him close to her heart and bent her head, laying her cheek against the bird's head. She whispered something to Eliot and then kissed him on the head. Suddenly, she bobbed down and back up, and with a swift, upward gesture like throwing confetti into the air, she released the bird. Sheer momentum carried him up, and at the apex, when gravity took hold and confetti would have fluttered downwards, Eliot extended his wings and with powerful strokes, rose high and triumphantly circled the yard.

"Go, Eliot!" Sam cried.

He landed on the topmost branch of the pear tree near Leo's house, took a moment to get his bearings, and then flew in a straight line across the yard to land on the fence near the mulberry tree, five feet from where Sam stood.

By nine-thirty on Saturday morning, Joshua was completely packed. All his worldly goods, save the desk, the chair, and the piano, were lined up in the foyer: three large suitcases, one garment bag containing his tuxes and suits, one duffel bag, one stuffed backpack, and four boxes filled with books and music.

Late the previous afternoon, he had brought Leo the check for the first month's rent and received the key in return. He and Leo had briefly inspected the apartment, which was in the process of vigorous cleaning by a large, imposing black woman. She was the color of *café au lait*, round-faced and muscular, with a short afro shot through with streaks of white. She turned off the vacuum cleaner when Leo spoke.

"Jerrica, this is Joshua Brightman, who is going to rent the apartment. Joshua, Jerrica Hobbs is my housecleaner and—"

"So you're the cause of all this trouble," she interrupted, giving Joshua a severe look.

"I am," he smiled. Her voice poured out like honey, thick and sweet and golden. Joshua wanted to hear her sing.

"Hmmph. So you play the piano?"

"I do."

"Know any Fats Waller, Scott Joplin, Eubie Blake, you know—the good stuff?"

"I sure do."

"Well, when you get that big piano up here, you make damn sure you play me a tune or two."

Joshua laughed, "I certainly will, and maybe then you can sing for me."

Jerrica's eyes widened in surprise. "Sing? How d'you know if I can sing? I might be tone deaf."

Joshua smiled and shook his head. "Nope, don't think so. I'm betting you've got a great big husky alto voice that can tear up a blues song."

Jerrica threw back her head and laughed. "I actually do!"

"See, I knew it," he grinned. "One of these days we'll have some fun. But in the meantime, thank you for all your good work."

"You're welcome. And check the refrigerator, boy, 'cause you lookin' kinda scrawny. I left you some tasty chicken gumbo."

"Why, thank you!"

Leo smiled, "Jerrica, you're the best."

"You know it, Dr. Leo."

The apartment was spacious and light; Joshua really liked it. He and Leo moved the sofa and recliner slightly to make room for the Steinway at one end of the living area. The kitchen had pots, pans, dishes and utensils in the cabinets. The bedroom housed a double bed, "with clean sheets," Jerrica loudly informed him, a dresser with a mirror, and one large closet. It was perfect. He could park George's truck on one side of the garage below.

He had left the apartment with a light heart to go home and pack. Only one more night to spend in the Beast's house.

And now the day had come. The piano movers were set to arrive at eleven, and they had agreed to take the desk and chair, as well as the suitcases, bags, and boxes in their truck, since Joshua would do the loading and unloading. He didn't have George's truck yet, so it was the best he could do.

His excitement and anxiety about the move worked together to produce an elevated heartbeat, a slight sheen of sweat, rapid breathing, and a butterfly stomach, just like waiting in the wings to perform. He had an hour and a half before the movers came. Since he hadn't eaten breakfast yet, he went to the kitchen, knowing he would probably encounter the Beast on the way.

He counted his steps:

1, 2, 3, 4, 5.

Avoid the weapon wall.

6, 7, 8, 9

"Moving out, eh?" The Beast sat on the sofa, cleaning one of his guns. The coffee table, overlaid with newspaper, was littered with cleaning oil, rods, cotton balls, and dirty rags.

Joshua could smell the sharp odor of gun oil. "Shortly. I'm going to eat breakfast now."

"Yeah, have some free grub before you leave."

It was never free, he wanted to shout. No, it had been paid for time and again in the coin of constant emotional and psychological abuse. But he put his head down and clamped his jaws together, hoping to get through ninety more minutes without incident.

Knock him down. Slam his head against the floor. Stop his mouth with dirty rags.

Made it to the kitchen—safe!

Joshua immediately went to the sink, lathered his hands and rinsed them, three times in a row. Feeling slightly better, he sliced an English muffin in half and put it into the toaster.

THRESHOLD OF EDEN

He heard the patio door open and saw his mother come in from outside. That was odd, since she rarely ventured out into the backyard. She must have seen him with her peripheral vision, but she did not look at him or greet him, which was also strange. Well, maybe she was upset, too.

The muffin popped up, and he retrieved it from the toaster, plopping both halves down on a plate. He smeared them with butter and topped that off with spoonfuls of strawberry preserves. He poured himself a mug of coffee and added some milk. Still feeling tense, he ate standing at the kitchen counter. He chewed doggedly, washing down each bite with rapid sips of coffee, eating more for fuel's sake than for pleasure.

He checked his watch. Ten o'clock—only sixty minutes between him and freedom. He had so little to move at such a short distance; he could be settled in by evening. He didn't even have to cook, thanks to Jerrica's gift of gumbo.

On Sunday, it would all be a *fait accompli*, and then with all the tension and the move behind him, he could focus on the concert. He'd have Sunday, Monday, Tuesday, and Wednesday morning as practice days to finish preparing the Beethoven. The orchestra management was giving him some time on Wednesday afternoon to practice alone on the piano in the hall, to get acclimated. Then there was the Thursday morning rehearsal with the orchestra, followed by the concert Thursday night.

Pop! Pop-pop!

Joshua slammed the mug down with such force that a hot brown wave of coffee sloshed over the top like a muddy flood tide breaching a levee. White-lipped, he turned and walked to the kitchen door to confirm what he knew was happening.

The Beast had positioned the recliner so that it faced the open patio door. Sitting relaxed, with his feet up, he held the .22 to his shoulder, ready to fire again. Sensing Joshua's presence, he remarked, "Just practice shots."

182

He had timed this display perfectly so Joshua could see it. And, of course, Joshua belatedly realized, his mother's part had been to strew the nuts on the ground to draw the squirrels. They were quite a team, his parents.

Joshua stood about five feet behind and to the right of the Beast, with the same line of sight. In the brilliant morning sunlight, he could clearly see the pile of light brown walnuts and darker pecans in the thick green grass, lying about halfway to the fence, directly in line with the mulberry tree. He crossed his arms and leaned against the kitchen door frame, waiting. All was quiet. He could hear the ticking of the kitchen clock and the songs of birds through the open door. Two full minutes passed. "What a pity," said Joshua, "looks like the great outdoors is short on game."

The Beast lowered the gun momentarily and glanced back over his right shoulder, smiling. "Oh, not for long."

In the distance, Joshua heard Sam's voice, high and clear, calling out something.

The Beast turned back and raised the gun to his shoulder, taking aim at what, Joshua could not tell, for there were no squirrels in sight.

"See, there's a nice target."

At the last second before his father fired, Joshua saw that the prey was not on the ground. The Beast aimed at a bright target perched on the top of the fence, a blue jay.

Pop-pop!

"No!" Joshua screamed and lunged headlong for the gun across five feet of space.

With the reflexes of an athlete, the Beast turned to meet him. Gripping the rifle like a staff, barrel in his left hand, stock in his right, he deflected Joshua's outstretched arms with an upward stroke of the barrel, then hammered his son's head with the wooden stock. There was a resounding crack, and Joshua crumpled to the floor.

CHAPTER 20

The Fallen

"Billy, what have you done?" Amy shrieked. She rushed to Joshua's side and knelt beside him. He lay face down, unmoving on the tile.

"I defended myself. You saw him attack me. What did you expect me to do?"

"You provoked him, and then you hit him way too hard." Her voice was bitter, "Don't try to blame this on him."

She gently rolled her son onto his back. "Get a kitchen towel and soak it with cool water. He's out cold, and his cheek is swelling." Amy's voice was low and angry. "And close the damn patio door!"

Propping the .22 upright in the recliner, Billy did as he was told.

As soon as he brought the soaked towel, Amy applied it gently to Joshua's face. "Joshua, wake up. Wake up, now."

"He's probably just faking it," Billy sneered, as he stood looking down at them.

"No, he is not, and you know it." When Amy's eye fell on the gun in the recliner, she raised her voice, "And put the goddamned rifle away!"

While Billy complied, Joshua moaned and blinked his eyes.

"That's it, wake up, honey."

"Oh, God," he whispered. Wincing, he raised one hand to his left cheek. Then he laid his palm lightly across his eyes. "God, that hurts."

"Joshua, can you sit up?"

Groaning softly, he did.

"All right, let's see if you can stand." Crouching beside him, Amy held his left hand in hers and put her right arm around his waist. "Ready?"

He nodded. First he got to his knees, and then putting his right foot under him, he leaned forward and tried to rise. Struggling to help him, Amy pulled upward on his hand and lifted him with her right arm. By the time he got to his feet, they were both breathing heavily.

Pretending not to notice them, or care, Billy tidied up the newspaper and cleaning equipment from the coffee table. Amy knew he was watching them with his peripheral vision.

Keeping her right arm locked around Joshua's waist as he caught his breath, she said, "When you're ready, let's go over to the sofa."

Billy walked out of the room.

Weak-kneed Joshua, with Amy's help, slowly and unsteadily walked to the sofa. He sat down heavily and gingerly touched the side of his face.

Looking toward the hall where her husband had gone, Amy called out in a loud voice, "Billy, get the ice bag out of the bathroom cabinet and fill it with ice." She was dismayed to see the entire left side of Joshua's face swelling. His left eye was completely bloodshot and the area above and below it was red and puffy.

"Looks like you're going to have a shiner."

Blinking repeatedly, he said, "I feel woozy."

"Sit back, honey. We're going to put ice on it to bring down the swelling. You're going to be fine," she said in a bright tone, while her mind raced. She had no idea of the extent or seriousness of his injuries, but first and foremost, she wanted to keep the incident quiet and treat Joshua at home if possible. If he had to be hospitalized, they would have a lot of explaining to do. Billy had a reputation to uphold.

Billy appeared with the ice bag and handed it to his wife.

"Oh!" Joshua exclaimed, sitting up straight and looking at the Beast with one wide eye, as the other had now closed. "The blue jay—did you kill it?"

The Beast glanced away and sniffed, "Nah, it flew off. Missed it by a mile."

"Here, put this on your eye," said Amy, offering the ice bag to Joshua.

He took it in his hand distractedly, wondering if the blue jay was Eliot or not. He knew Sam was going to release the bird soon, but he didn't know when. He prayed it was a different bird, but thankfully the Beast had missed his target. Even so, Joshua couldn't allow it to happen ever again.

He regarded the Beast, "It's got to be illegal to fire a gun in the city limits. And there's a young girl who lives next door." His voice wavered, and his whole body shook with suppressed rage. "She climbs the big tree by the fence where you shot. If you ever fire a gun from this house again, whether it's in the direction of her house, or any direction, I will have you arrested."

"Don't threaten me, you—"

"Billy, just stop it. You know he's right—you broke the law."

"What the fuck? Nobody got hurt."

Joshua shook his head and sat back with a sigh, holding the ice bag against his swollen cheek and eye. *Nobody got hurt.* Well, that was correct; to his father he was nobody. "Mom, could you please bring me some aspirin and a glass of water?" he mumbled. The swelling of his jaw made speaking difficult. "My whole face aches and I have a terrible headache."

"Your father will do it," she replied, giving Billy a meaningful glance. Sitting beside Joshua on the sofa, she said, "I'm going to stay right here with you."

Joshua glanced at his watch. "The movers are coming at eleven. I have to help them load and unload."

"You'll do no such thing," said Amy. "Your father has the day off and *he* will do the loading and unloading."

"He won't help me."

"Oh, yes, indeed he will," replied Amy, nodding firmly, relishing the fact that she now had the upper hand. "In fact, he'll do it all for you. I guarantee it."

Ever after, when she recalled the day, the memory was as hallucinatory and fragmented as a dream. Diana would always remember the colors, shimmering like jewels. The sapphire sky above, cloudless and resplendent with morning light, the emerald grass below, the darker malachite of the rustling mulberry leaves, the golden beryl of the wooden fence, and centered in the midst, the pearl of Sam's white blouse and the onyx of her hair, shining in the sun. Their summer dresses, Annie's jade and hers amethyst. The bird, a variegated lapis lazuli, beautiful, swift, and arrow-like in flight, rising toward the east, circling, swooping west, down to the fence, from flight into crystalized stillness for a heartbeat, then launched again, rising up, wings extended, but tumbling, pitching backwards in freefall. Sam running, catching the bird against her chest, and then at the center of it all, the most vivid jewel, the precious bright ruby upon her white breast, Eliot's blood.

Diana rose and Annie rose with her, both uncomprehending. Sam turned toward them, her mouth open in a silent scream, but no sound issued from it. Time slowed, halted. They stood immobilized, three figures in high relief, an ancient frieze depicting sacrifice.

Sam dropped to her knees and the sudden motion broke the spell, releasing Diana and Annie. Diana moved more quickly than Annie, covering the distance in a few long strides, her thoughts outpacing her body. What had happened? Had someone shot the bird? But she had heard no shot.

"Sam, let me take him."

Sam held out both hands, cupping the bird. His neck dangled down; his eyes were covered by ivory, opaque lids. He was clearly dead. *God have mercy*—Diana closed her eyes as her heart sank. Her shoulders slumped; she had hoped he might still be alive. She wanted to comfort her daughter, but she was struck dumb; no words came. What words could restore death to life and bring back the light in a young girl's eyes?

As she took the dead bird from Sam's hands, she saw his shattered breast and felt the warm, sticky wetness of his blood. Again, as in a dream, everything slowed, subsided into stillness. Only the wind moved, rustling the leaves of the mulberry tree, swaying the bird feeder slightly, and stirring the shimmering surface of the water in the basin below it.

The deep grass muted Annie's slow steps. She placed her hands on Sam's shoulders, "Come, *albi*. Come in the house and sit down."

Sam did not move or acknowledge her grandmother. Breathing rapidly, she remained on her knees, gazing at the ground. Her bloodied hands hung limply at her sides.

"Come, *albi*."

There was no response.

"Sam?" Diana bent down and tried to make eye contact, but Sam's gaze was blank.

Diana's heartache turned to fear. She held the bird in one hand and beckoned Annie a little distance away. In a barely audible voice, she murmured in Annie's ear, "Go quickly and call Leo. I think she's gone into shock."

Annie immediately turned and walked toward the house.

Diana laid the blue jay gently on the grass, behind Sam. She found a tissue in the pocket of her dress and wiped the blood from her hands. Kneeling next to Sam, she draped an arm around her. She watched Annie plod toward the house. She had asked Annie to hurry; why was she walking so slowly?

Diana turned her attention to Sam. "Let's go in, Sam. Stand up now."

Sam rose obediently, but without expression, shell-like and withdrawn, as though her soul had retreated to somewhere distant.

Diana looked toward the house and again, dreamlike, as if it happened in slow motion, she saw Annie stumble on the patio. As she lost her balance, the old woman grabbed the back of an Adirondack chair to right herself, but her weight and momentum tilted the chair sideways. Wood clattered against stone as the chair and Annie toppled heavily to the ground.

"Oh, no!" Caught between her fear for Sam and her alarm at Annie's fall, Diana put her arm around Sam and hurried her toward the house. When they reached the patio, she sat Sam down in an Adirondack chair and knelt beside her mother-in-law who lay unmoving on her side. "Annie, are you all right? Can you lie on your back?"

Grimacing in pain, Annie changed position. "I'm so sorry, *albi*. I don't know what happened." She laid a hand on her hip, "My leg. . ."

Afraid to move her, Diana hurried into the house and brought back a pillow for Annie's head. Using her mobile phone, she called Leo, who was thankfully at home.

He came immediately and took charge. "Diana, take Sam into the house. Have her lie down with her legs elevated and keep her warm. I'll take care of Annie."

As Annie lay on the stones of the patio, she described the severe pain in her hip and groin area, and he noticed how the leg on the injured side was turned outward. As he suspected Annie had a broken hip, he called for an ambulance. Leo kept her immobile until the EMT's arrived. As they lifted her carefully onto a gurney, she turned to Leo with desperation in her eyes, "Please don't take me to the hospital, Leo, you can treat me at home."

"No, I can't, Annie."

She grabbed his hand, squeezing it with amazing force. She begged, "Please, I don't want to go—please, please let me stay here with Sam and Diana."

Surprised by the depth of her fear, which seemed uncharacteristic and all out of proportion, Leo tried to explain, "Annie, we have to X-ray your hip to see how it's injured. Otherwise, we won't know how to treat it." Hoping to comfort her, he added, "I bet you'll be home tomorrow."

Annie shook her head and sighed, "No, no, no." She lapsed into a stream of Arabic, low and mournful-sounding. Then, as if to shut out reality, she closed her eyes, laid her head back on the gurney and accepted her fate.

As the EMT's rolled the gurney out the door, Diana called George at Levant House and told him what had happened. "Sam is physically uninjured, but Leo thinks Annie broke her hip. The ambulance came and they're taking her to Chalice General."

"I'm on my way to the hospital," George said.

"Call me later and let me know how she is."

While Diana spoke to George, Leo examined Sam. She lay ashen-faced on the sofa; her skin was clammy, and she stared with unfocused eyes. Diana had covered her with one of Annie's afghans and propped her legs up with pillows.

Diana clicked off the phone and asked Leo, "What do you think?"

"She's in shock," said Leo, shaking his head. "I'm so sorry this happened."

They kept her warm with her feet elevated until her pulse and breathing slowed. Diana sat beside her on the edge of the sofa. After a while, to Diana's great relief, Sam opened her eyes and drank a little water. But her face remained expressionless, and no matter what questions her mother asked her or how Diana coaxed her to talk, Sam spoke not a word for the rest of the day.

CHAPTER 21

Aftermath

On Sunday evening, George, Cat, and Leo came over to Diana's for dinner. Although she had recovered from the initial shock, Sam was still not herself. She sat with them at the table, but she was not really present. Distressed by Sam's listlessness, the adults kept the conversation light and humorous, like swimmers splashing in sunlight atop the water, while the dark, cold undercurrent of their fear swirled just beneath the surface. Expressionless and silent, Sam ate very little, and went to bed shortly after the meal.

When Diana was certain Sam had fallen asleep, they gathered in the living room to discuss the previous day's events. They ate the almond cookies George brought with coffee.

Diana got straight to the point. She leaned forward from her place on the loveseat and said, "Leo, Sam has not uttered a word since Eliot was shot. Why can't she speak? What's wrong with her?"

Leo rested his coffee mug on the arm of the sofa. "Diana, she can speak; there's no physical reason why not. Eliot's death was a trauma she simply couldn't bear. As a result, Sam has simply withdrawn, and part of that withdrawal is her refusal to speak. The term for it is elective mutism."

"Will she come out of it on her own?"

"I think so, but if she doesn't, we'll have to take her to see a specialist." He swirled the coffee in his mug. "We have to give her time to bounce back; it's only been thirty-six hours. Try to be patient. It was actually a double trauma. After Eliot was shot, Sam saw Annie fall, and then the EMT's came and took her grandmother away."

"Yes, that made it worse," said Diana. She rubbed her eyes. "It's the way Eliot died that shocked us. Sam wanted to release him so he could be free and have a good life. She let him go, and two minutes later he was a bloody carcass." She turned down the corners of her mouth, "She just couldn't endure another emotional shock so soon after Joseph's death. I'm so worried about her."

George spoke up, "Leo, do you know how long it might be before Sam speaks again?"

He shook his head, "Only time will tell. It depends on how long it takes her to process it all and heal."

"What can we do to help her?" Diana asked.

"Just treat her normally, and don't pressure her to speak. Talk to her and shower her with affection even if she doesn't respond outwardly. She's young and resilient; I believe she'll come out of it soon."

"It will help when Annie comes home," added Catherine.

Leo agreed. "Yes, it will. In fact, Diana, you ought to take Sam to visit Annie at the hospital. Just seeing her grandmother might put some of her anxiety to rest." He adjusted his glasses and then glanced at George, "How is Annie doing?"

"Her hip is broken and she's real unhappy to be at the hospital. She's fretting about Sam, but she's comfortable and resting for the time being. They'll decide this week if she's a candidate for surgery or not." George set his mug of coffee down, "What I wanna know is who the hell shot the bird, and who beat the shit out of Joshua."

"Joshua?" Diana frowned, "What happened to him?"

George explained, "We don't know. We just discovered he was hurt this mornin'. Last night, after I got home from seeing Mamma at the hospital, I remembered I promised Joshua the truck. After church this mornin', I dropped it off at his place and ran upstairs to give him the key. When he opened the door, he had the worst shiner I've ever seen. One eye was swollen shut and half his face was bruised.

"I said, 'Holy shit! What happened to you? Looks like you been in one helluva barroom brawl.'"

"'Not quite.'"

"'I brought the truck, by the way.'"

"He smiled and said, 'Believe me, I heard you coming.'"

"When I asked him what happened, he wouldn't answer. I said, 'Not talkin', eh? Well, have you seen a doctor?'"

"'No.'"

"'I know just the man.' I ran down the stairs and got Leo."

Leo took up the thread. "I examined him as best I could. I said, 'I hoped you gave as good as you got, Joshua, because whoever it was deserved it.' I think he has a fractured cheek, which may require surgery, but he refused to go in for treatment. He said he had to play the concert this Thursday no matter what, and that was that."

Leo finished his coffee. "By the way, I think I know who is responsible."

"You do?" asked Diana.

"Yes. As you know, Joshua moved in to the apartment yesterday."

"Joshua shot Eliot?" Diana was aghast.

Leo smiled, "No, of course not. This is what happened. About noon on Saturday, after we had done all we could for Sam, I went home. As I got to my house, the piano movers drove away in their big truck. They had left several boxes, a couple of suitcases, and a wooden desk sitting on the driveway in front of the garage, so I assumed Joshua was upstairs. But then a big, swarthy man with a shaved head came hustling down the stairs. He wore a black T-shirt with a white Yankees logo on it and khaki shorts.

"'Is Joshua upstairs?' I asked."

"'No, he's not. I'm his father, Billy Brightman. I'm helping him move.'"

"We shook hands, and I introduced myself as Joshua's landlord. From talking with Joshua at the party, I knew two things about his father. First, Brightman is an attorney for Leviathan Oil, and secondly, he forced his son to leave home because he and Joshua had a disagreement. It struck me as odd that Brightman was helping with the move, because Joshua implied that his father was quite angry with him.

"Anyway, Billy Brightman was sweating profusely, and there was a strong odor about him, that was familiar, not really unpleasant, but I couldn't place it at the time. I asked him when Joshua was coming. He hesitated and said, 'Uh, well, he had a little accident, and he's resting right now. He'll be over sometime tonight, I'm sure.'

"That sounded odd—what 'little accident,' I wondered. I left him to his work and went to eat lunch. It was later that day that I realized that the familiar odor was the smell of gun oil. My dad used to take me duck hunting, and now and again we would clean the guns. The smell of the oil is unmistakable."

"You think Billy Brightman did it?" asked Diana.

"It's possible. The shot had to have come from the direction of his house."

"Diana, did you hear a shot?" asked George.

"No, nothing. That's why it was so shocking when the bird catapulted backwards."

"Well," mused George, "if you didn't hear anything, it could have been a BB gun at close range—they don't make much sound, or a bigger gun like a .410 or a .22 from a greater distance."

"I vote for the bigger gun," said Leo. "A .22 would be powerful enough to knock the bird backwards off the fence. But the report should have been audible; it's strange no one heard it."

"And there's this—a blue jay is a damn small target," George added. "Whoever killed Eliot had to be relatively close by, not to mention out of his mind to fire a gun directly at another house inside the city limits. Even so, he must be either a very good shot, or, I hate to use the word, a lucky one." George folded his arms across his chest. "In either case, I'm rarin' to get my hands on the crazy, mean son of a bitch."

"Well, the simplest way to solve the shooter mystery is to ask Joshua," said Diana.

Leo shook his head vehemently. "No, Diana, not now. He's injured, upset, and under great pressure to perform this concerto on Thursday. Imagine if it *was* his father who shot Eliot—how do you think that makes him feel? I don't want to give him any more grief. He's got to rest and practice in peace this week."

Leo ran a hand through his hair, "What's done is done; we can wait until after the concert to ask him." He adjusted his glasses, "I think someone walloped him, and I have a bad feeling it was his father. That's probably why Joshua kept mum about the 'little accident,' as Billy Brightman put it."

Cat spoke up, "Did you tell Joshua what happened to Sam and Annie?"

"No, I didn't, for the same reason. I'm going to invite him to dinner at my house the night after the concert. I'll tell him the whole story then, and I'll also try to find out who hit him and who shot Eliot."

"If his father beat him up or shot Eliot," remarked George, with a fierce look in his eye Diana had never seen before, "I think I'll invite Billy Brightman over to my house for the dinner he deserves. We'll see if the bully boy enjoys an authentic Middle Eastern fist sandwich."

Diana took Sam to visit Annie the next day. They brought her roses from home to cheer up her room. Although Annie had witnessed Sam's shock at the death of Eliot, and George had prepared her for Sam's strange behavior, she was still taken aback by her granddaughter's listless demeanor. From the hospital bed, she held our her arms, "*Albi*, give your Sitti a kiss."

Sam obeyed, but there was a wooden quality about her that Annie had never seen before. Sam stood beside the bed and held onto Annie's hand, but she remained mute when her grandmother spoke to her or asked her questions. Diana's hopes rose briefly when Annie prayed for Sam, but there was no immediate change.

"How are you feeling, Annie?"

"Oh, they gave me pain medication; I'm not hurting at all, but I'm ready to go home. What about you, Diana, how are you feeling?"

Diana smiled, "I guess your prayers had a delayed reaction, Annie, because I feel great. The only way I can tell I was sick is by my weight loss. Otherwise, physically, I'm strong and healthy again."

Annie's face shone, "Diana, I am so happy for you." She squeezed Sam's hand. "*Albi*, see, the Lord answered our prayers in his own good time. Be thankful your mamma is healthy again."

Annie looked somehow diminished in the hospital bed, frailer and less substantial. Diana wondered if she was eating. "Is the food all right here?"

Annie laughed, "No, it's awful, but George brings me a plate from Levant House every evening." She smiled, "Don't worry about me, Diana, just take care of our Sam."

She laid her head back against the pillow as if she was suddenly fatigued.

Diana decided to cut the visit short. She knew a broken hip could have grave consequences for older people, but Annie had always had exceptional vitality. She would soon recover, Diana was sure.

Joshua rested all of Sunday, lying with the ice bag on his throbbing, aching face. He warmed up Jerrica's gumbo for lunch and dinner, and took extra strength ibuprofen at intervals to dampen the pain.

On Monday, despite the aching, he resumed practicing for the concert. Each day he felt somewhat better and was able to practice longer. Jerrica's gumbo lasted until Tuesday, and at that point he felt well enough to go out and buy groceries.

Nathan called the same day. "Hey, man, just checkin' on the Bad Boy of Classical Music before he wows 'em in New Orleans. How's it goin'? You got the rehearsal schedule and enough practice time in the hall?"

It cheered Joshua to hear Nathan's familiar accent and rapid-fire delivery. "Yeah, it's fine."

"Playin' goin' well?"

Joshua's tone was subdued, "Oh, pretty good." He sat down on the sofa.

"Man, you don't sound like yourself. Pretty good? That's not what your manager wants to hear! My sixth sense tells me something's goin' on down there. You got a problem?"

"Well, I had a disagreement with a man about a gun."

"Oh, shit, I'm nervous already. Tell me before I crap my pants—did he shoot you?"

"No."

"Well, what then?"

"He was shooting animals in the city limits, and I tried to stop him. He hit me in the head with the stock of the rifle."

"And?"

"And he fractured my left cheekbone and blacked my eye."

"Joshua, I'm sorry. When did this happen?"

"Two days ago."

Nathan exhaled loudly. "All right, two questions: One, are you sure you can play the concert, and two, did you file charges against the effing son of a bitch?"

"I had to rest all weekend, and I have to pace myself this week, but yes, I can play. And no, I didn't file charges."

"Professionally, I think it's probably good not to file charges because it could cause some trouble with BG Artists, especially after your San Francisco escapade. Bruce the boss wants his artists to keep a clean image. But personally, I gotta say, I think you oughta sue the ass off this guy for assault and battery. I'd like to come down there and beat the shit outta the guy myself. What's his name?"

"Who it is doesn't matter. It's done, so let's drop it."

"Okay, man." There was a heavy silence until Nathan changed conversational direction. "Hey, how's the romance comin' along?"

"Romance?"

"Yeah, with the athletic chick who says she's gonna marry you."

"Oh," Joshua smiled. "It's been great. We took a fishing trip in her boat—"

"Boat? She's got a boat?"

"Big white one with a high-powered outboard motor."

"Some guys have all the luck."

"And we partied on July Fourth and went out to see the fireworks over the Mississippi River. I met the whole family."

"What's her name again?"

"Sam."

"Hey, Joshua, I got another client call comin' in. Look, play well on Thursday, and let's talk after."

Sam. Joshua pocketed the phone. He didn't want Sam, Diana, or Annie to see him so disfigured, and he dreaded their questions. They were coming to the concert, and he would meet them for supper after, but he was going to avoid them until then. Maybe the discoloration and swelling would subside by Thursday. If not, they would ask him what had happened, and he would have to lie or refuse to answer. How could he tell them his father had fired a .22 at a blue jay on their fence and then battered his own son with the rifle?

With an aching heart, he slumped back on the sofa, leaden-limbed. Sorrow and depression threatened to overwhelm him. After a moment, he closed his eyes and shook his head to clear it, like a fighter on the ropes. No, he couldn't give in to those feelings; he had to resist—he was a professional and he had a job to do.

He rose and took his place at the piano. Hoping to dispel the heaviness in his heart, he drew in a deep breath and exhaled. He lifted his hands to the keyboard and played the powerful opening arpeggios of the Emperor Concerto's first movement, but feeling dispirited and dissatisfied, broke off. Hands in his lap, he closed his eyes, and waited several minutes in an effort to settle himself and still his thoughts.

And then, stealing on his mind in muted tones of strings and woodwinds, he heard the chorale, simple and so sublime, which opens the second movement, the quiet Adagio. Moved and inspired at last, he listened inwardly and then joined the imagined orchestra with a second melody, which cascaded gently downward against sustained chords. In his inner ear he heard the orchestral interlude that followed, and then he played the theme itself. The serene melody flowed from his fingers with an intensity that translated it to an outpouring of his soul. It became a prayer, wordless and pure. As he played, no longer aware of his fingers, the keys, or anything on the physical plane, Joshua yearned toward a realm it seemed he could never reach, a place of healing and peace, where sorrow ended and evil, pain, and fear could not enter. . .

The ending of the Adagio, interrogative, inconclusive, was like a question left hanging in the air. It mirrored his unfulfilled longing for the kingdom of peace—would he ever find it? Joshua dropped his hands and bowed his head. Where, he wondered, where stand the gates of Paradise?

CHAPTER 22

Concert

On the night of Joshua's concert, Leo dressed carefully and then walked over to Diana's house. This would be the first time they went out together. They had never made it to *Die Fledermaus*, due to Sam's trauma after Eliot was shot and Annie's injury. Leo rang the bell precisely at six forty-five, and Diana let him in. He wore a fawn-colored blazer with a light-blue shirt, a gaudy Tabasco tie patterned with orange crawfish and blue crabs, navy slacks and deep brown wingtips. He hoped he looked distinguished and solid, to somehow bring an air of stability and strength into Diana's topsy-turvy world.

"Hello, Leo."

He opened his mouth to reply, blinked several times, pushed his glasses up to the bridge of his nose, and closed his mouth in surprise, tongue-tied as a teenager on his first date. The air of sadness that veiled Diana's eyes and her fragile beauty stopped his speech. Dark smudges of fatigue underscored the dark blue of her eyes, but her fair skin was rosy and her hair, light brown and shining, curled in waves to her shoulders. She smelled of roses. Although his tongue refused to move, the muscles of his arms and shoulders contracted with a sudden impulse to embrace her. He was so powerfully drawn to her that he had to divert himself. Shifting his glance to Sam, who sat behind Diana on the sofa, Leo poured on his Irish Channel accent, "Sam, ya mamma's a chahmah, no, wait—an enchantress. Blue is huh culah." Finally able to address Diana, he added, "Your dress matches your eyes and you look lovely."

Surprised and pleased by his compliment, Diana felt the blood rise to her cheeks. "Well, thank you."

"Is everybody ready?" he asked.

"Yes, come on Sam."

Dressed in blue pumps and the white dress dotted with tiny blue and violet flowers, Sitti's gifts, Sam rose from the sofa like an automaton. Expressionless and mute since the day of Eliot's death, she was a beautiful, obedient young girl, but hollow as a conch shell and just as vacant of life.

"Hello, Sam," Leo said, taking her cold hand in both of his warm ones. "You're a chahmah, just like ya mamma. You look so grown up tonight." He was certain that it was best to treat her normally, even if she did not respond. "Let's go see our Joshua perform." He hoped that the concert, the music, might bring her out of herself, might help restore the old Sam. Keeping her hand in his, he led her out to the car.

As he drove out of the neighborhood and approached the Westbank Expressway, he kept the conversation with Diana light and neutral, talking about the surprising dearth of threatening tropical storms and the encouraging upswing of house renovations in the city. Then, remembering George's remark about her interest in politics, Leo asked Diana for her opinion of the current occupant of the White House.

Proving George right, Diana launched into a blow by blow analysis of the President's economic and foreign policies, and his erosion of Americans' constitutional rights that lasted all the way to the City Center.

As he followed the javelin-straight shot of her logic, Leo watched the fire in her eyes and her quick, vehement gestures. He even noticed a brown freckle in her left iris. Thankfully, her fervor for the subject temporarily dispelled the aura of worry and melancholy that had surrounded her since Sam had been traumatized and ceased to speak five days ago. Feeling the force of her passion affected him greatly; it called forth his own ardor. From some deep place within himself, he felt the welling up of strong emotions that he had not felt, or had not allowed himself to feel, for years. Drawn to Diana almost against his will, he was highly conscious of her nearness in the car, her scent, her elegant profile, the whiteness of her throat. She *was* an enchantress. He felt a kind of desire he had never even felt for his wife; he wanted to be all things to Diana: lover, protector, friend. And then there was Sam. He glanced back at her. Had she lived, his darling daughter Lisa would have loved her like a sister. Given the chance, he would treat Sam as his own.

Protection was part of his nature. He had taken the long, difficult road to become a physician so that he could help people. As trite as it sounded, his desire to help, to heal, to defend, had been and remained the core of his vocation. He thought about the plight of Foreman and Emma Clostio, Marshall and Regina Ross, and René Guilbeau's family. He could document the onset and duration of their symptoms and illnesses; he could suggest tests and refer them to local physicians, but other than that, he could not help them. But these two, lovely Diana and fragile Sam, he could help, and he would help them as much and for as long as they would allow.

"Leo, the exit!" Diana shouted.

"Oh, hell!" If she hadn't roused him, he would have ended up in Slidell. He cut over into the far right lane and took the O'Keefe Avenue exit.

Five minutes later, Leo parked his Chevy Blazer in the City Center parking lot. He and Diana, with Sam between them, walked toward the auditorium in the thick, humid air of evening. Leo pointed out George's pitiful old truck at the front of the lot. It was parked between a shiny silver Mercedes and a blue Corvette, like a leper in the company of angels. "Look, Sam, Joshua's here already, 'cause there's his truck." The sun was still high as they climbed the marble stairs to the gray stone Art Deco auditorium. The blessedly cool air of the broad foyer was a relief. People streamed through the doors, and as Leo picked up their tickets from the Will Call window, Diana scanned the crowd for George and Cat and their children.

She squeezed Sam's hand gently and leaned down, "Uncle George, Aunt Cat, and your cousins are coming tonight, too, and afterwards, Joshua is meeting us for crêpes at Marigold's Bistro in Uptown." Marigold's was a place Sam loved, which is why they had chosen it.

Sam did not blink or acknowledge her mother in any way.

Diana straightened, clenching her jaws. She was seized with so fierce a rage toward the person who had killed Eliot that she felt it as a burning wave rushing through her body with the power of a flash flood. She could taste bile in the back of her throat. Like George, she wanted to beat the shooter with her bare hands; she wanted to see him suffer. She felt so compelled to lash out, that she contracted both hands into fists and dug her nails into the palms of her hands until it hurt. That utter bastard—who gave him the right? If it was Billy Brightman, she would soon know. Leo had promised he would get the answer from Joshua after the concert, and now the night of the concert had arrived.

Leo appeared at her elbow with Joshua's complimentary tickets in his hand, just as she spotted George and Catherine across the foyer. Her brother-in-law and his wife made a handsome couple. The dramatic white streak in George's pitch-black hair was striking against his pale gray seersucker suit and red tie, and Cat, with her shoulder-length dark hair and long neck, looked elegant in a simple black dress with a string of pearls. Diana waved her arm, and caught Cat's attention. They met in the center of the foyer, under a large crystal chandelier.

"I hardly recognize you when you're all dressed up and cigar-less," Diana told George.

He smiled, but didn't reply, which was unusual for him. Cat stepped into the breach, "Don't worry," she said, "wherever George is, cigars cannot be far behind. He's got an entire box out in the car." She greeted Leo and Diana, and bent down and hugged Sam. "You look lovely, sweetheart." Sam showed no sign of recognition.

George shook hands with Leo, kissed Diana on the cheek, and then bent down and kissed Sam on the head. "Glad to see you, darlin'," he murmured.

"Let's go in," suggested Leo. "All our seats are in the same row, so Michael and Lucy will find us easily." They presented their tickets and took programs from the uniformed ushers at the door. Their seats, about halfway down in the orchestra, were slightly left of center, which was Leo's idea, so they would be able to see Joshua's hands at the keyboard. Sam sat between Leo and Diana, with Catherine and George to Diana's right. Settling comfortably in the plush red seats, they browsed through their programs and surveyed the auditorium's colorful interior.

The hall, an ornate jewel box built in 1925, was high and shallow, like a European opera house, with two balconies and four box seats on either side above the stage, two per balcony. Unlike the vast, barn-like American halls, built later in the century, every seat was close to the stage, and the acoustics were excellent. The nine muses, beautifully painted in a ceiling mural, presided over the theater. Their long gowns, in blues and greens with touches of white and ochre, fell from shoulder to feet in graceful folds. Each figure held some emblem, a scroll, lyre, flute, or mask, tragic or comic, representing her domain. Below them, one could read on a panel beginning high on the left wall, continuing above the stage, and onto the right wall, a gold-leaf, large-letter inscription from Milton's *Paradise Lost*:

> *Of Man's first disobedience, and the fruit*
> *Of that forbidden tree whose mortal taste*
> *Brought death into the World, and all our woe,*
> *With loss of Eden, till one greater Man*
> *Restore us, and regain the blissful Seat,*
> *Sing, Heavenly Muse!*

As the hall filled with people, musicians gradually populated the brilliantly lit stage. Dressed in tuxedos or long black gowns, the performers strolled in and warmed up in cheerful chaos, ignoring the audience and each other. The effect was high-spirited and rambunctious, akin to the grade school anarchy that inevitably occurs when the teacher leaves the room. The hall was pierced by trumpet calls, blaring trombones, clashing violin passages, flute riffs, grumbling basses, and the pungent squawking and crowing of oboes and bassoons.

The cacophony rose and fell in waves for about ten minutes. While Diana talked to Cat and George, Leo kept up a one-sided conversation with Sam. "See the nine muses painted on the ceiling?" he asked her. "To remember them, I just visualize a map of New Orleans, the city with streets named for the muses, even if everyone fractures their pronunciation. There's Terpsichore, the muse of dance, Melpomene, tragedy, Polymnia, choral poetry, Thalia, the muse of comedy," he held up four fingers, keeping a running count. "Urania, the muse of astronomy, Clio, for history, Erato for lyric poetry, Calliope the muse of. . . hmmmh. . ." He pursed his lips, "She is the muse of—calliopes." Regarding his eight fingers, he said, "There's one more. What's the last one, Sam?" He wiggled his fingers and closed his eyes. "Of course!" He glanced at her. "How could I forget my favorite one: Euterpe, the muse of ice cream?"

Sam's eyebrows contracted, and Leo saw a flicker of light in her eyes that disappeared almost as soon as it flared, like a firefly. Nonetheless, hope rose in his heart, high and shining, like the evening star.

Michael, Lucy, and her boyfriend Richard, a tall man with curly blond hair and a trimmed beard, slipped into the seats next to George just as the house lights dimmed, and the entire orchestra subsided into silence. The oboe gave its mournful A, and the orchestra tuned. Following a moment of expectant silence, the conductor appeared to enthusiastic applause, and the concert began.

Standing alone in the Artist Room, Joshua heard the applause swell for the conductor's entrance. After a short interval of silence, he heard the opening measures of Beethoven's Egmont Overture, dark and forte, in F minor. He knew he had about ten minutes before it was his turn to walk onstage and perform.

He adjusted his bow tie, ran a hand through his hair, and took stock of himself in the mirror. "You are a colorful dude, no doubt about it," he murmured. Except for the tuxedo, he resembled either a lightweight boxer who had lost his last bout badly, or a raccoon. The left side of his face was still puffy, discolored, and very tender, and his eye remained bloodshot. Against his fair skin, the purple bruising around his cheekbone and eye stood out like beet juice splattered on a white rug. He had considered applying liquid makeup, but the area was so large and so painful to the touch, that he abandoned the idea. At least when he sat at the piano, his bad side would be mostly hidden from the audience.

The stage manager tapped at the door, interrupting Joshua's musings. "Mr. Brightman, five minutes."

"Thank you."

Like a soldier preparing to go into battle, Joshua steeled himself for what he had to do. In perfect health and peak playing form, he needed every bit of mental focus, physical stamina, and emotional presence he could muster to play Beethoven's fifth piano concerto. The piece was forty minutes long and required a balance of formidable technique with exquisite control and delicacy. Now he had to go out there and do the same in spite of a fracture that had not had time to heal, fatigue, and the past week's load of mental and emotional turmoil.

Drawing on his experiences with Sam, Annie, and George, he bowed his head and clasped his hands before his chest. Quietly and hesitantly, he said, "Lord God, thank You for the chance to perform this sublime and beautiful music. I...uh, please...please grant me calmness of mind and the strength to play well. Bless the work of my hands and be with me now. Amen."

He drew in a deep breath and let his hands fall to his sides. Closing his eyes, he played the opening measures in his mind.

Tap-tap-tap. "Mr. Brightman, it's time."

"Coming." Squaring his shoulders, he opened the door and walked down a short hall to the backstage area where the conductor, William Steigerwalt, waited. The German-born maestro with blond page-boy hair greeted him with a smile.

As the orchestra tuned to the piano, Joshua looked out from the shadowy wings of the stage. He could see the black Steinway with raised lid, elegant and gleaming in the brilliant lights. Beyond it he saw people in the first few rows of the audience. He glanced at the box seat nearest the stage and immediately wished he hadn't. He recognized the blond Merrick family, his mother, and the bald head of the Beast. He hadn't seen his father since the day of the altercation. Well, so be it. The Faris family and Leo were also out there in the darkened hall; he would draw strength and comfort from his friends.

The sound of tuning instruments faded to silence. "Ready?" asked the Maestro.

Joshua breathed deeply, "Yes."

Followed by the conductor, Joshua Brightman strode into the light as swelling applause greeted him. He bowed quickly, keeping his face down as long as possible. He straightened, turned to the piano and sat down at the bench. Steigerwalt stepped onto the podium, greeted the orchestra silently, then turned and watched Joshua. He gave the pianist time to ready himself. When Joshua met his eyes and nodded slightly, the conductor faced the orchestra and gave a swift, strong downbeat.

After a fortissimo E-flat major chord from the orchestra, Joshua played the opening arpeggios which led into an improvisatory-sounding passage. The same introductory sequence happened twice more, and then the orchestra presented the majestic first theme while the soloist rested. During the rest, Joshua's mind and senses worked on several levels. He listened to the orchestra and felt and responded to the power of the music. Physically, he broke into a light sweat from nervous energy and the heat of the lights. He was aware of the energy and presence of the audience, and highly conscious that his father sat less than thirty feet away. Determined to block him out, Joshua forced himself to breathe slowly and deeply, keeping his focus fully in the moment.

The orchestra reached the final measures leading up to his entrance. With a quickening heartbeat, Joshua shifted slightly on the bench, set his foot on the pedal, and lifted his hands. *Bless the work of my hands and be with me. . .* The last word of the prayer coincided with the first notes of his entrance:...*now!* With power and concentration, he entered into the music.

The moment Joshua walked out onto the stage and faced the audience, Catherine placed her hand on Diana's arm. Under the cover of applause, Cat leaned toward her sister-in-law and said, "His face is awful."

Diana nodded, "And this is after five days. Can you imagine what he looked like last Saturday?" It was their first glimpse of his injury.

"Oh, my gosh, Dad!" Lucy exclaimed. She sat between George and Richard. "You said he was hurt, but someone beat him to a pulp, the poor guy."

Up in the box seat, Taylor Merrick smiled delightedly and used her phone to snap pictures of Joshua.

Lucinda immediately asked Amy, "What happened to your son?"

With an elevated pulse, Amy gave the agreed-upon lie. "Oh, he was cleaning leaves out of the gutters at the house when he reached too far over and fell off the ladder. He landed on the concrete patio."

When Lucinda looked doubtful, Amy smiled and shrugged, "Just one of those things." She added, "Don't worry, it looks bad, but he's fine," and fanned her sweaty brow with the program.

Taylor leaned over and whispered in her mother's ear, "He's probably a coke head who got beat up in a drug deal."

"Your boy looks a little rough," Charles Merrick remarked to Billy. Merrick was a member of the Louisiana Philharmonic's Board of Directors.

"Yeah, he had an accident at the house over the weekend," Billy chuckled. "Fell off a ladder. Naturally, it happened just before the concert. But I brought him up tough; he'll play fine."

After the orchestra's initial chord, Leo took Sam's hand in his. He knew the Emperor Concerto well. As a music lover, he was excited to hear Joshua play the piece, but as a physician, he worried the young man might crack under the emotional and physical strain. He glanced at Sam to gauge her reaction and caught Diana's eye. They smiled at each other, pleased to see Sam gazing directly at Joshua.

George watched intently, fascinated by Joshua's transformation from the troubled, tentative young man of the fishing trip to the bold artist who played with such assurance and power despite his injury. George was delighted; he wished concerts were like football games so he could light up a cigar and cheer: *Go, Joshua, go!*

At the same time, he wondered if Brightman, the S.O.B. who had likely beat up Joshua, was here in the hall, a witness to his gifted son's performance. He hoped the bastard could recognize courage when he saw it.

There were many different kinds of courage, George mused. He thought of his mother, suffering in the hospital. He had visited her each day and answered her questions about Sam as best he could. She inquired almost as much about Diana. Today, when he reminded her about the concert, she smiled and said, "I'm going to say a prayer for Joshua tonight." So in her way, his mother was present in the hall, too. His heart swelled with love for her, for he knew that despite her own suffering, and without applause or acclaim, she had done, and continued to do, all she could for others.

George sighed—if only he could do something for her. But her doctor's revelation earlier in the day had ruled that out. George had considered staying with Annie at the hospital, but since there was nothing he could do, he had left it in God's hands. He decided to attend the concert and keep the news to himself until later. *God bless and keep you, Mamma.*

He glanced at Diana, who had regained her strength and vitality so rapidly. She listened raptly, and even Sam seemed to be paying attention. He would describe it all to his mother tomorrow. He returned his attention to the stage, hoping the majestic, life-affirming music might comfort his heart.

The Merricks watched with varying degrees of inattention. Charles, yawning from long hours at Leviathan, two glasses of wine, and an eighteen-ounce, medium rare ribeye, laced his fingers over his mountainous belly and dozed off in the middle of the second movement. Lucinda spent her time people-watching and wondering if Amy's story about Joshua was true or not. Taylor took the conductor's downbeat as her cue to text her friends and surf the internet on her phone. The five-inch screen was a vortex that swallowed her alive for the duration of the concert.

A battle raged inside the Beast. He was torn between a reluctant pride in his son's ability and burning resentment at Joshua's professional success, achieved so early in life without struggle or sacrifice. Joshua had always had a father; he had never been responsible for supporting an entire family as a teenager. Even now he didn't know what it was like to have that burden. Billy glanced around the hall. All eyes were on his son, the star of the concert. The Beast fumed, remembering Joshua's taunts—*the war on squirrels. What bravery, what courage, what a superior man!* Billy would not tolerate disrespect. His anger swelled and he would have walked out if he could have left without offending Merrick. His boss had invited him; otherwise, he would never have come. He shifted restlessly in his seat, ready for the piece to end.

Amy didn't like Beethoven—his music had too many sudden shifts. He never let the listener get comfortable. She didn't like Lucinda or the bratty Taylor either, but most of all, she didn't like herself. Ashamed that Billy had injured Joshua, and ashamed of the lie she told to cover it up, she sat immersed in guilt. From the box seat, she could see Joshua's bruises and every expression on his battered face. It pained her to see him so disfigured. Even so, he didn't let his injury interfere with his playing. Her heart swelled with pride. She loved her son, but for so many years she had failed to protect him. She should have either stopped Billy's abuse years ago, or taken Joshua and left him. Out of weakness, she had done neither. As the music rose up from the stage, she knew she had a lot to make up for; she just didn't know if she had the courage to do it.

CHAPTER 23

To Hear or Not to Hear

S weat-soaked, utterly spent, in pain, and acutely conscious of his disfigured face, Joshua greeted audience members and some of the musicians who came backstage to speak to him after the concert. When his parents and the Merrick family got to the head of the line, Amy hugged him, "Beautiful playing, Joshua. We're very, very proud of you."

As she was rarely demonstrative, her fierce embrace surprised him. "Thanks, Mom."

The Beast seemed fidgety and quite ill at ease. He did not comment on the performance, but said, "Charles Merrick and his family invited us to come with them." Turning to the leonine presence beside him, he added, "Charles is a member of the Philharmonic's Board of Directors."

"Very fine," said Charles from under his shaggy blond forelock, shaking Joshua's hand firmly. "Sorry about the fall."

"Uh, thanks." Joshua had no idea what he meant.

"Loved it," said Lucinda, with a steely smile. "You'll have to play for us sometime at the country club."

Taylor, mobile phone in hand, smirked down at him. She turned her phone so that he, and he alone, could see the picture she had downloaded. "There you are," she said.

"Thanks, Taylor, how typical of you." It was the iconic picture of Boris Karloff as Frankenstein. Joshua shrugged it off; what could you expect from a college student with the mental maturity of a six-year-old?

Leo was not far behind them in the queue. His smile equaled the wattage of all the stage lights combined. Disregarding Joshua's extended hand, Leo embraced him. "Bravo, Joshua, bravo! You played so powerfully and with such expression. It was wonderful! I really don't know how you managed, because I'm sure you're in pain."

"That I am." Despite taking extra ibuprofen just beforehand, the pain resurfaced due to his physical exertion in the first movement. The throbbing ache, which he somehow disregarded, continued throughout the second movement, and then it receded as he gave himself over entirely to the music in the joyous, dance-like rondo. Now it had returned in full force.

"Take some medication as soon as you can. We have to have the honoree feeling good for the party, you know." Leo handed him a folded piece of paper. "Here are the directions to Marigold's Bistro. We're going ahead to get a table, and we'll wait for you there. But just so you know: Sam is not feeling well, so don't be surprised if she seems glum and doesn't talk. I'll explain later."

As soon as he could, Joshua returned to the Artist Room and hurriedly swallowed three ibuprofen to still the ache in his face and eye. Then he showered and changed into clean street clothes. With his garment bag over one arm, he walked out the stage door: *Mission accomplished.* He climbed into his vintage vehicle and cranked it up. "All right," he said, as he pulled out of the parking lot, "time to rock and roll." The truck, in a show of solidarity, punctuated his sentence with an enormous backfire. Joshua Brightman left the scene in triumph with flames shooting out of the tailpipe like glory.

Twenty minutes later, he walked into Marigold's Bistro, glad to see his friends, but fearful he would have to fend off a thousand questions about his disfigured face. To his relief, Leo and the Faris family greeted him with cheers and applause. They congratulated him loudly, showering him with compliments only—no questions. Only Sam remained silent, as Leo had forewarned; she didn't even make eye contact.

At first, Joshua was pleasantly surprised by her grownup appearance. The lipstick and pretty white dress Sam wore afforded him the merest glimmer of the woman she would be. But he was caught flat-footed by the slump in her back and the dullness of her gaze. Stunned, and trying to mask his dismay, Joshua greeted everyone with a smile and a wave while his mind churned. *What had happened to her? What in the world had stolen the life from her eyes?*

He sat between Michael and Leo, elbow to elbow at a round table covered with a clean white tablecloth. The bistro was quiet, less than half-filled on a Thursday night. While they awaited the arrival of their crêpes, they conversed and assuaged their thirst with wine, Scotch, ice water, and, in Sam's case, lemonade.

"Well, Joshua," remarked Leo, "I have to tease you a little bit; your spectacular shiner isn't pretty, but it certainly upholds your image as the Bad Boy of Classical Music." He smiled kindly, "But don't worry, no one's going to say any more about it than that."

Joshua felt a great sense of relief, "Thanks, Leo." He glanced around the table. "Where's Annie?"

"She fell and broke her hip," said George. "She's been in the hospital since Saturday."

Saturday, the same day the Beast battered him with the rifle. "Really?" Joshua was taken aback. Good Lord, another casualty—apparently it had been a week of calamities. "I had no idea."

"We didn't mention it because it was important for you to hibernate with the piano this week," said George, "and we didn't wanna disturb you."

"Is Annie going to be okay?" Even as he asked the question, Joshua glanced uneasily at Sam, impatient to find out what had happened to her. He hated to see her so listless.

"Knowing Mamma, I would say yes, no matter what," George replied. After swirling the ice cubes in his drink, he set it down abruptly, and waved impatiently to the waiter. When the young man came over, George gestured at Joshua and said, "Take this man's order. He's just played a helluva concert and he needs victuals."

While Joshua ordered his drink and crêpes, Michael and George continued to discuss the concert.

"That Steigerwalt is a really good conductor," Michael told George.

"You know what makes him so good?" George responded.

"His baton technique?"

"Naw, it's all in the hair."

"The hair?"

"Yeah, that pageboy cut. See, if he flopped it just right, the violins knew exactly when to come in and how loud and all that. The stick is nothin'; they watch the hair."

"What about all that bouncing and dancing around he did?"

"Well," said George, "since the orchestra's makin' the music while he's not producin' a damn bit of sound himself, I guess he figures he better do somethin' to work up a sweat, otherwise they'd realize he's not necessary and fire his fancy ass."

Michael smiled. "Good analysis, Dad."

George sipped his double Scotch. "What d'ya think, Joshua? Do I have it right?"

"A whole lot of orchestral musicians would agree with you."

"Ha!" exclaimed George.

"But, on the other hand," Joshua continued, "a really great conductor can make the musicians rise above themselves. Like a great coach, he can inspire them to play better than they ever thought they could—even if he's bald as an egg," Joshua laughed.

"Well, Dad," said Michael, "that shoots your theory to hell."

"Son," drawled George, "I saw what I saw."

As the waiter delivered Joshua's drink, Lucy, looking like a Renaissance angel with her cloud of dark, curling hair, leaned over from across the table and introduced her blond boyfriend Richard, a building contractor, who complimented Joshua on his performance. Then, with a teasing glint lighting her hazel eyes, she asked, "Be honest now, Joshua, did you make any mistakes?"

"I plead the fifth on that one." He smiled and sipped his scotch. Setting it down, he said, "Well, the truth is that all performances are imperfect. Modern recordings give the impression that the great orchestras and soloists play perfectly. They lie."

"But what about the performances recorded live?" asked Leo.

"If problems occur during the performance, the concert is followed by a patch session. The performers re-record the sections or passages that didn't go well, and these 'corrections' are patched in to the original live recording. Current technology is magic; with computers, recording engineers can hide all kinds of mistakes. But these doctored recordings create false expectations. People think live performances can only be good if they are mistake-free, like the so-called perfection of recorded music."

"What's your opinion on that?" Leo asked.

"Well, I think note-perfect playing is less important than playing with spirit and élan, even if it's flawed. Arthur Rubenstein dropped notes all over the floor, but people adored his playing. And in his day, performers recorded on a single take—no splicing."

As he spoke, Joshua glanced occasionally at Sam, masking his alarm at the changes in her. She had eaten only half of her crêpes and sat silent, dull-eyed, and aloof, like a displaced, shell-shocked war refugee rather than a young girl surrounded by her loving family at a post-concert party.

When the waiter set his own platter of crêpes before him, Joshua did not hesitate. He ate voraciously and with pleasure in the traditional manner of his profession. After concerts, musicians eat like locusts or marauding Visigoths; they devour everything in their path. Joshua had sweated under fire, battled nerves, self-doubt, fatigue, and physical pain. He had given of himself physically, spiritually, and emotionally, and he was ready to feast.

Diana's curiosity didn't let him eat for very long. "Are you aware of the audience's reaction as you play?"

Joshua swallowed a mouthful of his goat cheese and spinach crêpe and licked his lips in pleasure before he answered. "When there's a great quiet, a listening stillness, in the hall, then I know the audience is really engaged. But often I'm so completely immersed in the moment, I only know the audience's reaction at the end by the level of applause."

After another bite of his crêpe, he added, "But no matter how excellent the performance may be, a great artist knows that he is simply the servant of the creator, the composer of the music."

"And the creator, too, has his purposes," said Leo. "After the London premier of *Messiah*, when Lord Kinnoull complimented George Frideric Handel, calling the oratorio 'a noble entertainment' for the audience, Handel replied, 'I should be sorry, my Lord, if I only entertained them; I wished to make them better.'"

"There you have it, from one of the world's greatest performer-composers," smiled Joshua.

And on that note, Leo stood up and raised his glass, "To our own Joshua, the Brightest and Baddest Boy of Classical Music."

With much laughter and the cheerful clinking of glasses, they called out, "Hear, hear!"

Cat stayed with Sam while Diana met George for lunch at Levant House on Friday. The store imported foodstuffs from the Levant, the Mediterranean lands east of Italy, including Syria, Lebanon, Jordan, Israel, Palestine, and Cyprus. The region took its name from the French word *levant,* which means rising, or the point where the sun rises. The red brick building that housed the grocery store and café, located in the Warehouse District on Baronne Street, was built in the 1890's. It had high ceilings with overhead fans hanging down, a wooden plank floor, and large windows that made the store airy and bright. The grocery area was to the left of the entrance, six aisles stocked with spices of all types, packaged bulgur wheat, an entire wall of olive oil in gallon containers, canned goods from beans and tahini to baba ganoush, honey, fruit preserves, packaged cookies, candy, pita bread, and loose, bulk tea. In addition to the tea itself, they also sold ceramic and porcelain teapots and cups, long-handled coffee jugs, and coffee sets.

The intimate café area on the right, with its small, square wooden tables was enclosed on three sides. On the street side, just to the right of the entrance, there was a buffet serving area with its offerings of fresh tabouli, stuffed grape leaves, eggplant and other vegetable dishes, as well as sandwiches and plate lunches of beef, lamb, and chicken. A glass refrigerated case standing against the back wall housed Bulgarian, French, and Greek feta cheeses in long tubs, and great wheels of hard, pungent cheeses. The side wall included a double row of barrels with olives floating in brine, and barrels of almonds, pistachios, walnuts, pine nuts, dried apricots, Medjool and California dates, and a pastry case with walnut or pistachio baklava, bird's nest cookies, macaroons, and almond cookies.

Diana loved the Old World atmosphere and smell of Levant House, fragrant with the mingled odors of spices, baked goods, fresh bread, and savory meats. It felt like a mini-vacation to come into the city and take a break from her worries about Sam. She greeted Karim, the manager, who told her George was in his office. She walked through the door at the left rear which opened into the large stockroom. George's office, with two large windows, was immediately on the left. Diana looked wistfully at the accountant's office on the right, formerly Joseph's. Despite his faults, she missed him still.

George greeted her with a smile and a kiss on the cheek. His office contained a desk, computer, and filing cabinets, and, to one side, a sofa and small coffee table. He had Karim bring in lamb kebabs, Diana's favorite, with tabouli, stuffed grape leaves, and bottles of mineral water. Sitting on the sofa as they ate, they chatted about Sam, Joshua's concert, and the previous evening at Marigold's Bistro.

"Have you seen any improvement in Sam?" George asked.

"She showed a flicker of expression at the concert, Leo said. He pointed out the muses painted on the auditorium ceiling and told Sam that Euterpe was the muse of ice cream," Diana laughed. "That got a small reaction. So we're hopeful that she'll come out of this soon."

She took a bite of tabouli.

"What about you, George? You seemed rather subdued last night."

"I was worried about Mamma."

"Well, she seemed a little thin and pale on Monday when Sam and I visited her, but she was in good spirits. When we saw her on Wednesday morning, she said they were going to replace her hip."

"That was the plan originally, but the doctor didn't like her color and vital signs, so he ordered some blood tests. After he got the results of the blood tests, he ordered a CAT scan of her abdomen on Wednesday afternoon, and he called me late yesterday, a few hours before Joshua's concert."

Diana frowned, "Annie didn't say anything about blood tests or a CAT scan."

George smiled sadly, "She wouldn't, especially in Sam's presence. And I didn't want to spoil the concert for you, so that's why I waited until today to tell you. They're not gonna to do the hip surgery because Mamma has cancer."

"Cancer?" Diana's fork clattered against her plate and she sat back abruptly. "What kind of cancer and how advanced?"

"Pancreatic cancer, stage four. They asked me if she has a living will."

Diana's mouth worked, but no words came. Her thoughts fluttered without order or logic, like the pages of a discarded magazine in a capricious wind. *Annie picking at her food, sleeping late, moving slowly. . . aging, that's all, time taking its toll. She was almost eighty, for godsakes. She couldn't be ill.* Diana shook her head and whispered, more to herself than George, "Not pancreatic cancer. It can't be."

George sighed, and lines of worry and sorrow coursed deep paths from his nose to his chin and furrowed across his brow. Ignoring her remark, he said, "We have to make some decisions. She will stay at the hospital until I make the hospice arrangements and we can bring her home."

"Is there nothing they can do for her?"

Closing his eyes, he drew his thumb and forefinger from the outer corners of his eyes to the bridge of his nose. "All that's left is pain management."

The soft-spoken words paralyzed Diana. *All that's left is pain management.* Exactly what Dr. Wun had told her four weeks ago. Her mind reeled. It could not be true; she would not accept the news. "No, George, he must be wrong. Let's get another opinion."

"Diana, a second opinion is not necessary for a person whose internal organs are ravaged by cancer. Besides, the only other place we could take Mamma is Houston, which is almost six hours away by car. I don't want to put her through that." George cleared his throat. "She's gone downhill so fast, I can hardly believe it. She's barely eatin', she's fightin' nausea, and she just seems to get weaker every day. She's sleepin' a lot. . ." His voice faded away. Bending his head forward, he placed his hands on his knees. "It's a matter of a few weeks, if that."

Diana, breathing quickly and feeling inexplicable anger, shook her head several times. "George, this is impossible," she spat. "How can she have stage four cancer? It couldn't have happened so suddenly."

George pressed his lips together, "Diana, I think you know how it can be."

"What are you talking about?"

"Your cancer metastasized first to the liver and spleen, correct? And when Dr. Wun gave you his death sentence, it had already spread to the colon and stomach. But when you were tested last Friday, there was no sign of cancer."

"That's right. Dr. Wun was astounded."

"As well he should be." George regarded Diana. "According to her doctor, Mamma's cancer has metastasized to the liver, the spleen, the colon and the stomach."

"What is that supposed to mean?"

George searched Diana's eyes. "I think you know exactly what that means."

She turned her head away.

George sighed, "We're bringing Mamma home on Monday. Where do you want her to go, Diana, to my house or yours?"

CHAPTER 24

The Truth Revealed

Leo's home, like Sam's, was a wood frame antique house he had restored. The interior of the three-bedroom house had twelve foot ceilings, polished parquet floors, a small kitchen, a dining room, and a living room with a small wood-burning fireplace. Leo, wearing a red apron over his polo shirt and jeans, met Joshua at the door. Rosie wore her usual fur coat.

Looking down at the dog, Joshua said, "Well, Leo, if your car breaks down, you can saddle up Rosie. She's a horse!"

"She's a big 'un. Come on in."

Joshua inhaled the savory scent wafting from the kitchen. "Mmmmh, whatever you're cooking smells wonderful."

"It's chicken parmigiana."

Rosie lifted a very large paw, and Joshua bent down and took it in his hand. "Well, nice to meet you, too, Rosie. It's time we got acquainted, since I'm going to take care of you when Leo's away." He stroked the dog's thick white coat. "Is she a mix or a purebreed?"

"Purebreed Great Pyrenees. They originated in the Pyrenees Mountains as herd dogs for sheep. In spite of their size and the ferocity of their bark, they are gentle giants."

"This climate must be tough on her." Joshua looked into Rosie's deep brown eyes.

"Yes it is. In the summer, she stays indoors by day, and goes out at night. Once the weather cools off in October, she stays outside all the time. The colder it is, the better she likes it." He patted Rosie's head affectionately, and then glanced up at Joshua, "Dinner is almost ready. While I'm finishing up, why don't you take a look around?"

Naturally drawn to Leo's extensive opera collection in the living room, Joshua studied the titles of his LPs, CDs, and DVDs, while Rosie studied him. He sat for a moment in an armchair facing the fireplace and petted the dog. "Jerrica does a great job, Leo," he called. "The house is immaculate."

"Unlike my specs," Leo said, entering the room. As Rosie ambled to his side, he held his eyeglasses up to the light. "I think I got more tomato sauce on these than on the chicken."

Pointing to the stone hearth, Joshua asked, "Do you really need a fireplace in Louisiana? Does it ever get cold here?"

Cleaning the lenses with his apron, Leo replied, "Well, my friend from Alaska said the coldest he'd ever been in his life was duck hunting in a Louisiana marsh at thirty-five degrees. It's a damp, bone-chilling cold we get. But it's not the sustained cold of the North. Our winter comes in waves. A cold front descends from Canada and temperatures drop for a few days, but once the warm Gulf air takes over, the thermometer pops back up into the fifties or sixties until the next front comes through."

Placing his glasses back on his nose, he added, "And then we have our summertime bone-chilling cold. When it's a ninety-eight degree, ninety per cent humidity sauna outside, and you're covered in sweat, you step into a restaurant or public building where the air conditioning is set to sixty-five degrees and pumping out gale-force drafts, then it's jacket time in July. And speaking of restaurants, come on into the dining room. Dinner's ready." He removed his apron with a flourish.

When they were seated and Rosie had parked herself under the table, Leo blessed the food. In addition to the chicken parmigiana, he served a spinach salad and dinner rolls with white wine.

"Mmmmm, the chicken is delicious!" exclaimed Joshua, reveling in the taste of tender chicken and sharp parmesan cheese with tomato sauce.

"My mamma's recipe."

After he had eaten almost all his serving of chicken, Joshua broached the subject that was on his mind. "Leo, what's wrong with Sam? At the bistro last night, she sat there like a lamp extinguished. All the light's gone out of her."

"That's a good way to put it. Last Saturday, someone shot and killed Eliot, her blue jay."

Joshua's gut roiled and he almost threw up. "Oh, no." Laying down his fork and knife, he sat back in the chair. He groaned inwardly; the Beast had lied. *Missed it by a mile.*

Leo adjusted his glasses, "Sam and Diana bought a bird feeder and birdbath and set them up that morning, and then Sam released Eliot. Diana said he flew up to the pear tree near my house and then over to the fence by the mulberry tree close to where Sam stood. Just as he alighted, someone shot him, and the impact knocked the bird up and backwards. Sam caught him as he fell. . ." Leo's voice trailed off. "From that moment to this, she has not uttered a word."

"Why? Is there something physically wrong with her?"

"No, this is Sam's reaction to the emotional trauma. She has withdrawn and doesn't want to speak. The condition is called elective mutism."

Background noises filled in the silence that followed: the whirring of the overhead fans and the soft humming of the air conditioner, the click of Rosie's nails on the floor as she changed position.

Leo said quietly, "The shot came from the direction of your father's house, Joshua."

Joshua closed his eyes, bowed his head, and sighed. Outside, a truck passed by and the sound of changing gears was clearly audible in the room.

Leo regarded Joshua's bowed head. "I met your father that same day, around noon, when he helped move your things into the apartment, and he smelled of gun oil." Leo laid his fork and knife in his plate. Another silence descended, like a death pall. Leo took off his glasses and laid them on the table. "You tried to stop him, didn't you?"

"I couldn't stop him." When Joshua jerked his head up, the sudden movement dislodged the tears in his eyes. "By the time I realized he was aiming at the blue jay on the fence, he fired. I lunged at the rifle, and he struck me with the stock. I passed out. When I woke up and asked if he had hit the bird, my father told me it flew away; he said he missed it. I didn't know if the bird was Eliot or not." Joshua gingerly wiped his eyes, wincing at the pain on the left side of his face. "But now I do. I am so sorry, Leo. I would never have hurt Sam in any way, but especially like that."

Leo put his glasses on and shook his head. "You didn't hurt Sam, Joshua. Someone else did. You are not responsible for the actions of another person, a grown man." He blew out an explosive breath. "What's done is done, and it's not your fault. I suspected that he had done it, but I wanted confirmation."

He tapped his fingers on the table. "There's another question I have. Diana said she never heard a shot. What kind of gun was it?"

"It was a .22, and the reason she didn't hear the shot is because he fired from inside the house, about five feet from the open patio door."

"Well, that explains it."

The telephone rang and Leo got up to answer it. "Excuse me a minute." He disappeared into the living room.

Relief that Leo knew the truth gave Joshua some comfort, but he grieved for Sam's sake. He couldn't sit still. He got up and knelt down beside Rosie who lay on her side just under the edge of the table. She panted open-mouthed even though the inside temperature was seventy degrees. When she sat up on her haunches to greet Joshua, her head came up to the level of the table. Over and over, Joshua stroked the dog's thick, coarse coat from the side of her head, down across her shoulder and her back, drawing comfort from her presence and the warmth and softness of her fur. Rosie grinned and watched him with her deep brown, patient eyes. Animals—dogs, birds, squirrels—such beautiful, innocent creatures. How could anyone hurt them? And yet people did, every day.

Leo returned and stood by the table with a frown on his face. "Diana called about Annie." He took off his glasses and rubbed his eyes. "I was going to tell you what happened to Annie, since you didn't know. When Eliot was shot, Diana and Annie went out in the yard to comfort Sam. Diana stayed with Sam and she sent Annie back to the house to call me. But Annie stumbled and fell on the stone patio and broke her hip. Now Diana says that in addition to the broken hip, Annie has been diagnosed with end stage pancreatic cancer."

"Oh, no." Joshua stood up.

"At the party on the Fourth, I noticed Annie had lost weight, and she ate very little that day." Leo put his glasses back on. "It's so odd."

"What is?"

"She's got the same kind of cancer Diana had, and it has metastasized to the exact same organs."

"How are they going to treat her?" Joshua asked.

"They're not. No hip surgery, no radiation, no chemotherapy. On Monday, they're bringing her home to die."

August

L ike a vessel held in the hands of the Alchemist, the earth is a crucible for matter and its transformation. All matter is subject to the ancient and enduring laws. All that is proceeds from One and becomes many. All that is proceeds out of stillness into motion. All that is proceeds out of the invisible to form the visible. All that is visible is transient; that which is unseen endures. All matter that is and was created is made of four elements: earth, air, fire, and water. They are the foundations of the visible world, and as such, they can be measured. Substance-less ether, the fifth element, fills the void, but, like thought or will or love or grace, it cannot be weighed or measured.

The four sensible qualities of this world are heat, cold, wetness, dryness, and of these, heat is the motive, generative power behind all transformations. Being of one substance, matter can change its state without changing its essence, so that by heat, water becomes vapor (of the air) or by lack of heat, water becomes ice (solid, of the earth), but it is always itself. By heat, a substance can be evaporated and separated from a mixture to obtain its pure state. By fire, controlled at exactly the right temperature for the right duration, the refiner heats the impure ore to liquefy it, so that he may skim off the dross and obtain the purified silver.

Earth, air, water, fire of the sun, ether—body, breath, blood, fire of the heart, spirit: Are these not the same? The earth is a crucible for matter and its transformation. The earth is a crucible for the transformation of the soul.

CHAPTER 25

Fire

I n the South, August is the hottest month. The days are long, and the sun is a brilliant adversary cloaked in fire: unrelenting, insistent, and implacable. Day by day, the heat builds on the earth, in the sea, and in the air. Wild animals and birds feed only at dawn and dusk, seeking shade in which to rest, panting open-mouthed in the middle of the day. On the hard, burning sidewalks of the cities, people walk slowly, as if oppressed; even the rhythms of speech flag. There is a sense of patient enduring, of waiting, of anticipation for the relief to come, for a cool front from the North or a storm to break the relentless heat.

During the second week of August, in the midst of a searing heat wave in which the high temperature exceeded 100 degrees Fahrenheit for eight straight days, two events occurred: the Leviathan civil trial began in New Orleans, and Louisiana's public schools opened their doors. Samantha Faris was one of three hundred freshmen from two different middle schools to enter ninth grade at Jeffrey Lee Travasos High School in Chalice.

From kindergarten on, Sam had attended small Catholic schools, and she expected to attend the Catholic Cabrini High School in the city, but after her father died, as Diana explained, it proved to be too expensive, even with a scholarship. Very few of her classmates, and none of her friends, attended the public high school. Though Diana feared for her daughter, who had yet to utter a word since July, she thought the best course of action was to keep Sam in school and hope for a breakthrough.

The week before school began, Diana conferred privately with Principal Ronnie Bryant to explain the situation. He requested a doctor's excuse to be presented to him and to all Sam's teachers, explaining Samantha's muteness. On the first day of school, Sam gave identical copies of the excuse, signed by Dr. Leo DeLuca, to each of her teachers. No explanation was given to the students, but it didn't take long for her classmates to notice that the petite, dark-haired Sam never spoke.

Although they were not her friends, Caitlin Canard, Tetra Dugas, and Raye Ann Price had attended Sam's middle school, and they shared four classes with Sam at Travasos High School: Algebra I, French I, English I, and Chemistry. More interested in boys than academics, the three girls were indifferent students who regarded Sam's middle school feats of literary and athletic prowess with a mixture of awe and mild dislike.

After the summer break, seeing that Sam obviously was not her old self, they took note. Like predators seeking vulnerable prey, they observed all differences and weaknesses in others. Compassionate as coyotes, and gleefully malicious, as only high school girls can be, they took it upon themselves to plumb the depths of Sam's mysterious muteness by trying to make her speak. They came very close to succeeding, but not in the way they expected.

"Look at her; she's got to be fakin' it," plump, round-faced Caitlin assured her friends. Shaking her mane of sandy hair, she pursed her lips in disapproval and pointed a fleshy, freckled finger toward the back edge of the crowded, noisy school cafeteria. Tetra and Raye Ann turned to stare at Sam who sat alone at a table, isolated in her island of self-imposed silence. Shifting her gaze to her plate, Caitlin ate quickly and voraciously, heaping red beans and rice on her fork and chewing rapidly. With her mouth full, she added, "This whole week, she hasn't said a word in class. It's got to be some kind of attention-getting act."

"Yeah, she can talk all right," agreed green-eyed Raye Ann, who hardly touched her food. Tall, flat-chested, and pear-shaped, she was dieting to take pounds off her hips and the bane of her backside, her doughnut-derived derrière. "I got so tired of her at St. Catherine's. She always knew all the answers, wrote the best reports, and won all those stupid awards. She always had some smart remark to make." She sneered, "She's prob'ly bustin' her gut tryin' *not* to talk."

"Yeah, you right," agreed Tetra. "Remember that time you called her a little pill, and she looked up at you and said, 'If I'm a pill, you must be a tablet.'"

"Shut up, Tetra."

Tetra laughed, "Hey, did ya' see Tony Palmisano lookin' at her funny 'cause she's so quiet?"

"Maybe he was lookin' at her 'cause she's so cute," said Raye Ann with a sideways glance at Tetra. "Cuter than you."

"No, he was lookin' at her 'cause she's so quiet and sorta sad. Wish he'd look at me that way."

"Never mind about Tony, he's too tall for you," said Caitlin.

"No, he's not." Tetra, who wore her long brown hair in a ponytail, was almost as petite as Sam. "He's so handsome." She took a bite of a buttered roll and drank some milk, adding a white mustache to the light coating of hair on her upper lip. "Oh, my God, he just sat down at her table!" The school's star quarterback was so tall and broad-shouldered, he blocked their view of Sam.

"Well, are we gonna do somethin' about it, or what?" asked Caitlin through a mouthful of beans and rice.

"'Bout Tony?" asked Tetra.

"No, sug," she pronounced it *shoog*, "pay attention. 'Bout Sam."

"Yeah," said Raye Ann, "let's make 'er talk."

"How we gonna do that?" Tetra asked, wiping her mouth with a paper napkin.

"Here's how." Raye Ann pinched Tetra's arm hard with a violent twisting motion.

"Ow!" Tetra jerked her arm away. "Are ya crazy? What the hell d'you do that for?"

Raye Ann laughed, "Made you talk, din't I? Get it?"

They carried out their plan immediately. They followed Sam into the restroom and pushed her against the wall. Caitlin, the self-appointed spokeswoman, said, "We know you're fakin' it, Sam. Either say somethin' on your own, or we'll make you talk."

When Sam did not comply, Raye Ann and Tetra pinched her arms as hard as they could. Sam cried soundlessly, but she offered no resistance. Her lack of response unnerved the girls, and when the bell rang for class, the trio of bullies bolted.

By week two, they had pinched Sam so hard and so repeatedly that her arms, encircled by blue-black bruises edged with yellow and green, would have impressed a French Quarter tattoo artist. In order to conceal her condition from her mother, and despite the heat, Sam wore long sleeve blouses to school every day.

Frustrated that pinching elicited no sound and what was worse, no resistance, from their target, Caitlin, Tetra, and Raye Ann decided to up the ante. Working together like a trio of coyotes, they tripped Sam in the busy hallways, and stepped on her hands when she fell. They ambushed her from behind and sucker punched her in the back and stomach. The greatest reaction they got was silent tears, until one day after lunch when the stomach punch produced projectile vomit, and Sam spewed shrimp jambalaya all over Tetra's face. That ended the punching.

Raye Ann, however, came up with a plan for Mr. Musgrove's Chemistry class. By good fortune, or so she thought, Raye Ann sat on the last row of marble-topped lab tables between Sam and Tony Palmisano, who was six feet four, with hands as big as a side of beef. He had to repeat the class, which he had failed the previous year. Caitlin and Tetra sat one row ahead. When Mr. Musgrove disappeared into the supply room at the front to retrieve more flasks for the experiment, Raye Ann, who was six inches taller and forty pounds heavier, muttered to Sam, "Let's see if this'll make ya talk." She grabbed Sam's wrist and tried to force the smaller girl's hand over the flame of a Bunsen burner.

As Raye Ann bent forward, Tony Palmisano, with an athlete's split-second timing, reached under her skirt, clapped his huge hand around the left cheek of her ample fanny and kneaded it like a ball of dough.

Startled, pop-eyed, and open-mouthed as a hooked fish, Raye Ann jerked upright with a gasp, releasing Sam's wrist to strike at Tony's arm. "What are you doin'!" she hissed.

"Squeezin' your butt," he replied with an angelic smile.

"Get your hands off me!"

Hearing the commotion, Mr. Musgrove hurriedly emerged from the supply room with an armful of flasks. "Tony, what are you doin' back there?"

With a final satisfying squeeze, Tony jerked his hand away and raised his massive palms upwards to heaven. "Me? I ain't doin nothin'."

"Well, what you're supposed to be doin' is the experiment, so get to work."

"You jerk," Raye Ann whispered, venomous as a viper.

"Don't you say nothin', or I'll tell him what you have did," replied Tony, whose forte was football, not grammar. "And if you and dose dawgs you call friends don't quit bullyin' that little chahmah Sam, I'll pass by ya house and tell ya mamma how you been smokin' and drinkin' whiskey afta school out dere in da pahkin' lot."

"You better not."

"I will if you don't leave her alone."

When no retort came, Tony grinned and held his hands close to Raye Anne's face, flexing his fingers slowly and suggestively, "F'sure, you got a real nice ass."

A sputtering sound startled them both. They turned to find Sam, head down on the table, shaking with laughter.

That weekend, a passing thunderstorm broke the heat wave briefly. It rained on Saturday morning, holding the temperature down to the high seventies. Sam sat cross-legged on the sofa listening to the drumming of the rain on the roof, as she thought about the past week. After Tony's intervention and threat, the three girls had finally stopped harassing her. And somehow it seemed that a little light had pierced the perpetual grayness that had beset her for so long. Numb and isolated, she had walked in a fog devoid of feeling, caring, or desire. When the girls had pinched and punched her, she had felt it, but she hadn't cared. She had almost welcomed it. Physical pain meant she felt something; it was preferable to her state of walking death. Maybe they had done her a favor, because now that the fog had begun to lift, she didn't feel as numb anymore. But she was very glad to be away from school and at home with Sitti.

The day after Annie Faris came home, Sam handed her mother a paper with the question: *Why is Sitti so sick if she only broke her hip?* Diana decided to tell her the truth as she knew it. They sat on the sofa and Diana took her daughter's hands in hers.

"Sam, somehow, and we don't know when exactly it happened or why, Sitti developed cancer, the same kind I had. Because of that and her weak condition, they couldn't operate on her hip. We. . . uh, we had to bring her home because they say there's nothing more they can do to treat her." Diana tried to put the situation in a positive light. "She hated being in the hospital. Now she'll be here with us all the time, and we're going to do our best to take care of her. I want you to help. Will you do that?"

Sam nodded. She walked to Sitti's bedside, held her grandmother's hand, and laid her head facedown on the pillow beside Annie's head.

"*Albi*, it's all right. I'm glad to be home with you." Annie stroked Sam's hair and met Diana's worried gaze. After a few moments, Annie said, "Sam, will you bring me some black tea and a piece of Syrian bread?"

She did as Annie had asked, and thereafter, Sam attended her or sat by her side, silent, loving, and vigilant as a loyal dog.

Annie slept in the hospital bed they had set up in the living room, three feet away from Sam's perch on the sofa. Although she slept soundly, the rasp of her breathing was clearly audible above the sound of the rain. The lamp on the bedside table cast a golden glow in the dim room. Beside the lamp Diana had set a clock radio, a hairbrush, a glass of water, a straw, and a small brown bottle of morphine.

While her mother showered, Sam decided to check the weather on Diana's computer. The biggest weather topic that morning was the strengthening tropical storm in the Caribbean. Curious, and hoping to distract herself from her worries about Sitti, Sam decided to search for how such storms form. But first, she searched for *Joshua Brightman, concert pianist*, hoping to see a review of his concert. She did find a review, but her attention was caught by a related topic: *Classical pianist injured in drug deal*.

Frowning, she clicked on the link and Joshua's disfigured face materialized in glaring color. There was a brief article about him in the New Orleans online entertainment magazine *The Word on the Street*. The caption under the photo read: *Pianist Joshua Brightman plays concert with a spectacular black eye. Did he fall off a ladder or is it more likely he took a beating in a drug deal gone bad?* Sam inhaled sharply and drew her hands back from the keyboard as if it had shocked her.

At the same moment her mother entered the room. With a quickening pulse Sam closed the window and typed a question in the search bar: *how do hurricanes form?* She stared uncomprehending at the list of articles when Diana ousted her.

"I can see you want to read about hurricanes, Sam, but right now you have to scoot. I'm teaching five courses at Tulane this fall, and with my own illness and now Sitti's illness, I haven't prepared at all this summer. The semester starts next week and I need the computer to work on my syllabi. You can use the encyclopedias instead."

Banished, Sam searched the encyclopedias in Diana's library. When she found an article about hurricanes, she took the book back to the living room.

Disturbed by Sitti's labored breathing and her own chaotic thoughts about Joshua, Sam tried to focus on the hurricane article while questions buzzed in her mind, disturbing as a cloud of mosquitoes. Could it be true? Did Joshua use drugs? Was that why no one told her how he got the black eye? Glancing down at the book in her lap, she didn't even try to read. No, it couldn't be true. Thinking back, Sam remembered how everyone congratulated Joshua after his concert and seemed happy to talk with him. If he used drugs, she knew her mother and Uncle George would not associate with him; they would never approve of such behavior.

But then a chilling thought struck her. Maybe they didn't know what he had done—maybe he lied to them. Maybe. . . but no, how could an addle-brained drughead be a top-notch concert pianist? Drugs would interfere with his memory, his coordination, and his reliability. For a pianist, drug addiction would equal professional suicide.

Still, she couldn't stand it another minute. Shoving the encyclopedia aside, Sam got a piece of paper from her room and wrote a single question on it. She walked into her mother's room and handed the paper to Diana.

How did Joshua get a black eye?

Diana regarded her daughter's knitted brows and worried eyes as a positive sign, evidence that Sam might be emerging from her long apathy. At the same time, Diana wondered what had spurred her to ask the question out of the blue, long after Joshua's face had healed.

She took hold of Sam's hand and answered, "Honey, at first he wouldn't tell Uncle George and Leo what happened, but after his concert, he admitted to Leo that his father hit him."

Sam grabbed the paper and wrote: *Because he used drugs?*

Puzzled by the question, Diana tried to formulate an answer that wouldn't upset Sam, who still did not know Joshua's father had shot Eliot. "Uh, no. They had a bad argument about a gun."

To her astonishment, Sam smiled. Once again she grabbed the paper and wrote: *May I show you something on the computer?*

"Sure." Diana moved aside and Sam quickly pulled up the photograph of Joshua.

Standing beside Sam, Diana leaned forward to peer at the monitor. She immediately recognized the website of *The Word on the Street* and the gossip column by a well-known writer, a name-dropper *extraordinaire,* who chronicled the life and times of local celebrities, socialites, artists, and athletes. There was a lurid photograph of Joshua with its damning caption, followed by a short biography, and the fact that he performed with the Louisiana Philharmonic. The writer gleefully mentioned Joshua's drunken misbehavior prior to a recent concert in San Francisco. The only source cited was: *from one of our readers.*

"Now I see why you asked." Diana stood erect and shook her head. "Sam, that is pure unsubstantiated gossip; it's garbage. As I've told you before, you can't believe everything you see on the internet. I don't know about the San Francisco incident, but I can assure you that Joshua did not get beat up in a drug deal."

Sam rose from the computer and gave her mother a brief, hard hug, which surprised the hell out of Diana and pleased her mightily.

Satisfied and very relieved, Sam spun on her heels and returned to the living room, with her mind free to focus on the encyclopedia article. She read that hurricanes form when there is an area of low pressure over the ocean. Heated by the sun, the warm water evaporates into the air. As the saturated air rises, it cools, and the water vapor condenses into towering cumulonimbus clouds. Thunderstorms form, which begin to rotate slowly, counterclockwise in the northern hemisphere and clockwise in the southern, around the central low pressure area. The warm, moist air and the warm ocean water feed the storms, giving them energy. The rotation, Sam read, is due to the Coriolis Effect, caused by the earth's rotation. The turning of the planet causes the air drawn into the low pressure area to curve and begin the circular motion.

Sam sat up straight. It was easy to forget that even now as she sat in the living room reading a book, the earth was spinning on its axis and flying through space. How strange that despite all that speed and motion, she felt only stillness. She studied several photographs of hurricanes taken from space. The rotating white clouds covered huge areas; one shown in the Gulf of Mexico covered almost the entire body of water. In the center of each was the circular eye. More than anything, the pictures resembled photographs she had seen of spiral galaxies. Clearly, nature's principles remained the same regardless of size or makeup. A ball was a ball, be it a marble, an orange, or the earth itself.

Bending her head over the book again, she read on. The storm was called a tropical depression until the winds reached thirty miles per hour; then it became a tropical storm. When the winds reached seventy-five miles per hour, it became a hurricane.

Taking a break from her work, Diana came into the room and sat beside Sam on the sofa. "Still reading about hurricanes? I hope this latest storm in the Caribbean won't come our way."

When Sam did not respond, Diana put her arm around her daughter. "Did you know that when your dad was a boy, a hurricane passed directly over Chalice? He was six years old and he never forgot it. In the middle of the day, it became dark as night. Thunder boomed, lightning flashed, and the rain fell in sheets, rattling the windows. In the middle of the storm, the power went out, so they lit candles and used flashlights. The streets flooded and the wind gusted up to one hundred-twenty miles per hour. Sitti and Grandpa Albert thought the roof might blow off.

"Then, all of a sudden, it stopped—no wind, rain, thunder or lightning. The sun came out and the sky was cloudless, completely blue. When they went outside to check for damage, Grandpa Albert carried Joseph piggyback through the flooded yard to keep him dry. It seemed as if the storm had passed. It was a bright, calm, perfect day, except that it was eerily silent. No birds sang. Can you guess what happened?" Diana's question was answered by a tiny nod from Sam.

"Yes, you know." Diana kissed her daughter on the head. "Annie, Albert, George, and Joseph, and this very house stood in the eye of the storm. The calm lasted about thirty minutes and then the rain, thunder and lightning resumed, with the wind blowing just as fiercely from the opposite direction. The thing your dad remembered most, was the stillness in the eye of the storm."

With that, Diana and Sam regarded the sleeping Annie, who battled a storm they could not see. "Oh, how I wish she would get well," Diana murmured, as if to herself.

Sam looked up, surprised to see the sheen of unshed tears glistening in Diana's blue eyes.

At that moment, the rhythm of Annie's rasping breathing changed, and she awoke. "Diana," she whispered.

Diana vaulted up off the sofa. "I'm here, Annie." She felt a touch at her side. Sam had risen, soundlessly as a ghost, to stand beside her.

In the two weeks Annie had been home, she had eaten little, complained not at all, and slept at night and for many hours during the day. Diana had administered the morphine very sparingly. She simply put a drop under Annie's tongue if she groaned in her sleep or seemed restless with pain. The roundness and plumpness that was Annie had departed, bringing the bone structure of her face to prominence, and leaving her limbs stick-like and wasted. "Do you need something for pain?"

"No. Please ask Father David to come."

"Now?"

Annie nodded with as much vehemence as she could muster.

When Diana left to telephone the priest, Annie reached out a hand to Sam, "*Albi*, after Father David's visit, I want you to ask Joshua to come see me. Will you do that?"

"Yes. Want some water, Sitti?"

"Ah." On hearing Sam's first speech since the death of Eliot, a great knot relaxed in Annie's breast. Although the only food or drink she wanted was the sacrament, Annie smiled and said, "Yes, thank you, *albi*."

Sam turned the crank to raise the head of the hospital bed. She put a straw in the water and held the glass so her grandmother could drink. "Sitti," she confided, "you're the only one I'm going to talk to."

"All right, *albi*. But soon, I know you will speak to every-one." She sipped a little water. Then she took Sam's hand in hers. "Your voice will make a difference in the world. Will you remember?"

"I will."

"And remember this, too. I love you with all my heart."

Tears sprang to Sam's eyes, "I love you, too, Sitti."

"I had a dream," Annie began, but then she lay back with a small groan. The pain was relentless, but she did not want morphine to dull her mind. She would just have to endure it a little while longer. It was a great effort to speak, and the fatigue she felt was overwhelming. In the dream, the Lord had given her just that day, less than twenty-four hours, and she had much to do. She wanted to tell Sam about her dream of Albert, the garden and the vision of the shining city, but her tongue seemed leaden and heavy as an anchor. A great weight pressed on her whole body, and she faded into unconsciousness.

Father David, dressed all in black with a white clerical collar, arrived at one o'clock carrying a small briefcase. He was a calm presence, his light brown hair and beard flecked with white, his blue eyes serene behind horn-rimmed glasses. At Annie's bedside, he laid a white stole across his shoulders, took out his prayer book, a vial of healing oil, and set out bread and wine for Communion on the table.

With her eyes on the vial of consecrated oil, and Sam's hand locked in hers, Diana asked, "Are you going to try to heal her even now?"

Having presided over many rites of passage, from baptisms, marriages, confessions, illnesses, and deaths, Fr. David stood unruffled beside Annie's deathbed. "While it is true that the sacrament of holy unction is for healing and forgiveness, it is also true that God does not always grant physical healing. So I will administer the sacrament to Annie and pray that God's will for her be done. The anointing is a way of sanctifying her suffering and uniting it to the suffering of Christ."

"So she is going to die," murmured Diana.

"We all die," answered the priest, with a kindly look in his eye, "but as it is written: *Whether we live, we live unto the Lord;*

and whether we die, we die unto the Lord: whether we live therefore, or die, we are the Lord's."

Diana touched Annie gently to wake her. As soon as she saw the priest, Annie thanked him and then asked him to hear her confession. Diana and Sam left the room for a few minutes until Fr. David called them back. Then he celebrated the Eucharist, administering the consecrated bread and wine in their transformed state as the Body and Blood of Christ. Afterwards, they encircled Annie and laid their hands on her, while Fr. David prayed for healing and anointed her with oil.

Although Diana invited the priest to eat lunch with them, he had other appointments and could not stay. With no visible change in her condition, Annie fell asleep again, and Diana and Sam resumed their separate vigils.

CHAPTER 26

Air

A fter a long afternoon practice session with the Brahms first concerto, Joshua made coffee and a sandwich for a late lunch and then sat on the sofa to eat, with his feet propped on the coffee table. He was looking forward to the Seattle Symphony concert coming up in October, and then Detroit in November. Thankfully he had managed to play well in New Orleans in July; the review had been quite good.

He sipped his coffee and thought about the events of the past few weeks. First of all, he delighted in having his own place with its comfort and privacy. The concert had paid him a bundle, which ensured that he could make the payments for rent, the piano, and the student loans without worrying for a while. He had actually bought George's truck outright, at the reduced price of nine hundred, thanks to Catherine's pressure on George about "that heap," as she called it, so he had no car payments. He was even learning how to cook, with the help of Jerrica's recipes. After he had complimented her on the gumbo, she had taken him under her culinary wing. He actually had a flair for cooking.

His cheek had healed; the X-rays showed a fracture, but it did not require surgery. The black eye had long since faded, but invisible scars remained, not only for him, but for the Faris family as well. Thinking of them, he rose to look out at their house. From his apartment windows high above the garage, he could see the small green pears, the ball-like maturing pomegranates, the fig, mulberry, and mayhaw trees, and the sun-wasted garden in Sam's backyard. His injuries had healed, but Sam's wounds had not, and now Annie was dying.

He had visited her when she first came home from the hospital. He had played piano for her, a little ragtime interspersed with hymns from their hymnal, and short pieces by Mozart and Debussy. He hated to see Annie so frail and bedridden, a far cry from the robust woman he had met that first day in the kitchen. As she had prayed for him, so Joshua had prayed for Annie, and for Sam, too. But his prayers seemed to do no good.

Joshua regarded the empty Adirondack chairs on the patio. There, in that house, Annie lay dying. And the light has gone out of bright, cheerful Sam. And here I stand, he thought, powerless to do anything about it.

As he stood at the window, his thoughts returned to the root of all the trouble, the shot fired by the Beast, and the altercation that followed. Pondering Nathan's words, *I think you oughta sue the ass off this guy for assault and battery,* Joshua knew there was no way he could bring himself to take legal action against his own father. It would simply be his word against the Beast's, and his mother, he had no doubt, would back up any story his father concocted. The same problem would exist if Diana tried to take his father to court for killing Eliot. Why is it in this world, he wondered, that those who willfully injure the innocent so often go unpunished?

His mobile phone rang, and he hurried to the coffee table to answer it. Seeing Nathan's name on the lighted screen, he smiled. "Hey, Nathan, how're things in New York?"

"Ah, dude, not too good."

Surprised by the slow tempo of Nathan's speech and his mournful tone, Joshua felt a sudden apprehension. "What's wrong?"

"Well, after you got the great review from the New Orleans concert, somehow your photo ended up in a gossip column on the web. A New Orleans entertainment rag printed a lie about you gettin' beat up in a drug deal."

"What!"

"Bruce the boss got really pissed." Nathan paused, and in the background Joshua could hear the noise of traffic, car horns and roaring engines. "He's fired you, Joshua."

"Fired me?"

"Yeah, I got a call from the Utah Mountain Symphony and a Baptist college in the same town; they wanted to book you for a concert and a masterclass in October. I had the contract ready to sign, but they searched you on the internet, saw the article, and backed out. Bruce was furious. I had to mail you a letter givin' you thirty days' notice. He let you go for besmirching the squeaky-clean image of BG Artists Management."

"Nathan, you know it's not true."

"Yeah, it's libel, pure and simple. I fought Bruce about it, but I guess I went too far, 'cause he fired me, too."

"Oh, no!"

"Oh, yeah."

"Nathan where are you?"

"Fifty-seventh and Fifth, poundin' the pavement lookin' for another job. I called two agencies, and I got an interview with Virginia Webb Artists today in a few minutes and one with Moreno-Menzdorf Artist Management tomorrow."

Joshua tried to take in the news while his head buzzed with questions. "Nathan, what did you say to Bruce to make him fire you?"

"I was respectful. Not one profane word passed through the gate of my big mouth, but I knew the story was a lie, and I insisted that the firm stand up for you. He didn't give a shit for the truth," Nathan's voice cracked. "He only cared about the image, and so I said if they fired you, then I would resign. So he said, 'Don't bother finishing out the day.' I cleaned out my desk and left."

Nathan had stood up and defended him to the point of sacrifice: another casualty stemming from the Beast's acts of cruelty. Joshua felt anger shooting up like hot lava in his chest. How much damage could one man do? By fracturing his son's cheek, the Beast had jeopardized Joshua's career and left Nathan jobless. Would the fallout from that day never end?

"Nathan, thank you for standing up for me, I—"

"It's all right, dude, we'll get past this. And listen, your concerts in Seattle and Detroit are still a go. You'll play those, but after that, they're done with you. Well, here I am at Virginia Webb Artists. Talk to you later, Joshua."

Joshua sighed and sat down heavily on the sofa, knowing what was done was done, and there was nothing he could do to change it. But who had falsely accused him of drug dealing? At least that hadn't come from his father. He picked up the *Times-Picayune* from the Sunday after his concert to reread the review, and study the photographs.

Review: Louisiana Philharmonic

Two Bad Boys of Classical Music

Thursday night's program featured the music of Beethoven, the original nineteenth-century bad boy of music, and the inspired playing of pianist Joshua Brightman, a bad boy musician of the twenty-first century.

He skipped the review of the overture to read the comments about the concerto:

> Soloist Joshua Brightman replaced Tian-Tian Chang who returned to Taiwan to be with her ailing mother. Brightman, a twenty-four year old Juilliard-trained pianist, was recently dubbed the Bad Boy of Classical Music after vandalizing his hotel room and appearing late to rehearsal with the San Francisco Symphony in May. It seems he has a penchant for trouble, as he sported a spectacular facial bruise and black eye. Be that as it may, if he can avoid future conflicts, Joshua Brightman has an enormously promising future.
>
> Like Beethoven, Brightman is clearly devoted to his art. Although Mr. Brightman's technical abilities are impressive, the musicality, poetry, and dynamic power of his playing in both the delicate passages and the strong outbursts of the first movement were truly exquisite, keeping the house hushed and listening throughout. The subdued, melancholy theme of the second movement was beautifully played by the strings and woodwinds, only to be matched by Mr. Brightman's carefully shaded, liquid legato, and heartfelt playing.
>
> Although the third movement tempo seemed a bit on the slow side, lacking somewhat in impetuosity, Brightman and the orchestra still captured the dance-like energy and rhythmic drive which characterize so much of Beethoven's music. While there were some blurred notes in his playing, there was a spontaneity present that made the performance fresh and exciting. We hope Mr. Brightman will return for more engagements with the Louisiana Philharmonic. The evening was time well spent with two bad boys of classical music.

While the review was good, except for the embarrassing mention of his misbehavior in San Francisco, the pictures were painful to behold. Two photographs appeared above Jackson Schrumpf's review. In the first, Joshua, the conductor, and the orchestra stood onstage to acknowledge the audience's extended ovation. The second onstage photo was a striking close-up of Joshua. The facial bruise and black eye on one side of his face contrasted with his fair skin and flushed cheek on the other, to give the effect of a bizarre, asymmetrical Mardi Gras mask.

Wincing at the sight of himself, Joshua laid down the newspaper with purpose. He had to research this smear on his character—the drug deal story. After booting up his laptop and searching less than sixty seconds, Joshua found the website of *The Word on the Street*. There he was amongst local artists, celebrity chefs, jazz musicians, and visiting Hollywood actors. His picture, a different close-up, had obviously been taken backstage after the concert. The photo was bad enough, but the caption was the clincher: *Pianist Joshua Brightman plays concert with a spectacular black eye. Did he fall off a ladder or is it more likely he took a beating in a drug deal gone bad?*

"Either way," he murmured to himself, "why would anyone care?" *From one of our readers.* Really? Who? And why would someone want to smear him like that? Almost anyone who greeted him backstage could have taken the picture, but the person who sent it to *The Word on the Street* had malicious intent.

Suddenly, it hit him—*Taylor Merrick.* She had the means and the motive. She could have taken the picture with her phone, and she would have no qualms about libeling him. Spiteful Taylor— it had to be her. The bit about falling off a ladder brought to mind Charles Merrick's cryptic comment after the concert: *Sorry about the fall.* At the time, Joshua had no idea what he meant. The Beast must have used that story to explain his son's black eye. Taylor had discerned the lie, then added her own ugly accusation about the drug deal and sent it to the magazine.

He was ninety per cent certain she was the culprit, but maybe there was a way to know for sure. Joshua quickly looked up Taylor's Facebook page. He scrolled down through various pictures of her and her friends, and then he found it. Under the heading *Beat Up & Busted—Classical Coke Head,* she had posted three photos of him, two taken from the box seat when he first came out on the stage, and the post-concert close-up.

That clinched it. "Taylor, you vindictive nitwit." Joshua grinned, "Hoist on your own petard, you are."

He returned to the magazine website. Adding insult to injury and further chapping his ass, the short article below the photo also mentioned that Brightman had "trashed his hotel room in a drunken rampage" in San Francisco. He groaned. Would he ever live that down?

"Hope you shitheads have an army of attorneys, 'cause you must be sued on a daily basis, and I'll be the next in line." He didn't care about money; he wanted revenge for the damage Taylor had done him and Nathan.

He heard a quiet tapping at the door. Setting the laptop aside, Joshua opened the door to find Sam standing there. Wearing a black Saints T-shirt with gold lettering and blue jean shorts and sneakers, she frowned at him.

"Sam! Come in."

Shaking her head vehemently, she held out her hand to Joshua. As soon as he took her hand, she turned to go down the stairs, moving rapidly and tugging him after her. He barely had time to shut the door behind him. He had not seen her so animated in weeks. Leading him in a mad dash downstairs and along Leo's driveway, she crossed over into her front yard, threw open the front door and led Joshua directly to Annie's bedside.

Annie was so changed, it was painful to behold her. He felt his stomach muscles contract. The woman he saw before him was a wraith, simply skin on bones, with ropy blue veins rising like ridges on the plains of her hands and arms. Under sunken, shadowed eyes, her nose arched up above stark, protruding cheekbones. As she slept, her shuddering breaths rasped with long pauses in between. Annie, Joshua was certain, walked now through the valley of the shadow of death. Was that why had Sam brought him to her bedside with such urgency?

When Sam touched her grandmother's cheek, Annie's eyes fluttered open. She turned her head, saw Joshua, and a great smile transformed her face. "*Albi*, raise the bed for me," she whispered. Sam turned the crank to bring the head of the bed up.

"Joshua, some water, please," requested Annie. He held the glass and straw for her, and Annie drank small sips, pausing to breathe heavily in between, as if every action was a great effort. At last she sat back, and to Joshua's relief, her breathing eased and quieted. Then she cleared her throat and asked, "Joshua, do you still want me to pray for you?"

Startled that she remembered his request when she lay so close to death, he blurted, "Yes, Annie, but not if you feel too weak."

Without hesitation, she replied, "Let me lay my hands on your head."

In a movement similar to an onstage bow, he bent forward and down so she could reach his head. At the same time that Annie's hands touched his hair, he felt Sam's hands on his shoulder. Joshua waited for what seemed like eons for Annie to speak. He was keenly aware of her touch upon his head, and the warmth of Sam's hands on his shoulder. Just when he guessed Annie's strength had failed, she spoke with surprising power.

"Joshua, before I pray, I want you to forgive the ones who have harmed you. See them in your mind, and tell them that you forgive them everything."

The image of the Beast filled his mind. He could see his father's large, swarthy presence, his shaved head, goatee, and the judging, critical black eyes that had scrutinized Joshua all his life, pinpointing and mocking all his faults and weaknesses. He saw his mother, soft and fearful Amy, who oftentimes took the easy way out, loving her own comfort more than her son's welfare, rarely willing to confront the Beast's excesses and abuses.

How could he forgive them, especially now that the consequences of the Beast's last cruel act kept spreading outward like an oil sheen from a leaking well, staining everything it touched? The Beast had struck down Eliot, and with him, Sam; he had grieved the whole Faris family. Even Annie's fall and broken hip were part of the aftermath.

"Forgive us our trespasses, as we forgive those who trespass against us," murmured Annie.

It hit him like a line drive to the head. *Look at yourself, Joshua.*

How many times had he wished his father dead or tortured, injured, or struck down and humiliated? How many times had he recoiled at his own thoughts of malice, vengeance, and violence? How much rage against his parents had he stuffed down and hidden day in and day out?

"Do you see them in your mind?" Annie asked.

"Yes."

"Can you forgive them?"

Oh, God, he wanted to be free of it all, all the black thoughts, the rage and the guilt. "I want to, Annie; I want to try."

"Speak to them in your mind and tell them now that you forgive them."

As Joshua squeezed his eyes shut, he heard Annie praying for him to release all unforgiveness, and he marveled. On her deathbed, this uneducated, simple old woman interceded for him with the God of all creation. And she did this after his father had inflicted great injury on her and Sam and their whole family. In that moment, Joshua learned the meaning of grace. How, he wondered, had he ever deserved that?

He addressed his father silently: *Dad, I forgive you for all the times you hurt or mocked me or made me feel ashamed. I freely forgive you. I love you and wish you well. And I am sorry for all my anger and malicious thoughts.* He envisioned his mother and forgave her also.

Suddenly, he felt hands laid on his other shoulder, and he knew Diana had quietly joined them.

"I forgive them, Annie," Joshua said, feeling a great weight removed, like a mountain climber who reaches the summit and sheds his heavy pack.

Then, with astonishing intensity, in inverse proportion to her bodily weakness, Annie prayed, imploring the Holy Spirit to heal Joshua in his body, mind, and soul. She commanded the spirits of rejection, resentment, bitterness, and anger to depart from him. While Joshua wondered how she could have seen through him like that, how she could have discerned his innermost thoughts, Annie prayed with the force and authority of a general, expecting to see her orders carried out. And they were.

Joshua felt himself go hot, with a rising pressure in his chest, which quickly grew almost unbearable. He felt Sam and Diana holding on to him, gripping his arms. Annie's prayers only made the pressure and burning pain increase. He couldn't bear it. As he opened his mouth to scream, he felt a sudden sharp tearing in his chest and a convulsion snapped his head back, as if something wrenched itself out of him. He cried out in pain and fear; then his whole body went limp and he fell forward onto Annie as she lay in the hospital bed.

Knocked out momentarily like a prize fighter, he quickly came to. Diana and Sam held him by the arms and walked him a few steps over to the sofa where he sat heavily, blinking and disoriented. After a moment, he realized what had happened.

"It's gone," he said, astonished. "Annie, it's gone." Fear and anxiety, guilt, obsession and compulsion had fled like wraiths and shadows before the sun, leaving his mind as still and un-ruffled as a calm pool. He could not remember a time when he had felt such peace.

She smiled at him, "The Holy Spirit healed you."

"I feel so limp and weak," he said.

Watching him worriedly, Sam sat down beside him.

"Diana," Annie instructed, "give him some hot tea with bread, butter, and honey." Without questioning, Diana hurried to the kitchen.

To Joshua's great embarrassment, his eyes became artesian wells; he wept soundlessly and copiously in relief and release. Sam left his side and returned with a box of tissues.

"You are weak now, but soon you will be stronger than ever," said Annie.

"Thank you for remembering me, Annie, and for your prayers." While Joshua mopped his face with tissue after tissue, Sam sat beside him and threaded her arm through his. She leaned her head on his shoulder in mute comfort. This served to increase the flow of the artesian wells, and his nose ran to boot.

The tea kettle whistled, and shortly, Diana brought a tray laden with the yellow teapot, mugs, spoons, knives, and containers of cream and sugar. Then she returned to the kitchen and brought a second tray with saucers, a round loaf of Syrian bread, butter, and a jar of honey. She poured tea for Joshua and Sam, and some for herself. Glancing at the hospital bed, Diana asked, "Annie, can you drink a little tea?"

"Yes, *albi*, I think so."

Diana poured the tea in a mug, added cream and sugar, and brought it to Annie. She held the cup and helped her mother-in-law drink a few sips. Lying back on her pillow, Annie spoke very softly, "Diana, tell George and the whole family to come tonight. I'm going home."

Diana knew exactly what that meant. Remaining at Annie's side, she said quietly, "Annie, what about Sam?"

Understanding Diana's unspoken plea, the old woman took her hand and said cryptically, "There will be a storm, and in one week, Sam will be well." She squeezed Diana's hand, "In one week." Annie closed her eyes and loosed her grip. "Wake me when George comes," she murmured, and instantly drifted off to sleep.

Late that afternoon, after Joshua left, Diana and Sam ate a dinner of cold cuts, cheese, and salad. Diana called George and gave him Annie's message, and he promised to come later that evening. Around eight-thirty, tired from the emotional events of the day, Sam fell asleep on the sofa. Diana roused her and sent her to bed after she kissed her grandmother goodnight.

Diana kept a solo vigil on the sofa. She held a book in her hands, but couldn't read. She watched the wasted form of her mother-in-law, observing with alarm the shuddering rise and fall of her breaths, noisy and irregular, with long pauses in between. After the great energy surge that allowed her to pray for Joshua, Annie had spiraled downward precipitously. That show of strength, Diana realized, had been the last hurrah before death.

As she watched her mother-in-law die, Diana examined herself, her feelings of resentment and pent-up anger. She had held onto her anger at Annie and George because they had concealed Joseph's gambling and stealing. That anger had grown into a wall, blocking her sight, blinding her. Diana knew that she, not Annie, should have been the one taking her last breaths. As much as she resisted the thought, and denied it, as much as it defied logic, the truth, was plain and unavoidable: Annie lay dying in her place.

Standing back by the hall entrance earlier that day, Diana had heard Annie tell Joshua to forgive all those who had harmed him, which he clearly had done. Couldn't she do the same? How long could she hold a grudge against the family who had given her a home, a daughter, and now, and now. . .

What is wrong with you, Diana? For God's sake! Joseph was dead, the money was long gone, and she knew that part of the reason Annie and George withheld the truth was to try to shield her and make it right. *Diana, it's over. It's done. Let it go!*

She thought of the time Annie had prayed for her in Arabic, concealing the content of her prayer and how on another occasion she had angrily told Annie to stop praying for her. Now Diana knew what Annie's petitions had been and she knew those petitions had been granted.

Diana recalled her conversation with Sam in Café Massenet the day Annie took them shopping. Sam had been so sure: *God can do the impossible if people believe.*

What happens if they don't believe?

Then God goes to Plan B.

Annie's prayers for Diana's healing had no effect because Diana's anger and resentment had blocked her healing, so Annie, with God's help, had turned to plan B, as Sam said. Annie had asked God to take Diana's illness upon herself. She had given her life for her angry, resentful daughter-in-law.

As Diana's vision blurred with tears, she laid aside the book, drew her knees up and clasped them with her arms. Then she just let go—all the pent-up anger, resentment, the sorrow over Joseph's lies, betrayal, and death, the sadness and worry about Sam, her guilt that Annie was dying in her place, and the shame that she had denied it. The emotions battled their way out of her body. The spasm-like contractions of her diaphragm forced air up from her heaving lungs, through the aching knot in her throat and out of her open mouth. Her tears, like liquid fire, burned their way through her eyes. She heaved and sobbed until her eyes were swollen, her throat was raw, her body ached, and she was entirely spent.

The box of tissues Sam had brought for Joshua still sat on the coffee table. Diana wiped her eyes and blew her nose, feeling emptied, exhausted, but free of all the darkness that had inhabited her soul. She rose on wobbly legs and walked to Annie's bedside. Clasping the old woman's hand in hers, she said quietly, "Annie, can you open your eyes?"

There was no response.

Knowing that hearing was the last sense to go, she tried again, "Can you hear me, Annie?" Diana waited while a shuddering breath shook Annie. "Squeeze my hand if you can hear me."

Diana's pulse jumped when Annie's hand briefly tightened on hers.

Quickly, with a great sense of urgency, Diana confessed, "Annie, I am sorry for all my anger towards you and Joseph and George. It's gone; I'm not angry anymore. I loved Joseph, and I love you. Can you forgive me?"

When she felt the pressure of Annie's grip, Diana's tears flowed again. "Thank you, Annie, for your prayers and for giving me my life back."

Annie squeezed Diana's hand once more, and then her hand went limp.

George and Catherine arrived shortly after. They tried to rouse Annie gently, but she remained unresponsive. Taking turns, they spoke to her quietly, telling her they loved her, and then they held hands and George prayed aloud for peace to enfold her, for cessation of all pain, and for her release into the Lord's keeping.

About midnight, as the three of them stood at her bedside, Annie's breathing slowed greatly. After a long pause, she took a great breath, and, surprising them all, exclaimed in a tone of wonder, "My Jesus!" as though she saw Him face to face. And then she was gone.

George bowed his head and closed his eyes. Then he bent down and kissed his mother gently on the forehead. Cat put an arm around George's waist to comfort him.

"George, I'm so sorry," Diana said. "I denied it for so long, but I know she took my illness on herself. . . and . . ."

"Diana," he replied, "first of all, it wouldn't have happened if the Lord didn't will it. And secondly, Mamma wanted to do it; it was her gift to you and to Sam. She never spoke to me about her decision, or told me this, but I believe she did it so Sam would have her mother."

Keeping her arm around George, Cat looked toward the hall and said quietly, "And here she is, Diana."

Sam, dressed in pajamas, entered the room as slowly as a sleepwalker, holding a thin book against her chest. It was as if she already knew.

Diana hurried to her daughter and embraced her, "Sam, Sitti has gone to be with the Lord."

Sam held out the book to her mother.

Puzzled, Diana took it, opened it, and turned a few pages.

"What is it, Diana?" asked Cat.

"This is Annie's journal. She's written down all her recipes for us."

Sam's face remained an expressionless mask. To everyone's surprise, it was Diana who burst into tears.

CHAPTER 27

Earth

On Monday, the front page of the *Times-Picayune* carried two reports which captivated the local populace. The lead article covered the progress of the Leviathan civil trial, in which the oil company, if found grossly negligent, was at risk to pay billion dollar fines for violating the Clean Water Act. The other article chronicled the approach of Hurricane Delilah. The hurricane, upgraded from tropical storm status, had entered the Gulf on a track to threaten New Orleans in the next few days. A third brief notice, found on a back page and significant to only a few, was Annie Faris' obituary. Her funeral was scheduled for ten a.m., on Wednesday at St. Basil's Orthodox Church in Metairie.

By Wednesday morning, the cloud cover from the hurricane was extensive and the rains came. During the funeral service,

Diana and Sam stood, as was customary in the Orthodox Church, in the front right hand pew beside George, Cat, Michael, and Lucy. Leo, Joshua, and Richard, Lucy's boyfriend, stood just behind the family. Annie's open coffin, draped in a heavy white pall pulled to her chest, rested at the head of the center aisle near the altar steps. The church seated about three hundred people and it was two-thirds full despite the inclement weather.

To enter St. Basil's Antiochian Orthodox Church was to leave the jarring, jangling Western world and step into a hushed haven, a sanctuary sprung from the East like Christ Himself. It was a small stone church with wooden pews and a slate floor. Above the wainscoting, the white plaster walls soared to a vaulted ceiling. The rich, pungent smells of incense and beeswax candles lingered in the atmosphere like the prayers of the faithful. The *iconostasis*, a screen covered in icons at the front, separated the nave from the altar. It contained a central door, called the Beautiful Gate, used only by the clergy, and two doors for the servers on either side.

Diana recognized the life-size full figure icons: to the right, Christ, St. John the Baptist, and the archangel Michael, and to the left, the Theotokos holding the Christ child, the archangel Gabriel, and St. Basil. Framed in rich brown wood, each image, in colors of crimson, blue, and white, stood out against backgrounds of shimmering gold. In this place of unchanging, eternal mysteries, the holy presences kept a serene and ceaseless vigil.

Intermittent lightning illuminated the jewel-like colors of the icons and the beautiful stained glass windows depicting Saints and Apostles. Thunderclaps and the rattle of rain on the roof and windows played an irregular counterpoint to the singing of the choir and the priest's chanting. The music, whether unison chant or stark two-part harmony consisting of a droning bass overlaid with mournful and pungent Middle Eastern melodies, added to the solemn, otherworldly atmosphere.

As Fr. David, in full length, brocaded white robe, celebrated the Divine Liturgy, Diana's thoughts returned to the night of Annie's death. She relived her own tearful confession and request for pardon from Annie, and the pressure of Annie's hand, a sign that she forgave Diana.

A tug on her sleeve brought Diana's attention back to the present. Sam pointed to a question she had written on a scrap of paper: *What does* Eucharist *mean?* Embarrassed that she did not know, Diana quickly and unobtrusively looked up the word using her mobile phone. She held the display so Sam could read it. *Eucharist is a Greek word which means thanksgiving.* Diana leaned over and whispered in Sam's ear, "It's a thanksgiving and remembrance of Christ's sacrifice for us."

She clicked off the phone, and put it in her pocket, struck by her own words. *A thanksgiving and remembrance of Christ's sacrifice for us.* The Eucharist recalls the crucifixion; the direct intervention of God into the story of mankind. It is the intersection of time and eternity: it makes Christ's sacrifice for our sins always and ever present. By obedience to the demands of love, regardless of personal suffering, the Innocent One atoned for all our sins and opened the gates of Paradise. Forever after, Diana knew, the Eucharist would have an added meaning for her, because of what Annie had done. And it was a gift freely given. Following Christ's example, Annie had offered her life for Diana's; she had given all that she had.

At the conclusion of the service, members of the congregation approached the open coffin. The family came last, and each one kissed Annie's forehead in farewell. Father David anointed Annie with the sign of the cross, reciting from Psalm 51, "Sprinkle me with hyssop and I shall be clean. Wash me and I shall be whiter than snow." When he laid earth upon her body, also in the form of the cross, he quoted Psalm 24, "The earth is the Lord's, and the fullness thereof; the world and all that dwell in it." Then, from the third chapter of Genesis, "You are dust and to dust you shall return."

Although she saw before her the inert and lifeless body of her mother-in-law, Diana knew with absolute certainty that Annie was not in that white-draped coffin. It was far too small to contain one who lived, Diana was sure, forever with the Lord. And where was the Lord, whom Heaven and earth could not contain? He was always present in the sanctified bread and wine; he was present here and now in his splendid and holy creation. He was everywhere and always present. Diana's fears, doubts, and guilt faded away like smoke before the wind. Like an overflowing cup, she brimmed with thanks for the gift of her life. She draped an arm around Sam's shoulders and prayed a silent prayer, as heartfelt and humble as it was brief: *O Lord, thank You for my life. Please make me better than I am.*

As she followed the coffin out of the church, Diana realized that her physical recovery was only part of her healing; the Diana who walked out of the church was a new and different person from the one who had entered. She smiled, hearing Annie's voice in her mind: *And,* albi, *isn't that the point?*

Thankfully, the squall that had deluged the area had passed by the time they arrived at the gravesite. There was a light rain falling that was negligible by Louisiana's usual monsoon standards, but because of the threatening hurricane, few people followed the hearse to the cemetery. So in the end, it was almost a private service, with just family and a handful of friends present. They stood crowded together under a light canopy beside the tomb.

Father David continued with the Trisagion, intoning three times, "Holy God, Holy Mighty, Holy and Immortal, have mercy on us." He asked Christ to "give rest with the Saints to the soul of Your servant where there is neither pain, grief, nor sighing but life everlasting."

Let it be so, thought Diana.

Diana held her daughter's hand in the car as George and Cat drove them home. She glanced down at Sam's wild mane of dark brown hair. Sam had not spoken, cried, or visibly grieved for Annie, but Diana had hope. On Saturday, Annie had predicted a storm, which was now upon them, and she had also predicted that Sam would speak within one week. Diana calculated mentally: today was Wednesday, so the breakthrough would be Thursday, Friday, or Saturday. If Annie predicted it, Diana knew it would happen. Sam would soon speak; she would talk to them, and she would be herself again.

The break in the weather ended, and they drove through heavy, driving rain. The windshield wipers fought off the torrential downpour, and the headlights cut a narrow path of light through the darkening day. The storm was coming, as storms would always come, but Diana felt unafraid and calm. *Earth, ashes, and dust*—that was all they had buried. Annie lived, and so did she, and Diana knew without a doubt that somehow, despite earthquake, fire and storm, or any other adversities life might bring, all would be well.

CHAPTER 28

Water

L ike wars, but on a smaller scale, hurricanes are big business. And business boomed on Thursday in the greater New Orleans area. Lumberyards, hardware stores, and grocery stores were swamped with people making last-minute preparations for the approaching hurricane. The hottest commodities were sheets of plywood, hammers, nails, masking tape, gas generators, flashlights and batteries, bags of ice, bottled water, candles, matches, bread, and, true to the tradition of south Louisiana, alcohol, in all its various and sundry forms. Delilah was on her way, now upgraded to a category four storm, forecast to make landfall along the Louisiana coast in the wee hours of the night.

Diana and Sam were spared the long lines at the grocery store because George was bringing them supplies from Levant House later that day. He and his crew boarded up the store windows and closed at noon so everyone could get home and make their own preparations. In the meantime, Joshua and Leo finally located a lumberyard that had not sold out of plywood. It was the first time Joshua had used the pickup to haul something. After they loaded the bed with sheets of plywood and tied them down, Joshua threaded his way out of the crowded parking lot through the steady rain.

Leo patted the dashboard, "So did you buy this beauty for twelve hundred?"

Joshua laughed, "That was George's original price, but Catherine wouldn't have it. She made him come down to nine hundred."

"Whoa, can't go much cheaper than that for a vehicle that actually runs," said Leo. "And actually, aside from a pirogue, a pickup is the best vehicle to have in these parts because of days like today."

"What's a pirogue?"

"Originally, they were cypress dugouts the Cajuns used to navigate the shallow waters of the swamps and marshes, but nowadays they're narrow, flat-bottomed boats. So, in lieu of a pirogue, when the streets flood, like today, a truck is a lot safer than a car because it sits up high."

Joshua discovered the truth of Leo's words on the way home. The trip should have taken fifteen minutes, but it took forty-five. Water flowed in rivers down the sides of some streets, while others were already completely awash and almost impassable. Traffic slowed to a crawl as the vehicles venturing into deep water left wakes like boats, threatening to swamp those around them. Some cars were already flooded out and abandoned on the sides of the road.

"I might have to drive up there on the median, if the water gets deeper."

"Hate to tell ya, but in New Orleans, there ain't no median," said Leo.

"Sure there is," replied Joshua, "right there." He pointed to the raised, grassy divider between the two lanes of traffic.

"In this town, my boy, that is called the neutral ground, and don't you forget it."

Being a fast learner, Joshua replied emphatically, "Yeah, you right," in his best New Orleans-ese. And as it turned out, he never had to drive on the neutral ground; Joshua's truck stayed high and dry.

When they got home, Leo opened the garage doors and set up two sawhorses where he could work out of the rain. While he and Joshua unloaded the plywood, Diana and Sam, wearing rubber boots and yellow raincoats, came over to help. Using his circular saw, Leo cut the plywood sheets down to window-size segments. Diana held them over the windows while Sam and Joshua, wearing a hooded green raincoat, perched on ladders and nailed them into place. The north side of the house was somewhat sheltered by the eaves, but on the south side they battled gusting wind and heavy rain. To Joshua's surprise, while he managed to pound his left thumb and forefinger nearly as often as he hit the nail heads, Sam handled a hammer with the authority and economy of an experienced carpenter.

"Shit!" He did it again.

Sam gave him a stern look.

"I know," he replied to her dark-eyed, silent censure, "I remember the first time we met you told me that those words are not polite. I replied that I am not polite." He smiled at her and Diana, "And, although I am feeling worlds better, thanks to your Sitti, that statement is still unfortunately true."

By three o'clock, with only a quick break for sandwiches and coffee, they had finished the windows in Leo's house, Joshua's apartment, and Diana's house. Joshua and Leo were still at Diana's when George and Catherine arrived. They brought ice, bottled water, groceries, two ice chests, and extra flashlights and batteries. George, with Michael's help, had boarded up his house. Lucy was staying the night at Michael's apartment, and George and Catherine had decided to ride out the storm with Diana and Sam.

While they discussed their plans, Joshua went into the kitchen and called his mother. Since his parents were not hurricane veterans like Leo and the Faris family, he asked his mother if she wanted him to come over and board up the windows or bring some supplies.

"Hold on, honey, and let me ask Billy. He's here. Leviathan sent everyone home at noon today, and the judge suspended the trial until Monday."

Joshua heard his mother's muffled voice as she addressed Billy. After a brief pause, his father erupted, shouting in the background. "Hell, no, I don't want his help! He probably doesn't know which end of a hammer to hold. If I need groceries or something done around this house, you can be damn sure I'll do it myself."

His mother cleared her throat, and said, "Uh, Joshua, your dad said to thank you, but he's going to take care of it himself."

"I see." Well, he had tried, and that was all he could do.

Catherine volunteered to cook chicken and dumplings to feed the tired, hungry crew. Since everyone was off work on a weekday, there was a kind of subdued party atmosphere, on the lines of a wake, since it was the day after Annie's funeral. While Catherine worked in the kitchen, George handed out cold bottled beers, and Diana sent Sam to shower.

"How is Sam doing," Leo asked, "since Annie passed away?" He sat beside Diana on the sofa.

"Well, as you saw yesterday, she showed almost no emotion. Just before Annie's death, though, she had been a little more expressive and active. She actually gave me a hug one day, but now she seems to have withdrawn again." Diana didn't mention why Sam hugged her because then she would have had to discuss the online magazine article with Joshua's photo and the false allegation about a drug deal. She wondered if Joshua had seen it himself, but she didn't ask; she didn't want to surprise or embarrass him.

Joshua took a seat on the piano bench. "Sam was a great help today, hammering like a carpenter," he said, taking a sip of his cold brew.

"Well, we've been through hurricanes before, so she's had plenty experience."

George held his beer in one hand and took a cigar out of his pocket with the other. Weary from the labors of the day and quietly grieving for his mother, he leaned back on the loveseat across from Diana and Leo. "Has she spoken at all since the day Eliot was killed?"

Diana shook her head, "Not as far as I know." She frowned. "George, you're not going to smoke that cigar in my house, are you?"

"No, just holding it for comfort," he smiled. "You know, Sam's been mute for over a month." George rolled the cigar between his thumb and index finger. "Have you thought about taking her to a specialist?"

"I was on the verge of doing that when Annie told me Sam would speak again in one week."

George raised his eyebrows and sat up straight, "When did Mamma say that?"

"The day she died."

"Hmmph. So Sam's gonna speak sometime in the next three days." George smiled and sat back in the loveseat, "Well, if Mamma said it, that's good enough for me." He put the cigar in his shirt pocket. "How's Sam doin' in school?"

Diana lifted her shoulders and both palms toward the ceiling and then dropped them. "I'm not sure; it's too soon to tell as far as grades go. I explained the situation to the principal, and Leo prepared a medical excuse which Sam presented to all her teachers. How the students are treating her, I don't know. I hope they're leaving her alone, but kids can be quite cruel, especially teenage girls."

The conversation ended when Sam returned pink-cheeked from the hot shower, dressed in shorts and a bulky Saints sweatshirt.

"Aren't you gonna be too hot in that sweatshirt, Sam?" asked Catherine.

Sam shook her head vehemently.

"Well, that's a definite *no*," remarked George.

"My turn," Diana announced, and left to take her shower.

Sam walked directly to the piano, looked at Joshua, and wiggled her fingers above the keys without touching them.

"Do you want me to play?" Joshua asked.

She nodded and stood expectantly beside him.

"Scott Joplin," Joshua announced. He played *The Entertainer* because he liked it, and then he played *The Cascades* in honor of the pouring rain.

When the applause died, George prompted Joshua, "Don't stop now; you're just gettin' warmed up."

Swiveling around on the bench to face his audience, Joshua replied, "Okay, but now I'm gonna switch gears. This one's for Annie. It's from a Mozart Sonata in A Major. The last movement is his tribute to Middle Eastern music, a Rondo in the Turkish style, imitating the trumpets, drums, bells, and cymbals of the Turkish military bands, played by Joshua Brightman, with his hammer-battered thumb." He whirled around to the keyboard and launched into the highly rhythmic piece, with its quick-turning melody accompanied in a jaunty, jangling, percussive style. Leo, George and Cat instantly recognized the familiar theme. They smiled as they listened, nodding in time to the irresistible music, all the way through.

Just as Joshua struck the final chords, Diana entered the room, and everyone applauded. Seizing the moment, Diana stopped in her tracks, glanced at them all, and said, "Why, thank you!"

Joshua and Sam turned and looked at Diana, scrubbed and flushed from her shower.

"Were they all clapping for me, Sam?"

Sam shook her head and pointed at Joshua.

"Oh," said Diana, feigning disappointment, "and I thought everyone missed me while I was gone."

"I certainly did," said Leo.

Diana glanced at him and to cover her surprise, quickly said, "Joshua, play on."

But Leo and sharp-eyed George noticed the deepening pink of her cheeks.

At dinner, as they ate Catherine's chicken and dumplings with a green salad, Leo confessed to Joshua, "Hope you don't mind, but I had to record the two Joplin rags on my phone."

"You *had* to?"

"Mm-hmmh. Otherwise Jerrica would have killed me."

Joshua laughed, "You are a prudent man, Leo."

"Indeed. Completely invested in self-preservation."

After dinner, they crowded around Diana's computer for a hurricane update. Delilah was still a category four storm, three hundred-fifty miles in diameter with winds of one hundred forty-five miles per hour. She lay about seventy-five miles southeast of Grand Isle on the Louisiana coast, moving in a northeasterly direction at twenty-five miles per hour.

Leo thought of the Clostio family, and all those he had interviewed on the coast. He prayed they had evacuated to higher ground.

"Well, unless things change, it looks like we're in for a direct hit in about four or five hours," said George. "I hope we don't get the northeast quadrant."

"Why is that?" asked Joshua.

"Then we got the greatest chance of tornados, and I'm more worried about them than the hurricane itself."

Leo and Joshua left not long after to go home, shower, and get ready for whatever the storm might bring. By nine o'clock, fatigued from her hard-working day, Sam fell asleep sitting up on the sofa. Diana woke her and sent her off to bed. By that time, the strengthening wind howled around the corners of the house and the rain whipped through the air in sheets. When Diana peered out the front windows, the submerged street looked like a fast-flowing river.

An hour later, hearts aching for the loss of Annie, exhausted from the physical labor of the day, and knowing they could do nothing more to prepare, they went to bed. Diana slept in her room and George and Cat settled down in the third bedroom.

She walked in the most beautiful garden she had ever seen. The flowers and grass seemed to glow with color and light. The air was alive with their delicate perfumes. The trees were unlike any trees she had ever seen; she did not know their names. The rustling of their leaves in the light breeze was like soft and comforting music. She followed a white stone path that curved gently through the garden, which seemed very large.

Sam didn't know where she was, but she felt intensely happy; she wanted to stay there forever. In the distance, she could hear the sound of flowing water, and she hoped the path would lead her to it. When she rounded a bend, she saw the shining stream, and a lady who stood on the far bank.

Sam quickened her pace and came to the stream's edge. It was only about eight feet wide and a few feet deep. The crystal clear water rushed and sparkled over a bed of brightly colored stones. The rapid current made its own music, joyful and bright.

Captivated by the stream, Sam almost forgot the young woman standing only a few feet away on the other bank. She lifted her eyes to the woman and was struck by her beauty. Like everything in the garden, the lady seemed to glow with an inner light. Sam guessed she might be thirty years old, about Lucy's age, and she wore a long white gown with a wide, shining rose-gold band around her waist. Her hair was dark and tumbled thickly in deep curls from her head to her shoulders, reminding Sam again of Lucy. Her eyes seemed so kind and loving that Sam wanted to cross the stream and go to her, but something held her back.

"Do you live here?" Sam asked.

"Yes, I do."

"I wish I lived here. It is so beautiful and so peaceful."

"Someday you will live here, too."

"Well, since I'm already here, do you think I could just stay? I really don't want to go back. Maybe I could stay with you." As she spoke the words, Sam realized that she had probably overstepped her bounds. Her mother would not want her to speak so trustingly to a stranger, but somehow she knew the lady was kind and loving and would do her no harm.

"Someday, Sam, you will stay with me, but not yet. You have much to do when you go back."

"How did you know my name? And what do I have to do?"

"I will tell you, but first I want to show you something." The lady sang a wordless, flute-like melody, and held out her hand.

Sam heard an answering call, and she saw what she thought was a flash of blue and silver light. Suddenly a glistening bird, more beautiful than any Sam had ever seen, alighted on the lady's outstretched hand. The bird looked at Sam and burst into a song suffused with sweetness and joy and recognition.

Suddenly she knew him. "Eliot!" she exclaimed. "You're alive!"

The bell-like peal of the lady's laughter, the bird's song, and the countermelody of the brook made the sweetest music Sam had ever heard. Her heart, which had been sad for so long, was healed in an instant.

"Do you know now what you have to do when you go back?" asked the lady.

"Does it have to do with my voice?" asked Sam.

"Yes it does. There are many who wish to hear you speak and sing again. Will you do that?"

"Yes."

"It is important, Sam, for your voice will make a difference in the world." The lady turned to go.

"But wait," Sam said, "how did you know my name?"

Her smile was glorious, like a flash of light, and she said, "*Albi*, do you not know me?"

And then Sam awoke, and it was night.

Rain and gusts of wind rattled the windows; lightning flashed, followed by thunder crackling with enough power to split the sky. Disoriented at first, she remembered she had decided to sleep in Sitti's bed, and she had cried herself to sleep. Under the covers, she held Sitti's journal hard against her chest, the journal she had discovered under her grandmother's pillow. She missed Sitti terribly; she longed to see her again.

As she rubbed the sleep out of her swollen eyes, she suddenly remembered the beautiful dream, and her heart leapt. Her wish had been answered; she *had* seen Sitti, but she hadn't recognized her at first. She had seen her grandmother as she must have looked as a young woman. And she had seen Eliot, more alive and beautiful than ever. Wide awake and elated, Sam decided the news couldn't wait until morning; she had to tell her mother immediately.

She sat up, switched on the lamp, and heard the heavy rumble of a train. Sam wrinkled her brow; how could that be? There was no railroad nearby, but the powerful sound grew in volume and intensity as though a freight train bore down on the house. When the lamp blinked out and the air conditioning cut off, adrenaline shot through her body. Terrified, Sam realized the noise was not a train—it was the roar of an oncoming tornado.

She ripped off the covers and darted to Diana's room. Flinging open the door with such force that it slammed into the wall, she screamed, "Mamma, wake up—a tornado is coming!"

Diana vaulted out of bed, dragging the bed covers with her. "Go get George and Cat."

Sam dashed back down the hall and pounded on the bedroom door, "Uncle George, Aunt Cat, a tornado!"

Seconds later, George and Cat charged out of the room holding their pillows. George slammed the door shut behind him. "Close all the doors to the hall and lie down on the floor," he yelled over the roar of the maelstrom. Once that was done, in the utter blackness, Diana pulled Sam down and lay on top of her. Cat lay beside Diana, and George lay on top of his wife and draped the bed covers and pillows over them all. "Lord Jesus, protect this house," he prayed.

His voice was drowned out by the deafening roar. They heard debris pounding the roof and the outer walls and the sound of breaking glass. They lay in total darkness with eyes squeezed shut and muscles tensed, starting at every thud and crack against the house, expecting the roof to collapse and bury them. Fear and heart-pounding dread expanded every second to a hellish eternity. The wind shrieked around the house demonically, seeking entrance. Sudden, terrific gusts buffeted the old house, rattling the windows and shaking the doors. Even the floor and the walls vibrated in the assault. As Diana gripped her hard around the waist, Sam covered her ears with her hands and trembled.

Then, abruptly, it was over. The wind and terrible roar subsided, leaving them sweating and panting for breath. George threw off the blankets. "So far, so good. Thank God we're all right."

As they scrambled to their feet, Diana said, "And thank God Sam is speaking again."

Catherine, still on her knees, hugged Sam, "If it took a tornado to do it," she said, "then I'm very glad to have endured one."

"It was my dream that did it," said Sam.

"This is a dream I want to hear about," said George, "but first, I think we'd better take flashlights and have a look around to check for damage. Everybody get dressed and put on shoes in case there's any broken glass on the floor."

When they were ready, with flashlights shining, they walked from room to room through the house. Rain still battered the roof, and the wind moaned and wailed like a lost soul.

"No leaks I can see," said George, "so the roof must be intact. And looks like the plywood saved all the windows."

"But what about the sound of breaking glass we heard?" asked Diana.

"The sound was close," he said. "It must have been Leo's house or the Brightman's."

Then they heard the screams.

George grabbed his raincoat, ran out the front door, and shone the flashlight first to the right at Leo's house, which stood, and then to the left. The Brightman house was a heap of rubble. The woman's screams came from there. "Brightman's house is destroyed. I'm going over there," he shouted. "Diana, call Leo. We may need medical help."

When her mobile phone didn't work, Diana used the landline to call Leo. In the meantime, Cat and Sam pulled on their raincoats, and Sam got one for her mother. Diana quickly told Leo what had happened and asked him to meet them at the Brightman's house. She hung up the phone and said, "We should call Joshua, but I don't have his number."

"I'll go get him!" exclaimed Sam. The three Faris women hurried out the front door into darkness, rain, and wind. Diana and Cat ran left, and Sam ran right.

With her flashlight clutched in her hand, Sam bolted across the sodden grass of her front yard to Leo's driveway. She splashed through puddles of water on the slippery concrete, and then ran up the stairs to Joshua's apartment. The power was off everywhere, and without street lights and porch lights, the night was very dark.

"Joshua, Joshua!" she shouted, as she pounded on his door with the butt of the flashlight.

Barefoot, wearing jeans and a T-shirt, he opened the door with a startled expression, "Sam, you're talk—"

"Joshua, your parents need help! The tornado destroyed their house."

He ran for the bedroom, drew on shoes and socks.

Sam called out, "Mamma, Uncle George, and Aunt Cat went to help them. And Mamma called Dr. Leo."

Joshua grabbed his raincoat and ran back to the living room where Sam waited. "Let's go!" he said, and holding hands, they bounded down the stairs.

They ran up Leo's driveway, crossed Sam's front yard, and came to a dead stop in the Brightman's front yard. Shocked, they struggled to make sense of the scene, astonished by the utter destruction of the brick house that had seemed so imposing. The house was an unrecognizable pile of debris. In the middle of the rubble heap, where the living room had been, George and Leo frantically lifted bricks, broken sheetrock, and splintered lumber, while Diana held two flashlights on the debris pile so they could see. Amy stood in darkness on the front lawn beside Cat, engulfed in the taller woman's raincoat. Cat, drenched by the downpour, kept her arm around Amy, whose teeth chattered in shock.

Seeing her distress, Joshua ran to embrace his mother.

Without a word, Sam turned and ran back home.

Amy cried out when she saw her son, "Joshua, he's pinned under debris. They got me out first, but Billy. . ." She leaned against him and sobbed.

"Mom, are you all right?"

Amy nodded, "Yes, but your father. . ."

He hugged her and then pushed her gently back toward Catherine, "I have to help them dig." He clambered up onto the ruins of the house, stepping over broken timbers, exposed nails, heaps of brick, mortar, insulation, shingles, and sheetrock.

A few minutes later, Sam reappeared and climbed onto the pile to stand beside her mother. She trained her flashlight on the scene as well.

With the three men working and lifting the heavier pieces together, they finally unearthed Billy Brightman. A massive beam pinned him down. With tremendous strain, they lifted the beam, only to discover a great sword underneath which had severed his right arm just below the elbow. Billy lay gashed, bruised, and unconscious in a pool of his own blood.

By this time, Amy had made her way across the pile of debris. Seeing her husband unresponsive and bloody, she fainted, but Cat caught her before she fell.

Joshua stripped off his raincoat and his T-shirt and knelt beside Billy to staunch the blood pumping from his arm.

"Here, let me do it," said Leo.

"Diana, go call 9-1-1," said George.

"I already did," said Sam.

"Good girl," said Diana, giving her a fierce hug.

Improvising a tourniquet, Leo tied Joshua's T-shirt just above Billy's elbow, while Joshua cradled his father's head to keep it out of the bloody pool. George covered Billy with their raincoats to keep him warm and shield him from the rain.

Seeing the unconscious Amy, George lifted her in his arms, "Let's get her into the house." Diana, Sam, and Cat went with him, while Joshua and Leo stayed with Billy.

"Where did the sword come from?" asked Leo.

"My dad had a weapon collection mounted on a wall in the living room. This area here is about where the living room used to be. Dad had swords, bayonets, revolvers, rifles, and knives." Joshua nodded toward the sword lying beside his father, "That's a

Civil War sword. I guess it flew off the wall when the tornado hit the house, but I don't know how it could have severed his arm."

"I do," said Leo. "I have seen pine needles pierce the trunks of trees after a tornado. The sword could have flown off the wall with enough force to sever anything in its path." Leo blew out an explosive breath, "Anyway, what's done is done. We may never know what happened."

"Will he die?" asked Joshua.

"He's lost a lot of blood, but he's a big man. If the ambulance can get here fast enough, he'll live, I think. Let's pray, Joshua."

In the darkness and pouring rain, they knelt beside Billy Brightman and prayed to God that he might live. Before the prayer ended, they heard the shrill, high-pitched wail of an ambulance siren. In all his life, Joshua had never heard sweeter music.

CHAPTER 29

Equilibrium

J oshua rode in the ambulance with his father while Leo
followed in his Blazer. Aside from the injured man and
the two Emergency Medical Technicians, Joshua's only
companion on that harrowing ride was fear. Fear was the icy vise
that gripped his heart, tensed his muscles, and made him shiver
in the stifling heat. He did not know if his father would live.

He held onto the seat on the bumpy ride as the driver
navigated through debris and flooded streets. "How is he?" he
asked the EMT's sitting beside him as they kept their eyes fixed
on the gurney.

One, a young man about his own age with a blond buzz
cut, answered, "Well, his blood pressure is low, due to blood
loss, but his pulse and breathing rate are unusually slow. With an
injury like this, I would expect him to be in hypovolemic shock."

"What does that mean?"

"Usually, with this kind of blood loss, the heart races and breathing is rapid and shallow, not close to normal like this."

Joshua didn't know if that was good or bad, and he was too fearful to ask.

As they arrived at Chalice General Hospital, other ambulances carrying critically injured people also converged on the emergency entrance. Amidst the flashing lights and the noise of the gusting wind, driving rain, and the shouts of medical personnel, Billy remained unmoving and unconscious. For Joshua, the whole process of admitting him to the hospital remained a blur revolving around the still, pasty-white center that was his father's bloodless face.

By five a.m., with the hospital powered by emergency generators, the doctors had stabilized Billy Brightman. He had lost his right forearm, but he was alive. They had cleaned and bandaged his stump, wrapped his three broken ribs, treated his multiple cuts and contusions, and given him prodigious amounts of antibiotics, fluids, and AB positive blood, some of which Joshua donated. Exhausted, disoriented, but relieved, both Joshua and Leo rested in bedside chairs on either side of Billy's hospital bed. Leo slept open-mouthed, leaning back with his spectacles propped on top of his head. Joshua kept a bleary-eyed vigil, wondering at the speed and sudden violence of the tornado that in a matter of seconds had mutilated his father, destroyed his house, and launched them all into an uncertain future.

Shortly after the ambulance left, Amy regained consciousness. When she learned Billy had been taken to the hospital, she wanted to drive there to be with him. George told her she was in no shape to drive. "Besides, traveling now is very dangerous, Amy. The roads are flooded, full of debris, and there are plenty of downed power lines out there." He clinched the argument by adding, "If something happens to you, who will take care of Billy?" She agreed to stay the night at Diana's on the condition that he and Cat would drive her to the hospital at first light.

While Amy showered, George and Sam rested in the living room. Diana made a pot of tea, and Cat lit two large pillar candles and set them on the coffee table. When everyone had a cup of tea, Diana sat on the sofa and prompted Sam, "Come sit with me and tell us about your dream."

Smiling, Sam sat beside her mother and described every detail of her meeting in the garden with the young Annie Faris and Eliot, both transformed and more beautiful than ever. "Because I saw them, Mamma, I don't feel sad anymore, and that's why I can talk again."

"Darlin', I can't tell you how good that makes me feel," said George. He rose from the loveseat and enveloped Sam in his arms. "Mamma's okay, Eliot's okay, and you're on track to be just as sassy as ever," he said, making them all laugh. After Diana and Cat hugged and kissed Sam, Diana sent her off to bed.

When Amy emerged from the shower, Cat applied disinfectant to her cuts and abrasions, and Diana gave her a cup of hot, sweet tea. Battling fatigue, they gathered in the living room. In the flickering candlelight, they carried on a quiet conversation punctuated by the rattle of the rain and wind, as they waited anxiously to hear news of Billy from Leo or Joshua.

The torrential rain continued all through the night, and in the sodden, gray dawn after Delilah's departure, the citizenry emerged out of hiding, as hesitantly as the Munchkins of Oz after Dorothy's crash-down, trying to comprehend the violent destruction that for many, had altered the face of the visible world.

Four people in the greater New Orleans area died. Floodwaters breached a levee and swept away and drowned two teenaged boys. An ancient live oak uprooted by the tornado smashed into a house in Gretna, killing the owner and rendering his widow and their three school-age children homeless. A woman died when her car hydroplaned across an elevated highway and struck the railing, ejecting her through the windshield onto the unforgiving concrete seventeen feet below.

At five a.m., the power came back on, to everyone's relief. At five-thirty, Joshua called to tell them that the medical staff had got Billy stabilized; he was going to live. Amy was overjoyed and everyone was relieved. They ate a quick, light breakfast, and then George and Cat drove Amy to the hospital to be with her husband.

Diana laid down to rest a moment and woke up five hours later. After her shower, she and Sam sat on the sofa to look through Annie's journal together. The journal began with a brief letter followed by all the recipes:

Dear Sam and Diana,

The Lord has answered my prayers, and I have only a short time to live. Do not grieve for me. I visited Heaven in a dream and saw my Albert, and I am going there to be with him and Joseph soon. My heart is very glad because you will be well and healthy, Diana, and as my dearest Sam grows up, she will have her mother. That is how it should be.

Here are all my recipes so you don't forget how to make Syrian food! I love you both, and George, Cat, Michael, and Lucy with all my heart.

God bless you all,
Annie +

Laban   (Yoghurt)

Heat a half gallon of milk until the bubbles begin to surface. Cool the pot in cold water for seven minutes, or until it feels lukewarm. Put the starter yoghurt in a large container, pour in the warm milk and mix. Seal it and put it in a warm place (on top of the water heater). Let it stand for several hours or overnight. In other words, albi, just put in the ingredients, treat them right, and then let God and bacteria do the rest!

Smiling, Diana browsed through the pages of handwritten recipes for making Syrian bread, kibbeh, tabouli, mahshi, fig preserves, pear preserves, and even mayhaw jelly.

"Mamma, she knew she was going to die for a long time. Remember when Sitti took us shopping in July? That was the day she bought the journal, and remember I told you that she sat up late every night writing in it?"

"Yes, I remember. She knew she had very little time to live, so she wrote down all her recipes for us, and she took us shopping because she wanted to give us gifts we would like while she still could."

Sam snapped her fingers, "That's right! She told me the Lord told her to take us shopping."

Diana gazed at her daughter, "She was a simple, uneducated woman, but so very wise. She knew how to heal me, even when I was angry and unforgiving. She knew Joshua needed healing, and she knew you would recover. On the night she died, she told me you would be speaking again within one week."

"And she was right!" Sam rested her hand on the open page of Annie's journal; it was the closest thing to Annie herself. "Mamma, are you going to learn how to cook Syrian food?"

"I am," answered Diana. And then, thinking of Joseph and his unfinished business, Diana added, "But I am going to do much more than that. I'm going to make this collection of recipes into a very attractive cookbook; I'm going to publish it."

Sam's eyes lit up, "Really? Do you think it will sell?"

"I hope so, but that's not the point. I want to do this to honor your grandmother and your father. Years ago, when Joseph and I first met, he had the idea to publish Annie's recipes, but he never followed through on it." She tapped the thin book. "But now Annie has made it easy. Her recipes are all here, and with the current interest in the Mediterranean diet, which is considered one of the healthiest in the world, we might have a bestseller."

As she visualized her plan, Diana's eyes sparkled, "We'll begin at Levant House. An attractive Middle Eastern cookbook at the counter might sell very well indeed."

After two days in Chalice General, Billy Brightman's doctors moved him to Touro Infirmary in New Orleans, which had the best in-patient Orthopedic Rehabilitation Center in Louisiana. Early on that Saturday after the storm, Joshua drove west on St. Charles Avenue, looking for Foucher Street where the hospital and his mother's hotel were located. At the hotel, which faced St. Charles, he made a left down Foucher and was hunting a parking space when Nathan called.

"Hey, man, I got good news all round."

"Yeah, what's that?"

"Well, Virginia Webb hired me, and, as you know, her firm is to Bruce's agency as Carnegie Hall is to the local high school auditorium."

"Congratulations, Nathan!"

"Yeah, and it's a big boost in salary too."

"Even better."

"Dude, New Orleans is a dangerous city, I know, but it sounds like you're in a war zone. Who's shootin'?"

Joshua laughed, "My truck—it backfires."

"Whoa, what'd it cost you—five ninety-nine?"

"You're close," Joshua laughed. "Nine hundred."

"This heap I gotta see; send me a photo. All right, where was I? Oh yeah, speakin' of money, with my extra bucks, I hired an attorney to contact the entertainment magazine that printed the lie about you. After he threatened to sue them unless they could prove the allegation, they agreed to retract the story and print an apology. But they refused to reveal the source."

"Nathan, thank you! I intended to hire a lawyer, but you beat me to it. I'm gonna reimburse you the attorney's fees. But don't worry, I know who did it. Her name is Taylor Merrick."

Joshua spotted the red brick hospital on Prytania. As he pulled into the parking garage across the street and took a ticket, he said, "She's the daughter of my dad's boss at Leviathan Oil. It's a long story, but I pissed her off the first time we met and it's been downhill ever since. Being equal parts malice and stupidity, she posted the same photo on her Facebook page."

"I believe it. Sheesh!" Nathan paused, and as Joshua found a parking space and killed the engine, he could visualize Nathan shaking his head.

"Well, here's the deal, Joshua. After I told Virginia Webb the article was false and the magazine is going to retract it, I pitched you as a new client for her agency. The agencies keep tabs on all up-and-coming artists, so they already knew about you, and, Joshua, they want to take you on."

"Holy shit, Nathan, that's great!"

"Ain't it? And now we can both tell Bruce to go to hell."

Joshua fairly shouted with laughter, while Nathan whooped and egged him on.

Finally catching his breath, Joshua said, "Nathan, I want you to come down soon and visit me. We can tour the town in my elegant truck, and try out the local cuisine. The airfare is on me; I owe you big time."

"Thanks, man. Let's do it soon before the season starts in September."

After they worked out a date, Nathan said, "Hey, what about the hurricane? Everything okay down there?"

"Ah," said Joshua, "that's quite a story." Sitting in the parked truck, Joshua retold the events and aftermath of the previous Thursday.

"So, how's your dad doin' now?" asked Nathan.

"So far, so good," Joshua replied. "Well, I'm here at the hospital to see him, and I'd better go up."

He locked the truck and went up to the Beast's room, feeling nervous and uncertain about his father's condition, despite his words to Nathan. When he walked in, his mother glanced up from her bedside chair. Her blue eyes were underscored by dark circles of fatigue, and he noticed the worry lines drawn deep between her eyes and furrowing down from her nose to her chin.

Looking almost as pale as the white hospital pillow, Billy Brightman lay on his back, eyes closed, with drip bags attached to his left arm and a drainage tube protruding from under the white-bandaged stump to carry off excess fluids. A plastic bag half-filled with urine hung on the metal rail of the bed.

Joshua spoke softly, "Is he sleeping or just resting?"

"He's sound asleep. The move this morning wore him out."

"Any news?"

"Well, his new physician, Dr. Ferucci, said he is doing quite well and all his vital signs are good. He expects a rapid recovery."

"Excellent!" he said, in a hearty tone, trying to convey confidence and cheer to his mother. But he sensed something was wrong. If the doctor's report was good, why was she so worried and depressed? A vague uneasiness descended on him like a pall.

Joshua observed the steady tempo of the drips from two plastic bags suspended above his father. "What are those?"

"More antibiotics and fluids, and they just gave him a shot for pain."

"He'll sleep for quite a while, then."

Amy nodded and rubbed her eyes as if it were midnight. It was ten-thirty a.m.

Joshua wanted to get her out of the room so they could talk. "Mom, you look like you could use some coffee. There's nothing we can do right now, so while he's sleeping, let's go down to the cafeteria and get some coffee and something to eat," Joshua suggested. "I've got some news."

In the hospital cafeteria, they purchased two cups of coffee, a Hubig's fried pie with its Savory Simon wrapping, and a slice of strawberry pie that proved beyond Joshua's willpower to resist. They sat at a window table. He hoped his news would cheer her up. "Mom, I'll start with the bad part. Nathan and I both got canned from BG Artists."

"Oh, no." She wrinkled up her forehead, "I hope there's some good news."

"There is." Joshua took a big bite of pie and then waved his fork in the air. "Mmmmm, that is delish," he mumbled, through a mouthful of strawberries, piecrust, and whipped cream. He swallowed and added, "The good news is that Nathan got hired by Virginia Webb Artists, and they're taking me on, too. Her firm is one of the best artist management companies in New York. They manage the careers of some very high-profile musicians."

"That's great, Joshua." She smiled at him, but her tone was flat, and she seemed fidgety and preoccupied. She drank the coffee, but she had only taken two bites of the lemon pie.

Joshua sipped his coffee, puzzled. "Mom, what's wrong? Dad is going to be fine. There's no infection, and he's healing well. So what's the matter?" He took an enormous bite of pie.

Amy sighed. "Leviathan let him go."

Joshua laid down his fork. "He lost his job because of his arm?"

"They say not. Billy wasn't the only one to lose his job; the company laid off over two thousand workers. They say it's because of the huge fine they had to pay."

"Who made the decision to fire Dad?"

Amy's nostrils flared and the corners of her mouth dived. "Charles Merrick."

He leaned forward, "Charles Merrick and family. I don't like any of them." Picturing Charles, Lucinda, and Taylor in his mind, Joshua smashed the remaining piecrust crumbs with his fork, taking special care to grind them to smithereens against the plate. Suddenly he inhaled sharply and looked at his mother. "Mom, maybe I can help him get his job back. Do you have Merrick's phone number?"

"Yes, but, Joshua, there's nothing you can do. Please don't beg. Your dad would be humiliated."

Joshua smiled, "Oh, don't worry, Mom, there's no need to beg. See, the reason I got fired from BG Artist Management was that someone took a picture of me after the concert when I had the black eye and my face was still bruised. That person emailed the photo to a local entertainment magazine. The caption was, and I quote: *Pianist Joshua Brightman plays concert with a spectacular black eye. Did he fall off a ladder or is it more likely he took a beating in a drug deal gone bad?*"

"What?"

"Bruce, the CEO at BG Management, found out, and because of my bad behavior in San Francisco, he believed it. Then an orchestra and a college in Utah were interested in hiring me, but when they saw the online picture and article, they canceled. For Bruce, that was the last straw. When Nathan stood up for me, Bruce fired him too."

"It's a lie."

"It's two lies. Did Dad tell the Merricks I fell off a ladder to explain my black eye?"

Amy dropped her gaze and her face flushed. "Yes, I'm sorry, Joshua, we both did. We couldn't face telling the truth."

He nodded, "That's what I guessed from Merrick's comment after the concert. Well, at any rate, the drug deal story is libel, an offense that can be prosecuted. The source is Taylor Merrick."

Amy's mouth dropped open. "Why?"

"She was furious at me for pointing out her rudeness at the lunch party you and Dad gave. She called me an asshole."

"Yes, I heard her say it. But Joshua, what does this have to do with your father?"

"I can prove Taylor is responsible and take her to court. But I won't do that if Charles Merrick will give Dad his job back."

"I see." Amy sipped her coffee. "You know, Billy may not want to work for Leviathan anymore."

"Has he discussed it with you?"

"Not really, but I know he's terrified he'll never work again."

"He'll have a prosthetic arm and hand eventually."

"Joshua, I don't know how long it will take for him to learn to use the arm and hand, or if he will be able to write or use a computer ever again."

"Mom, he can learn to type with one hand if necessary. His work is mostly mental, not physical. Besides, there are voice recognition software programs that will type dictated notes."

Amy frowned and swirled the milky coffee in her paper cup. "I guess so. It's just going to be an enormous change for him whatever happens."

"I know it is, but he'll handle it. It may take a long time of transition, but he will adapt. He's no stranger to adversity. Remember how he supported his mother and sisters as a schoolboy by working construction jobs nights, weekends and summers? He kept his grades up and managed to pitch for the baseball team, too."

Amy smiled. "He did."

"It's the same guy, up in that hospital bed. He's a fighter; he's gonna rise to the occasion." Joshua smiled, "I'm sure the path will be paved with profanities, but I swear, he'll rise."

Joshua drained his cup, and added, "We can discuss all this with Dad later. If he wants to go back to Leviathan, I'll contact Charles Merrick and put my plan into action."

"Joshua, let's go back; I don't like leaving him for too long."

As they walked down the hall toward the elevators, Joshua said, "Mom, next weekend, Nathan's coming for a short visit. I intend to invite him, the Faris family and Leo DeLuca to go out and eat some Louisiana specialties as a way of thanking them for all they've done. I'd like you to come, too. I'm going to make reservations for us at Creole Louie's. I want to do something for them, and I feel like celebrating."

"You feel like celebrating when your dad has lost his job, his right arm, and his home?"

"Look, Mom, I'm not minimizing any of those losses, but we have to be thankful for what remains. Unlike several people who died as a result of the storm, Dad is alive and recovering. The house is gone, but the insurance will allow you to rebuild or buy another. As to his job, we'll see what he wants to do; let's not worry about that now. But I'm certain he will be able to work for many years to come. And then there's the fact that I am newly represented by one of the most powerful artist management firms in New York."

He smiled down at his mother, "Mom, it's going to be all right."

Amy's face crumpled and she burst into tears. Turning to her son, she threw her arms around him. "Oh, Joshua, I hope so. It's been awful to see your father so weak and injured. I am so grateful you're here with me now. And. . . and I'm so very sorry that Billy hit you with the rifle and that he was always so harsh toward you. I should have stopped him so many times." She reached into her purse for a tissue to wipe her eyes. "I have a lot to make up for."

Sniffing, she said, "Let's go to his room. I hate blubbering in public."

In the privacy of the elevator, Amy continued, "You know, I realized that in the end it was a good thing he threw you out of the house, because it kept you safe from the tornado. I don't know what I'd do if you were injured, too." Her nose turned watermelon red, while her pale blue eyes swam in water like melting New Orleans snowballs. "I want you to know I love you and I am so very proud of you."

Joshua embraced his mother, holding her tightly while the aching lump in his throat subsided. After a long moment, he kissed her on the cheek. "Thanks, Mom. You just gave me another reason to celebrate."

CHAPTER 30

A Reckoning

To give his mother a respite from her all-day sojourns at the hospital, Joshua sat with his father every evening that first week. In the apartment by day, he practiced intensely for his upcoming performances. In the hospital by night, he studied his new book about the history and beliefs of Judaism or murmured the prayers from his *siddur* while his father slept or silently watched television.

At first, due to the painkillers, Billy seemed to have short term memory loss; any conversations he had with Joshua he forgot the next day. But as the week drew toward its close, Dr. Ferucci reduced the dosage. Billy complained little, but he seemed distant, brooding, keeping his feelings to himself. Joshua had no idea what was going through his father's mind. That changed on

Friday night, eight days after the storm and one week since Billy Brightman had been transferred to Touro Infirmary.

That evening, when his dad fell asleep right after eating his dinner, Joshua clicked off the television and opened his prayer book to the *Shema*. He murmured, "*Shema Yisrael, Adonai Eloheinu. Adonai Echad. . .*" When he finished, he repeated the last line softly to himself in English, "And you shall love the Lord your God with all your heart and with all your soul and with all your might."

And no one had done that better than Annie. Sighing, he laid his head against the back of the chair, thinking of her and her great goodness toward him. She had healed him and set him on the right path, and he had hardly had time to thank her before she died. Seeking comfort, he thumbed through the book and found a prayer for the dead. He recited it softly, supplying her name. "O God, full of compassion, Who dwells on high, grant true rest upon the wings of the Shekinah, in the exalted spheres of the holy and pure, who shine as the resplendence of the firmament, to the soul of Annie. . . may her place of rest be in Gan Eden."

The Garden of Eden. Joshua smiled. Yes, Annie would be at home in a garden, she surely would. *O Lord, may she dwell forever with You in Paradise.* Satisfied, Joshua closed his eyes, thinking he would rest just a moment.

Two hours later, he woke with a crick in his neck. It was eleven o'clock. He grimaced in pain as he rubbed his neck. He glanced at his father and froze. Billy had Joshua fixed in his black, laser-like unsmiling gaze, a gaze full of clarity and force; he didn't appear confused, drugged, or groggy. Apparently the good old days had returned.

Sitting up straight, Joshua asked, "How are you, Dad?" He felt wary and uneasy, not knowing what to expect.

"Just peachy, son. My arm's chopped off, my house is a pile of rubble, and Leviathan canned my ass."

And then to Joshua's surprise, a deep rumble started in his father's chest that erupted into laughter. Amazed at Billy's good humor, and greatly relieved, Joshua smiled.

"Hell, this is like a vacation—not my first choice, of course—but look at the benefits: I'm the center of attention; I get breakfast in bed; I got good-lookin' women takin' care of my every need, and what a view!" He gestured toward the window and the lights of New Orleans. "Plus, I have all the time in the world to shoot the breeze with my family."

Here it comes. Joshua's smile died and he braced himself for the attack like a soldier in the trenches. Quickly and silently, he prayed for strength and equanimity.

"Hell, I don't give a shit about Leviathan. Who needs 'em? I'll be better off without 'em and that condescending pot-bellied asshole Merrick. Once I get out of here," his voice cracked as he gestured at the hospital room, "I'll find another job. . ."

"Dad, that's someth—"

"Don't interrupt me, goddammit!" The corners of Billy's mouth dived and he glared at Joshua. He repeated his statement as if to reassure himself, "Like I said, I'll find another job. As for the house, the insurance will cover rebuilding. Or maybe we'll buy a new house. We'll see what the best option is after I get out of the hospital. We might even move back to Brooklyn. But wherever we are, once we get settled, you can move back in. I know we don't see eye to eye on much, but you'll always have a place with us."

It seemed like a peace offering. Hoping his father might be receptive, Joshua seized the opportunity to explain himself and to try to set things right. "Dad, thank you for the offer, but I think it's time I earned my own way."

Billy snorted, "Big talk from someone who's never paid his own way. You know you can't make it on your income with the debt you have."

Joshua met his father's gaze calmly. "Well, I'm getting by so far. And now I've got new and better management—"

Billy cut him off, "I know, your mother told me."

Joshua swallowed, "Well, you're right about our differences—they are many. I know I disappointed you because I'm a musician, not an athlete or a lawyer. But I want to explain some of my actions to you." With sweating palms and heat rising to his face, Joshua revealed something he had been ashamed of and concealed for years. He steadfastly kept his eyes on his father's face, "You know about my compulsive hand washing?"

Billy nodded.

"Well, I washed my hands to relieve myself of stress. The stress came from intrusive, violent thoughts. And. . . and. . ." Joshua stopped himself. It was too painful to disclose that his thoughts were various ways of killing or torturing his father. He dropped his eyes. "The thoughts were just thoughts. I was never going to act on any of them, but they popped up in my head all the time, out of repressed anger, I guess. They practically paralyzed me with fear and guilt. That's why I never wanted to handle the guns and knives in your collection. The weapons reminded me of all the violent thoughts I wanted to avoid."

He shoved his hands in his pockets. "Just before the hurricane hit, our neighbor Annie prayed for me, and when she did, the thoughts, the fears, and the compulsions left, and they haven't returned."

"Prayer did it?" Billy looked skeptical.

"That and forgiveness."

Billy sniffed, "Well, I guess you're special, son; most people don't need healing to pick up a .22."

The statement was like a steel door slammed shut in his face. It was an outright rejection, a refusal to understand. Joshua clenched his teeth and sighed. Well, he had tried.

"What are you reading?"

Surprised by the abrupt change of subject, Joshua sat back in the chair and fingered his *siddur*. "It's a Jewish prayer book."

Billy laughed, "Didn't know you were interested in fairytales."

"God is not a fairytale, Dad."

"How can you look at this world and all the crap that happens and still believe that there's a God?"

"How can I look at creation and believe a Creator doesn't exist?"

"Bullshit."

Joshua knew better than to engage in an argument. He could not alter his father's lack of faith, and he didn't want to argue with him while he was still weak.

Billy picked at the sheet. "If the drugs and the drips haven't addled my brain, seems like back in July we parted in anger. I'm sorry about it, but, you know, son, if you hadn't attacked me, I wouldn't have hit you. Besides, it wasn't much of a blow. You only got a black eye out of it. And naturally Amy blew it all out of proportion—she got hysterical." Billy pursed his lips and shook his head, "Just like a woman." Satisfied with himself, he shifted his pillow, laid his head back, and closed his eyes.

Joshua gazed thoughtfully at his father, seeing him clearly for the first time. Despite his bluster and size, Billy was a weak, insecure, and fearful man who only felt powerful when he controlled and ridiculed others. He dodged responsibility for the abuse he handed out, placing blame on anyone but himself, even if it meant lying and twisting the facts. In that moment, Joshua felt engulfed by a great pity for his father. How miserable he must be.

On another level, his father was a lawyer and a Jew. And Joshua had just recited the *Shema*, the ancient law entrusted to the Hebrew people: *Hear, O Israel: The Lord is our God, the Lord is one. Love the Lord your God with all your heart and with all your soul and with all your might.* And from Leviticus: *You shall love your neighbor as yourself.* Two laws, so pure and simple, which human beings chose daily to disobey.

How easy it was to seek the dark and not the light, to turn from the highest, the purest, and the true in order to worship the desires of one's own heart above everything else.

Billy yawned and pulled the bed covers up to his chest, while Joshua took stock of the present state of affairs. On the surface it seemed that nothing between them had changed, and yet everything had changed. Joshua had forgiven Billy on the night Annie healed him. Forgiveness didn't mean he forgot or condoned or excused the wrongs. It meant that he chose to release all resentments and any desire for vengeance. He was free; Billy had no more power over him.

Joshua took a deep breath and steeled himself for what he had to do next. "Dad, before I go, there's one thing I have to tell you. Remember the blue jay on the fence that day? Maybe you didn't realize it, but you did hit it and kill it."

Billy glared at his son, "So what if I did? It was just a bird."

"The blue jay's name was Eliot, and he had been raised and kept as a tame bird by the girl who lives next door. She decided to set him free that day, and she had just released the bird when you shot him. She caught the blue jay as he fell, and it traumatized her."

Billy shrugged. "Look, I had no idea. I really don't think I hit the damn bird anyway."

"I'm afraid you did. And that's the family who helped you after the tornado."

"I know what they did," Billy snapped. "And I'm going to thank them for it."

"Do you want me to invite them to come here to the hospital to visit you?"

"Sure, do that."

Two days later, on the last day of August, a Sunday afternoon ten days after the onslaught of Hurricane Delilah, the people who had saved Billy's life stood gathered around his upraised hospital bed. The wall of windows in Billy's private room flooded the black and white tiled floor and the ivory walls with cheerful natural light as a wan and thin Billy surveyed them all. The bandaged stump of his right arm was a painful reminder of what he had endured.

Joshua introduced everyone to his father, while Amy, who knew them all, stood smiling and watchful to Billy's right. "Dad, this is my friend Sam, Samantha Faris, and her mother Diana, and this is Sam's Uncle George and Aunt Catherine, and you already know Leo DeLuca, my landlord."

Billy glanced at Joshua, "Sam and George, the friends who took you fishing?"

"Yes," Sam replied. She stepped forward and handed Billy three red roses in a slender glass vase. "These are from our rose bushes—one from me, one from my mother, and one from Sitti, my grandma." She added solemnly, "If my grandma were here, she'd pray for you and you'd heal faster."

"Is that so?" Billy set the vase on the side table with his left hand.

"It's the truth."

Watching her interaction with his father, Joshua noticed a difference in Sam. Childish ebullience had given way to more restraint. She seemed quieter and more reticent, and she chose her words with care.

"Well, thank you for the roses. What's your grandma's name?"

"Annie Faris."

"Annie Faris?" Billy Brightman tilted his head forward, knit his eyebrows together and opened his mouth in surprise, as if Sam had said something shocking. He took a deep breath and nodded in wide-eyed affirmation, "Annie Faris! That was her name! I met her during the storm. When the roof and the wall collapsed on me and pinned me down, I could hardly breathe." His speech gathered momentum, "I had terrible pain in my side, and I knew something really bad had happened to my arm. I had never felt pain like that. I panicked; my heart was racing, and the next thing I knew, there was a beautiful woman kneeling beside me."

"Dad, why didn't you tell us about this before?" Joshua's brows collided in a frown. Obviously his father had hallucinated. How could a woman kneel beside him when he was buried under a great pile of debris?

Billy faced his son, "I didn't remember until just now. All the drugs have kept me in a haze."

He turned back toward Sam who still stood at his bedside. "Sweetheart, her name was Annie Faris, but she looked so young. She was only about thirty years old."

Sam seemed unperturbed. "Did she speak to you?"

"Yes, she held my hand, and she said, 'It's going to be all right, William. They're coming to help you right now. It's going to be all right.' And she called me a name, something like sadeek—sa—"

"*Sadeeqy*," said George. "It means *my friend* in Arabic."

"Yes, she said 'Rest, *sadeeqy*' and put her palm on my forehead. The moment she did that, the most blessed calm descended on me. Just before I fell asleep, I asked, 'Who are you?'"

"She told me her name and then I blacked out. I woke up in the hospital almost twenty-four hours later."

Billy shook his head slightly, smiling at the memory. Then he lifted his chin and glanced at his visitors. "When can she come and see me? I'd like to thank Annie in person."

During the awkward silence that ensued, George cleared his throat and said, "Mr. Brightman, Annie was my mother. She died on August 17th, five days before Delilah struck."

Billy's eyebrows lifted and he leaned forward, "She died?"

"We buried her the day before the storm."

Billy looked bewildered, "But if Annie was dead, how. . ."

No one spoke until Catherine said quietly, "Mr. Brightman, you didn't know her, but Annie was a gifted healer. Three years ago, I had a brain tumor, and it disappeared after she prayed for me. She healed many people in our community."

"But why would she want to help me?"

Exactly, thought George. That his mother *could* help, he had no doubt, but why *would* she help such a mean bastard?

"And how would she even know I was hurt?"

After a protracted silence, Leo said, "I don't think anyone can answer your questions, Mr. Brightman." He pushed his spectacles up toward the bridge of his nose. "But let's go back to Annie's appearance at your side. It's important from a medical standpoint to remember she was there before any of us even knew you were injured. She calmed you and slowed your pulse. That reduced the blood loss from the moment of the injury until we dug you out of the rubble and applied a tourniquet."

"On the way to the hospital, Dad, the EMT told me your slow pulse and breathing rate were unusual. He said most people with great blood loss go into hyper—hypo—"

"Hypovolemic shock," supplied Leo.

"Are you *Doctor* Leo Deluca?" Billy asked.

"Yes," answered Leo, adjusting his glasses.

"Who provided the research data for the Leviathan trial on the illnesses of the coastal residents after the oil spill?"

"The very one."

Billy tapped the fingers of his left hand on the sheet that covered him. "Well, you did a damn good job for the prosecution, Dr. DeLuca, because, as you know, we lost the trial. The company has to pay the biggest fine in the history of the world. Billions." Sighing, Billy laid his head back on the pillow and looked up at the ceiling.

After a moment, Billy broke the silence, "Well, the fact that I had a slow pulse can't be disputed, but the woman who calmed me was far too young to be your grandmother, Samantha."

Sam stood her ground. "When people die, they're not old anymore. On the night of the storm, I saw my grandmother in a dream, but I didn't recognize her because her hair was long and black, not white anymore. It fell in deep curls from the top of her head past her shoulders."

Sam glanced back at her family, "Uncle George, she reminded me of Lucy."

George explained to Billy, "Lucy is my daughter, Annie's granddaughter and Sam's cousin. She's a beautiful girl."

"I can vouch for that," Joshua smiled.

George dug his wallet out of his back pocket, while Sam recounted her dream. She described the beautiful lady's wordless song and the appearance of the bird, blue and silver as light. Sam smiled, "It was Eliot, my blue jay, and he was changed, too. He looked more beautiful than any bird on this earth. When I saw him alive and well, I was all right again. I didn't feel sad or numb anymore."

Billy dropped his eyes and shifted uncomfortably in the bed, while Amy glanced at him anxiously.

"The only way I knew the beautiful lady was my grandmother was when she called me *albi*. Then I realized who she was."

"*Albi* is an Arabic term of endearment; it means *my heart*," said Catherine.

"Take a look at this, Mr. Brightman." George stepped forward with a snapshot of Lucy. "This is a photo of my daughter, taken last year in Audubon Park."

Billy studied the photograph for a long time. Amy leaned over and gazed at it too. At last, Billy nodded his head, "Yes, Annie Faris looked very much like that."

"Mr. Brightman, it *was* my grandma."

"All right, Samantha, though it defies logic, I believe you."

He handed the photograph back to George and sank back against the pillow.

After a moment, he lifted his head and cleared his throat, "Well," he said quietly and slowly, "I want to thank you all. Amy told me what happened. If you hadn't dug me out and applied the tourniquet, and if Sam hadn't called 9-1-1, I would have bled to death. Without you, and I guess without Annie's intervention, I would be a dead man. Thank you for saving my life."

He cleared his throat, "Joshua and I have had a lot of time to talk since I've been in the hospital." Billy gazed straight ahead; he didn't glance at his son. "He, uh, he, well. . . he told me that I. . . that I shot your blue jay, Samantha. But you have to understand it was just a very unfortunate accident. When I aimed at a squirrel on the ground, Joshua thought I was aiming at the blue jay. And just as I fired, he bumped my arm, knocking the rifle upwards, and apparently the shot hit the bird. It was a fluke; I never would have done that on purpose."

The lie rose up and reared its head, grimfaced and ugly, as if Tyrannosaurus Rex had materialized in their midst. In the charged silence that followed, only Sam and Billy seemed unaffected. White-lipped Joshua nodded almost imperceptibly and locked eyes with Leo. Amy glanced at the floor and shifted position nervously. George shook his head while Catherine and Diana looked anxiously at Joshua.

Billy kept his eyes on Sam, "I am so sorry. Can you forgive me, Sam?"

She nodded, "I forgive you, Mr. Brightman. I know my Eliot is all right."

"Thank you. Is there anything I can do to make it up to you?"

Sam frowned and shook her head.

George intervened, "Uh, Mr. Brightman, there is one request from the Faris family for reparations."

Cat, Diana, and Sam cast surprised glances at George.

"We request that as reparation, you would pay fifty per cent of Joshua's student loans and the loan for his piano."

Joshua's quick intake of breath was clearly audible.

Two brilliant pink spots kindled and burned in Billy Brightman's cheeks as he lowered his gaze and shifted uncomfortably in the bed. His nostrils flared and the muscles in his jaw worked as he clenched and unclenched his teeth. When Amy placed her hand on his shoulder, Joshua wondered if it was for moral support or to contain a forthcoming explosion.

"Billy has lost—"

"Amy, hush!" Billy blurted, with a sharp upward thrust of his head. He regarded George and spoke forcefully, "I will." He glanced at his son. "We'll work this out in private."

"Thank you, Dad," Joshua replied, unsure if Billy's statement was a promise or a threat.

"Well," said Leo, "speaking as a doctor, it is never good to tire out the patient, so I think we should let you rest now, Mr. Brightman. Joshua, we'll see you at Creole Louie's in a couple of hours."

When Leo and the Faris family left, Billy, scowling and surly, asked Joshua, "What's this about Creole Louie's?"

"I've invited all of them, and George's children Michael and Lucy to dinner to thank them." And pre-empting his father, he added, "And, yes, I can afford it."

"Well, in that case, go off with your friends. Amy will stay here with me."

Amy stepped close to her son and threaded her arm through his. "Actually, Billy, I'm going to eat with Joshua. And speaking of food, you'll have a *lovely* hospital dinner, and then you can rest easy and think about the fabulous fiction you just fed that young girl."

"What the hell do you mean?" Billy spat.

Amy replied pleasantly, "You know exactly what I mean, dear."

And then, looking up at her son, Amy gently tugged on his arm. "Well, Joshua, let's go celebrate."

Joshua's smile as they left the room was as wide and free as the mighty Mississippi.

CHAPTER 31

The Feast at Creole Louie's

Amy's hotel stood on the corner of St. Charles Avenue and Foucher Street, just a block and a half from Touro Infirmary. As they walked back to the hotel, Joshua said, "Mom, if you're worried about Dad paying fifty per cent of my loans—don't. I can do it myself. I won't hold him to it."

Amy's blue eyes met his. "*He* will hold himself to it. He's promised, and he will deliver. I know him; he's a very proud man."

As she changed clothes and reapplied her makeup in the bathroom, Joshua lay spread-eagled on the bed, staring at the ceiling and thinking about his father. After rehabilitation, what would Billy Brightman do? Aside from Leviathan, what opportunities existed in New Orleans for a laid-off oil and gas attorney missing most of his right arm? Maybe a little networking with George and family would give him some ideas.

Billy's lies about the "very unfortunate accident" of shooting Eliot made him wince. Typical—his father couldn't confess his mistakes or take responsibility, so he distorted the truth and blamed his son. Joshua sighed. He, his mother, and God knew what really happened that day, and thankfully, innocent Sam bore no resentment. Joshua shook his head. Poor Billy. Lies were a short-term solution; one paid dearly for them in the end. As the Psalmist wrote: *The mouth of them that speak lies shall be stopped.*

He thought about Annie's mysterious appearance at his father's side. Why had she done that? It remained an unanswered question—maybe he would never understand. He closed his eyes and rested a moment. And then, in his spirit, he clearly heard the words: *Dead men can't repent.* Startled, he opened his eyes and sat up. *Dead men can't repent.* Was that the real reason Annie had kept his father alive? Joshua felt a flicker of hope. It made sense—as long as Billy remained alive, the chance for change existed.

Well, only time would tell. At the moment, there was nothing Joshua could do or say to soften his father's heart, so he did the only thing he could; he left it in the hands of God. He said a quick prayer for the healing of the insecure, frightened man he had formerly, and mistakenly, called the Beast.

When Amy was ready, they left the hotel and crossed St. Charles Avenue to the neutral ground. As he stood near the rail tracks, watching a streetcar approach, Joshua felt a rising excitement, akin to the exhilaration he had felt as a six-year-old waiting to board the Staten Island Ferry for the first time. Holed up "ova da rivuh" in Chalice since May, he hadn't really explored the city of New Orleans, and this was his first time to take the St. Charles line. For 150 years, these streetcars had carried passengers in a thirteen-mile crescent-shaped circuit from Carondelet at Canal Street in the Central Business District, past the Garden District through Uptown to Carrollton at Claiborne Avenue.

Although it lacked the speed and sleekness of a subway train, the olive green streetcar with its shiny brass fittings breathed the life of an earlier era; it was simply irresistible in presence, charm, and character. Joshua and Amy climbed aboard and sat in one of the mahogany seats. As the car rumbled and swayed down the avenue through the dappled shade tunnel formed by the interlaced branches of ancient live oaks, he could not stop smiling. Passengers chattered and peered out the windows as they passed block after block of gorgeous homes, antebellum mansions, restaurants, churches, schools, and libraries. For Joshua, the ride ended far too soon, when he and his mother exited the streetcar at the Loyola University stop.

They crossed over St. Charles Avenue again and strolled down Exposition Boulevard, parallel to Audubon Park. Joggers ran along the paths through the park and children crowded the playgrounds shaded by the graceful, majestic oaks. Audubon Park was situated between St. Charles Avenue on one side, directly across from Tulane and Loyola Universities, and the Mississippi River on the other.

Joshua had chosen Creole Louie's for his party, because it was Michael Faris' favorite bar and grill. As a newcomer, aware of the city's culinary reputation, but ignorant of its best restaurants, Joshua trusted that a New Orleans native would know the best place for authentic Louisiana cuisine. As they strolled up to Creole Louie's, Joshua was glad to see it was an attractive, upscale restaurant facing the park near Prytania Street.

He opened the heavy beveled glass door for his mother, and they entered the cool foyer where the host waited at his station. The restaurant's antique white hexagonal tile floor contrasted with the dark, gleaming mahogany bar, crowded with customers. Joshua immediately noticed the lingering musty smell that pervades old buildings in the humid South, along with a faint odor of wood polish. Overlaying it all, he breathed in the smell of spices, onions, garlic, grilled seafood, and alcohol, the staples of Louisiana kitchens. His mouth watered in anticipation of the repast to come.

The host, a young man with the dark eyes, prominent nose, and rich black hair of a French aristocrat, directed them to the dining area. The Farises and Leo awaited them at a large round table near the bank of windows. The elegant table, covered by a snowy white table cloth and set with plates, glasses, cloth napkins, and shining silverware, had a vase of blue irises as its centerpiece. When they were seated, Joshua introduced Michael and Lucy to his mother.

Watching Amy interact with the Farises, Joshua felt comforted by her presence. She had just stood up for the truth and launched a stinging, surprise attack on Billy. She had also chosen to accompany her son to dinner, pleasing him greatly. It finally occurred to Joshua that ever since the move, his mother had been almost as isolated as he. To see her conversing happily and easily with Diana and Catherine, as with old friends, gladdened his heart.

Feeling content, he surveyed the restaurant. Four waiters, dressed in black trousers, white long-sleeved shirts, and black bow ties moved about the room, quiet, well-oiled, and elegant as Bentleys.

Their waiter, young and muscular, glided over with a stack of menus and introduced himself, "Good afternoon, everyone, my name is Chad." Gazing directly at Diana, he surprised her. "And you're Ms. Faris," he said, smiling, "the best and kindest English professor at Tulane. I took your Expository Writing class last spring, and you let me take the final exam early so I could leave for a gymnastics competition in Michigan. If you hadn't done that, I would have failed the course."

Diana smiled, "I remember. Well, I try to be merciful, because I hope to obtain mercy myself."

After they had ordered drinks, Michael asked Joshua, "How is your father doing and what's his prognosis?"

"Physically, he's healing well, and he's going to get a prosthetic limb, but I'm more worried about his mental and emotional recovery."

"Once he's back to work, which will happen sooner than you think," Leo reassured Joshua, "he'll regain his confidence and—"

"But see, Leo, that's the problem," Joshua interrupted, "Leviathan let him go."

Michael smiled and slowly shook his head. "Typical for those heartless corporate bastards. Human beings are worth shit; the only thing that matters is profit."

"You're right about that," agreed Amy, with an angry edge to her voice, "although they claim it had nothing to do with his injury. Supposedly, he was laid off with many others as part of their downsizing."

"As I told Mom, I think I have a way to get him his job back," said Joshua. "That is, if he *wants* to go back and work for them."

"What's your plan?" asked George.

"I'll explain that a little later," Joshua demurred, checking the time on his wristwatch, "when Nathan arrives."

"Well, if your dad decides not to return to Leviathan," said George, "then what?"

"Surely he can find another position," said Amy. "He's an experienced attorney in the oil and gas industry."

Michael lowered his menu, "He could come and work for me."

"What do you do?" asked Amy.

Michael smiled. "I am an overworked attorney in private practice, and I currently have beaucoup clients who hope to sue the hell out of Leviathan Oil. As a former lawyer for that firm, your husband couldn't directly litigate against Leviathan, but he could handle all other cases."

Joshua smiled, "Thus freeing you to battle Leviathan."

With his dark eyes sparkling behind his spectacles, Michael inclined his head in a genteel Southern bow. "Counsel for the plaintiff concurs."

At that moment, a short, wiry, freckle-faced young man burdened by an overstuffed backpack rushed up to the table, short of breath, but not volume. "Joshua! Dude, where ya been all my life!"

Joshua shot up out of his chair, almost overturning it, to hug his friend. "Nathan, you made it." After slapping him on the back, Joshua faced the table, "Everyone, this is Nathan Weiss, my courageous friend and manager. He's visiting for a few days, and I want him to meet all the important people in my life."

No sooner had Nathan placed his backpack against the wall and sat down than Chad appeared with an extra menu in one hand and an enormous circular tray with their drinks held aloft in the other. After taking Nathan's order for a draft beer, he stood poised to take their food orders.

"Why don't we order platters of various dishes," suggested Joshua, "and then we can share." Everyone agreed, and Chad took their orders.

While they sipped their drinks, Joshua introduced Nathan to his mother.

"Good to meet you, Nathan," Amy said. "My husband Billy and I heard about you often. Thank you for all you've done for Joshua."

"My pleasure. Careerwise, we've both hit major turbulence lately, but I think we've outflown the storm."

"Well, as you may know, his father Billy has been, uh, how should I say it. . . less than supportive of Joshua's career, but that has just changed. The trauma my husband suffered has made him quite a bit more malleable, and with some friendly persuasion by George here, Billy has agreed to help Joshua financially. And I. . . well, I'm sad to say I didn't stand up for my son the way I should have either, and I regret that." Her nose reddened, and her blue eyes swam in tears.

"Women!" exclaimed Joshua. "And I'm thinking of one in particular named Delilah."

"Delilah? As in Samson's ex?" asked Nathan.

"That one, too, but I meant Hurricane Delilah, a troublesome female we have to thank for pulling us together as family."

Amy took a tissue out of her purse, blew her nose, and told Joshua, "Go on with the introductions."

Joshua made it entertaining. "All right, Nathan, pay attention. The guy with the white streak in his hair and two cigars sticking up out of his pocket is George Faris who owns a Middle Eastern import business. Next to him is his very gracious, long-suffering, cigar-immune wife Catherine. Their children are the drop-dead gorgeous Lucy here and Michael the shyster law—I mean the brilliant attorney. The fair-haired lady is Diana Faris, renowned English professor at Tulane (even the waiter knows her). The petite brunette with sparkling eyes and untamable hair is Diana's daughter, an incredible bookwor—I mean, the well-read, articulate Samantha. The handsome curly-haired guy in the glasses is Leo DeLuca, physician and landlord—my landlord. So be prepared to behave yourself; he owns the garage apartment where you'll be staying.

"Got that, Nathan?"

"Let me see, there's your mom Amy, George and Catherine, Lucy and Michael. Hold it!" He stopped himself, raising one hand like a traffic cop. Leaning toward Lucy, he asked in a stage whisper, "No boyfriend, I hope?"

She laughed. "Out of luck, Nathan, his name is Richard."

He slammed his open palm against his chest, "Shot through the heart and I haven't even had an *hors d'oeuvre* yet. Okay, then there's Diana and Samantha." He tapped his fingers on the snowy tablecloth. "Samantha."

"Everyone calls me Sam," she said.

Nathan narrowed his eyes and stared at Joshua. "Seems like Joshua mentioned you before. Now, what did he say? Hmmm, it'll come to me."

Joshua held his breath and endured Nathan's keen gaze.

"Well, I can't remember now. And Dr. Deluca."

"Call me Leo."

"You're pretty good at remembering names," said Sam.

"Have to be," replied Nathan. "People are my business, and I make it a point to remember their names."

"Names are important, and words are important."

"They are. Words can build up or tear down. They can strengthen or destroy."

"I'm going to be a writer," Sam declared. "My grandma told me that my voice will make a difference in the world."

"What's her name?"

"Annie Faris. She died earlier this month, but she healed my mom, my Aunt Catherine, and Joshua."

"Joshua?" He glanced at his friend. "What was wrong with you?"

"Well, I can give you the details later, but I had a severe obsessive-compulsive problem. She prayed over me and now it's gone."

"I didn't know," said Nathan, slightly taken aback, "but I'm glad to hear you're cured." He turned and regarded Sam, "I wish I could have met your grandmother. I would have thanked her for helping my friend Joshua." After a moment he added, "So if you're going to be a writer, maybe you can tell her story some day."

"I will."

Nathan smiled, "Then write well, Sam, and make her proud."

Chad returned with trays of steaming food and placed them in the center of the table. When the waiter left, Joshua said, "Before we eat, I would like to say a blessing."

To Amy's utter astonishment, her son bowed his head and prayed:

"Lord God, King of the Universe, the great commandments are to love You with all our hearts and with all our souls and with all our might, and to love our neighbors as ourselves. I thank you with my whole heart for all my friends gathered here, and for your servant Annie, may she rest in peace. For by their actions towards us, each of them has followed your commandment. They have loved us, my mother, my father, and me, as themselves. And so, Lord, bless them all, bless my parents and me, and bless this food.

"*Baruch hatah Adonai Elohainu melech haolam.* Blessed are You, Lord our God, King of the Universe, Who has created all the fruits of the earth. Amen."

While the tears in Amy's blue eyes spilled over and ran down her cheeks, George smiled proudly.

Nathan said, "I barely remember anything from Hebrew school. How did you?"

"Never went to Hebrew school, Nathan. I've been studying. I intend to carry on the tradition of our people in the world." With a wide grin, Joshua lifted his mug of beer, "Enjoy!"

And they did. They began with small bowls of seafood gumbo, followed by salad, and then they dived into platters of crawfish étoufée, stuffed crab, grilled red snapper topped with crab, fried catfish, fried shrimp, and a platter of boiled shrimp, with hush puppies, dirty rice, corn on the cob, baked potatoes, and sliced lemons on the side. The Louisiana seafood industry took a dent that night.

For the next few minutes, with silent and intense concentration, Joshua peeled boiled shrimp and dipped them into the cocktail sauce Michael made at the table with Tabasco, ketchup, and lemon juice. He followed that with chunks of red snapper topped with crab. When he had satisfied his initial hunger, he drank some beer and sat back in his chair. "George," he said, wiping his hands on his napkin, "now that Nathan's here, I'll explain my plan to get my dad his job back."

Joshua glanced at Nathan, "I'm gonna tell them about Taylor Merrick."

"Ah, yes," replied Nathan, sipping his beer, "the Empress of Spite. Let me help you tell the tale."

Joshua explained how Taylor had taken the infamous post-concert picture, and then emailed it to *The Word on the Street* website, with the damning caption about a drug deal gone bad.

Sam said, "I saw it online, and I showed it to Mamma!"

Michael smiled sheepishly, and said, "I did too. A colleague of mine sent me the link a couple of weeks ago."

Nathan took up the story from there. "Yeah, a concert pianist beat up in a drug deal is scrumptious news for a gossip column. The lie spread faster than bird flu in the henhouse. Joshua lost two bookings over it. Bruce, the CEO, saw it as a stain on his management firm, and he fired Joshua."

"And when Nathan defended me, Bruce fired him, too."

"Well, how is that going to help your dad get his job back?" asked George.

"Taylor's father Charles Merrick was Dad's boss at Leviathan," answered Joshua.

"He's the one who let Billy go," added Amy.

"The magazine agreed to retract the story, but I could make a big legal stink for Taylor."

"You could press charges for defamation of character," said Michael.

"But I won't do it if Charles Merrick gives Dad his job back."

"You should do it anyway," said Amy. "That miserable girl should pay."

"Actually, I think we should pay her," said Nathan, "because when Bruce let me go, I interviewed with The Virginia Webb Agency, one of the best artist management firms in New York and maybe the whole freakin' world. They hired me, and when I told 'em what had happened to Joshua, they decided to offer him a contract, too." Nathan threw back his head and laughed. "Hell, thanks to Taylor, we're much better off now than we were before!"

He and Joshua clinked glasses in agreement.

"Amy," said Diana, "what do you think Billy will do?"

Amy laid down her fork and drew in a deep breath before she answered. "I think his pride will prevent him from going back to Leviathan, and, frankly, I hope he never works for a big corporation again. He might be interested in Michael's offer, but I just don't know."

"Well," said George, "it's gotta be his call." Then glancing down at Sam, he remarked, "You've been awfully quiet, Miss Faris. What do you think?"

As the focus of everyone's attention, Sam milked the moment. She glanced up at the ceiling, pursed her lips and stroked her imaginary beard in a sage-like manner. "Having considered the gravity of the issue with all its ramifications," she intoned with furrowed brow, "it is my studied opinion, that we have got as far as we can get, and therefore it's time for dessert."

Amid laughter and spontaneous applause, Michael shouted, "The judge has spoken—summon the waiter!"

There was no need; Chad had already appeared at Joshua's elbow. Beginning of course with Sam, they chose their desserts and ordered gallons of *café au lait.*

Before the desserts came, Joshua excused himself to go to the restroom. Like a cattle egret flying after a Brahman bull, Nathan was immediately at his back. As they walked, Nathan said, "Samantha Faris, the babe that lives next door, sporty, a fit athletic type?" He stared at Joshua. "The one who declared she would marry you? She's a babe, all right. What is she—twelve?"

Joshua glanced at his friend and smiled, "Nah, Nathan, she's thirty; it's a hormonal problem."

"She damn well talks like thirty."

"Okay, so I put you on, but, it was all true. She is all of the above, and she did declare she was going to marry me."

"You pisser."

"Just what I had in mind." Joshua opened the door to the Men's Room.

On the way back, Nathan said, "Regarding Sam, don't count her out as a girlfriend; in three years she may look like Lucy, and you'll have to fight off all the eligible men in the City of New Orleans."

"You may be right, but whether she grows up beautiful or not, she's already a rare one indeed."

When they returned, the table was laden with Chocolate Doberge Cake, Bananas Foster, Cherries Jubilee, strawberry shortcake, pecan pie, and bread pudding with Bourbon sauce.

Amidst the clinking of silverware, the rattle of cups and saucers, and the teasing, good-natured banter, Joshua felt a great freedom, an expansion, a lifting up taking place within him. At peace with himself, he was no longer isolated, no longer a stranger in a strange land. Encircled by friends, he presided over a table of abundance. Whatever it was in him that had been dark, mean, frightened, shriveled, and ugly had departed, and in its place grew a young and sturdy plant, full of life and seeking light. He felt the pouring down of grace upon his head, warm and smooth as the oil of anointing.

Realizing he had another responsibility before the evening ended, Joshua tapped a spoon against his glass. With all eyes on him, he rose from his chair, surveyed the company, and announced, "I have to ask your opinion on a question that has been nagging at me for days." He waited a beat. "Is it possible for a Jewish boy to have a Lebanese grandmother?"

After a split-second of silence, they all responded at once.

"Absolutely," shouted George.

"Why not?" said Leo.

Amy smiled, "I hope so."

"Okay, dude, but don't change your stage name," cried Nathan.

"That makes Joshua our first cousin," Lucy told Michael.

"Mamma, can first cousins marry?" asked Sam.

"Oh, my gosh!" exclaimed Diana.

"Yes, indeed," laughed Michael, answering Sam and Joshua in one fell swoop.

"Sounds like it's a go," replied Joshua. Standing at the threshold of his life, he smiled and raised his glass, which mirrored his thankful heart, brimful to overflowing. "To Annie."

Chairs scraped against the floor as they stood spontaneously. "To Annie." They lifted high their glasses and drank.

Thereafter the celebration continued with equal parts mirth and massive caloric intake, while high above them in a company of silver stars, a shining crescent moon arose, as if the soul of the city itself had risen, luminous and purified in the sky.

Epilogue: September

It was the morning of an ordinary day. The trees of the garden, planted in rich earth, watered by plenteous rains, and warmed by the light and heat of an ancient, incandescent star, bore their abundant fruit: pomegranates, pears, persimmons, figs, and pecans. The first cold front had arrived, breaking the heat of summer, and the brisk north wind, cool, sharp and reviving, set the trees to dancing and stirred the sap. Flurries of dry, yellow leaves quivered and broke off, sailing in the breeze, skittering and rustling on the ground. Under a sky of pure, luminescent sapphire, brilliant dew diamonds sparkled in the grass; they shimmered on the last of summer's velvety roses, and the scarlet trumpets of the hibiscus. Even the birds seemed roused by the heady wind; the songs of cardinals, blue jays, mockingbirds and sparrows bespangled the air: trills, roulades, chirps, whistles, calling and answering.

With his new pocketknife, Joshua harvested pomegranates, red and round, from the tree. Sam stood beside him, gripping the handles of a large wicker basket partly filled with fruit. She watched Joshua intently, memorizing the glint of light on his auburn hair and the way the muscles of his arms stood out from strain as the thick stems resisted the blade. Beads of sweat formed on his brow, despite the cool air.

"Once, I would have counted every stroke of the knife," he said, glancing at Sam and wiping his brow. "Numbers and rapid calculations used to buzz in my mind like bees around a hive. But lately, it's the quality of numbers that interests me."

Sam furrowed her brow. "What do you mean?"

"Numbers are not just a means of counting; they have a greater significance. Here's *one* pomegranate," he said, putting it in her basket, "but the number *one* stands for unity and primacy. If I cut the fruit in half, there will be two parts. *Two* shows division or difference. *Three* has geometrical possibilities. The pomegranate, like every solid, has three dimensions, height, width, and depth. So *three* has to do with solidity or completeness. *Four* is important in creation."

"How is that?"

"Our world is made from four great elements: earth, air, fire (or heat), and water. It took all those elements for the tree to produce the fruit. The earth has four regions: north, south, east, and west, and we have four seasons." Joshua cut through the stem of the last pomegranate, and the supple branch, thick with lance-like leaves, sprang back, free of the weight.

He handed the fruit to Sam. "Remember when you told me we live in the midst of a cosmic clock?"

"Yes."

"Well, according to that grand and peerless clock, today is the fall equinox, when the day and the night are equal in length. The pendulum of light swings between the longest day, the summer solstice in June, to the shortest day, the winter solstice in

December, with the equinoxes falling midway between in March and September. The cycle keeps repeating itself, and the year forms a circle. See, here it is."

Joshua knelt at the base of the pomegranate tree and used a twig to draw a circle in the dirt showing the four cardinal directions.

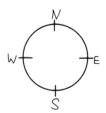

"The summer solstice is at the top and going clockwise, there is the fall equinox, the winter solstice at the bottom, and the spring equinox to the left. Summer, fall, winter, and spring. As you said, Sam, the great cycles move in perfect clockwork. The earth spins on its axis and, at the same time, travels through space circling the sun. And the whole solar system is moving. Everything is pure and ordered motion."

At that moment, a blue jay, stroking the air with powerful wings, swooped down from the mulberry tree, sailed just above them and then, in a steep blue and silver arc, banked up toward the east.

Sam smiled, watching the bird's unerring flight. Kneeling on the ground beside Joshua, she lifted her face to his, "And we are all part of it."

"Yes, we are." He gazed into her earnest eyes, as a gust of wind swirled her dark hair about her upraised face. "We are enclosed and enfolded by a great perfection. As the poet said, in it we live and move, and have our being."

Sam studied the drawing. "A circle has no beginning or end, so how can you tell when the year begins?"

"Good question, and I don't know the answer. But now is the time of the Jewish New Year, Rosh Hashanah. It means *head of the year.*"

"A time for new beginnings." Sam sat cross-legged upon the grass with the basket in her lap and Joshua sat beside her.

Taking a pomegranate in her hand, she asked, "Have you ever eaten one of these?"

"No," he smiled, "another first for Joshua Brightman. But I do know it's a significant fruit. In ancient times, the Hebrew High Priests wore robes with the images of pomegranates woven into the hems, interspersed with bells of pure gold. Hundreds of pomegranates on gold chains were depicted on the capitals of the two bronze pillars standing before Solomon's Temple in Jerusalem."

The sound of their voices rose up in the garden and blended into the music that surrounded them, the songs, chirps, whistles and calls of birds, the buzzing of bees, and the humming of the wind through the trees.

"Time to taste one," she said, reaching into the basket. "Here we go."

Riding on a planet spinning at one thousand miles per hour and hurtling through space at untold velocity, she held a warm, round pomegranate in the palm of her hand, as though it was the center, the very heart, of the universe.

Curious, with care and intent, he pierced the pomegranate's leathery skin with the knife's sharp blade, to reveal the hidden jewels within: seeds of ruby and garnet. Taking turns, they tasted the sweet juice that flowed from the wound, red as blood, and precious and holy as sacrifice.

Poised on the cusp between the life that had been and the life that would be, in a world created for them, watched over by Presences unseen, they and their story, written long ago, were known, as they traveled, borne at high velocity on a spinning planet, warmed and bathed in the light of an ancient star, on the morning of an ordinary day.

Notes and Acknowledgements

All Scripture quotations are from the *King James Version*.

In Chapter 4, the beginning of Annie's Arabic prayer is translated as follows: *Lord Almighty, God of our fathers, we pray to You, hear us and have mercy. Have mercy on us, O God in your great mercy; we pray to You, hear us and have mercy.*

The facts about the number 3 in the design of the bee and the multiples of 11 in the frequencies of the musical scale come from Chapter 1: The Works of God in E. W. Bullinger's *Number in Scripture; Its Supernatural Design and Spiritual Significance.* Joshua's explanation of the significance of the numbers 1, 2, 3, and 4 in the Epilogue is derived from Part II: Spiritual Significance in the same book.

Annie's expression of surprise, *tatheedi,* in Chapter 11 is my transliteration of an Arabic word I heard as a child. I have no idea what it means literally, but that's how it sounded, and its usage is akin to *Oh, my gosh!*

I extend my heartfelt thanks to editor Matthew Arkin of My Two Cents Editing for his thoughtful, sensitive, and thorough critique which gave me a fresh perspective on the story. I am grateful also to those who read the manuscript in its early stages. Annette Stadelmann's gentle criticism and Nicholas Bergin's no-holds-barred honesty were most helpful.

Thanks to Michael Cosgrove, New Orleans native and engineer, who helped clarify the local accent, its derivation and pronunciation, as well as unique terms used in the city. I appreciate the help of two attorneys: my cousin Oliver Jackson Schrumpf, who advised me on legal language, and Margaret Shannon, who explained the rules of litigation regarding former employees.

Many thanks to my neighbors Traci and Michael Burke and their daughters Tabitha and Sabrina for allowing me to make Eliot the blue jay an important character in the novel. They found him in the backyard as a fledgling, named him Eliot, raised him to maturity, and eventually set him free, *successfully*.

References

Bridge the Gulf: Voices from the Gulf Coast; http://bridgethegulf project.org/blog

Bullinger, Ethelbert W. *Number in Scripture; Its Supernatural Design and Spiritual Significance.* Eyre and Spottiswoode: London, 1894. Reprinted: Martino Publishing: Mansfield Centre, CT, 2011.

Jamail, Dahr. "People Are Dropping Dead from BP Dispersants: Toxicologist," *Al Jazeera*, October 27, 2010. https://coto2.word press.com/2010/10/27/people-are-dropping-dead-from-bp-dispersants-toxicologist/

Juhasz, Antonia. "Investigation: Two Years After the BP Spill, A Hidden Health Crisis Festers," *The Nation*, May 7, 2012.

Lake Pontchartrain Basin Foundation; www.saveourlake.org

A Lexicon of New Orleans Terminology and Speech; http://www.gumbopages.com/yatspeak.html

New Orleans Colloquial Speech; http://joeykelly.net/neworleans speech.html

Orthodox Christianity.net; http://www.orthodoxchristianity.net/forum/index.php?topic=13343.0

Tolino, Vanessa. "Letter from the Gulf: The View from Plaquemines Parish," *The Brooklyn Rail*, June 3, 2010.

Water: Estuaries and Coastal Watersheds; http://water.epa.gov/type/oceb/nep/about.cfm#content

CPSIA information can be obtained at www.ICGtesting.com
Printed in the USA
LVOW07s0914250216

476673LV00005B/269/P